It was written that I should
be loyal to the nightmare of my choice—

Joseph Conrad
Heart of Darkness

THE BIG NOWHERE

The prowler's low beams crisscrossed the lot, picking out booze empties, sodden lumber and paper debris. Danny cleared his throat; one of the men wheeled and pulled his gun, spastic twitchy. Danny said, 'Easy, Gibbs. It's me, Upshaw.'

Gibbs reholstered his piece; the other cops separated. Danny looked down at the corpse, felt his knees buckle and made like a criminologist so he wouldn't pass out or vomit:

'Deffrey, Henderson, keep your lights on the decedent. Gibbs, write down what I say verbatim.

'Dead male Caucasian, nude. Approximate age thirty to thirty-five. The cadaver is lying supine, the arms and legs spread. There are ligature marks on the neck, the eyes have been removed and the empty sockets are extruding a gelatinous substance . . .'

Eyes poked out. Sex organs mauled. Bare flesh gored down to the quick. Danny followed the morgue wagon downtown, wishing his car had a siren to get him there faster.

THE BIG NOWHERE

James Ellroy

ARROW BOOKS

To
Glenda Revelle

Arrow Books Limited
20 Vauxhall Bridge Road, London SW1V 2SA

An imprint of Random Century Group

London Melbourne Sydney Auckland
Johannesburg and agencies throughout
the world

First published in Great Britain in 1989 by Mysterious Press UK

Arrow edition 1990

Phototypeset by Input Typesetting Ltd, London
Printed and bound in Great Britain by
Courier International Ltd, Tiptree, Essex

ISBN 0 09 964920 9

1

Red Crosscurrents

CHAPTER ONE

Thundershowers hit just before midnight, drowning out the horn honks and noisemaker blare that usually signalled New Year's on the Strip, bringing 1950 to the West Hollywood Substation in a wave of hot squeals with meat wagon backup.

At 12:03, a four-vehicle fender bender at Sunset and La Cienega resulted in a half dozen injuries; the deputies who responded got eyewitness testimony: the crash was caused by the clown in the brown DeSoto and the army major in the Camp Cooke staff car racing no-hands with dogs wearing paper party hats on their laps. Two arrests; one call to the Verdugo Street Animal Shelter. At 12:14, an uninhabited vet's shack on Sweetzer collapsed in a heap of drenched prefab, killing a teenaged boy and girl necking under the foundation; two County Morgue DOA's. At 12:29, a neon lawn display featuring Santa Claus and his helpers short-circuited, shooting flames along the electrical cord to its inside terminus – a plug attached to a maze of adapters fueling a large, brightly lit Christmas tree and nativity scene – severely burning three children heaping tissue-wrapped presents on a glow-in-the-dark baby Jesus. One fire truck, one ambulance and three Sheriff's prowl cars to the scene, a minor jurisdictional foul-up when the LAPD appeared in force, a rookie dispatcher mistaking the Sierra Bonita Drive address as City – not County – territory. Then five drunk drivings; then a slew of drunk and disorderlies as the clubs on the Strip let out; then a strongarm heist in front of Dave's Blue Room, the victims two Iowa yokels in town for the Rose Bowl, the muscle two niggers who escaped in a '47 Merc with purple fender skirts. When the rain petered out shortly after 3:00, Detective Deputy

1

Danny Upshaw, the station's acting watch commander, predicted that the 1950's were going to be a shit decade.

Except for the drunks and nonbooze misdemeanants in the holding tank, he was alone. Every black-and-white and unmarked was out working graveyard; there was no chain of command, no switchboard/clerical girl, no plainclothes deputies in the squadroom. No khaki and olive drab patrolmen strutting around, smirking over their plum duty – the Strip, glossy women, Christmas baskets from Mickey Cohen, the real grief over the city line with the LAPD. No one to give him the fisheye when he picked up his criminology textbooks: Vollmer, Thorwald, Maslick – grid-searching crime scenes, blood spatter marks explained, how to toss an 18-foot-by–24-foot room for hard evidence in an hour flat.

Danny settled in to read, his feet up on the front desk, the station-to-prowler two-way turned down low. Hans Maslick was digressing on how to roll fingerprints off severely burned flesh, the best chemical compounds to remove scabbed tissue without singeing the skin below the surface of the print pattern. Maslick had perfected his technique during the aftermath of a prison fire in Düsseldorf in 1931. He had plenty of stiffs and fingerprint abstracts to work from; there was a chemical plant nearby, with an ambitious young lab assistant eager to help him. Together, they worked rapid fire: caustic solutions burning too deep, milder compounds not penetrating scarred flesh. Danny jotted chemical symbols on a notepad as he read; he pictured himself as Maslick's assistant, working side by side with the great criminologist, who would give him a fatherly embrace every time he made a brilliant logical jump. Soon he was transposing the scorched nativity scene kids against his reading, going solo, lifting prints off tiny fingers, double-checking them against birth records, the hospital precaution they took in case newborns got switched around –

'Boss, we got a hot one.'

Danny glanced up. Hosford, a uniformed deputy

working the northeast border of the division, was in the doorway. 'What? Why didn't you call it in?'

'I did. You mustn't of – '

Danny pushed his text and notepad out of sight. 'What is it?'

'Man down. I found him – Allegro, a half mile up from the Strip. Jesus dog, you ain't ever seen noth – '

'You stay here, I'm going.'

Allegro Street was a narrow residential road, half Spanish bungalow courts, half building sites fronted by signs promising DELUXE LIVING in the Tudor, French Provincial and Streamline Moderne styles. Danny drove up it in his civilian car, slowing when he saw a barrier of sawhorses with red blinkers, three black-and-whites parked behind it, their headlights beaming out into a weed-strewn vacant lot.

He left his Chevy at the curb and walked over. A knot of deputies in rain slickers were pointing flashlights at the ground; cherry lamp glow fluttered over a sign for the ALLEGRO PLANTATION ARMS – FULL TENANCY BY SPRING 1951. The prowlers' low beams crisscrossed the lot, picking out booze empties, sodden lumber and paper debris. Danny cleared his throat; one of the men wheeled and pulled his gun, spastic twitchy. Danny said, 'Easy, Gibbs. It's me, Upshaw.'

Gibbs reholstered his piece; the other cops separated. Danny looked down at the corpse, felt his knees buckle and made like a criminologist so he wouldn't pass out or vomit:

'Deffry, Henderson, keep your lights on the decedent. Gibbs, write down what I say verbatim.

'Dead male Caucasian, nude. Approximate age thirty to thirty-five. The cadaver is lying supine, the arms and legs spread. There are ligature marks on the neck, the eyes have been removed and the empty sockets are extruding a gelatinous substance.'

Danny squatted by the corpse; Deffry and Henderson moved their flashlights in to give him some close-ups.

'The genitals are bruised and swollen, there are bite marks on the glans of the penis.' He reached under the dead man's back and felt wet dirt; he touched the chest near the heart, got dry skin and a residue of body heat. 'There is no precipitation on the cadaver, and since it rained heavily between midnight and three A.M., we can assume the victim was placed here within the past hour.'

A siren wailed toward the scene. Danny grabbed Deffry's flashlight and went in extra close, examining the worst of it. 'There is a total of six oval, irregular, circumscribed wounds on the torso between the navel and rib cage. Shredded flesh outlines the perimeters, entrails coated with congealed blood extruding from them. The skin around each wound is inflamed, directly outlining the shred marks, and – '

Henderson said, 'Hickeys sure as shit.'

Danny felt his textbook spiel snap. 'What are you talking about?'

Henderson sighed. 'You know, love bites. Like when a dame starts sucking on your neck. Gibbsey, show plainclothes here what that hat check girl at the Blue Room did to you Christmas.'

Gibbs chuckled and kept writing; Danny stood up, pissed at being patronized by a flunky harness bull. Not talking made the stiff sucker-punch him; his legs were rubber and his stomach was flip-flops. He flashed the five-cell at the ground surrounding the dead man, saw that it had been thoroughly trampled by LASD-issue brogans and that the prowl cars had obliterated any possible tire tracks. Gibbs said, 'I ain't sure I got all them words spelled right.'

Danny found his textbook voice. 'It doesn't matter. Just hold on to it and give it to Captain Dietrich in the morning.'

'But I'm off at eight. The skipper don't come in till ten, and I got Bowl tickets.'

'Sorry, but you're staying here until daywatch relieves you or the lab techs show up.'

4

'The County lab's closed New Year's, and I've had them tickets – '

A Coroner's wagon pulled to a stop by the sawhorses, killing its siren; Danny turned to Henderson. 'Crime scene ropes, no reporters or rubberneckers. Gibbs stays posted here, you and Deffry start shaking down the locals. You know the drill: witnesses to the dumping, suspicious loiterers, vehicles.'

'Upshaw, it is four-twenty fucking A.M.'

'Good. Start now, and you may be finished by noon. Leave a report in duplicate with Dietrich, and write down all the addresses where no one was home, so they can be checked later.'

Henderson stormed over to his cruiser; Danny watched the Coroner's men place the body on a stretcher and drape it with a blanket, Gibbs talking a blue streak to them, Rose Bowl odds and a number on the Black Dahlia case, still unsolved, still a hot topic. The profusion of cherry lights, flashlights and headbeams darted over the lot, picking out details: mud puddles reflecting moonlight and shadows, the neon haze of Hollywood in the distance. Danny thought of his six months as a detective, his own two homicides open-and-shut family jobs. The morgue men loaded the body, hung a U-turn and took off sans siren. A Vollmer maxim hit home: 'In murders of extreme passion, the killer will always betray his pathology. If the detective is willing to sort physical evidence objectively and then *think* subjectively from the killer's viewpoint, he will often solve crimes that are baffling in their randomness.'

Eyes poked out. Sex organs mauled. Bare flesh gored down to the quick. Danny followed the morgue wagon downtown, wishing his car had a siren to get him there faster.

The LA City and County morgues occupied the bottom floor of a warehouse on Alameda just south of Chinatown. A wooden partition separated the two operations: examination slabs, refrigerators and dissecting tables for

5

bodies found within City confines, a different set of facilities for stiffs from the unincorporated area patrolled by the Sheriff's Department. Before Mickey Cohen sent the LAPD and Mayor's Office topsy-turvy with his Brenda Allen revelations – the high brass taking kickbacks from LA's most famous whores – there had been solid City/County cooperation, pathologists and cadaver caddies sharing plastic sheets, bone saws and pickling fluid. Now, with the County cops giving Cohen shelter on the Strip, there was nothing but interagency grief.

Edicts had come down from City Personnel: *no* loanouts of City medical tools; *no* fraternizing with the County crew while on duty; *no* Bunsen burner moonshine parties, for fear of mistagged DOA's and body parts snatched as souvenirs resulting in scandals to back up the Brenda Allen job. Danny Upshaw followed the stretcher bearing John Doe # 1–1/1/50 up the County loading dock, knowing his chance of getting his favorite City pathologist to do the autopsy was close to nil.

The County side was bustling: traffic fatalities lined up on gurneys, morgue jockeys tagging big toes, uniformed deputies writing dead body reports and Coroner's men chaining cigarettes to kill the stench of blood, formaldehyde and stale chink takeout. Danny side-stepped his way over to a fire exit, then hooked around to the City loading dock, interrupting a trio of LAPD patrolmen singing 'Auld Lang Syne.' Inside, the scene was identical to the one on the County turf, except that the uniforms were navy blue – not olive drab and khaki.

Danny headed straight for the office of Dr. Norton Layman, Assistant Chief Medical Examiner for the City of Los Angeles, author of *Science Against Crime* and his instructor for the USC night school course 'Forensic Pathology for Beginners.' A note was tacked to the door: 'I'm on days starting 1/1. May God bless our new epoch with less business than the first half of this rather bloody century – N. L.'

Cursing to himself, Danny got out his pen and notepad and wrote:

6

'Doc – I should have known you'd take the busiest night of the year off. There's an interesting 187 on the County side – male, sexually mutilated. Grist for your new book, and since I caught the squeal I'm sure I'll get the case. Will you try to get the autopsy? Capt. Dietrich says the ME on the County day shift gambles and is susceptible to bribes. Enough said – D. Upshaw.' He placed the sheet of paper on Layman's desk blotter, anchored it with an ornamental human skull and walked back to County territory.

Business had slacked off. Daylight was starting to creep across the loading dock; the night's catch was lined up on steel examination slabs. Danny looked around and saw that the only live one in the place was an ME's assistant propped up in a chair by the dispatch room, alternately picking his teeth and his nose.

He walked over. The old man, breathing raisinjack, said, 'Who are you?'

'Deputy Upshaw, West Hollywood Squad. Who's catching?'

'Nice duty. Ain't you a little young for a gravy job like that?'

'I'm a hard worker. Who's catching?'

The old man wiped his nose-picking finger on the wall. 'I can tell conversation ain't your strong suit. Doc Katz was catching, only a snootful of juice caught him. Now he's catching a few winks in that kike kayak of his. How come the hebes all drive Cadillacs? You're a detective, you got an answer for that?'

Danny felt his fists jam into his pockets and clench, his warning to ease down. 'It beats me. What's your name?'

'Ralph Carty, that's – '

'Ralph, have you ever done a preautopsy prep?'

Carty laughed. 'Sonny, I done them all. I did Rudy Valentino, who was hung like a cricket. I did Lupe Velez and Carole Landis, and I got pictures of both of them. Lupe shaved her snatch. You pretend they ain't dead,

7

you can have fun. What do you say? Lupe and Carole, five-spot a throw?'

Danny got out his billfold and peeled off two tens; Carty went for his inside jacket pocket, whipping out a deck of glossies. Danny said, 'Nix. The guy I want is on a tray over there.'

'What?'

'I'm doing the prep. *Now.*'

'Sonny, you ain't a certified County morgue attendant.'

Danny added a five-spot to his bribe and handed it to Carty; the old man kissed a faded snapshot of a dead movie star. 'I guess you are now.'

Danny got his evidence kit from the car and went to work, Carty standing sentry in case the duty ME showed up pissed.

He stripped the sheet off the corpse and felt the limbs for postmortem lividity; he held the arms and legs aloft, dropped them and got the buckle that indicated rigor mortis coming on. He wrote, 'Death around 1:00 A.M. likely,' on his notepad, then smeared the dead man's fingertips with ink and rolled his prints onto a piece of stiff cardboard, pleased that he got a perfect spread the first time around.

Next he examined the neck and head, measuring the purpled ligature marks with a caliper, writing the specs down. The marks encompassed the entire neck; much too long and broad to be a single- or double-hand span. Squinting, he saw a fiber under the chin; he picked it off with a tweezer, nailed it as white terrycloth, placed it in a test tube and on impulse forced the half-locked jaws open, holding them wide with a tongue depressor. Shining his penlight into the mouth, he saw identical fibers on the roof, tongue and gums; he wrote, 'Strangled and suffocated with white terrycloth towel,' took a deep breath and checked out the eye sockets.

The penlight beam picked out bruised membranes streaked with the gelatinous substance he'd noticed at

8

the building site; Danny took a Q-tip and swabbed three slide samples from each cavity. The goo had a minty medicinal odor.

Working down the cadaver, Danny spot-checked every inch; scrutinizing the inside crook of the elbows, he tingled: old needle scars – faded, but there in force on both the right and left arms. The victim was a drug addict – maybe reformed – none of the tracks were fresh. He wrote the information down, grabbed his caliper and braced himself for the torso wounds.

The six ovals measured to within three centimeters of each other. They all bore teeth mark outlines too shredded to cut casts from – and all were too large to have been made by a human mouth biting straight down. Danny scraped congealed blood off the intestinal tubes that extended from the wounds; he smeared the samples on slides and made a speculative jump that Doc Layman would have crucified him for:

The killer used an animal or animals in the postmortem abuse of his victim.

Danny looked at the dead man's penis; saw unmistakable human teeth marks on the glans, what Layman called 'homicidal affection,' working for laughs in a classroom packed with ambitious off-duty cops. He knew he should check the underside and scrotum, saw Ralph Carty watching him and did it, getting no additional mutilations. Carty cackled, 'Hung like a cashew'; Danny said, 'Shut the fuck up.'

Carty shrugged and went back to his *Screenworld*. Danny turned the corpse onto its back and gasped.

Deep, razor-sharp cuts, dozens of them crisscrossing the back and shoulders from every angle, wood splinters matted into the narrow strips of caked blood.

Danny stared, juxtaposing the front and backside mutilations, trying to put them together. Cold sweat was soaking his shirt cuffs, making his hands twitch. Then a gruff voice. 'Carty, who is this guy? What's he doing here?'

Danny turned around, putting a pacify-the-locals grin

on; he saw a fat man in a soiled white smock and party hat with '1950' in green spangles. 'Deputy Upshaw. You're Dr. Katz?'

The fat man started to stick out his hand, then let it drop. 'What are you doing with that cadaver? And by what authority do you come in here and disrupt my workload?'

Carty was shrinking into the background, making with supplicating eyes. Danny said, 'I caught the squeal and wanted to prep the body myself. I'm qualified, and I lied and told Ralphy you said it was kosher.'

Dr. Katz said, 'Get out of here, Deputy Upshaw.'

Danny said, 'Happy New Year.'

Ralph Carty said, 'It's the truth, Doc – if I'm lyin', I'm flyin'.'

Danny packed up his evidence kit, wavering on a destination: canvassing Allegro Street or home, sleep and dreams: Kathy Hudgens, Buddy Jastrow, the blood house on a Kern County back road. Walking out to the loading dock, he looked back. Ralph Carty was splitting his bribe money with the doctor in the rhinestone party hat.

CHAPTER TWO

Lieutenant Mal Considine was looking at a photograph of his wife and son, trying not to think of Buchenwald.

It was just after 8:00 A.M.; Mal was in his cubicle at the DA's Criminal Investigation Bureau, coming off a fitful sleep fueled by too much Scotch. His trouser legs were covered with confetti; the roundheeled squadroom steno had smeared kisses on his door, bracketing EXECUTIVE OFFICER in Max Factor's Crimson Decadence. The City Hall sixth floor looked like a trampled parade ground; Ellis Loew had just awakened him with a phone call: meet him and 'someone else' at the Pacific Dining

Car in half an hour. And he'd left Celeste and Stefan at home alone to ring in 1950 – because he knew his wife would turn the occasion into a war.

Mal picked up the phone and dialed the house. Celeste answered on the third ring – 'Yes? Who is this that is calling?' – her bum phrasing a giveaway that she'd been speaking Czech to Stefan.

'It's me. I just wanted to let you know that I'll be a few more hours.'

'The blonde is making demands, Herr Lieutenant?'

'There's no blonde, Celeste. You know there's no blonde, and you know I always sleep at the Hall after the New Year's – '

'How do you say in English – rotkopf? Redhead? Kleine rotkopf scheisser schtupper – '

'Speak English, goddamn it! Don't pull this with me!'

Celeste laughed: the stage chortles that cut through her foreign-language routine and always made him crazy. 'Put my son on, goddamn it!'

Silence, then Celeste Heisteke Considine's standard punch line: 'He's not your son, Malcolm. His father was Jan Heisteke, and Stefan knows it. You are my benefactor and my husband, and the boy is eleven and must know that his heritage is not amerikanisch police talk and baseball and – '

'*Put my son on, goddamn you.*'

Celeste laughed softly. Mal knew she was acknowledging match point – him using his cop voice. The line went silent; in the background he could hear Celeste cooing Stefan out of sleep, singsong words in Czech. Then the boy was there – smack in the middle of them. 'Dad – Malcolm?'

'Yeah. Happy New Year.'

'We saw the fireworks. We went on the roof and held umb-umb – '

'You held umbrellas?'

'Yes. We saw the City Hall light up, then the fireworks went, then they . . . fissured?'

11

Mal said, 'They fizzled, Stefan. F-i-z-z-l-e-d. A fissure is a kind of a hole in the ground.'

Stefan tried the new word. 'F-i-s-u-r-e?'

'Two s's. We'll have a lesson when I get home, maybe take a drive by Westlake Park and feed the ducks.'

'Did you see the fireworks? Did you look out the window to see?'

He had been parrying Penny Diskant's offer of a cloakroom quickie then, breasts and legs grinding him, wishing he could do it. 'Yeah, it was pretty. Son, I have to go now. Work. You go back to sleep so you'll be sharp for our lesson.'

'Yes. Do you want to speak to Mutti?'

'No. Goodbye, Stefan.'

'Goodbye, D-D-Dad.'

Mal put down the phone. His hands were shaking and his eyes held a film of tears.

Downtown LA was shut down tight, like it was sleeping off a drunk. The only citizens in view were winos lining up for doughnuts and coffee outside the Union Rescue Mission; cars were erratically parked – snouts to smashed fenders – in front of the hot-sheet hotels on South Main. Sodden confetti hung out of windows and littered the sidewalk, and the sun that was looming above the eastern basin had the feel of heat, steam and bad hangovers. Mal drove to the Pacific Dining Car wishing the first day of the new decade an early death.

The restaurant was packed with camera-toting tourists wolfing the 'Rose Bowl Special' – hangtown fry, flapjacks, Bloody Marys and coffee. The headwaiter told Mal that Mr. Loew and another gentleman were waiting for him in the Gold Rush Room – a private nook favored by the downtown legal crowd. Mal walked back and rapped on the door; it was opened a split second later, and the 'other gentleman' stood there beaming. 'Knock, knock, who's there? Dudley Smith, so Reds beware. Please come in, Lieutenant. This is an auspicious assemblage of police brain power, and we should mark the occasion with proper amenities.'

Mal shook the man's hand, recognizing his name, his style, his often imitated tenor brogue. Lieutenant Dudley Smith, LAPD Homicide. Tall, beefside broad and red-faced; Dublin born, LA raised, Jesuit college trained. Priority case hatchet man for every LA chief of police dating back to Strongarm Dick Steckel. Killed seven men in the line of duty, wore custom-made club-figured ties: 7's, handcuff ratchets and LAPD shields stitched in concentric circles. Rumored to carry an Army .45 loaded with garlic-coated dumdums and a spring-loaded toad stabber.

'Lieutenant, a pleasure.'

'Call me Dudley. We're of equal rank. I'm older, but you're far better looking. I can tell we're going to be grand partners. Wouldn't you say so, Ellis?'

Mal looked past Dudley Smith to Ellis Loew. The head of the DA's Criminal Division was seated in a thronelike leather chair, picking the oysters and bacon out of his hangtown fry. 'I would indeed. Sit down, Mal. Are you interested in breakfast?'

Mal took a seat across from Loew; Dudley Smith sat down between them. The two were dressed in vested tweed suits – Loew's gray, Smith's brown. Both men sported regalia: Phi Beta Kappa key for the lawyer, lodge pins dotting the cop's lapels. Mal adjusted the crease in his rumpled flannels and thought that Smith and Loew looked like two mean pups out of the same litter. 'No thanks, counselor.'

Loew pointed to a silver coffeepot. 'Java?'

'No thanks.'

Smith laughed and slapped his knees. 'How about an explanation for this early morning intrusion on your peaceful family life?'

Mal said, 'I'll guess. Ellis wants to be DA, I want to be Chief DA's Investigator and you want to take over the Homicide Bureau when Jack Tierney retires next month. We've got venue on some hot little snuff that I

13

haven't heard about, the two of us as investigators, Ellis as prosecuting attorney. It's a career maker. Good guess?'

Dudley let out a whooping laugh; Loew said, 'I'm glad you didn't finish law school, Malcolm. I wouldn't have relished facing you in court.'

'I hit it, then?'

Loew forked an oyster and dipped it in egg juice. 'No. We've got our tickets to those positions you mentioned, though. Pure and simple. Dudley volunteered for his own – '

Smith interrupted: 'I volunteered out of a sense of patriotism. I hate the Red filth worse than Satan.'

Mal watched Ellis take one bit of bacon, one of oyster, one of egg. Dudley lit a cigarette and watched him; Mal could see brass knuckles sticking out of his waistband. 'Why am I thinking grand jury job?'

Loew leaned back and stretched; Mal knew he was reaching for his courtroom persona. 'Because you're smart. Have you been keeping abreast of the local news?'

'Not really.'

'Well, there's a great deal of labor trouble going on, with the Hollywood movie studios in particular. The Teamsters have been picketing against the UAES – the United Alliance of Extras and Stagehands. They've got a long-term contract with RKO and the cheapie studios on Gower. They're picketing for more money and profit points, but they're not striking, and – '

Dudley Smith slammed the tabletop with two flattened palms. 'Subversive, mother-hating Pinks, every one of them.'

Loew did a slow burn; Mal sized up the Irishman's huge hands as neck snappers, ear gougers, confession makers. He made a quick jump, pegged Ellis as being afraid of Smith, Smith hating Loew on general principles: as a sharpster Jew lawyer son of a bitch. 'Ellis, are we talking about a *political* job?'

Loew fondled his Phi Beta Kappa key and smiled.

14

'We are talking about an extensive grand jury investigation into Communist influence in Hollywood, you and Dudley as my chief investigators. The investigation will center around the UAES. The union is rife with subversives, and they have a so-called brain trust that runs things: one woman and a half dozen men – all heavily connected to fellow travelers who went to jail for pleading the Fifth before HUAC in '47. Collectively, UAES members have worked on a number of movies that espouse the Commie line, *and* they're connected to a veritable Dun and Bradstreet of other subversives. Communism is like a spider's web. One thread leads to a nest, another thread leads to a whole colony. The threads are names, and the names become witnesses and name more names. And you and Dudley are going to get me all those names.'

Silver captain's bars danced in Mal's head; he stared at Loew and ticked off objections, devils advocate against his own cause. 'Why me instead of Captain Bledsoe? He's Chief DA's Investigator, he's Mr. Toastmaster for the whole goddamn city and he's everybody's favorite uncle – which is important, since you come across like a shark. I'm a detective specializing in collecting homicide evidence. Dudley is Homicide brass flat out. Why *us*? And why now – at nine A.M. New Year's morning?'

Loew counted rebuttal points on his fingers, the nails coated with clear polish and buffed to a gloss. 'One, I was up late last night with the District Attorney. The Bureau's final fiscal 1950 budget has to be submitted to the City Council tomorrow, and I convinced him that the odd forty-two thousand dollars we had left over should be used to fight the Red Menace. Two, Deputy DA Gifford of the Grand Jury Division and I have agreed to switch jobs. He wants criminal prosecution experience, and you know what I want. Three, Captain Bledsoe is going senile. Two nights ago he gave a speech to the Greater Los Angeles Kiwanis Club and lapsed into a string of obscenities. He created quite a stir when he announced his intention to "pour the pork" to Rita Hayworth, to "hose her till she bleeds." The DA checked with Bledsoe's doctor, and learned that our dear Captain has had a series of small strokes that he's kept under wraps. He will be retiring on April fifth – his twentieth anniversary with the Bureau – and he is strictly a figurehead until then. Fourth, you and Dudley are damn good, damn smart detectives, and an intriguing contrast in styles. Fifth – '

Mal hit the tabletop à la Dudley Smith. 'Fifth, we both know the DA wants an outside man for Chief Investigator. He'll go to the Feds or fish around the LAPD before he takes me.'

Ellis Loew leaned forward. 'Mal, he's agreed to give it to you. Chief Investigator and a captaincy. You're thirty-eight?'

'Thirty-nine.'

'A mere infant. Do well at the job and within five years you'll be fending off police chief offers with a stick. And *I'll* be District Attorney and McPherson will be Lieutenant Governor. Are you in?'

Ellis Loew's right hand was resting flat on the table; Dudley Smith covered it with his and smiled, all blarney. Mal reviewed his caseload: a hooker snuff in Chinatown, two unsolved shine killings in Watts, a stickup and ADW at a coon whorehouse frequented by LAPD brass. Low priority, no priority. He put his hand on the pile and said, 'I'm in.'

The pile dispersed; Dudley Smith winked at Mal. 'Grand partners in a grand crusade.' Ellis Loew stood up beside his chair. 'First, I'll tell you what we have, then I'll tell you what we need.

'We have sworn depositions from Teamster members, stating Red encroachment within the UAES. We've got Commie front membership lists cross-filed with a UAES membership list – with a lot of matching names. We've got prints of pro-Soviet films made during the war – pure Red propaganda – that UAES members worked on. We've got the heavy artillery that I'll mention in

16

a minute and I'm working on getting a batch of Fed surveillance photos: UAES brain trusters hobnobbing with known Communist Party members and HUAC indictees at Sleepy Lagoon protest activities back in '43 and '44. Good ammo, right from the gate.'

Mal said, 'The Sleepy Lagoon stuff might backfire. The kids that were convicted were innocent, they never got the real killer and the cause was too popular. Republicans signed the protest petition. You might want to rethink that approach.'

Dudley Smith doused his cigarette in the remains of his coffee. 'They were guilty, lad. All seventeen. I know that case. They beat José Diaz half to death, dragged him out to the Lagoon and ran him down with an old jalopy. A pachuco passion job, pure and simple. Diaz was sticking it to somebody's cousin's brother's sister. You know how those taco benders intermarry and breed. Mongoloid idiots, all of them.'

Mal sighed. 'It was a railroad, Lieutenant. It was right before the zoot suit riots, and everyone was cuckoo about the mexes. And a Republican governor pardoned those kids, not the Commies.'

Smith looked at Loew. 'Our friend here takes the word of the fourth estate over the word of a brother officer. Next he'll be telling us the Department was responsible for all our pooooor Latin breathren hurt during the riot. A popular Pinko interpretation, I might add.'

Mal reached for a plate of rolls – keeping his voice steady to show the big Irishman he wasn't afraid of him. 'No, a popular LAPD one. I was on the Department then, and the men I worked with tagged the job as horseshit, *pure and simple*. Besides – '

Loew raised his voice – just as Mal heard his own voice start to quiver. '*Gentlemen, please*.'

The interruption allowed Mal to swallow, dredge up a cold look and shoot it at Dudley Smith. The big man shot back a bland smile, said, 'Enough contentiousness over a worthless dead spic,' and extended his hand. Mal shook it; Smith winked.

Ellis Loew said, 'That's better, because guilty or not guilty isn't germane to the issue here. The fact is that the Sleepy Lagoon case attracted a lot of subversives and *they* exploited it to their ends. That's *our* focus. Now I know you both want to go home to your families, so I'll wind this up for today.

'Essentially, you two will be bringing in what the Feds call "friendly witnesses" – UAESers and other lefties willing to come clean on their Commie associations and name names. You've got to get admissions that the pro-Red movies UAES worked on were part of a conscious plot – propaganda to advance the Communist cause. You've got to get proof of venue – subersive activities within LA City proper. It also wouldn't hurt to get some big names. It's common knowledge that a lot of big Hollywood stars are fellow travelers. That would give us some . . .'

Loew paused. Mal said, 'Marquee value?'

'Yes. Well put, if a bit cynical. I can tell that patriotic sentiment doesn't come easy to you, Malcolm. You might try to dredge up some fervor for this assignment, though.'

Mal thought of a rumor he'd heard: that Mickey Cohen bought a piece of the LA Teamsters off of their East Coast front man – an ex-syndicate trigger looking for money to invest in Havana casinos. 'Mickey C. might be a good one to tap for a few bucks if the City funding runs low. I'll bet he wouldn't mind seeing the UAES out and his boys in. Lots of money to be made in Holly-wood, you know.'

Loew flushed. Dudley Smith tapped the table with a huge knuckle. 'No dummy, our friend Malcolm. Yes, lad. Mickey would like the Teamsters in and the studios would like the UAES out. Which doesn't negate the fact that the UAES is crawling with Pinks. Did you know, lad, that we were almost colleagues once before?'

Mal knew: Thad Green offering him a transfer to the

Hat Squad when his sergeantcy came through back in '41. He turned it down, having no balls for armed robbery stakeouts, going in doors gun first, gunboat diplomacy police work: meeting the Quentin bus at the depot, pistol-whipping hard boys into a docile parole. Dudley Smith had killed four men working the job. 'I wanted to work Ad Vice.'

'I dont' blame you, lad. Less risk, more chance for advancement.'

The old rumors: Patrolman/Sergeant/Lieutenant Mal Considine, LAPD/DA's Bureau comer, didn't like to get his hands dirty. Ran scared as a rookie working 77th Street Division – the heart of the Congo. Mal wondered if Dudley Smith knew about the gas man at Buchenwald. 'That's right. I never saw any percentage there.'

'The squad was wicked fun, lad. You'd have fit right in. The others didn't think so, but you'd have convinced them.'

He's got the old talk nailed. Mal looked at Ellis Loew and said, 'Let's wrap this up, okay? What's the heavy ammo you mentioned?'

Loew's eyes moved back and forth between Mal and Dudley. 'We've got two men assisting us. The first is an ex-Fed named Edmund J. Satterlee. He's the head of a group called Red Crosscurrents. It's on retainer to various corporations and what you might want to call "astute" people in the entertainment industry. It screens prospective employees for Communist ties and helps weed out subversive elements that may have wormed their way in already. Ed's an expert on Communism, and he's going to give you a rundown on how to most effectively collate your evidence. The second man is a psychiatrist, Dr. Saul Lesnick. He's been the "approved" headshrinker for the LA Communist Party since the '40s, and he's been an FBI informer for years. We've got access to his complete file of psychiatric records – all the UAES bigwigs – their personal dirt going back to before the war. *Heavy artillery*.'

Smith slapped the table and stood up. 'A howitzer, a

barrage weapon, maybe even an atom bomb. We're meeting them at your house tomorrow, Ellis? Ten o'clock?'

Loew cocked a finger at him. 'Ten sharp.'

Dudley aped the gesture to Mal. 'Until then, partner. It's not the Hats, but we'll have fun nonetheless.'

Mal nodded and watched the big man exit the room. Seconds passed; Loew said, 'A rough piece of work. If I didn't think the two of you would be great together, I wouldn't have let him sign on.'

'He volunteered?'

'He's got a pipeline to McPherson, and he knew about the job before I got the go-ahead. Do you think you can keep him on a tight leash?'

The question was like a road map to all the old rumours. Ellis Loew had him down straight as a Nazi killer and probably believed that he was behind the botched snuff attempt on Buzz Meeks. They had to blow the Ad Vice and 77th Street stories out of the water. Dudley Smith knew better. 'I don't see any problem, counselor.'

'Good. How's things with Celeste and Stefan?'

'You don't want to know.'

Loew smiled. 'Cheer up, then. Good things are coming our way.'

CHAPTER THREE

Turner 'Buzz' Meeks watched rental cops patrol the grounds of Hughes Aircraft, laying four to one that Howard hired the ineffectual bastards because he liked their uniforms, two to one he designed the threads himself. Which meant that the Mighty Man Agency was an RKO Pictures/Hughes Aircraft/Tool Company 'Stray Dog' – the big guy's tag for tax-write-off operations that he bought and meddled in out of whim. Hughes owned a brassiere factory in San Ysidro – 100 percent wetback-run; he owned a plant that manufactured electroplate trophies; he owned four strategically located snack stands – essential to the maintenance of his all-cheese-burger/chili dog diet. Buzz stood in his office doorway, noticed pleated flaps on the pockets of the Mighty Man standing by the hangar across from him, made the style as identical to a blouse Howard designed to spotlight Jane Russell's tits, and called the odds off. And for the three trillionth time in his life, he wondered why he always cut bets when he was bored.

He was now very bored.

It was shortly after 10:00 New Year's morning. Buzz, in his capacity as Head of Security at Hughes Aircraft, had been up all night directing Mighty Men in what Howard Hughes called 'Perimeter Patrol.' The plant's regular guards were given the night off; boozehound specters had been crisscrossing the grounds since yesterday evening. The high point of their tour was Big Howard's New Year's bonus – a flatbed truck loaded with hot dogs and Cokes arriving just as 1949 became 1950 – compliments of the burger write-off in Culver City. Buzz had put down his sheet of bookie calculations to watch the Mighty Men eat; he laid six to one that Howard would hit the roof if he saw their custom-embroidered uniforms dotted with mustard and sauerkraut.

Buzz checked his watch – 10:14 – he could go home and sleep at noon. He slumped into a chair, scanned the walls and studied the framed photos that lined them. Each one made him figure odds for and against himself, made him think of how pefect his figurehead job and what he *really* did were.

There was himself – short, broad, running to fat, standing next to Howard Hughes, tall and handsome in a chalk stripe suit – an Oklahoma shitkicker and a millionaire eccentric giving each other the cuckold's horns. Buzz saw the photo as the two sides of a scratchy hillbilly record: one side about a sheriff corrupted by

21

women and money, the flip a lament for the boss man who bought him out. Next was a collection of police shots – Buzz trim and fit as an LAPD rookie in '34; getting fatter and better dressed as the pictures jumped forward in time: tours with Bunco, Robbery and Narcotics divisions; cashmere and camel's hair blazers, the slightly nervous look in his eyes indigenous to bagmen everywhere. Then Detective Sergeant Turner Meeks in a bed at Queen of Angels, high brass hovering around him, pointing to the wounds he survived – while *he* wondered if it was a fellow cop who'd set him up. A string of civilian pics on the wall above his desk: a fatter, grayer Buzz with Mayor Bowron, ex-DA Buron Fitts, Errol Flynn, Mickey Cohen, producers he'd pimped for, starlets he'd gotten out of litigation and into abortions, dope cure doctors grateful for his referrals. Fixer, errand boy, hatchet wielder.

Stony broke.

Buzz sat down at his desk and jotted credits and debits. He owned fourteen acres of Ventura County farmland; parched and worthless, he'd bought it for his parents to retire to – but they foiled him by kicking in a typhus epidemic in '44. The real estate man he'd been talking to said thirty bucks an acre tops – better to hold on to it – it couldn't go much lower. He owned a mint green '48 Eldo coupé – identical to Mickey C.'s, but without the bullet-proof plating. He had a shitload of suits from Oviatt's and the London Shop, the trousers all too tight in the gut – if Mickey bought secondhand threads he was home free – he and the flashy little hebe were exactly the same size. But the Mick threw away shirts he'd worn twice, and the debit list was running off the page and onto his blotter.

The phone rang; Buzz grabbed it. 'Security. Who's this?'

'It's Sol Gelfman, Buzz. You remember me?'

The old geez at MGM with the car thief grandson, a nice boy who clouted convertibles out of Restaurant Row parking lots, raced Mulholland with them and always left his calling card – a big pile of shit – in the back seat. He'd bought off the arresting officer, who altered his report to show two – not twenty-seven – counts of GTA, along with no mention of the turd drop MO. The judge had let the kid off with probation, citing his good family and youthful verve. 'Sure. What can I do for you, Mr. Gelfman?'

'Well, Howard said I should call you. I've got a little problem, and Howard said you could help.'

'Your grandson back to his old tricks?'

'No, God forbid. There's a girl in my new picture who needs help. These goniffs have got some smut pictures of her, from before I bought her contract. I gave them some money to be nice, but they're persisting.'

Buzz groaned – it was shaping up as a muscle job. 'What kind of pictures?'

'Nasty. Animal stuff. Lucy and this Great Dane with a schlong like King Kong. I should have such a schlong.'

Buzz grabbed a pen and turned over his debit list to the blank side. 'Who's the girl and what have you got on the blackmailers?'

'On the pickup men I got bubkis – I sent my production assistant over with the money to meet them. The girl is Lucy Whitehall, and listen, I got a private detective to trace the calls. The boss of the setup is this Greek she's shacking with – Tommy Sifakis. Is that chutzpah? He's blackmailing his own girlfriend, calling in his demands from their cute little love nest. He's got pals to do the pickups and Lucy don't even know she's being had. Can you feature that chutzpah?'

Buzz thought of price tags; Gelfman continued his spiel. 'Buzz, this is worth half a grand to me, and I'm doing you a favor, 'cause Lucy used to strip with Audrey Anders, Mickey Cohen's squeeze. I coulda gone to Mickey, but you did me solid once, so I'm giving you the job. Howard said you'd know what to do.'

Buzz saw his old billy club hanging by a thong from the bathroom doorknob and wondered if he still had the touch. 'The price is a grand, Mr. Gelfman.'

'What! That's highway robbery!'

'No, it's felony extortion settled out of court. You got an address for Sifakis?'

'Mickey would do it for free!'

'Mickey would go batshit and get you a homicide conspiracy beef. What's Sifakis' address?'

Gelfman breathed out slowly. 'You goddamn okie lowlife. It's 1187 Vista View Court in Studio City, and for a grand I want this thing wiped up clean.'

Buzz said, 'Like shit in the back seat,' and hung up. He grabbed his LAPD-issue equalizer and headed for the Cahuenga Pass.

The run to the Valley took him an hour; the search for Vista View Court another twenty minutes of prowling housing developments: stucco cubes arrayed in semi-circles gouged out of the Hollywood Hills. 1187 was a peach-colored prefab, the paint already fading, the aluminum siding streaked with rust. Identically built pads flanked it – lemon yellow, lavender, turquoise, salmon and hot pink alternating down the hillside, ending at a sign proclaiming, VISTA VIEW GARDENS! CALIFORNIA LIVING AT ITS FINEST! NO $ DOWN FOR VETS! Buzz parked in front of the yellow dive, thinking of gumballs tossed in a ditch.

Little kids were racing tricycles across gravel front yards; no adults were taking the sun. Buzz pinned a cereal-box badge to his lapel, got out and rang the buzzer of 1187. Ten seconds passed – no answer. Looking around, he stuck a bobby pin in the keyhole and gave the knob a jiggle. The lock popped; he pushed the door open and entered the house.

Sunlight leaking through gauze curtains gave him a shot at the living room: cheapsky furniture, movie pinups on the walls, stacks of Philco table radios next to the sofa – obvious proceeds from a warehouse job. Buzz pulled the billy club from his waistband and walked through a grease-spattered kitchen-dinette to the bedroom.

24

More glossies on the walls – strippers in g-strings and pasties. Buzz recognized Audrey Anders, the 'Va Va Voom Girl,' alleged to have a master's degree from some Podunk college; next to her, a slender blonde took up space. Buzz flicked on a floor lamp for a better look; he saw tame publicity stills: 'Juicy Lucy' in a spangly one-piece bathing suit, the address of a downtown talent agency rubber-stamped on the bottom. Squinting, he noticed that the girl had unfocused eyes and a slaphappy grin – probably jacked on some kind of hop.

Buzz decided on five minutes to toss the pad, checked his watch and went to work. Scuffed drawers yielded male and female undergarments tangled up indiscriminately and a stash of marijuana cigarettes; an end cabinet held 78s and dime novels. The closet showed a woman on her way up, a man running second: dresses and skirts from Beverly Hills shops, mothball-reeking navy uniforms and slacks, dandruff-flecked jackets.

With 3:20 down, Buzz turned to the bed: blue satin sheets, upholstered headboard embroidered with cupids and hearts. He ran a hand under the mattress, felt wood and metal, grabbed and pulled out a sawed-off pump shotgun, big black muzzle, probably a 10 gauge. Checking the breech, he saw that it was loaded – five rounds, double-aught buckshot. He removed the ammo and stuffed it in his pocket; played a hunch on Tommy Sifakis' brain and looked under the pillow.

A German Luger, loaded, one in the chamber.

Buzz ejected the chambered round and emptied the clip, pissed that he didn't have time to prowl for a safe, find the doggy stuff to shove in Lucy Whitehall's face later, a jolt to scare her away from Greeks with dandruff and bedroom ordnance. He walked back to the living room, stopping when he saw an address book on the coffee table.

He leafed through it, no familiar names until he hit the G's and saw Sol Gelfman, his home and MGM numbers ringed with doodles; the M's and P's got him Donny Maslow and Chick Pardell, dinks he rousted working Narco, reefer pushers who hung out at studio commissaries – not the extortionist type. Then he hit S and got his lever to squeeze the Greek dry and maybe glom himself a few solids on the side:

Johnny Stompanato, Crestview–6103. Mickey Cohen's personal bodyguard. Rumored to have financed his way out of lowball duty with the Cleveland Combination via strongarm extortion schemes; rumored to front Mexican marijuana to local dealers for a 30 percent kickback.

Handsome Johnny Stomp. *His* name ringed in dollar signs and question marks.

Buzz went back to his car to wait. He turned the ignition key to Accessory, skimmed the radio dial across a half dozen stations, found Spade Cooley and his Cowboy Rhythm Hour and listened with the volume down low. The music was syrup on top of gravy – too sweet, too much. It made him think of the Oklahoma sticks, what it might have been like if he'd stayed. Then Spade went too far – warbling a tune about a man about to go to the state prison gallows for a crime he didn't commit. That made him think of the price he paid to get out.

In 1931 Lizard Ridge, Oklahoma, was a dying hick town in the lungs of the Dustbowl. It had one source of income: a factory that manufactured stuffed souvenir armadillos, armadillo purses and Gila monster wallets, then sold them to tourists blowing through on the highway. Locals and Indians off the reservation shot and skinned the reptiles and sold them to the factory piecework; sometimes they got carried away and shot each other. Then the '31 dust storms closed down U.S. 1 for six months straight, the armadillos and Gilas went crazy, ate themselves diseased on jimson weed, crawled off to die or stormed Lizard Ridge's main drag and got squashed by cars. Either way, their hides were too trashed and shriveled to make anyone a dime. Turner Meeks, ace Gila killer, capable of nailing the bastards with a .22 from thirty yards out – right on the spine where the

26

factory cut its master stitches – knew it was time to leave town.

So he moved to LA and got work in the movies – revolving cowboy extra – Paramount one day, Columbia the next, the Gower Gulch cut-rate outfits when things got tight. Any reasonably presentable white man who could twirl a rope and ride a horse for real was skilled labor in Depression Hollywood.

But in '34 the trend turned from westerns to musicals. Work got scarce. He was about to take a test offered by the LA Municipal Bus Company – three openings for an expected six hundred applicants – when Hollywood saved him again.

Monogram Studio was being besieged by picketers: a combine of unions under the AFL banner. He was hired as a strike-breaker – five dollars a day, guaranteed extra work as a bonus once the strike was quelled.

He broke heads for two weeks straight, so good with a billy club that an off-duty cop nicknamed him 'Buzz' and introduced him to Captain James Culhane, the head of the LAPD's Riot Squad. Culhane knew a born policeman when he saw one. Two weeks later he was walking a beat in downtown LA; a month later he was a rifle instructor at the Police Academy. Teaching Chief Steckel's daughter to shoot a .22 and ride a horse earned him a sergeantcy, tours in Bunco, Robbery and the big enchilada – Narcotics.

Narco duty carried with it an unwritten ethos: you roust the lowest forms of humanity, you walk your tour knee-deep in shit, you get a dispensation. If you play the duty straight, you don't rat on those who don't. *If* you don't you lay off a percentage of what you confiscate direct to the coloreds or the syndicate boys who sell to shines only: Jack Dragna, Benny Siegel, Mickey C. And you watch the straight arrows in other divisions – the guys who want you out so they can get your job.

When he came on Narco in '44, he struck his deal with Mickey Cohen, then the dark horse in the LA rackets, the hungry guy coming up. Jack Dragna hated

Mickey; Mickey hated Jack; Buzz shook down Jack's niggertown pushers, skimmed five grams on the ounce and sold it to Mickey, who loved him for giving Jack grief. Mickey took him to Hollywood parties, introduced him to people who needed police favors and were willing to pay; fixed him up with a roundheeled blonde whose cop husband was serving with the MPs in Europe. He met Howard Hughes and started bird-dogging for him, picking up star-struck farm girls, ensconcing them in the fuck pads the big guy had set up all over LA. It was going aces on all fronts: the duty, the money, the affair with Laura Considine. Until June 21, 1946, when an anonymous tip on a storefront operation at 68th and Slauson led him into an alleyway ambush: two in the shoulder, one in the arm, one through the left cheek of his ass. And a speedy wound ticket out of the LAPD, full pension, into the arms of Howard Hughes, who just happened to need a man . . .

And he still didn't know who the shooters were. The slugs they took out of him indicated two men; *he* had two suspects: Dragna triggers or contract boys hired by Mal Considine, Laura's husband, the Administrative Vice sergeant back from the war. He had Considine checked out within the Departments, heard that he turned tail from bar brawls in Watts, that he got his jollies sending in rookies to operate whores when he ran the night watch in Ad Vice, that he brought a Czech woman and her son back from Buchenwald and was planning to divorce Laura. Nothing concrete – one way or the other.

The only thing he had down for sure was that Considine knew about the deal with his soon-to-be ex and hated him. He'd taken a retirement tour of the Detective Bureau, a chance to say goodbye and pick up his courtesy badge, a chance to get a take on the man he cuckolded. He walked by Considine's desk in the Ad Vice squadroom, saw a tall guy who looked more like a lawyer than a cop and stuck out his hand. Considine

28

gave him a slow eyeball, said, 'Laura always did have a thing for pimps,' and looked away.

Even odds: Considine or Dragna, take your pick.

Buzz saw a late-model Pontiac ragtop pull up in front of 1187. Two women in crinoline party dresses got out and rocked toward the door on high high heels; a big Greek in a too-tight suitcoat and too-short trousers followed them. The taller of the skirts caught her stiletto spike in a pavement crack and went down on one knee; Buzz recognized Audrey Anders, hair in a pageboy, twice as beautiful as her picture. The other girl – 'Juicy Lucy' from the publicity stills – helped her up and into the house, the big man right behind them. Buzz laid three to one that Tommy Sifakis wouldn't respond to the subtle approach, grabbed his billy club and walked up to the Pontiac.

His first shot sheared off the Indian-head hood ornament; his second smashed the windshield. Three, four, five and six were a Spade Cooley refrain that dented the grille into the radiator, causing steam clouds to billow all around him. Seven was a blind swing at the driver's side window, the crash followed by a loud 'What the fuck!' and a familiar metal-on-metal noise: a shotgun slide jacking a shell into the chamber.

Buzz turned and saw Tommy Sifakis striding down the walkway, the sawed-off held in trembling hands. Four to one the Greek was too mad to notice the weapon's light weight; two to one he didn't have time to grab his box of shells and reload. Bluff bet, straight across.

His baton at port arms, Buzz charged. When they were within heavy damage range, the Greek pulled the trigger and got a tiny little click. Buzz countered, swinging at a hairy left hand frantically trying to pump in ammo that wasn't there. Tommy Sifakis screamed and drooped the shotgun; Buzz brought him down with a forehand/backhand to the rib cage. The Greek spat blood and tried to curl into a ball, cradling his wounded parts. Buzz knelt beside him and spoke softly, accentuat-

29

ing his okie drawl. 'Son, let's let bygones be bygones. You rip up them pictures and shitcan the negatives and I won't tell Johnny Stomp you fingered him on the squeeze. Deal?'

Sifakis spat a thick wad of blood and 'F-f-fuck you'; Buzz whacked him across the knees. The Greek shrieked gobbledy-gook; Buzz said, 'I was gonna give you and Lucy another chance to work things out, but now I think I'm gonna advise her to find more suitable lodging. You feel like apologizin' to her?'

'F-f-f-y-y-you.'

Buzz drew out a long sigh, just like he did playing a homesteader who'd taken enough shit in an old Monogram serial. 'Son, here's my last offer. You apologize to Lucy, or I tell Johnny you snitched him, Mickey C. you're extortin' his girlfriend's pal and Donny Maslow and Chick Pardell you snitched them to Narco. Deal?'

Sifakis tried to extend a smashed middle finger; Buzz stroked his baton, catching a sidelong view of Audrey Anders and Lucy Whitehall in the doorway, jaws wide. The Greek lolled his head on the pavement and rasped, 'I p-pologize.'

Buzz saw flashes of Lucy and her canine co-star, Sol Gelfman botching her career with grade Z turkeys, the girl crawling back to the Greek for rough sex. He said, 'Good boy,' popped the baton into Sifakis' gut and walked over to the women.

Lucy Whitehall was shrinking back into the living room; Audrey Anders was blocking the doorway, barefoot. She pointed to Buzz's lapel. 'It's a phony.'

Buzz caught the South in her voice; remembered locker room talk: the Va Va Voom Girl could twirl her pastie tassels in opposite directions at the same time. 'Wheaties. You from New Orleans? Atlanta?'

Audrey looked at Tommy Sifakis, belly-crawling over to the curb. 'Mobile. Did Mickey send you to do that?'

'No. I was wonderin' why you didn't seem surprised. Now I know.'

'You care to tell me about it?'

30

'No.'

'But you've done work for Mickey?'

Buzz saw Lucy Whitehall sit down on the couch and grab a stolen radio for something to hold. Her face was blotchy red and rivers of mascara were running down her cheeks. 'I certainly have. Mickey disapprove of Mr. Sifakis there?'

Audrey laughed. 'He knows trash when he sees it, I'll give him that. What's your name?'

'Turner Meeks.'

'*Buzz* Meeks?'

'That's right. Miss Anders, have you got a place for Miss Whitehall to stay?'

'Yes. But what – '

'Mickey still hang out New Year's at Breneman's Ham 'n' Eggs?'

'Yes.'

'You get Lucy to pack a grip, then. I'll run you over there.'

Audrey flushed. Buzz wondered how much of her smarts Mickey put up with before he jerked the chain; if she ever did the tassel trick for him. She went over and knelt beside Lucy Whitehall, smoothing her hair, prying the radio out of her grasp. Buzz got his car and backed it up on the gravel front yard, one eye on the Greek, still moaning low. Neighbor people were peering out their windows, spread venetian blinds all around the cul-de-sac. Audrey led Lucy out of the house a few minutes later, one arm around her shoulders, one hand carrying a cardboard suitcase. On the way to the car, she stopped to give Tommy Sifakis a kick in the balls.

Buzz took Laurel Canyon back to Hollywood – more time to figure out the play if Johnny Stompanato turned up at his boss's side. Lucy Whitehall mumbled litanies on Tommy Sifakis as a nice guy with rough edges, Audrey cooing 'There, there,' feeding her cigarettes to shut her up.

It was coming on as a three-horse parlay: a grand

31

from Gelfman, whatever Mickey slipped him if he got sentimental over Lucy and a shakedown or favor pried out of Johnny Stomp. Play it soft with the Mick – he hadn't seen him since he quit the Department and their percentage deal. Since then the man had survived a pipe bomb explosion, two IRS audits, his right-hand goon Hooky Rothman stubbing his face on the business end of an Ithaca .12 gauge and the shootout outside Sherry's – chalk that one up to Jack Dragna or shooters from the LAPD, revenge for the cop heads that rolled over the Brenda Allen job. Mickey had half of bookmaking, loan-sharking, the race wire and the dope action in LA; he owned the West Hollywood Sheriff's and the few City high brass who didn't want to see him crucified. And Johnny Stomp had stuck with him through all of it: guinea factotum to a Jew prince. Play them both *very* soft.

Laurel Canyon ended just north of the Strip; Buzz took side streets over to Hollywood and Vine, dawdling at stoplights. He could feel Audrey Anders eyeing him from the back seat, probably trying to get a take on him and the Mick. Pulling up in front of Breneman's, he said, 'You and Lucy stay here. I got to talk to Mickey in private.'

Lucy dry-sobbed and fumbled with her pack of ciga-rettes; Audrey reached for the door handle. 'I'm going, too.'

'No, you're not.'

Audrey flushed; Buzz turned to Lucy. 'Sweetheart, this is about them pictures of you and that big old dog. Tommy was tryin' to squeeze Mr. Gelfman, and if you go inside looking distraught, Mickey just might kill him and get all of us in heaps of trouble. Tommy's got them rough edges, but the two of you just might be able to work things – '

Lucy bawled and made him stop; Audrey's look said he was lower than the dog. Buzz headed into Brene-man's at a trot. The restaurant was crowded, the radio crew for 'Tom Breneman's Breakfast in Hollywood' packing up equipment and hustling it toward a side exit. Mickey Cohen was sitting in a wraparound booth, Johnny Stompanato and another muscle boy sandwiching him. A third man sat alone at an adjoining table, eyes constantly circling, a newspaper folded open on the seat beside him – obviously camouflaging a monster piece.

Buzz walked over; the gunman's hand slid under his morning *Herald*. Mickey stood up, smiling; Johnny Stomp and the other guy pasted identical grins on their faces and slid over to let him into the booth. Buzz stuck out his hand; Cohen ignored it, grabbed the back of his head and kissed him on both cheeks, scraping him with razor stubble. 'Big fellow, it has been too long!'

Buzz recoiled from a blast of cologne. 'Much too long, big fellow. How's business?'

Cohen laughed. 'The haberdashery? I got a florist's shop and an ice cream parlor now, too.'

Buzz saw that Mickey was giving him a shrewd once-over; that he'd caught his frayed shirt cuffs and a home manicure. 'No. *Business.*'

Cohen nudged the man on his left, a bony guy with wide blue eyes and a jailhouse pallor. 'Davey, business he wants. Tell him.'

Davey said, 'Men got to gamble and borrow money and schtup women. The shvartzes got to fly to cloud nine on white powder airlines. Business is good.'

Mickey howled with laughter. Buzz chuckled, faked a coughing attack, turned to Johnny Stompanato and whispered, 'Sifakis and Lucy Whitehall. *Keep your fucking mouth shut.*'

Mickey pounded his back and held up a glass of water; Buzz kept coughing, enjoying the look on Stompanato's face – a guinea Adonis turned into a busted schoolboy, his perfectly oiled pompadour about to wilt from fright. Cohen's back slaps got harder; Buzz took a gulp of water and pretended to catch his breath. 'Davey, you're a funny man.'

Davey half smiled. 'Best in the West. I write all Mr.

Cohen's routines for the smokers at the Friar's Club. Ask him, "How's the wife?" '

Buzz saluted Davey with his glass. 'Mickey, how's the wife?'

Mickey Cohen smoothed his lapels and sniffed the carnation in the buttonhole. 'Some women you want to see, my wife you want to flee. These two Dragna humps were staking out my house after the Sherry's job, my wife brought them milk and cookies, told them to shoot low, she ain't had it from me since Lucky Lindy crossed the Atlantic, she don't want nobody else getting it either. My wife is so cold that the maid calls our bedroom the polar icecap. People come up to me and ask, "Mickey, are you getting any," and I pull a thermometer out of my jockey shorts, it says twenty-five below. People say, "Mickey, you're popular with the ladies, you must get reamed, steamed and dry-cleaned regularly." I say, "You don't know my wife – hog-tied, fried and swept to the side is more like it." Some women you *got* to see, some you *got* to flee. Oops – here she comes now!'

Mickey ended his schtick with a broad grab for his hat. Davey the gagster collapsed on the table, convulsed with laughter. Buzz tried to drum up chortles and couldn't; he was thinking that Meyer Harris Cohen had killed eleven men that he knew of and had to rake in at *least* ten million a year tax free. Shaking his head, he said, 'Mickey, you're a pisser.'

A group of squarejohns at the next table was giving the routine a round of applause; Mickey tipped his hat to them. 'Yeah? Then why ain't you laughing? Davey, Johnny, go sit someplace.'

Stompanato and the gagster slid silently out of the booth. Cohen said, 'You need work or a touch, am I right?'

'Nix.'

'Howard treating you right?'

'He treats me fine.'

Cohen toyed with his glass, tapping it with the six-carat rock on his pinky. 'I know you're in hock to some handbooks. You should be with me boychik. Good terms, no sweat on the payback.'

'I like the risk the other way. It gets my juices goin'.'

'You're a crazy fuck. What do you want? Name it.'

Buzz looked around the room, saw Stompanato at the bar belting a stiff one for guts and solid citizen types giving Mickey surreptitious glances, like he was a zoo gorilla who might bolt his cage. 'I want you not to lean on a guy who's about to make you real mad.'

'What?'

'You know Audrey's friend Lucy Whitehall?'

Mickey traced an hourglass figure in the air. 'Sure. Solly Gelfman's gonna use her in his next picture. He thinks she's going places.'

Buzz said, 'Hell in a bucket maybe,' saw Mickey going into his patented low simmer – nostrils flaring, jaw grinding, eyes trawling for something to smash – and handed him the half-full Bloody Mary Johnny Stompanato left behind. Cohen took a gulp and licked lemon pulp off his lips. 'Spill it. *Now*.'

Buzz said, 'Lucy's shack job's been squeezing Solly with some dirty pictures. I broke it up, strong-armed the boy a little. Lucy needs a safe place to flop, and I know for a fact that the Greek's got pals on the West Hollywood Sheriff's – your pals. I also know he used to push reefer in Dragna territory – which made old Jack D. real mad. Two damn good reasons for you to leave him alone.'

Cohen was gripping his glass with sausage fingers clenched blue-white. 'What . . . kind . . . of . . . pictures?'

The big wrong question – Mickey might be talking to Sol Gelfman and get the true skinny. Buzz braced himself. 'Lucy and a dog.'

Mickey's hand popped the glass, shards exploding all over the table, tomato juice and vodka spritzing Buzz. Mickey looked at his bloody palm and pressed it flat on the tabletop. When the white linen started to turn red, he said, 'The Greek is fucking dead. He is fucking dog food.'

Two waiters had approached; they stood around shuffling their feet. The squarejohns at the next table were
making with shocked faces – one old lady with her jaw
practically down to her soup. Buzz waved the waiters
away, slid next to Cohen and put an arm around his
twitching shoulders. 'Mickey, you can't, and you know
it. You put out the word that anybody who bucks Jack
D. is your friend, and the Greek did that – in spades.
Audrey saw me work him over – and *she'd* know. And
the Greek didn't know how stand-up you are – that your
woman's friends are like kin to you. Mickey, you got to
let it go. You got too much to lose. Fix Lucy up with a
nice place to stay, someplace where the Greek can't find
her. Make it a mitzvah.'

Cohen took his hand from the table, shook it free of
glass slivers and licked lemon goo off his fingers. 'Who
was in it besides the Greek?'

Buzz showed him his eyes, the loyal henchman who'd
never lie; he came up with two gunsels he'd run out of
town for crashing Lew the Jew Wershow's handbook at
Paramount. 'Bruno Geyer and Steve Katzenbach. Fair-
ies. You gonna find Lucy a place?'

Cohen snapped his fingers; waiters materialized and
stripped the table dervish fast. Buzz sensed wheels turning behind the Mick's blank face – in *his* direction. He
moved over to cut the man some slack; he stayed deadpan when Mickey said, 'Mitzvah, huh? You fucking
goyishe shitheel. Where's Audrey and Lucy now?'

'Out in my car.'

'What's Solly pay you?'

'A grand.'

Mickey dug in his pants pockets and pulled out a roll
of hundreds. He peeled off ten, placed them in a row
on the table and said, 'That's the only mitzvah you
know from, you hump. But you saved me grief, so I'm
matching. Buy yourself some clothes.'

Buzz palmed the money and stood up. 'Thanks,
Mick.'

'Fuck you. What do you call an elephant who moonlights as a prostitute?'

'I don't know. What?'

Mickey cracked a big grin. 'A two-ton pickup that lays for peanuts.'

'That's a riot, Mick.'

'Then why ain't you laughing? Send the girls in – *now*.'

Buzz walked over to the bar, catching Johnny Stompanato working on another shot. Turning, he saw Cohen being glad-handed by Tom Breneman and the maître d', out of eyeshot. Johnny Stomp swiveled around; Buzz put five Mickey C-notes in his hand. 'Sifakis snitched you, but I don't want him touched. And I didn't tell Mickey bubkis. *You owe me*.'

Johnny smiled and pocketed the cash. 'Thanks, pal.'

Buzz said, 'I ain't your pal, you wop cocksucker,' and walked outside, stuffing the remaining hundreds in his shirt pocket, spitting on his necktie and using it to daub the tomato juice stains on his best Oviatt's worsted. Audrey Anders was standing on the sidewalk watching him. She said, 'Nice life you've got, Meeks.'

CHAPTER FOUR

Part of him knew it was just a dream – that it was 1950, not 1941; that the story would run its course while part of him grasped for new details and part tried to be dead still so as not to disrupt the unraveling.

He was speeding south on 101, wheeling a hot La Salle sedan. Highway Patrol sirens were closing the gap; Kern County scrubland loomed all around him. He saw a series of dirt roads snaking off the highway and hit the one on the far left, figuring the prowl cars would pursue straight ahead or down the middle. The road wound past farmhouses and fruit pickers' shacks into a box canyon; he heard sirens to his left and right, behind him and in front of him. Knowing any roadway was capture, he down-shifted and plowed across furrowed dirt, gaining distance on the wheeirr, wheeirr, wheeirr. He saw stationary lights up ahead and made them for a farmhouse; a fence materialized; he down-shifted, swung around in slow second gear and got a perfect view of a brightly lit picture window:

Two men swinging axes at a young blonde woman pressed into a doorway. A half-second flash of an arm severed off. A wide-open mouth smeared with orange lipstick screaming mute.

The dream speeded up.

He made it to Bakersfield; unloaded the La Salle; got paid. Back to San Berdoo, biology classes at JC, nightmares about the mouth and the arm. Pearl Harbor, 4F from a punctured eardrum. No amount of study, cash GTAs or *anything* can push the girl away. Months pass, and he returns to find out how and why.

It takes a while, but he comes up with a triangle: a missing local girl named Kathy Hudgens, her spurned lover Marty Sidwell – dead on Saipan – questioned by the cops and let go because no body was found. The number-two man most likely Buddy Jastrow. Folsom parolee, known for his love of torturing dogs and cats. Also missing – last seen two days after he tore across the dry cabbage field. The dream dissolving into typescript – criminology texts filled with forensic gore shots. Joining the LASD in '44 to know WHY; advancing through jail and patrol duty; other deputies hooting at him for his perpetual all-points want on Harlan 'Buddy' Jastrow.

A noise went off. Danny Upshaw snapped awake, thinking it was a siren kicking over. Then he saw the stucco swirls on his bedroom ceiling and knew it was the phone.

He picked it up. 'Skipper?'

'Yeah,' Captain Al Dietrich said. 'How'd you know?'

'You're the only one who calls me.'

Dietrich snorted. 'Anyone ever call you an ascetic?'

'Yeah, you.'

Dietrich laughed. 'I like your luck. One night as acting watch commander and you get floods, two accident deaths and a homicide. Want to fill me in on that?'

Danny thought of the corpse: bite marks, the missing eyes. 'It's as bad as anything I've seen. Did you talk to Henderson and Deffry?'

'They left canvassing reports – nothing hot. Bad, huh?'

'The worst I've seen.'

Dietrich sighed. 'Danny, you're a rookie squadroom dick, and you've never worked a job like this. You've only seen it in your books – in black and white.'

Kathy Hudgen's mouth and arm were superimposed against the ceiling – in Technicolor. Danny held on to his temper. 'Right, Skipper. It was bad, though. I went down to the morgue and . . . watched the prep. It got worse. Then I went back to help Deffry and Hender – '

'They told me. They also said you got bossy. Shitcan that, or you'll get a rep as a prima donna.'

Danny swallowed dry. 'Right, Captain. Any ID on the body?'

'Not yet, but I think we've got the car it was transported in. It's a '47 Buick Super, green, abandoned a half block up from the building site. White upholstery with what looks like bloodstains. It was reported stolen at ten this morning, clouted outside a jazz club on South Central. The owner was still drunk when he called in – you call him for details.'

'Print man dusting it?'

'Being done now.'

'Is SID going over the lot?'

'No. The print man was all I could wangle downtown.'

'Shit. Captain, I want this one.'

'You can have it. No publicity, though. I don't want another Black Dahlia mess.'

'What about another man to work with me?'

Dietrich sighed – long and slow. 'If the victim warrants it. For now, it's just you. We've only got four detectives,

Danny. If this John Doe was trash, I don't want to waste another man.'

Danny said, 'A homicide is a homicide, sir.'

Dietrich said, 'You're smarter than that, Deputy.'

Danny said, 'Yes, sir,' hung up, and rolled.

The day had turned cool and cloudy. Danny played the radio on the ride to Allegro; the weatherman was predicting more rain, maybe flooding in the canyons – and there was no news of the horrific John Doe. Passing the building site, he saw kids playing touch football in the mud and rubberneckers pointing out the scene of last night's spectacle – an SID prowl of the lot would now yield zero.

The print wagon and abandoned Buick were up at the end of the block. Danny noticed that the sedan was perfectly parked, aligned with the curb six inches or so out, the tires pointed inward to prevent the vehicle from sliding downhill. A psych lead: the killer had just brutally snuffed his victim and transported the body from fuck knows where, yet he still had the calm to coolly dispose of his car – *by the dump scene* – which meant that there were probably no witnesses to the snatch.

Danny hooked his Chevy around the print car and parked, catching sight of the tech's legs dangling out the driver's side of the Buick. Walking over, he heard the voice the legs belonged to: 'Glove prints on the wheel and dashboard, Deputy. Fresh caked blood on the back seat and some white sticky stuff on the side headliner.'

Danny looked in, saw an old plainclothesman dusting the glove compartment and a thin patch of dried blood dotted with white terrycloth on the rear seat cushion. The seat rests immediately behind the driver were matted with crisscross strips of blood – the terrycloth imbedded deeper into the caking. The velveteen sideboard by the window was streaked with the gelatinous substance he'd tagged at the morgue. Danny sniffed the goo, got the same mint/medicinal scent, clenched and unclenched his fists as he ran a spot reconstruction:

40

The killer drove his victim to the building site like a chauffeur, the stiff propped up in his white terry robe, eyeless head lolling against the sideboard, oozing the salve or ointment. The crisscross strips on the seat rests were the razorlike cuts on his back soaking through; the blood patch on the cushion was the corpse flopping over sideways when the killer made a sharp right turn.

'Hey! Deputy!'

The print man was sitting up, obviously pissed that he was taking liberties. 'Look, I have to dust the back now. Do you mind . . .'

Danny looked at the rear-view mirror, saw that it was set strangely and got in behind the wheel. Another reconstruction: the mirror held a perfect view of the back seat, blood strips and goo-streaked sideboard. The killer had adjusted it in order to steal glances at his victim as he drove.

'What's your name, son?'

Now the old tech was really ticked. Danny said, 'It's Deputy Upshaw, and don't bother with the back seat – this guy's too smart.'

'Do you feel like telling me how you know that?'

The two-way in the print wagon crackled; the old-timer got out of the Buick, shaking his head. Danny memorized the registration card laminated to the steering column: Nestor J. Albanese, 1236 S. St. Andrews, LA, Dunkirk–4619. He thought of Albanese as the killer – a phony car theft reported – and nixed the idea as far-fetched; he thought of the rage it took to butcher the victim, the ice it took to drive him around LA in New Year's Eve traffic. *Why?*

The tech called out, 'For you, Upshaw.'

Danny walked over to the print car and grabbed the mike. 'Yeah?'

A female voice, static-filtered, answered. 'Karen, Danny.'

Karen Hiltscher, the clerk/dispatcher at the station; *his* errand girl – occasional sweet talk for her favors. She hadn't figured out that he wasn't interested and persisted in using first names over the County air. Danny pushed the talk button. 'Yeah, Karen.'

'There's an ID on your 187. Martin Mitchell Goines, male Caucasian, DOB 11/9/16. Two convictions for marijuana possession, two years County for the first, three to five State for the other. Paroled from San Quentin after three and a half, August of '48. His last known address was a halfway house on 8th and Alvarado. He was a State parole absconder, bench warrant issued. Under employment he's listed as a musician, registered with Union Local 3126 in Hollywood.'

Danny thought of the Buick stolen outside a darktown jazz club. 'Have you got mugs?'

'Just came in.'

He put on his sugar voice. 'Help me with paperwork, sweet? Some phone calls?'

Karen's voice came out whiny and catty – even over the static. 'Sure, Danny. You'll pick up the mugshots?'

'Twenty minutes.' Danny looked around and saw that the print tech was back at work. He added, 'You're a doll,' hoping the girl bought it.

Danny called Nestor J. Albanese from a pay phone on Allegro and Sunset. The man had the raspy voice and skewed speech of a hangover sufferer; he told a booze-addled version of his New Year's Eve doings, going through it three times before Danny got the chronology straight.

He was club-hopping in darktown from 9:00 or so on, the bop joints around Slauson and Central – the Zombie, Bido Lito's, Tommy Tucker's Playroom, Malloy's Nest. Leaving the Nest around 1:00 A.M., he walked over to where he thought he left his Buick. It wasn't there, so he retraced his steps, drunk, figuring he'd ditched the car on a side street. The rain was drenching him, he was woozy from mai tais and champagne, he took a cab home and woke up – still smashed – at 8:30. He took another cab back to South Central, searched for the Buick for a solid hour, didn't find it and called the police

42

to report it stolen. He then hailed another taxi and returned home again, to be contacted by the watch sergeant at the West Hollywood substation, who told him his pride and joy was a likely transport vehicle in a homicide case, and now, at 3:45 P.M. New Year's Day, he wanted his baby back – and that was that.

Danny 99 percent eliminated Albanese as a suspect – the man came off as legit stupid, professed to have no criminal record and seemed sincere when he denied knowing Martin Mitchell Goines. He told him the Buick would be kicked loose from the County Impound inside three days, hung up and drove to the Station for mugshots and favors.

Karen Hiltscher was out on her dinner break; Danny was grateful she wasn't around to make goo-goo eyes and poke his biceps, copping feels while the watch sergeant chuckled. She'd left the mugshot strip on her desk. Alive and with eyes, Martin Mitchell Goines looked young and tough – a huge, Butch-Waxed pompadour the main feature of his front, right and left side pics. The shots were from his second reefer roust: LAPD 4/16/44 on a mugboard hanging around his neck. Six years back; three and a half of them spent in Big Q. Goines had aged badly – and had died looking older than thirty-three.

Danny left Karen Hiltscher a memo: 'Sweetheart – will you do this for me? 1 – Call Yellow, Beacon and the indy cab cos. Ask about pickups of single males on Sunset between Doheny and La Cienega and side sts. between 3:00 to 4:00 a.m. last nite. Ditto pickups of a drunk man, Central and Slauson to 1200 block S. St. Andrews, 12:30 – 1:30 a.m. Get all log entries for pickups those times and locations. 2 – Stay friendly, ok? I'm sorry about that lunch date I cancelled. I had to cram for a test. Thanks – D.U.'

The lie made Danny angry at the girl, the LASD and himself for kowtowing to teenaged passion. He thought of calling the 77th Street Station desk to tell them he was going to be operating in City territory, then kiboshed the idea – it was too much like bowing to the LAPD and their pout over the Sheriff's harboring Mickey Cohen. He held the thought, the contempt. A killer-hoodlum who longed to be a nightclub comic and got weepy over lost dogs and crippled kids brought a big-city police department to its knees with a wire recording: Vice cops taking bribes and chauffeuring prostitutes; the Hollywood Division nightwatch screwing Brenda Allen's whores on mattresses in the Hollywood Station felony tank. Mickey C. putting out his entire smear arsenal because the City high brass upped his loan shark and bookmaking kickbacks 10 percent. Ugly. Stupid. Greedy. *Wrong*.

Danny let the litany simmer on his way down to darktown – Sunset east to Figueroa, Figueroa to Slauson, Slauson east to Central – a hypothetical route for the car thief/killer. Dusk started coming on, rain clouds eclipsing late sunshine trying to light up Negro slums: ramshackle houses encircled by chicken wire, pool halls, liquor stores and storefront churches on every street – until jazzland took over. Then loony swank amidst squalor, one long block of it.

Bido Lito's was shaped like a miniature Taj Mahal, only purple; Malloy's Nest was a bamboo hut fronted by phony Hawaiian palms strung with Christmas-tree lights. Zebra stripes comprised the paint job on Tommy Tucker's Playroom – an obvious converted warehouse with plaster saxophones, trumpets and music clefs alternating across the edge of the roof. The Zamboanga, Royal Flush and Katydid Klub were bright pink, more purple and puke green, a hangarlike building subdivided, the respective doorways outlined in neon. And Club Zombie was a Moorish mosque featuring a three-story-tall sleepwalker growing out of the facade: a gigantic darky with glowing red eyes high-stepping into the night.

Jumbo parking lots linked the clubs; big Negro bouncers stood beside doorways and signs announcing 'Early Bird' chicken dinners. A scant number of cars was stationed in the lots; Danny left his Chevy on a side street and started bracing the muscle.

The doormen at the Zamboanga and Katydid recalled seeing Martin Mitchell Goines 'around'; a man setting up a menu board outside the Royal Flush took the ID a step further: Goines was a second-rate utility trombone, usually hired for fill-in duty. Since 'Christmas or so' he'd been playing with the house band at Bido Lito's. Danny read every suspicious black face he spoke to for signs of holding back; all he got was a sense that these guys thought Marty Goines was a lily-white fool.

Danny hit Bido Lito's. A sign in front proclaimed DICKY MCCOVER AND HIS JAZZ SULTANS – SHOWS AT 7:30, 9:30 AND 11:30 NITELY – ENJOY OUR DELUXE CHICKEN BASKET. Walking in, he thought he was entering a hallucination.

The walls were pastel satin bathed by colored baby spotlights that hued the fabric garish beyond garish; the bandstand backing was a re-creation of the Pyramids, done in sparkly cardboard. The tables had fluorescent borders, the high-yellow hostesses carrying drinks and food wore low-cut tiger costumes, the whole place smelled of deep-fried meat. Danny felt his stomach growl, realized he hadn't eaten in twenty-four hours and approached the bar. Even in the hallucinatory lighting, he saw the barman make him for a cop.

He held out the mugshot strip. 'Do you know this man?'

The bartender took the strip, examined it under the cash register light and handed it back. 'That's Marty. Plays 'bone with the Sultans. Comes in before the first set to eat, if you wants to talk to him.'

'When was the last time you saw him?'

'Las' night.'

'For the band's last set?'

The barman's mouth curled into a tight smile; Danny sensed that 'band' was square nomenclature. 'I asked you a question.'

The man wiped the bartop with a rag. 'I don' think

so. Midnight set I remember seein' him. Sultans played two late ones las' night, on account of New Year's.'

Danny noticed a shelf of whiskey bottles without labels. 'Go get the manager.'

The bartender pressed a button by the register; Danny took a stool and swiveled to face the bandstand. A group of Negro men was opening instrument cases, pulling out sax, trumpet and drum cymbals. A fat mulatto in a double-breasted suit walked over to the bar, wearing a suck-up-to-authority smile. He said, 'Thought I knew all the boys on the Squad.'

Danny said, 'I'm with the Sheriff's.'

The mulatto's smile evaporated. 'I usually deal with the Seven-Seven, Mr. Sheriff.'

'This is County business.'

'This ain't County territory.'

Danny hooked a thumb in back of him, then nodded toward the baby spots. 'You've got illegal booze, those lights are a fire hazard and the County runs Beverage Control and Health and Safety Code. I've got a summons book in the car. Want me to get it?'

The smile returned. 'I surely don't. How can I be of service, *sir*?'

'Tell me about Marty Goines.'

'What about him?'

'Try everything.'

The manager took his time lighting a cigarette; Danny knew his fuse was being tested. Finally the man exhaled and said, 'Not much to tell. The local sent him down when the Sultans' regular trombone fell off the wagon. I'd have preferred colored, but Marty's got a rep for getting along with non-Caucasians, so I said okay. Except for ditching out on the guys last night, Marty never did me no dirt, just did his job copacetic. Not the world's best slideman, not the worst neither.'

Danny pointed to the musicians on the bandstand. 'Those guys are the Sultans, right?'

'Right.'

'Goines played a set with them that ended just after midnight?'

The mulatto smiled, 'Dicky McCover's up-tempo "Old Lang Syne." Even Bird envies that – '

'When was the set finished?'

'Set broke up maybe 12:20. Fifteen-minute break I give my guys. Like I said, Marty ditched out on that and the 2:00 closer. Only time he did me dirt.'

Danny went in for the Sultans' alibi. 'Were the other three men on stage for the final two sets?'

The manager nodded. 'Uh-huh. Played for a private party I had going after that. What'd Marty do?'

'He got murdered.'

The mulatto choked on the smoke he was inhaling. He coughed the drag out, dropped his cigarette on the floor and stepped on it, rasping, 'Who you think did it?'

Danny said, 'Not you, not the Sultans. Let's try this one: was Goines feeding a habit?'

'Say what?'

'Don't play dumb. Junk, H, horse, a fucking heroin habit.'

The manager took a step backward. 'I don't hire no god-damned hopheads.'

'Sure you don't, just like you don't serve hijack booze. Let's try this: Marty and women.'

'Never heard nothing one way or the other.'

'How about enemies? Guys with a hard-on for him?'

'Nothing.'

'What about friends, known associates, men coming around asking for him?'

'No, no and *no*. Marty didn't even have no family.'

Danny shifted gears with a smile – an interrogation technique he practiced in front of his bedroom mirror. 'Look, I'm sorry I came on so strong.'

'No, you ain't.'

Danny flushed, hoping the crazy lighting didn't pick it up. 'Have you got a man watching the parking lot?'

'No.'

'Do you remember a green Buick in the lot last night?'

47

'No.'

'Do your kitchen workers hang out in the lot?'

'Man, my kitchen people is too busy to hang out anyplace.'

'What about your hostesses? They sell it outside after you close?'

'Man, you are out of your bailiwick and way out of line.'

Danny elbowed the mulatto aside and threaded his way through the dinner crowd to the bandstand. The Sultans saw him coming and exchanged looks: cop-wise, *experienced*. The drummer quit arranging his gear; the trumpeter backed off and stood by the curtains leading backstage; the saxophone man stopped adjusting his mouthpiece and stood his ground.

Danny stepped onto the platform, blinking against the hot white light shining down. He sized up the sax as the boss and decided on a soft tack – his interrogation was playing to a full house. 'Sheriff's. It's about Marty Goines.'

The drummer answered him. 'Marty's clean. Just took the cure.'

A lead – if it wasn't one ex-con running interference for another. 'I didn't know he had a habit.'

The sax player snorted. 'Years' worth, but he kicked.'

'Where?'

'Lex. Lexington State Hospital in Kentucky. This about Marty's parole?'

Danny stepped back so he could eyeball all three men in one shot. 'Marty got snuffed last night. I think he was snatched from around here right after your midnight set.'

Three clean reactions: the trumpeter scared, most likely afraid of cops on general principles; the drummer trembling; the sax man spooked, but coming back mad. 'We all gots alibis, 'case you don't already know.'

Danny thought: RIP Martin Mitchell Goines. 'I know, so let's try the usual drill. Did Marty have any enemies that you know of? Woman trouble? Old dope buddies hanging around?'

The sax said, 'Marty was a fuckin' cipher. All I knew about him was that he hung up his Quentin parole, that he was so hot to kick he went to Lex as a fuckin' absconder. Big balls if you asks me – that's a Fed hospital, and they mighta run warrant checks on him. Fuckin' cipher. None of us even knew where he was stayin'.'

Danny kicked the skinny around and watched the trumpet player inch over from the curtains, holding his horn like it was an ikon to ward off demons. He said, 'Mister, I think I got something for you.'

'What?'

'Marty told me he had to meet a guy after the midnight set, and I saw him walking across the street to the Zombie parking lot.'

'Did he mention a name?'

'No, just a guy.'

'Did he say *anything* else about him? What they were going to do – anything like that?'

'No, and he said he'd be coming right back.'

'Do you think he was going to buy dope?'

The saxophone player bored into Danny with blue eyes lighter than his own brown ones. 'Man, I fuckin' told you Marty was clean, and intended to stay clean.'

Boos erupted from the audience; paper debris hit Danny's legs. He blinked against the spotlight and felt sweat creeping down his rib cage. A voice yelled, 'Ofay motherfuck'; applause followed it; a half-chewed chicken wing struck Danny's back. The sax man smiled up at him, licked his mouthpiece and winked. Danny resisted an urge to kick the horn down his throat and quick-walked out of the club by a side exit.

The night air cooled his sweat and made him shiver; pulsating neon assaulted his eyes. Little bursts of music melded together like one big noise and the nigger sleepwalker atop the Club Zombie looked like doomsday. Danny knew he was scared, and headed straight for the apparition.

The doorman backed off from his badge and let him in to four walls of smoke and dissonant screeching – the combo at the front of the room heading toward a crescendo. The bar was off to the left, shaped like a coffin and embossed with the club's sleepwalker emblem. Danny beelined there, grabbing a stool, hooking a finger at a white man polishing glasses.

The barkeep placed a napkin in front of him. Danny yelled, 'Double bonded!' above the din. A glass appeared; Danny knocked the bourbon back; the barman refilled. Danny drank again and felt his nerves go from sandpapered to warm. The music ended with a *thud-boom-scree*; the house lights went on amid big applause. When it trailed off, Danny reached in his pocket and pulled out a five-dollar bill and the Goines mugshot strip.

The bartender said, 'Two spot for the drinks.'

Danny stuffed the five in his shirt pocket and held up the strip. 'Look familiar?'

Squinting, the man said, 'Is this guy older now? Maybe a different haircut?'

'These are six years old. Seen him?'

The barman took glasses from his pocket, put them on and held the mugshots out at arm's length. 'Does he blow around here?'

Danny missed the question – and wondered if it was sex slang he didn't know. 'Explain what you mean.'

'I mean does he gig, jam, play music around here?'

'Trombone at Bido Lito's.'

The barman snapped his fingers. 'Okay, I know him then. Marty something. He juices between sets at Bido's, been doing it since around Christmas, 'cause the bar at Bido's ain't supposed to serve the help. Hungry juicer, sort of like – '

Like *you*. Danny smiled, the booze notching down his temper. 'Did you see him last night?'

'Yeah, on the street. Him and another guy heading over to a car down by the corner on 67th. Looked like he had a load on. Maybe . . .'

50

Danny leaned forward. 'Maybe *what*? Spell it out.'

'Maybe a junk load. You work jazz clubs awhile, you get to know the ropes. This Marty guy was walking all rubbery, like he was on a junk nod. The other guy had his arm around him, helping him over to the car.'

Danny said, 'Slow and easy now. The time, a description of the car and the other man. Real slow.'

Customers were starting to swarm the bar – Negro men in modified zoot suits, their women a half step behind, all made up and done up to look like Lena Horne. The barkeep looked at his business, then back at Danny. 'Had to be 12:15 to 12:45, around in there. Marty what's his face and the other guy were cutting across the sidewalk. I know the car was a Buick, 'cause it had them portholes on the side. All I remember about the other guy was that he was tall and had gray hair. I only saw them sort of sideways, and I thought, "I should have such a nice head of hair." Now can I serve these people?'

Danny was about to say no; the barkeep turned to a bearded young man with an alto sax slung around hid neck. 'Coleman, you know that white trombone from Bido's? Marty what the fuck?'

Coleman reached over the bar, grabbed two handfuls of ice and pressed them to his face. Danny checked him out: tall, blond, late twenties and off-kilter handsome – like the boy lead in the musical Karen Hiltscher dragged him to. His voice was reedy, exhausted. 'Sure. A from-hunger horn, I heard. Why?'

'Talk to this police gentleman here, he'll tell you.'

Danny pointed to his glass, going two shots over his nightly limit. The barman filled it, then slid off. The alto said, 'You're with the Double Seven?'

Danny killed his drink, and on impulse stuck out his hand. 'My name's Upshaw. West Hollywood Sheriff's.'

The men shook. 'Coleman Healy, late of Cleveland, Chicago and the planet Mars. Marty in trouble?'

The bourbon made Danny *too* warm; he loosened his

tie and moved closer to Healy. 'He was murdered last night.'

Healy's face contorted. Danny saw every handsome plane jerk, twitch and spasm; he looked away to let him quash his shock and get hepcat again. When he turned back, Healy was bracing himself into the bar. Danny's knee brushed the alto's thigh – it was taut with tension. 'How well did you know him, Coleman?'

Healy's face was now gaunt, slack under his beard. 'Chewed the fat with him a couple of times around Christmas, right here at this bar. Just repop – Bird's new record, the weather. You got an idea who did it?'

'A lead on a suspect – a tall, gray-haired man. The bartender saw him with Goines last night, walking toward a car parked on Central.'

Coleman Healy ran fingers down the keys of his sax. 'I've seen Marty with a guy like that a couple of times. Tall, middle-aged, dignified looking.' He paused, then said, 'Look, Upshaw, not to besmirch the dead, but can I give you an impression I got – on the QT?'

Danny slid his stool back, just enough to get a full-face reaction – Healy wired up, eager to help. 'Go ahead, impressions help sometimes.'

'Well, I think Marty was fruit. The older guy looked like a nance to me, like a sugar daddy type. The two of them were playing footsie at a table, and when I noticed it, Marty pulled away from the guy – sort of like a kid with his hand caught in the cookie jar.'

Danny tingled, thinking of the tags he eschewed because they were too coarse and antithetical to Vollmer and Maslick: PANSY SLASH. QUEEN BASH. FRUIT SNUFF. HOMO PASSION JOB. 'Coleman, could you ID the older man?'

Healy played with his sax. 'I don't think so. The light here is strange, and the queer stuff is just an impression I got.'

'Have you seen the man before or since those times with Goines?'

'No. Never solo. And I was here all night, in case you think I did it.'

Danny shook his head. 'Do you know if Goines was using narcotics?'

'Nix. He was too interested in booze to be a junk fiend.'

'What about other people who knew him? Other musicians around here?'

'Ixnay. We just gabbed a couple of times.'

Danny put out his hand; Healy turned it upside down, twisting it from a squarejohn to a jazzman shake. He said, 'See you in church,' and headed for the stage.

Queer slash.

Fruit snuff.

Homo passion job.

Danny watched Coleman Healy mount the bandstand and exchange back slaps with the other musicians. Fat and cadaverous, pocked, oily and consumptive looking, they seemed wrong next to the sleek alto – like a crime scene photo with blurs that fucked up the symmetry and made you notice the wrong things. The music started: piano handing a jump melody to the trumpet, drums kicking in, Healy's sax wailing, lilting, wailing, drifting off the base refrain into chord variations. The music digressed into noise; Danny spotted a bank of phone booths next to the powder room and rolled back to police work.

His first nickel got him the watch boss at the 77th Street Station. Danny explained that he was a Sheriff's detective working a homicide – a jazz musician and possible dope addict slashed and dumped off the Sunset Strip. The victim was probably not currently using drugs – but he wanted a list of local H pushers anyway – the snuff might be tied to dope intrigue. The watch boss said, 'How's Mickey these days?,' added, 'Submit request through official channels,' and hung up.

Pissed, Danny dialed Doc Layman's personal number at the City Morgue, one eye on the bandstand. The pathologist answered on the second ring. 'Yes?'

'Danny Upshaw, Doctor.'

Layman laughed. 'Danny Upstart is more like it – I just autopsied the John Doe you tried to usurp.'

Danny drew in a breath, turning away from Coleman Healy gyrating with his sax. 'Yes? And?'

'And a question first. Did you stick a tongue depressor in the corpse's mouth?'

'Yes.'

'Deputy, never, *ever*, introduce foreign elements into interior cavities until after you have thoroughly spotted the exterior. The cadaver had cuts with imbedded wood slivers all over his back – pine – and you stuck a piece of pine into his mouth, leaving similar slivers. Do you see how you could have fouled up my assessment?'

'Yes, but it was obvious the victim was strangled by a towel or a sash – the terrycloth fibers were a dead giveaway.'

Layman sighed – long, exasperated. 'The cause of death was a massive heroin overdose. The shot was administered into a vein by the spine, by the killer himself – the victim couldn't have reached it. The towel was placed in the mouth to absorb blood when the heroin hit the victim's heart and caused arteries to pop, which means the killer had at least elementary anatomical knowledge.'

Danny said, 'Jesus fuck.'

Layman said, 'An appropriate blasphemy, but it gets worse. Here's some incidentals first:

'One, no residual heroin in the bloodstream – Mr. Doe was not now addicted, although needle marks on his arms indicate he once was. Two, death occurred around 1:00 to 2:00 A.M., and the neck and genital bruises were both postmortem. The cuts on the back were postmortem, almost certainly made by razor blades attached to something like a pine slab or a 2 by 4. So far, brutal – but not past my ken. However . . .'

Layman stopped – his old classroom orator's pause. Danny, sweating out his jolts of bonded, said, 'Come on, Doc.'

'All right. The substance in the eye sockets was KY Jelly. The killer inserted his penis into the sockets and ejaculated – at least twice. I found six cubic centimeters of semen seeping back towards the cranial vault. O+ secretor – the most common blood type among white people.'

Danny opened the phone booth door; he heard wisps of bebop and saw Coleman Healy going down on one knee, sax raised to the rafters. 'The bites on the torso?'

Layman said, 'Not human is what I'm thinking. The wounds were too shredded to make casts from – there's no way I could have lifted any kind of viable teeth marks. Also, the ME's assistant who took over after you pulled your little number swabbed the affected area with alcohol, so I couldn't test for saliva or gastric juices. The victim's blood – AB+ – was all I found there. You discovered the body when?'

'Shortly after 4:00 A.M.'

'Then scavenging animals down from the hills are unlikely. The wounds are too localized for that theory, anyway.'

'Doc, are you sure we're dealing with teeth marks?'

'Absolutely. The inflammation around the wounds is from a mouth sucking. It's too wide to be human – '

'Do you think – '

'Don't interrupt. I'm thinking that – *maybe* – the killer spread blood bait on the affected area and let some kind of well trained vicious dog at the victim. How many men are working this job, Danny?'

'Just me.'

'ID on the victim? Leads?'

'It's going well, Doc.'

'Get him.'

'I *will*'

Danny hung up and walked outside. Cold air edged the heat off his booze intake and let him collate evidence. He now had three solid leads:

The homosexual mutilations combined with Coleman Healy's observation of Marty Goines being 'fruit'; his 'nance' 'sugar daddy type' – who resembled the tall, gray-haired man the bartender saw with Goines, heading toward the stolen Buick last night – an hour or so before the estimated time of death; the heroin OD cause of death; the bartender's description of Goines weaving in a junk nod – that jolt of dope a probable precurser to the shot that burst his heart; Goines' previous addiction and recent dope cure. Putting the possible animal mutilations out of mind, he had one *hard* lead: the tall, gray-haired man – a sugar daddy capable of glomming heroin, hypodermic syringes and talking a reformed junkie into geezing up on the spot and ditching his New Year's Eve gig.

And no LAPD cooperation – yet – on local horse pushers; a junkie squeeze was the only logical play.

Danny walked across the street to Tommy Tucker's Playroom, found an empty booth and ordered coffee to kill the liquor in his system and keep him awake. The music/motif was ballads and zebra-striped upholstery, cheap jungle wallpaper offset by tiki torches licking flames up to the ceiling, another fire hazard, a blaze to burn the whole block to cinder city. The coffee was black and strong and made inroads on the bonded; the bop was soft – caresses for the couples in the booths: lovebirds holding hands and sipping rum drinks. The total package made him think of San Berdoo circa '39, him and Tim in a hot Olds ragger joy-riding to a hicktown prom, changing clothes at his place while the old lady hawked *Watchtowers* outside Coulter's Department Store. Down to their skivvies, horseplay, jokes about substitutes for girls; Timmy with Roxanne Beausoleil outside the gym that night – the two of them bouncing the Olds almost off its suspension. Him the prom wallflower, declining seconds on Roxy, drinking spiked punch, getting mawkish with the slow grind numbers and the hurt.

Danny killed the memories with police work – eyeball prowls for Health and Safety Code violations, liquor infractions, *wrongness*. The doorman was admitting minors; high yellows in slit gowns were oozing around soliciting business, there was only one side exit in a huge room sixteen seconds away from fireballing. Time passed; the music went from soft to loud to soft again; coffee and constant eye circuits got his nerves fine-honed. Then he hit paydirt, spotting two Negroes by the exit curtains pulling a handoff: cash for something palmable, a quick segue into the parking lot.

Danny counted to six and followed, easing the door open, peering out. The spook who took the money was striding toward the sidewalk; the other guy was two rows of cars down, opening the door of a rig topped by a long whip antenna. Danny gave him thirty seconds to geez up, light up or snort up, then pulled his .45, hunkered down and approached.

The car was a lavender Merc; marijuana smoke was drifting out the wind wings. Danny grabbed the driver's door and swung it open; the Negro shrieked, dropped his reefer and recoiled from the gun in his face. Danny said, 'Sheriff's. Hands on the dashboard slow or I'll kill you.'

The youth complied, in slow motion. Danny jammed the .45's muzzle under his chin and gave him a frisk; inside and outside jacket pockets, a waistband pat for weaponry. He found a lizardskin wallet, three marijuana cigarettes and no hardware; popped the glove compartment and flicked on the dashlight. The kid said, 'Look, man'; Danny dug his gun in harder, until it cut off his air supply and forced him mute.

The reefer stench was getting brutal; Danny found the butt on the seat cushion and snuffed it. With his free hand he opened the wallet, pulled out a driver's license and over a hundred in tens and twenties. He slipped the cash in his pocket and read the license: Carlton W. Jeffries, M.N., 5' 11", 165, DOB 6/19/29, 439 1/4 E. 98 St., L.A. A quick toss of the glove compartment got him DMV registration under the same name and a slew of unpaid traffic citations in their mailing envelopes. Danny put the license, reefers, money and registration into an envelope and dropped it on the pavement; he pulled his .45 out from under the boy's chin and used the muzzle to turn his head toward him. Up close, he saw a chocolate brown punk next to tears, lips flapping, Adam's apple bobbing up and down as he struggled for breath.

Danny said, 'Information or five years State time minimum. You call it.'

Carlton W. Jeffries found a voice: high, squeaky. 'What you think?'

'I think you're smart. Give me what I want, and I'll put that envelope in the mail to you tomorrow.'

'You could give it back now. Please. I need that money.'

'I want a hard snitch. If you play both ends and I get hurt, I've got you nailed. Evidence, and the confession you just made.'

'Man, I didn't make no confession to you!'

'Sure you did. You've been selling a pound a week. You're the A-number-one Southside grasshopper.'

'Man!'

Danny rested his gun barrel on Carlton W. Jeffries' nose. 'I want names. Heroin pushers around here. Give.'

'Man – '

Danny flipped the .45 up and grabbed the muzzle, reversing his grip so the gun could be used as a bludgeon. '*Give, goddamn you.*'

Jeffries took his hands off the dash and wrapped his arms around himself. 'Only guy I know is a guy name of Otis Jackson. Lives above the laundromat on One-o-three and Beach and please don't give me no rat jacket!'

Danny holstered his piece and backed out the car door. His foot hit the DMV envelope just as he heard Carlton W. Jeffries start bawling. He picked the evidence up, tossed it on the seat and double-timed to his Chevy so he wouldn't hear the sad little fuck blubber his gratitude.

103rd and Beach was a run-down intersection in the

heart of Watts: hair-straightening parlors on two corners, a liquor store on the third, the Koin King Washeteria occupying number four. Lights were burning in the apartment above the laundromat; Danny parked across the street, doused his headbeams and scoped out the only possible access: side steps leading up to a flimsy-looking door.

He walked over and up them, tiptoes, no hand on the railing for fear it would creak. At the top, he pulled his gun, put an ear to the door and listened, picking up a man's voice counting: eight, nine, ten, eleven. Tapping the door, he faked a drawl straight from Amos 'n' Andy: 'Otis? You there, man? It's me, man.'

Danny heard 'Shit!' inside; seconds later the door opened, held to the jamb by a chain. A hand holding a switchblade stuck out; Danny brought his gun barrel down on the shiv, then threw his weight inward.

The switchblade hit the top step; a voice screeched; the door caved in, Danny riding it. Then it was a crash to teh carpet and a topsy-turvy shot of Otis Jackson scooping junk bindles off the floor, stumbling to the bathroom, a toilet flushing. Danny got to his knees, sighted in and yelled, 'Sheriff's!' Otis Jackson flipped him his middle finger and weaved back to the living room wearing a shiteater grin.

Danny stood up, his head pounding with jazz chords. Otis Jackson said, 'The fuckin' Sheriff's ain't fuckin' shit around here.'

Danny lashed the .45 across his face. Jackson hit the rug, moaned and spit out cracked bridgework. Danny squatted beside him. 'You sell to a tall, gray-haired white man?'

Jackson spat bloody phlegm and a slice of his tongue. 'I'm with Jack D. and the Seven-Seven, mother – '

Danny held his gun at eye level. 'I'm with Mickey and the County, so what? I asked you a question.'

'I deal Hollywood, man! I know lots of gray-haired suckers!'

'Name them, and name everyone else you know who unloads at the clubs on South Central.'

'I'll let you kill me first, sucker!'

The jazz noise was coming back, soundtracking images: Coleman Healy fondling his sax, the reefer guy about to beg. Danny said, 'One more time. I want skinny on a tall white man. Middle-aged, silver hair.'

'An' I told you – '

Danny heard footsteps coming up the stairs, grunts and the unmistakable sound of revolvers being cocked. Otis Jackson smiled; Danny glommed the gist, holstered his piece and reached for his badge holder. Two big white men popped in the doorway aiming .38's; Danny had his shield out and a peace offering ready. 'Sheriff's. I'm a Sheriff's detective.'

The men walked over, guns first. The taller of the two helped Otis Jackson to his feet; the other, a fat guy with curly red hair, took Danny's ID buzzer, examined it and shook his head. 'Bad enough you guys get in bed with Mickey Kike, now you gotta beat up my favorite snitch. Otis, you are one lucky nigger. Deputy Upshaw, you are one stupid white man.'

The tall cop helped Otis Jackson into the bathroom. Danny stood up and grabbed his badge holder. The fat redhead said, 'Get the fuck back to the County and beat up your own niggers.'

CHAPTER FIVE

'. . . And the most pervasive aspect of Communism, its single most insidiously efficacious tool, is that it hides under a million banners, a million different flags, titles and combinations of initials, spreading its cancer under a million guises, all of them designed to pervert and corrupt in the name of compassion and goodness and social justice. UAES, SLDC, NAACP, AFL-CIO,

League for Democratic Ideals and Concerned Americans Against Bigotry. All high-sounding organizations that all good Americans should be proud to belong to. All seditious, perverted, cancerous tentacles of the Communist Conspiracy.'

Mal Considine had been sizing up Edmund J. Satterlee, ex-Fed, ex-Jesuit seminarian, for close to half an hour, taking occasional glances at the rest of the audience. Satterlee was a tall man, pear-shaped, in his early forties; his verbal style was a cross between Harry Truman homespun and Pershing Square crackpot – and you never knew when he was going to shout or whisper. Dudley Smith, chain-smoking, seemed to be enjoying his pitch; Ellis Loew kept looking at his watch and at Dudley – probably afraid that he was going to drop ash all over his new living room carpet. Dr. Saul Lesnick, psychiatrist/longtime Fed informant, sat as far away from the Red Chaser as possible while remaining in the same room. He was a small, frail old man with bright blue eyes and a cough that he kept feeding with harsh European cigarettes; he had the look native to stool pigeons everywhere – loathing for the presence of his captors – even though he had allegedly volunteered his services.

Satterlee was pacing now, gesticulating to them like they were four hundred, not four. Mal squirmed in his chair, reminding himself that this guy was his ticket to a captaincy and Chief DA's Investigator.

'. . . and in the early days of the war I worked with the Alien Squad relocating Japs. I gained my first insights into how anti-American sentiment breeds. The Japs who wanted to be good Americans offered to enlist in the armed forces, most were resentful and confused, and the subversive element – under the guise of patriotism – attempted to coerce them into treason by concerted, heavily intellectualized attacks on alleged American racial injustices. Under a banner of American concerns: liberty, justice and free enterprise, the seditious Japs portrayed this democracy as a land of

61

lynched Negroes and limited opportunities for coloreds, even though the Nisei were emerging as middle-class merchants when the war broke out. After the war, when the Communist Conspiracy emerged as the number-one threat to America's internal security, I saw how the same kind of thinking, of manipulation, was being used by the Reds to subvert our moral fiber. The entertainment industry and business were rife with fellow travelers, and I founded Red Crosscurrents to help weed out radicals and subversives. Organizations that want to keep themselves Red-free pay us a nominal fee to screen their employees and prospective employees for Commie associations, and *we* keep an exhaustive file on the Reds we uncover. This service also allows innocent people accused of being Pink to prove their innocence and gain employment that they might have been denied. Further – '

Mal heard Dr. Saul Lesnick cough; he looked at the old man sidelong and saw that the eruption was half laughter. Satterlee paused; Ellis Loew said, 'Ed, can we gloss the background and get down to business?'

Satterlee flushed, picked up his briefcase and took out a stack of papers, four individually clipped sheafs. He handed one each to Mal, Loew and Dudley Smith; Dr. Lesnick declined his with a shake of the head. Mal skimmed the top sheet. It was a deposition detailing picket line scuttlebutt: members of the United Alliance of Extras and Stagehands mouthing Pinko platitudes overheard by counter-pickets from the Teamsters. Mal checked the signees' names, recognizing Morris Jahelka, Davey Goldman and Fritzie 'Icepick' Kupferman – known Mickey Cohen strongarms.

Satterlee resumed his position in front of them; Mal thought he looked like a man who would kill for a lectern – or any resting place for his long, gangly arms. 'These pieces of paper are our first wave of ammunition. I have worked with a score of municipal grand juries nationwide, and the sworn statements of patriotic citizens always have a salutary effect on Grand Jury members. I think we have a great chance for a successful one here in Los Angeles now – the labour infighting between the Teamsters and the UAES is a great impetus, a shot at the limelight that will probably not come again. Communist influence in Hollywood is a broad topic, and the picket line trouble and UAES's fomenting of subversion within both contexts is a good device to get the public interested. Let me quote from the deposition of Mr. Morris Jahelka: 'While picketing outside Variety International Pictures on the morning of November 29, 1949, I heard a UAES member, a woman named "Claire," tell another UAES member: "With the UAES in the studios we can advance the cause better than the entire Red Guard. Movies are the new opiate of the people. They'll believe anything we can get on the screen." ' Gentlemen, Claire is Claire Katherine De Haven, a consort of Hollywood 10 traitors and a known member of no fewer than fourteen organizations that have been classified as Communist Fronts by the California State Attorney General's Office. Is that not impressive?'

Mal raised his hand. Edmund J. Satterlee said, 'Yes, Lieutenant Considine? A question?'

'No, a statement. Morris Jahelka has two convictions for felony statch rape. Your patriotic citizen screws twelve-year-old-girls.'

Ellis Loew said, 'Goddamnit, Malcolm.'

Satterlee tried a smile, faltered at it and stuck his hands in his pockets. 'I see. Anything else on Mr. Jahelka?'

'Yes. He also likes little boys, but he's never been caught at it.'

Dudley Smith laughed. 'Politics makes for strange bedfellows, which doesn't negate the fact that in this case Mr. Jahelka is on the side of the angels. Besides, lad, we'll be damn sure his jacket is sealed, and the goddamn Pinks probably won't bring in lawyers for redirect questioning.'

Mal concentrated on keeping his voice calm. 'Is that true, Ellis?'

Loew fanned away plumes of Doc Lesnick's cigarette smoke. 'Essentially, yes. We're trying to get as many UAESers as possible to volunteer as witnesses, and hostile witnesses – subpoenaed ones – tend to try to assert their innocence by not retaining counsel. Also, the studios have a clause in their contract with UAES, stating that they can terminate the contract if certain areas of malfeasance can be proven against the contractee. Before the grand jury convenes – if our evidence is strong enough – I'm going to the studio heads to get UAES ousted on that clause – which should make the bastards hopping mad and rabid when they hit the witness stand. An angry witness is an ineffectual witness. You know that, Mal.'

Cohen and his Teamsters in; UAES out. Mal wondered if Mickey C. was a contributor to Loew's six-figure slush fund – which should hit the half million mark by the time of the '52 primaries. 'You're good, counselor.'

'So are you, *Captain*. Down to brass tacks, Ed. I'm due in court at noon.'

Satterlee handed Mal and Dudley mimeographed sheets. 'My thoughts on the interrogation of subversives,' he said. 'Guilt by association is a strong lever on these people – they're all connected up – everyone on the far left knows everyone else to one degree or another. In with your depositions I've got lists of Commie front meetings cross-filed with donation lists, which are excellent levers to procure information and get Reds to inform on other Reds to save their own damn skin. The donations also mean bank records that can be subpoenaed as evidence. Proffering suveillance photos to potential witnesses is my personal favorite technique – being shown at a subersive meeting puts the fear of God into the most Godless Pinks, and they'll inform on their own mother to stay out of jail. I may be able to get us some extremely damaging photos from a friend who works for Red Channels – some exremely good pictures of Sleepy Lagoon Defense Committee picnics. In fact, I've been told the photos are the Rembrandts of Federal surveillance – actual CP bigwigs and Hollywood stars along with our friends in UAES. Mr Loew?'

Loew said, 'Thank you, Ed,' and gave his standard one finger up, indicating everybody stand. Dudley Smith practically leaped to his feet; Mal stood and saw Doc Lesnick walking to the bathroom holding his chest. Awful wet coughs echoed from the hallway; he pictured Lesnick retching blood. Satterlee, Smith and Loew broke up their circle of handshaking; the Red Chaser went out the door with the DA kneading his shoulders.

Dudley Smith said, 'Zealots are always tiresome. Ed's good at what he does, but he doesn't know when to quit performing. Five hundred dollars a lecture he gets. Capitalist exploitation of Communism, wouldn't you say so, Captain?'

'I'm not a captain yet, Lieutenant.'

'Ha! And a grand wit you have, too, to go with your rank.'

Mal studied the Irishman, less scared than he was yesterday morning at the restaurant. 'What's in this for you? You're a case man, you don't want Jack Tierney's job.'

'Maybe I just want to get next to you, lad. You're odds on for Chief of Police or County Sheriff somewhere down the line, all that grand work you did in Europe, liberating our persecuted Jewish brethren. Speaking of which, here comes the Hebrew contingent now.'

Ellis Loew was leading Lesnick into the living room and settling him into an easy chair by the fireplace. The old man arranged a pack of Gauloises, a lighter and ashtray on his lap, crossing one stick leg over the other to hold them in place. Loew pulled up chairs around him in a semicircle; Smith winked and sat down. Mal saw cardboard boxes packed with folders filling up the dining alcove, four typewriters stacked in one corner to accommodate the grand jury team's paperwork. Ellis

Loew was preparing for war, his ranch house as head-quarters.

Mal took the leftover chair. Doc Lesnick lit a cigarette, coughed and started talking. His voice was highbrow New York Jew working with one lung; Mal made his pitch as processed, spieled to a load of other cops and DAs.

'Mr Satterlee did you a disservice by not going back further in his rather threadbare history of subversive elements in America. He neglected to mention the Depression, starvation and desperate people, concerned people, who wanted to change terrible conditions.' Lesnick paused, got breath and stubbed out his Gauloise. Mal saw a bony chest heaving, nailed the old man as gravebait and sensed that he was wavering: the pain of speech versus a chance to justify his fink duty. Finally he sucked in a huge draft of air and kept going, some kind of fervor lighting up his eyes.

'I was one of those people, twenty years ago. I signed petitions, wrote letters and went to labor meetings that accomplished nothing. The Communist Party, despite its evil connotations, was the only organization that did not seem ineffectual. Its reputation gave it a certain panache, a cachet, and the self-righteous hypocrites who condemned it in a blanket manner made me want to belong to it in order to assert my defiance of them.

'It was an injudicious decision, one that I came to regret. Being a psychiatrist, I was designated the official CP analyst here in Los Angeles. Marxism and Freudian analysis were very much in the intellectual vogue, and a number of people whom I later realized were conspirators against this country told me their . . . secrets, so to speak, emotional and political. Many were Hollywood people, writers and actors and their satellites – working-class people as deluded as I was regarding Communism, people who wanted to get close to the Hollywood people because of their movie connections. Just before the time of the Hitler-Stalin pact I became disillusioned with the Party. In '39, during the California State HUAC probe,

66

I volunteered to serve the FBI as an undercover informant. I have served in that capacity for over ten years,
while concurrently acting as CP analyst. I secretly made
my private files available to the 1947 House Un-American Activities Committee probers, and I am doing the
same for this grand jury probe now. The files are for
UAES members essential to your probe, and should you
require assistance in interpreting them, I would be happy
to be of service.'

The old man nearly choked on his last words. He
reached for his cigarette pack; Ellis Loew, holding a
glass of water, got to him first. Lesnick gulped, coughed,
gulped; Dudley Smith walked into the dining alcove and
tapped the filing boxes and typewriters with his spit-
shined brogues – uncharacteristically idle footwork.

A horn honked outside. Mal stood up to thank Lesnick and shake his hand. The old man looked away and
pushed himself to his feet, almost not making it. The
horn beeped again; Loew opened the door and gestured
to the cab in the driveway. Lesnick shuffled out, gulping
fresh morning air.

The taxi drove away; Loew turned on a wall fan.
Dudley Smith said, 'How long does he have, Ellis? Will
you be sending him an invitation to your victory cele-
bration come '52?'

Loew scooped big handfuls of files off the floor and
laid them out on the dining room table; he repeated the
process until there were two stacks of paper halfway to
the ceiling. 'Long enough to suit our purposes.'

Mal walked over and looked at their evidence: information extraction thumbscrews. 'He won't testify before
the grand jury though?'

'No, never. He's terrified of losing his credibility as a
psychiatrist. Confidentiality, you know. It's a good
hiding place for lawyers, and doctors covet it too. Of
course, it's not legally binding for them. Lesnick would
be kaput as a psychiatrist if he testified.'

Dudley said, 'You would think he would like to meet
his maker as a good patriotic American, though. He did

volunteer, and that should be a grand satisfaction for someone whose next life looms so imminently.'

Loew laughed. 'Dud have you *ever* taken a step without spotting the angles?'

'The last time *you* did, counselor. Captain Considine, yourself?'

Mal said, 'Sometime back in the Roaring Twenties,' thinking that mano a mano, brain to brain, he'd favor the Dublin street thug over the Harvard Phi Bete. 'Ellis, when do we start approaching witnesses?'

Loew tapped the file stacks. 'Soon, after you've digested these. Based on what you learn here, you'll be making your first approaches – on weak points – weak people – who'd seem most likely to cooperate. If we can build up an array of friendly witnesses fast, fine. But if we don't get a fair amount of initial cooperation, we'll have to put in a plant. Our friends on the Teamsters have heard picket line talk – that the UAES is planning strategy meetings aimed at coercing exorbitant contract demands out of the studios. If we get a string of balks right off the bat, I want to pull back and put a decoy into the UAES. I want both of you to think of smart, tough, idealistic-looking young cops we can use if it comes to that.'

Chills grabbed Mal. Sending in decoys, *operating*, had made his rep at Ad Vice – it was what he was best at as a policeman. He said, 'I'll think on it. There's just Dudley and me as investigators?'

Loew made a gesture that took in his whole house. 'Clerks from the City pool here to handle the paperwork, Ed Satterlee for the use of his contracts, Lesnick for our psychiatric edification. You two to interrogate. I might get us a third man to prowl for criminal stuff, rattle cages, that kind of thing.'

Mal got itchy to read, think, operate. He said, 'I'm going to clear up some loose ends at the Hall, go home and work.'

Loew said, 'I'm going to prosecute a real estate man for drunk driving on his son's motorcycle.'

Dudley Smith toasted his boss with an imaginary glass. 'Have mercy. Most real estate men are good patriotic Republicans, and you might need his contribution one day.'

Back at City Hall, Mal made calls to satisfy his curiosity on his two new colleagues. Bob Cathcart, a savvy Criminal Division FBI man he'd worked with, gave him the scoop on Edmund J. Satterlee. Cathcart's take: the man was a religious crackpot with a wild hair up his ass about Communism, so extreme in his views that Clyde Tolson, Hoover's number-two man at the Bureau, repeatedly issued gag orders on him when he served as Agent in Charge at the Waco, Texas, field office. Satterlee was estimated to earn fifty thousand dollars a year in anti-Communist lecture fees; Red Crosscurrents was 'a shakedown racket' – 'They'd clear Karl Marx if the dough was right.' Satterlee was rumored to have been bounced off the Allen Squad for attempting a kickback operation: cash vouchers from interned Japanese prisoners in exchange for his safeguarding their confiscated property until they were released. Agent Cathcart's summation: Ed Satterlee was a loony, albeit a rich and very efficient one – very adept at advancing conspiracy theories that stood up in court; very good at gathering evidence; very good at running outside interference for grand jury investigators.

A call to an old pal working the LAPD Metropolitan Squad and one to an ex-DA's man now with the State Attorney General's office supplied Mal with the true story on Saul Lesnick, MD, PhD. The old man was, and remained, a CP card carrier; he had been a Fed snitch since '39 – when he was approached by two LA office agents, who made him a deal: provide confidential psychiatric dirt to various committees and police agencies, and his daughter would be sprung from her five-to-ten-year sentence for hit and run drunk driving – one year down, four more to go minimum – the girl then currently hardtiming in Tehachapi. Lesnick agreed; his daughter was released and placed on indeterminate Federal parole – which would be revoked if the good doctor ever broke his cover or otherwise refused to cooperate. Lesnick, given six months tops in his fight with lung cancer, had secured a promise from a high-ranking Justice Department official: upon his death, all the confidential files he had loaned out would be destroyed; his daughter's vehicular manslaughter conviction and parole records would be expunged and all Fed/Municipal/State grand jury notations currently on official paper vis-à-vis Lesnick and his breaches of confidentiality with subversive patients would burn. No one would know that for ten years Saul Lesnick, Communist, psychiatrist, had played both ends against the middle – and had won his holding action.

Mal segued, new colleagues to old business, thinking that the lunger got what he paid for in spades, that his dance with the Feds was good value: a daughter spared broomstick rape and pernicious anemia from Tehachapi's famous all-starch cuisine in exchange for the rest of his life – shortened by suicide via French tobacco. And *he'd* have done the same thing for Stefan – he wouldn't have thought twice.

Paperwork was arrayed neatly across his desk; Mal, stealing glances at the huge grand jury pile, got to it. He wrote memos to Ellis Loew suggesting investigators to dig for backup evidence; he typed routing slips: case files to the green young Deputy DAs who would be prosecuting now that Loew was engaged full-time in battling Communism. A Chinatown hooker killing went to a kid six months out of the worst law school in California; the perpetrator, a pimp known for his love of inflicting pain with a metal-studded dildo, would probably walk on the charge. Two shine snuffs were routed to a youth still short of his twenty-fifth birthday – smart, but naive. This perp, a Purple Cobra warlord, had fired into a crowd of kids outside Manual Arts High School on the off-chance that there might be members of the Purple Scorpions in it. There weren't; an honor student and her

70

boyfriend went down dead. Mal gave the kid a fifty-fifty chance for a conviction – Negroes killing Negroes bored white juries and they often dropped their verdicts on whim.

The armed robbery/ADW at Minnie Roberts' Casbah went to a Loew protégé; writing evidence summaries on the three cases took four hours and gave Mal finger cramps. Finishing, he checked his watch and saw that it was 3:10 – Stefan would be home from school. If he was lucky, Celeste would be visiting her crony down the street, bullshitting in Czech, gabbing about the old country before the war. Mal grabbed his stack of psychiatric dirt and drove home, resisting a kid's urge: to stop at an army-navy store and buy himself a pair of silver captain's bars.

Home was in the Wilshire District: a big white two-story that devoured his savings and most of his salary. It was the house that was too good for Laura – a kid marriage based on rutting didn't warrant the tariff. He'd bought it when he returned from Europe in '46, knowing that Laura was out and Celeste was in, sensing that he loved the boy more than he could ever love the woman – that the marriage was for Stefan's safety. There was a park with basketball hoops and a baseball diamond nearby; the neighborhood's crime rate was near zero and the local schools had the highest academic standing in the state. It was his happy ending to Stefan's nightmare.

Mal parked in the driveway and walked across the lawn – Stefan's lackluster mowing job, Stefan's softball and bat weighing down the hedge that he'd neglected to trim. Going in the door, he heard voices: the two-language fight he'd refereed a thousand times before. Celeste was running down verb conjugations in Czech, sitting on the divan in her sewing room, gesturing to Stefan, her captive in a straight-backed chair. The boy was fiddling with objects on an end table – thimbles and thread spools – arranging them by progression of color, so smart that he had to keep occupied even while on the receiving

71

end of a lecture. Mal stood aside from the doorway and watched, loving Stefan for his defiance; glad that he was dark and pudgy like his real father was supposed to be – not lean and sandy-haired like Celeste – even though Mal was blond, and it clued people in that they weren't blood relations.

Celeste was saying, '. . . and it is the language of your people.'

Stefan was stacking the spools, making a little house out of them – dark colors the foundation, pastels on top. 'But I am to be an American now. Malcolm told me he can get me cit-cit-citizenship.'

'Malcolm is a minister's son and a policeman who does not understand our old country traditions. Stefan, your heritage. Learn to make your mother happy.'

Mal could tell this boy wasn't buying it; he smiled when Stefan demolished the spool house, his dark eyes fired up. 'Malcolm said Czechoslovakia is a . . . a . . . a . . .'

'A what, darling?'

'A Bohunk rubble heap! A shit pile! Scheiss! Scheiss! In German for mutti!'

Celeste raised a hand, stopped and hit her own pinched-together knees. 'In English for you – little ingrate, disgrace to your real father, a cultured man, a doctor, not a consort of whores and hoodlums – '

Stefan knocked over the end table and ran out of the room, straight into Mal, blocking the doorway. The small fat boy careened off his six-foot-three stepfather, then grabbed him around the waist and buried his head in his vest. Mal held him there, one hand steadying his shoulders, the other ruffling his hair. When Celeste stood up and saw them, he said, 'You'll never give it up, will you?'

Celeste mouthed words; Mal knew they were native tongue obscenities she didn't want Stefan to hear. The boy held on tighter, then let go and ran upstairs to his room. Mal heard ting-ting-ting – Stefan's toy soldiers

72

being hurled at the door. He said, 'You know what it makes him think of, and you still won't give it up.'

Celeste adjusted her arms inside her overslung cardigan – the single European affectation Mal hated the most. 'Nein, herr Leutnant' – pure German, pure Celeste – Buchenwald, the gas man, Major Considine, cold-blooded killer.

Mal braced himself into the doorway. 'Captain soon, *Fräulein* Chief DA's Investigator, and climbing. Juice, *Fräulein*. Just in case I think you're ruining my son and I have to take him away from you.'

Celeste sat down, knees together, a finishing school move, Prague 1934. 'To the mother the child belongs. Even a failed lawyer like you should know that maxim.'

A line that couldn't be topped. Mal kicked up the carpeting on his way outside; he sat on the steps and watched rain clouds hover. Celeste's sewing machine started to whir; upstairs, Stefan's soldiers were still dinging his already cracked and dented bedroom door. Mal thought that soon they'd be stripped of paint, dragoons without uniforms, and that simple fact would tear down everything he'd built up since the war.

In '45 he was an army major, stationed at a temporary MP barracks near the recently liberated Buchenwald concentration camp. His assignment was to interrogate surviving inmates, specifically the ones the medical evacuation teams deemed terminally ill – the husks of human beings who would most likely never live to identify their captors in court. The question and answer sessions were horrific; Mal knew that only the stony cold presence of his interpreter was keeping him frosty, contained, a pro. News from the home front was just as bad: friends wrote him that Laura was screwing Jerry Dunleavy, a buddy from the Homicide Bureau, and Buzz Meeks, a crooked Narcotics Squad dick and bagman for Mickey Cohen. And in San Francisco, his father, the Reverend Liam Considine, was dying of congestive heart disease and sending daily telegrams begging him to embrace Jesus before he died. Mal hated the man too much to give him the satisfaction and was too busy praying for the speedy and painless deaths of every single Buchenwald survivor, for the complete cessation of their memories and his nightmares. The old man died in October; Mal's brother Desmond, the used-car king of Sacramento, sent him a telegram rich in religious invective. It ended with words of disownment. Two days later Mal met Celeste Heisteke.

She came out of Buchenwald physically healthy and defiant, and she spoke enough English to render the interpreter unnecessary. Mal conducted his interrogations of Celeste solo; they spoke on only one topic: her whoredom with an SS lieutenant colonel named Franz Kempflerr – his price for her survival.

Celeste's stories – graphically told – killed his nightmares better than the contraband phenobarbital he'd been blasting for weeks. They excited him, disgusted him, made him hate the Nazi colonel and hate himself for being a voyeur eight thousand miles away from his legendary whore sweep operations in Ad Vice. Celeste sensed his excitement and seduced him; together, they reenacted all of her adventures with Franz Kempflerr. Mal fell in love with her – because he knew she had his number better than dumb sexpot Laura ever did. Then, when she had him hooked, she told him of her dead husband and her six-year-old son, who might still be alive somewhere in Prague. Would he, a veteran detective, be willing to search for the boy?

Mal agreed, for the challenge and the chance to become more to Celeste than a voyeur-lover, more than the sewer crawler cop his family considered him to be. He made three trips to Prague, blundering around asking questions in pidgin Czech and German. Networks of Heisteke cousins resisted him; twice he was threatened with guns and knives and retreated, fear at his back like he was walking a beat in LA niggertown, whispers and catcalls from the okie cops who dominated the nightwatch there: college boy chickenshit, nigger scared, coward. On his final trip he located Stefan Heisteke, a pale, dark-haired child with a distended belly, sleeping outside a cigarette vendor's stall in a rolled-up carpet lent to him by a friendly black marketeer. The man told Mal that the boy became frightened if people spoke to him in Czech, the language he seemed to best understand; phrases in German and French elicited simple yes or no answers. Mal took Stefan to his hotel, fed him and attempted to bathe him – stopping when he started to scream.

He let Stefan wash himself; he let him sleep for seventeen uninterrupted hours. Then, armed with German and French phrase books, he began his most gruelling interrogation. It took a week of long silences, long pauses and halting questions and answers with half the room between them for Mal to get the story straight.

Stefan Heisteke had been left with trusted first cousins just before Celeste and her husband, gentile anti-Nazis, were captured by the Germans; they, fleeing, had shunted him to distant in-laws, who left him with friends who gave him to acquaintances sequestered in a deserted factory basement. He was there for the better part of two years, accompanied by a man and woman gone cabin-fevered. The factory processed dog food, and cans of horsemeat were all Stefan ate during that time. The man and woman used him sexually, then goo-goo-talked to him in Czech, lover's endearments to a five-and-six-year-old child. Stefan could not tolerate the sound of that language.

Mal brought Stefan back to Celeste, gave her a mercifully abbreviated account of his lost years and told her to speak French to him – or teach him English. He did not tell her that he considered her cousins accomplices to the boy's horror, and when Stefan himself told his mother what had happened, Celeste capitulated to Mal. He knew she had been using him before; now she loved him. He had a family to replace his shattered one at home in America.

Together, they began teaching Stefan English; Mal wrote to Laura, requested a divorce and got the paperwork ready to bring his new family stateside. Things were going very smoothly; then they went haywire.

Celeste's whoremaster officer had escaped before Buchenwald was liberated; just as Mal was about to take his discharge, he was captured in Kraków and held at the MP barracks there. Mal went to Kraków just to see him; the stockade duty officer showed him the Nazi's confiscated property, which included unmistakable locks of Celeste's hair. Mal walked back to Franz Kempflerr's cell and emptied his sidearm into the man's face.

A tight net was thrown over the incident; the military governor, an Army one-star, liked Mal's style. Mal took an honorable discharge, brought Celeste and Stefan to America, returned to his LAPD sergeantcy and divorced Laura. Of his two cuckolders, Buzz Meeks was wounded in a shootout and pensioned off to civilian life; Jerry Dunleavy stayed on the job – but out of his way. Rumor had it that Meeks thought Mal was behind the shooting – revenge for the affair with Laura. Mal let the talk simmer: it played a good counterpoint to the coward innuendo he'd inspired in Watts. Word leaked out here and there on the gas man; Ellis Loew, DA's comer, Jew, draft dodger, took an interest in him and offered to swing some gravy his way once he aced the lieutenant's exam. In '47 he made lieutenant and transferred to the DA's Bureau of Investigations, cop protégé to the most ambitious Deputy District Attorney the City of Los Angeles ever saw. He married Celeste and settled into family life, a ready-made child part of the deal. And the closer father and son became, the more mother resented it; and the more he pressed to formally adopt the boy the more she refused – and tried to mold Stefan in the manner of the old Czech aristocracy that was yanked out from under her by the Nazis – language lessons and European culture and customs, Celeste oblivious to the memories they'd uprooted.

'To the mother the child belongs. Even a failed lawyer like you should know that maxim.'

Mal listened to Celeste's sewing machine. Stefan's toy

soldiers hitting the door. He came up with his own epigraph: saving a woman's life only induces gratitude if the woman has something to live for. All Celeste had was memories and a hated existence as a cop's hausfrau. All she wanted was to take Stefan back to the time of his horror and make him part of the memories. His final epigraph: he wouldn't let her.

Mal walked back in the house to read the Commie snitch's files: his glory grand jury and all it would reap.

Juice.

CHAPTER SIX

The two picket lines moved slowly down Gower, past the entrances of the Poverty Row studios. The UAES hugged the inside, displaying banners stapled to plywood strips: FAIR PAY FOR LONG HOURS, CONTRACT NEGOTIATIONS *NOW*! PROFIT SHARES FOR ALL WORKERS. The Teamsters paced beside them, a strip of sidewalk open, their signs – REDS OUT! NO CONTRACTS FOR COMMUNISTS – atop friction-taped two-by-four's. Talk between the factions was constant; every few seconds, 'Fuck' or 'shit' or 'Traitor' or 'Scum' would be shouted, a wave of garbled obscenities following. Across the street, reporters stood around, smoking and playing rummy on the hoods of their cars.

Buzz Meeks watched from the walkway outside Variety International Pictures' executive offices – three stories up, a balcony view. He remembered busting union heads back in the '30s; he sized up the Teamsters versus the UAES and saw a bout to rival Louis and Schmeling Number Two.

Easy: the Teamsters were sharks and the UAES were minnows. The Teamster line featured Mickey Cohen goons, union muscle and hard boys hired out of the day labor joints downtown; the UAES was old leftie types, stagehands past their prime, skinny Mexicans and a woman. If push came to shove, no cameras around, the Teamsters would use their two-by-four's as battering rams and charge – brass knuckle work in close, blood, teeth and nose cartilage on the sidewalk, maybe a few ears ripped off of heads. Then vamoose before the lackluster LAPD Riot Squad made the scene. *Easy*.

Buzz checked his watch. 4:45; Howard Hughes was forty-five minutes late. It was a cool January day, light blue sky mixed with rain clouds over the Hollywood Hills. Howard got sex crazy in the winter and probably wanted to send him out on a poontang prowl: Schwab's Drugstore, the extra huts at Fox and Universal, Brownie snapshots of well-lunged girls naked from the waist up. His Majesty's yes or no, then standard gash contracts to the yes's – one-liners in RKO turkeys in exchange for room and board at Hughes Enterprises' fuck pads and frequent nighttime visits from The Man himself. Hopefully, bonus money was involved: he was still in hock to a bookie named Leotis Dineen, a six-foot-six jungle bunny who hated people of the Oklahoma persuasion worse than poison.

Buzz heard a door opening behind him; a woman's voice called out, 'Mr. Hughes will see you now, Mr. Meeks.'

The woman had stuck her head out of Herman Gerstein's doorway; if the Variety International boss was involved, then bonus dough was a possible. Buzz ambled over; Hughes was seated behind Gerstein's desk, scanning the pictures on the walls: semicheesecake shots of Gower Gulch starlets going nowhere. He was dressed in his usual chalk stripe business suit, sporting his usual scars – facial wounds from his latest airplane crash. The big guy cultivated them with moisturizing lotion – he thought they gave him a certain panache.

And no Herman Gerstein; and no Gerstein's secretary. Buzz dropped the formalities that Hughes required when other people were present. 'Getting any, Howard?'

Hughes pointed to a chiar. 'You're my bird dog, you should know. Sit, Buzz. This is important.'

Buzz sat down and made a gesture that took in the whole office: cheescake, rococo wall tapestries and a knight's suit of armor hatrack. 'Why here, boss? Herman got a job for me?'

Hughes ignored the question. 'Buzz, how long have we been colleagues?'

'Goin' on five years, Howard.'

'And you've worked for me in various capacities?'

Buzz thought: fixer, bagman, pimp. 'That's right.'

'And during those five years have I given you profitable referrals to other people in need of your talents?'

'You surely have.'

Hughes cocked two finger pistols, his thumbs the hammers. 'Remember the premiere of *Billy the Kid*? The Legion of Decency was outside Grauman's shouting 'Whoremonger' at me and little old ladies from Pasadena were throwing tomatoes at Jane Russell. Death threats, the whole megillah.'

Buzz crossed his legs and picked lint off a trouser cuff. 'I was there, boss.'

Hughes blew imaginary smoke off his fingertips. 'Buzz, that was a dicey evening, but did I ever describe it as dangerous, or *big*?'

'No, boss. You surely didn't.'

'When Bob Mitchum was arrested for those marijuana cigarettes and I called you in to help with the evidence, did I describe *that* as dangerous or big?'

'No.'

'And when *Confidential Magazine* was getting ready to publish that article that alleged that I like well-endowed underage girls, and you took your billy club down to the office to reason with the editor, did I describe *that* as dangerous or big?'

Buzz winced. It was late '47, the fuck pads were at full capacity, Howard was a pork-pouring dervish and was filming his teenaged conquests' endorsing his prowess – a ploy aimed at getting him a date with Ava

Gardner. One of the film cans was snatched out of the RKO editing department and ended up at *Confidential*; he broke three sets of scandal mag fingers quashing the story – then blew Hughes' bonus betting stupid on the Louis-Walcott fight. 'No, Howard. You didn't.'

Hughes shot Buzz with his finger guns. 'Pow! Pow! Pow! Turner. I am telling you that that seditious spectacle down on the street is both dangerous *and* big, and *that* is why I called you here.'

Buzz looked at the pilot/inventor/mogul, exhausted by his theatrics, wanting to get to it. 'Howard, is there any cash money involved in all this big danger? And if you're askin' me to break some union heads, take another think, 'cause I am too old and too fat.'

Hughes laughed. 'Solly Gelfman wouldn't say that.'

'Solly Gelfman is too goddamned kind. Howard, what do you want?'

Hughes draped his long legs over Herman Gerstein's desk. 'What's your opinion of Communism, Buzz?'

'I think it stinks. Why?'

'The UAES down there, they're all Commies and Pinkos and fellow travelers. The City of Los Angeles is getting a grand jury together to investigate Communist influence in Hollywood, concentrating on the UAES. A bunch of studio heads – myself, Herman and some others – have formed a group called 'Friends of the American Way in Motion Pictures' to help the City out. I've contributed to the kitty, so has Herman. We thought you'd like to help out, too.'

Buzz laughed. 'With a contribution out of my meager salary?'

Hughes aped the laugh, putting an exaggerated okie twang on it. 'I knew appealing to your sense of patriotism was a long shot.'

'Howard, you're only loyal to money, pussy and airplanes, and I buy you as a good buddy of the American Way like I buy Dracula turning down a job at a blood bank. So this grand jury thing is one of the three, and my money's on money.'

Hughes flushed and fingered his favorite plane crash scar, the one a girl from the Wisconsin boonies was in love with. 'Brass tacks then, Turner?'

'Yes, sir.'

Hughes said, 'The UAES is in at Variety International, RKO, three others here on Gower and two of the majors. Their contract is ironclad and has five more years to run. That contract is costly, and escalation clauses will cost us a fortune over the next several years. Now the goddamn union is picketing for extras: bonuses, medical coverage and profit points. Totally unacceptable. *Totally.*'

Buzz locked eyes with Hughes. 'So don't renew their goddamned contract or let them strike.'

'Not good enough. The escalation clauses are too costly, and they won't strike – they'll pull very subtle slow dances. When we signed with UAES in '45, no one knew how big television was going to get. We're getting reamed at the box office, and we want the Teamsters in – despite the goddamned Pinko UAES and their goddamned ironclad contract.'

'How you gonna get around that contract?'

Hughes winked, scars and all, the act made him look like a big kid. 'There's a fine-print clause in the contract that states the UAES can be ousted if criminal malfeasance – and that includes treason – can be proved against them. And the Teamsters will work much cheaper, if certain payments are made to certain silent partners.'

Buzz winked. 'Like Mickey Cohen?'

'I can't shit a shitter.'

Buzz put his feet on Gerstein's desk, wishing he had a cigar to light up. 'So you want the UAES smeared, before the grand jury convenes or sometime during the proceedings. That way you can boot them on the malfeasance clause and put in Mickey's boys without them Commies suin' you – for fear of gettin' in more shit.'

Hughes nudged Buzz's feet off the desk with his own immaculate wing tips. ' "Smeared" is a misnomer. In this case we're talking about patriotism as the handmaid to good business. Because the UAES are a bunch of card-carrying Pinko subversives.'

'And you'll give me a cash money bonus to – '

'And I'll give you a leave of absence from your duties at the plant and a cash bonus to help the grand jury investigating team out. They've already got two cops as political interrogators, and the Deputy DA who's running the show wants a third man to rattle for criminal skeletons and make money pickups. Buzz, there's two things you know exceedingly well: Hollywood and our fair city's criminal elements. You can be very valuable to this operation. Can I count you in?'

Dollar signs danced in Buzz's head. 'Who's the DA?'

'A man named Ellis Loew. He ran for his boss's job in '48 and lost.'

Jewboy Loew, he of the colossal hard-on for the State of California. 'Ellis is a sweetheart. The two cops?'

'An LAPD detective named Smith and a DA's Bureau man named Considine. Buzz, are you in?'

The old odds: 50–50, either Jack Dragna or Mal Considine set up the shooting that got him two in the shoulder, one in the arm and one through the left cheek of his ass. 'I don't know, boss. There's bad blood between me and that guy Considine. Cherchez la femme, if you follow my drift. I might have to need money *really* bad before I say yes.'

'Then I'm not worried. You'll get yourself into a bind – you always do.'

CHAPTER SEVEN

Captain Al Dietrich said, 'I got four phone calls about your little escapades in City territory night before last. At home yesterday. *On my day off.*'

Danny Upshaw stood at parade rest in front of the station commander's desk, ready to deliver an oral rundown on the Goines homicide – a memorized pitch, to end in a plea for more Sheriff's manpower and an LAPD liaison. While Dietrich fumed, he scotched the ending and concentrated on making his evidence compelling enough so that the old man would let him work the snuff exclusively for at least two more weeks.

'. . . and if you wanted information on heroin pushers, you should have had *our* Narco guys contact *theirs*. You don't beat up the pushers, colored or otherwise. And the manager of Bido Lito's runs another club inside the County, and he's very simpatico with the watch sergeant at Firestone. And you were seen drinking on duty, which I do myself, but under more discreet circumstances. Follow my drift?'

Danny tried to look sheepish – a little trick he'd taught himself – eyes lowered, face scrunched up. 'Yes, sir.'

Dietrich lit a cigarette. 'Whenever you call me sir, I know you're jerking my chain. You're very lucky I like you, Deputy. You're very lucky I think your gifts exceed your arrogance. Report on your homicide. Omit Dr. Layman's findings, I read your summary and I don't like gore this early in the morning.'

Danny drew himself ramrod stiff in reflex – he'd wanted to play up the horror aspects to impress Dietrich. 'Captain, so far I've got two half-assed eyewitness descriptions of the killer – tall, gray-haired, middle-aged O+ blood typed from his semen – very common among white people. I don't think either witness could ID the man from mugs – those jazz clubs are dark and have distorted lighting. The print man who dusted the transport car got no latents except those belonging to the owner and his girlfriend. He did eliminations based on Civil Defense records – both Albanese and the girlfriend had CD jobs during the war. I checked taxi logs around the time the body was dumped and the car abandoned, and nothing but couples leaving the after-hours clubs on the Strip were picked up. Albanese's story of going back to darktown to look for his car has been verified by cab records, which eliminates him as a suspect. I spent all day yesterday and most of the evening recanvassing Central Avenue, and I couldn't find any other eyewitnesses who saw Goines with the tall, gray-haired man. I looked for the two eyewitnesses I talked to before, thinking I'd try to get some kind of composite drawing out of them, but they were gone – apparently these jazz types are mostly fly-by-nights.'

Dietrich stubbed out his cigarette. 'What's your next move?'

'Captain, this is a fag killing. The better of my two eyewitnesses pegged Goines as a deviant, and the mutilations back it up. Goines was killed with a heroin OD. I want to run mugshots of known homos by Otis Jackson and other local pushers. I want – '

Dietrich was already shaking his head. 'No, you cannot go back to City territory and question the man you pistol-whipped, and LAPD Narco will never cooperate with a list of local pushers – thanks to your escapades.' He picked a copy of the *Herald* off his desk, folded it over and pointed to a one-column piece: 'Vagrant's Body Found Dumped Off Sunset Strip New Year's Eve.' 'Let's keep it at this – low-key, no name on the victim. We've got great duty here at this division, we thrive on tourism, and I don't want it bollixed up because some queer slashed another queer hophead trombone player. Comprende?'

Danny twisted his fingers together behind his back, then shot his CO a Vollmer maxim. 'Uniform codes of investigation are the moral foundation of criminology.'

Captain Al Dietrich said, 'Human garbage is human garbage. Go to work, Deputy Upshaw.'

Danny went back to the squadroom and brainstormed in his cubicle, partition walls bracketing him, the station's other three detectives – all at least ten years his senior – typing and jabbering into phones, the noise coming at him like gangbusters, then subsiding into a lull that was like no sound at all.

A mug blowup of Harlan 'Buddy' Jastrow, Kern

County axe murderer and the jolt that made him a cop, glared from the wall above his desk; some deputy who'd heard about his all-point want on the man had drawn a Hitler mustache on him, a speech balloon extending from his mouth: 'Hi! I'm Deputy Upshaw's nemesis! He wants to fry my ass, but he won't tell anybody why! Watch out for Upshaw! He's a college boy prima donna and he thinks his shit don't stink!' Captain Dietrich had discovered the artwork; he suggested that Danny leave it there as a reminder to hold on to his temper and not high-hat the other men. Danny agreed; word got back to him that his fellow detectives liked the touch – it made them think he had a sense of humor that he didn't have – and it made him angry and somehow able to brainstorm better.

So far, two and a half days in, he had the basics covered. The Central Avenue jazz strip had been canvassed around the clock; every bartender, bouncer, musician and general hepcat on the block had been braced – ditto the area where the body was dumped. Karen Hiltscher had called San Quentin and Lexington State Hospital for information on Goines and his buddies, if any, there; they were waiting the results of those queries. Rousting H pushers inside City confines was out for the time being, but he could put in a memo to Sheriff's Narco for a list of dinks dealing in the County, press on that and see if he got any crossover leads back to LAPD turf. Goines' musicians' union would be reopening after the holiday this morning, and for now he had nothing but his instincts – what was true, what wasn't true, what was too farfetched to be true and so horrible that it *had* to be true. Going eyeball to eyeball with Buddy Jastrow, Danny reconstructed the crime.

The killer meets Goines somewhwere on the jazz block and talks him into geezing up – despite Marty's recent dope cure. He's got the Buick already staked out, door jimmied open or unlocked, wires unhooked and ready to be juiced together for a quick start. They drive someplace quiet, someplace equidistant from darktown and the Sunset Strip. The killer jacks enough horse into a vein near Goines' spine to pop his heart arteries, a terrycloth towel right there to shove into his mouth and keep blood from drenching him. Figure, by the Zombie barman's estimate, that the killer and Goines left Central Avenue around 12:15 to 12:45 A.M., took a half hour to drive to the destination, ten minutes to set the snuff up and accomplish it.

1:00 to 1:30 A.M.

The killer throttles his victim postmortem; fondles his genitals until they bruise, slashes his backside with the razor blade device, pulls out his eyes, screws him in the sockets at least twice, bites – or has an animal bite – through his stomach to the intestines, then cleans him up and drives him to Allegro Street, a rainy night, no moisture atop the body, the rain having stopped shortly after 3:00, the stiff discovered at 4:00 A.M.

An hour to an hour and forty-five minutes to mutilate the body, depending on the location of the killing ground.

The killer so sex-crazed that he ejaculates twice during that time.

The killer – maybe – taking a circuitous route to the Strip, rearview mirror hooked backward so he can view the corpse he is chauffeuring.

Flaw in the reconstruction so far: Doc Layman's tenuous 'blood bait' theory doesn't fit. Well-trained vicious dogs did not jibe with the scenario – they would be too difficult to deal with, a nuisance, a mess, too noisy at a murder scene, too hard to contain during moments of psychotic duress. Which meant that the teeth marks on the torso had to be human, even though the mouth imprints were too large to have been made by a human being biting down.

Which meant that the killer bit and gnawed and swiveled and gnashed his teeth to get a purchase on his victim's entrails, sucking the flesh upward to leave inflamed borders as he ravaged –

Danny bolted out of his cubicle and back to the records alcove adjoining the squadroom. One battered cabinet held the division's Vice and sex offender files – West Hollywood crime reports, complaint reports, arrest reports and trouble call sheets dating back to the station's opening in '37. Some of the folders were filed alphabetically under 'Arrestee'; some under 'Complainant'; some numerically by 'Address of Occurrence.' Some held mugshots, some didn't; gaps in the 'Arrestee' folders indicated that the arrested parties had bribed deputies into stealing reports that might prove embarrassing to them – and West Hollywood was only a small fraction of County territory.

Danny spent an hour scanning 'Arrestee' reports, looking for tall, gray-haired, middle-aged men with violence in their MOs, knowing it was a long shot to keep him busy while Musician's Local 3126 opened at 10:30. The slipshod paperwork – rife with misspellings, smudged carbons and near illiterate recountings of sex crimes – had him to the point of screaming at LASD incompetence; turgid accounts of toilet liaisons and high school boys bribed into back seat blow jobs kept his stomach churning with a bile that tasted like fried coffee grounds and last night's six shots of bonded. The time got him four possibles – men aged forty-three to fifty-five, 6' 1" to 6' 4", with a total of twenty-one sodomy convictions among them – most of the beefs stemming from fruit tank punkings – jailhouse coitus interruptus that resulted in additional County charges being filed. At 10:20, he took the folders up to the dispatcher's office and Karen Hiltscher, sweaty, his clothes wilted before the day had hardly started.

Karen was working the switchboard, plugging in calls, a headset attached to her Veronica Lake hairdo. The girl was nineteen, bottle blonde and busy – a civilian LASD employee flagged for the next woman's opening at the Sheriff's Academy. Danny pegged her as bad cop stuff: the Department's mandatory eighteen-month jail tour would probably send her off the deep end and into the arms of the first male cop who promised to take her away from dyke matrons, Mex gang putas and white trash mothers in for child abuse. The heartthrob of the West Hollywood Substation wouldn't last two weeks as a policewoman.

Danny straightened his tie and smoothed his shirtfront, his beefcake prelude to begging favors. 'Karen? You busy, sweetheart?'

The girl noticed him and took off her headset. She looked pouty; Danny wondered if he should lube her with another dinner date. 'Hi, Deputy Upshaw.'

Danny placed the sex offender files up against the switchboard. 'What happened to "Hi, Danny"?'

Karen lit a cigarette à la Veronica Lake and coughed – she only smoked when she was trying to vamp the cops working day watch. 'Sergeant Norris heard me call Eddie Edwards 'Eddie' and said I should call him Deputy Edwards, that I shouldn't be so familiar until I get rank.'

'You tell Norris I said you can call me Danny.'

Karen made a face. 'Daniel Thomas Upshaw is a nice name. I told my mother, and she said it was a really nice name, too.'

'What else did you tell her about me?'

'That you're really sweet and handsome, but you're playing hard to get. What's in those files?'

'Sex offender reports.'

'For that homicide you're working?'

Danny nodded. 'Sweet, did Lex and Quentin call back on my Marty Goines queries?'

Karen made another face – half vixen, half coquette. 'I would have told you. Why did you give me those reports?'

Danny leaned over the switchboard and winked. 'I was thinking of dinner at Mike Lyman's once I get some work cleared up. Feel like giving me a hand?'

Karen Hiltscher tried to return the wink, but her false eyelash stuck to the ridge below her eye, and she had to fumble her cigarette into an ashtray and pull it free.

Danny looked away, disgusted; Karen pouted, 'What do you want on those reports?'

Danny stared at the muster room wall so Karen couldn't read his face. 'Call Records at the Hall of Justice Jail and get the blood types for all four men. If you get anything other than O+ for them, drop it. On the O+'s, call County Parole for their last known addresses, rap sheets and parole disposition reports. Got it?'

Karen said, 'Got it.'

Danny turned around and looked at his cut-rate Veronica Lake, her left eyelash plastered to her plucked left eyebrow. 'You're a doll. Lyman's when I clear this job.'

Musician's Local 3126 was on Vine Street just north of Melrose, a tan Quonset hut sandwiched between a doughnut stand and a liquor store. Hepcat types were lounging around the front door, scarfing crullers and coffee, half pints and short dogs of muscatel.

Danny parked and walked in, a group of wine guzzlers scattering to let him through. The hut's interior was dank: folding chairs aligned in uneven rows, cigarette butts dotting a chipped linoleum floor, pictures from *Downbeat* and *Metronome* scotch-taped to the walls – half white guys, half Negroes, like the management was trying to establish jazzbo parity. The left wall held a built-in counter, file cabinets in back of it, a haggard white woman standing guard. Danny walked over, badge and Marty Goines mugshot strip out.

The woman ignored the badge and squinted at the strip. 'This guy play trombone?'

'That's right. Martin Mitchell Goines. You sent him down to Bido Lito's around Christmas.'

The woman squinted harder. 'He's got trombone lips. What did he do for you?'

Danny lied discreetly. 'Parole violation.'

The slattern tapped the strip with a long red nail. 'The same old same old. What can I do for you?'

Danny pointed to the filing cabinets. 'His employment record, as far back as it goes.'

The woman about-faced, opened and shut drawers, leafed through folders, yanked one and gave the top page a quick scrutiny. Laying it down on the counter, she said, 'A nowhere horn. From Squaresville.'

Danny opened the folder and read through it, picking up two gaps right away: '38 to '40 – Goines' County jolt for marijuana possession: '44 to '88 – his Quentin time for the same offense. Since '48 the entries had been sporadic: occasional two-week engagements at Gardena pokerino lounges and his fatal gig at Bido Lito's. Prior to Goines' first jail sentence he got only *very* occasional work – Hollywood roadhouse stints in '36 and '37. It was the early '40s when Marty Goines was a trombone-playing fool.

Under his self-proclaimed banner, 'Mad Marty Goines & His Horn of Plenty,' he'd gigged briefly with Stan Kenton; in 1941, he pulled a tour with Wild Willie Monroe. There were a whole stack of pages detailing pickup band duty in '42, '43 and early '44 – one-night stands with six- and eight-man combos playing dives in the San Fernando Valley. Only the bandleaders and/or club managers who did the hiring were listed on the employment sheets – there was no mention of other musicians.

Danny closed the folder; the woman said, 'Bubkis, am I right?'

'You're right. Look, do you think any of these guys around here might have known – I mean know – Marty Goines?'

'I can ask.'

'Do it. Would you mind?'

The woman rolled her eyes up to heaven, drew a dollar sign in the air and pointed to her cleavage. Danny felt his hands clenching the edge of the counter and smelled last night's liquor oozing out of his skin. He was about to come on strong when he remembered he was on City ground and his CO's shit list. He fished in his pockets for cash, came up with a five and slapped it down. 'Do it now.'

The slattern snapped up the bill and disappeared behind the filing cabinets. Danny saw her out on the sidewalk a few seconds later, talking to the bottle gang, then moving to the doughnut and coffee crowd. She zeroed in on a tall Negro guy holding a bass case, grabbed his arm and led him inside. Danny smelled stale sweat, leaves and mouthwash on the man, like the knee-length overcoat he was wearing was his permanent address. The woman said, 'This is Chester Brown. He knows Marty Goines.'

Danny pointed Brown to the nearest row of chairs. Miss Hepcat went back to her counter and the bass man shuffled over, plopped down and whipped out a bottle of Listerine. He said, 'Breakfast of champions,' gulped, gargled and swallowed; Danny sat two chairs over, close enough to hear, far away enough to defuse the stink. 'Do you know Marty Goines, Chester?'

Brown burped and said, 'Why should I tell you?'

Danny handed him a dollar. 'Lunch of champions.'

'I feed three times a day, officer. Snitching gives me an appetite.'

Danny forked over another single; Chester Brown palmed it, chugalugged and patted the Lysterine bottle. 'Helps the memory. And since I ain't seen Marty since the war, you gonna need that memory.'

Danny got out his pen and notepad. 'Shoot.'

The bass man took a deep breath. 'I gigged pickup with Marty, back when he called himself the Horn of Plenty. Hunger huts out in the Valley when Ventura Boulevard was a fuckin' beanfield. Half the boys toked sweet lucy, half took the needle route. Marty was strung like a fuckin' dog.'

So far, his seven-dollar story was running true – based on Goines' union jacket and what he knew of his criminal record. 'Keep going, Chester.'

'Weeell, Marty pushed reefers – not too good, since I heard he did time for it, and he was a righteous boss mothafuckin' burglar. All the pickup boys that was strung was doin' it. They'd grab purses off barstools and

91

tables, get the people's addresses and swipe their house keys while the bartender kept them drinkin'. One set you'd have no drummer, one set no trumpet, and so forth, 'cause they was utilizizin' their inside skinny to be burglarizizin' the local patrons. Marty did lots of that, solo stuff, steal a car during his break, burglarize, then be back for his next set. Like I tol' you, he was a righteous boss mothafuckin' burglar.'

Righteous new stuff – even to an ex-car thief cop who thought he knew most of the angles. 'What years are you talking about, Chester? Think hard.'

Brown consulted his Listerine. 'I'd say this was goin' on from summer of '43 to maybe sometime in '44.'

Goines copped his second marijuana beef in April of '44. 'Did he work alone?'

'You mean on the burglarizizin'?'

'Right. And did he have running partners in general?'

Chester Brown said, ''Cept for this one kid, the Horn of Plenty was a righteous loner. He had this sidekick, though – a white blondy kid, tall and shy, loved jazz but couldn't learn to play no instrument. He'd been in a fire and his face was all covered up in bandages like he was the fuckin' mummy. Just a fuckin' kid – maybe nineteen, twenty years old. Him and Marty pulled a righteous fuckin' fuckload of burglaries together.'

Danny's skin was tingling – even though the kid couldn't be the killer – a youth in '43-'44 wouldn't be gray and middle-aged in '50. 'What happened to the sidekick, Chester?'

'I dunno, but you sure askin' a lot of questions for a parole violation, and you ain't asked me where I think Marty might be stayin'.'

'I was getting to that. You got any ideas?'

Brown shook his head. 'Marty always stayed to himself. Never socializized with the boys out of the club.'

Danny dry-swallowed. 'Is Goines a homosexual?'

'Say what?'

'Queer, fruit, homo! Did he fucking like boys!'

Brown killed the bottle of Listerine and wiped his

lips. 'You don't gots to shout, and that's a nasty thing to say about somebody never did you harm.'

Danny said, 'Then answer my question.'

The bass man opened his instrument case. There was no fiddle inside, only bottles of Listerine Mouthwash. Chester Brown cracked the cap on one and took a long, slow drink. He said 'That's for Marty, 'cause I ain't the fool you think I am, and I know he's dead. And he wasn't no queer. He may not have been much for trim, but he sure as fuck wasn't no fuckin' fruitfly.'

Danny took Chester Brown's old news and rolled with it to a pay phone. First he called City/County R&I, learned that Martin Mitchell Goines had no detainments on suspicion of B&E and that no blond youths were listed as accomplices on his two marijuana rousts; no blond youths with distinguishing burn marks were arrested for burglary or narcotics violations anywhere in the San Fernando Valley circa 1942–1945. The call was a fishing expedition that went nowhere.

A buzz to the West Hollywood Station switchboard got him a pouty conversation with Karen Hiltscher, who said that the four long shots from the sex offender files proved to be just that – a toss of their jail records revealed that none of the men had O+ blood. Administrators had called in from both San Quentin and Lexington State Hospital; they said that Marty Goines was an institutional loner, and his counselor at Lex stated that he was assigned a Fed case worker in LA – but hadn't reported to him yet, and left no word about where he would be staying when he got to Los Angeles. Even though the lead was probably a big nothing, Danny told Karen to check the station's burglary file for B&E men with jazz musician backgrounds and for mention of a burned-face burglar boy – a jazz aficionado. Rankling, the girl agreed; Danny hung up thinking he should raise the dreaded dinner ante from Mike Lyman's to the Coconut Grove to keep her happy.

At just after 1:00 P.M. there was nothing he could do

93

but pound familiar pavement one more time. Danny drove to darktown and widened his canvassing area, talking Goines and the gray-haired man to locals on the side streets adjoining Central Avenue, getting four solid hours of nothing; at dusk he drove back to West Hollywood, parked on Sunset and Doheny and walked the Strip, west to east, east to west, residential streets north into the hills, south to Santa Monica Boulevard, wondering the whole time why the killer picked Allegro Street as his place to dump the body. He wondered if the killer lived nearby, desecrated Goines' corpse for that much more time and chose Allegro so he could gloat over the police and their efforts to nail him – the abandoned car a partial ruse to convince them he lived elsewhere. That theory played with led to others – subjective thinking – a Hans Maslick fundamental. Danny thought of the killer with his real car parked nearby for a quick getaway; the killer walking the Strip New Year's morning, sheltered by swarms of revelers, depleted from his awful back-to-back explosions. And that was when it got scary.

In a famous essay, Maslick described a technique he had developed while undergoing analysis with Sigmund Freud. It was called Man Camera, and involved screening details from the perpetrator's viewpoint. Actual camera angles and tricks were employed; the investigator's eyes became a lens capable of zooming in and out, freezing close-ups, selecting background motifs to interpret crime-scene evidence in an aesthetic light. Danny was crossing Sunset and Horn when the idea struck him – transpose 3:45 New Year's morning to now, himself as a sex slasher, walking home or to his car or to an all-night market to get calm again. But he didn't see the other people strolling the Strip or lining up to get in the Mocambo or sitting at the counter at Jack's Drive Inn. He went straight for Marty Goines' eyes and guts and groin, an ultra close-up in Technicolor, his preautopsy prep magnified ten million times. A car swerved in front of him then; he twitched with heebie-jeebies, saw a kaleidoscope of Coleman the alto man, his look-alike from the movie with Karen, Tim. When he pointed his Man Camera at the passerby he was supposed to be viewing, they were all gargoyles, all wrong.

It took long moments for him to calm down, to get it right. He hadn't eaten since yesterday; he'd postponed his bourbon ration in order to tread the Strip clear-headed. Hitting late-night clubs and restaurants with questions on a tall, gray-haired man New Year's would be straightforward police work to keep him chilled.

He did it.

And got more nothing.

Two hours' worth.

The same accounts at Cyrano's, Dave's Blue Room, Ciro's, the Mocambo, La Rue, Coffee Bob's, Sherry's, Bruno's Hideaway and the Movieland Diner: every single place was packed until dawn New Year's. No one remembered a solitary, tall, gray-haired man.

At midnight, Danny retrieved his car and drove to the Moonglow Lounge for his four shots. Janice Modine, his favorite snitch, was hawking cigarettes to a thin weeknight crowd: lovebirds necking in wraparound booths, dancers necking while they slow-grinded to juke-box ballads. Danny took a booth that faced away from the bandstand; Janice showed up a minute later, holding a tray with four shot glasses and an ice water backup.

Danny knocked the drinks back – bam, bam, bam, bam, eyes away from Janice so she'd take the hint and leave him alone – no gratitude for the prostie beefs he'd saved her from, no overheard skinny on Mickey C. – useless because West Hollywood Division's most aus-picious criminal was greasing most of West Hollywood's finest. The ploy didn't work; the girl squirmed in front of him, one spaghetti strap sliding off her shoulder, then the other. Danny waited for the first blast of heat, got it and saw all the colors of the lounge go from slightly wrong to right. He said, 'Sit down and tell me what you want before your dress falls off.'

Janice hunched into her straps and sat across the table

from him. 'It's about John, Mr. Upshaw. He was arrested again.'

John Lembeck was Janice's lover/pimp, a car thief specializing in custom orders: stolen chassis for the basic vehicle, parts stolen to exact specifications. He was a San Berdoo native like Danny, knew from the grapevine that a County plainclothes comer used to clout cars all over Kern and Visalia and kept his mouth shut about it when he got rousted on suspicion of grand theft auto. Danny said, 'Parts or a whole goddamn car?'

Janice pulled a Kleenex out of her neckline and fretted it. 'Upholstery.'

'City or County?'

'I – I think County. San Dimas Substation?'

Danny winced. San Dimas had the most rowdy detective squad in the Department; in '46 the daywatch boss, jacked on turpen hydrate, beat a wetback fruit picker to death. 'That's the County. What's his bail?'

'No bail, because of John's last GTA. See, it's a parole violation, Mr. Upshaw. John's scared because he says the policemen there are really mean, and they made him sign a confession on all these cars he didn't really steal. John said I should tell you a San Berdoo homeboy who loves cars should go to bat for another San Berdoo homey who loves cars. He didn't say what it meant, but he said I should tell you.'

Pull strings to save his career from its first hint of dirt: call the San Dimas bulls, tell them John Lembeck was his trusted snitch and that a nigger hot car gang had a jail bid out on him, shiv time if the stupid shit ever made it to a County lockup. If Lembeck was docile at the holding tank, they'd let him off with a beating. 'Tell John I'll get on it in the morning.'

Janice had pinched her Kleenex into little wispy shreds. 'Thanks, Mr. Upshaw. John also said I should be nice to you.'

Danny stood up, feeling warm and loose, wondering if he should muscle Lembeck for going cuntish on him.

'You're always nice to me, sweetheart. That's why I have my nightcap here.'

Janice vamped him with wide baby blues. 'He said I should be *really* nice to you.'

'I don't want it.'

'I mean, like really *extra* nice.'

Danny said, 'It's wrong,' and placed his usual dollar tip on the table.

CHAPTER EIGHT

Mal was in his office, on his twelfth full reading of Dr. Saul Lesnick's psychiatric files.

It was just after 1:00 A.M.; the DA's Bureau was a string of dark cubicles, illuminated only by Mal's wall light. The files were spread over his desk, interspersed with pages of notes splashed with coffee. Celeste would be asleep soon – he could go home and sleep in the den without her pestering him, sex offers because at this time of the morning he was her only friend, and giving him her mouth meant they could talk until one of them provoked a fight. Offers he'd accept tonight: the dirt in the files had him riled up like back in the Ad Vice days, when he put surveillance on the girls before they took down a whorehouse – the more you knew about who they were the better chance you had to get them to finger their pimps and money men. And after forty-eight hours of paper prowling, he felt he had a pulse on the Reds in the UAES.

Deluded.

Traitorous.

Perverse.

Cliché shouters, sloganeers, fashion-conscious pseudoidealists. Locusts attacking social causes with the wrong information and bogus solutions, their one legit gripe – the Sleepy Lagoon case – almost blown through guilt by association: fellow travelers soliciting actual Party members for picketing and leaflet distribution, nearly discrediting everything the Sleepy Lagoon Defense Committee said and did. Hollywood writers and actors and hangers-on spouting cheap trauma, Pinko platitudes and guilt over raking in big money during the Depression, then penancing the bucks out to spurious leftist causes. People led to Lesnick's couch by their promiscuity and dipshit politics.

Deluded.

Stupid.

Selfish.

Mal took a belt of coffee and ran a mental overview of the files, a last paraphrase before getting down to tagging the individual brain trusters he and Dudley Smith should be interrogating and the ones who should be singled out for their as yet unfound operative: Loew's project possibility, his favored tool already. What he got was a lot of people with too much money and too little brains pratfalling through the late '30s and '40s – betraying themselves, their lovers, their country and their own ideals, two events galvanizing their lunacy, spinning them out of their orbit of parties, meetings and sleeping around:

The Sleepy Lagoon case.

The 1947 House Un-American Activities Committee probe into Communist influence in the entertainment industry.

And the funny thing was – the two events gave the Pinkos some credibility, some vindication.

In August of 1942 a Mexican youth named José Diaz was beaten to death and run over with a car out at the Sleepy Lagoon – a grass-knolled meeting place for gang members in the Williams Ranch area of Central LA. The incident was allegedly sparked by Diaz being ejected from a nearby party earlier that night; he had allegedly insulted several members of a rival youth gang, and seventeen of them hauled him out to the Lagoon and snuffed him. Evidence against them was scant; the

LAPD investigation and trial were conducted in an atmosphere of hysteria: the '42-'43 zoot suit riots had produced a huge wave of anti-Mexican sentiment throughout Los Angeles. All seventeen boys received life sentences, and the Sleepy Lagoon Defense Committee – UAES brain trusters, Communist Party members, leftists and straight citizens – held rallies, circulated petitions and raised funds to employ a legal team – which ultimately got all seventeen pardoned. Hypocrisy within the idealism: Lesnick's male patients, hearts bleeding over the poor railroaded Mexicans, complained to him of Communist Party white women screwing 'proletariat' taco benders – then assailed themselves as rabid bigots moments later.

Mal made a mental note to talk to Ellis Loew about the Sleepy Lagoon angle: Ed Satterlee wanted to procure SLDC rally pictures from the Feds – but since the kids were exonerated, it might backfire. Ditto the info the shrinkees poured out over '47 HUAC. Better for him and Dudley to keep it sub rosa, not jeopardize Lesnick's complicity and use the info only by implication: to squeeze the UAESers' suspected weak points. Going with the HUAC stuff full-bore might jeopardize their grand jury: J. Parnell Thomas, the Committee's chairman, was currently doing time on bribery charges; hotshot Hollywood stars had protested HUAC's methods and Lesnick's files were rife with nonpetty trauma deriving from the spring of '47 – suicides, attempted suicides, frantic betrayals of friendship, booze and sex to kill the pain. If the '50 LA City grand jury team attempted to use the juice of '47 HUAC – *their first precedent* – they might engender sympathy for UAES members and subsidiary hostile witnesses. Better not to dip into old HUAC testimony for conspiracy evidence; imperative that the lefties be denied a chance to boo-hoo the grand jury's tactics to the press.

Mal felt his overview sink in as solid: good evidence, good thoughts on what to use, what to hold back. He killed his coffee and went to the individuals – the half dozen of the twenty-two most ripe for interrogation and operation.

His first was a maybe. Morton Ziffkin: UAES member, CP member, member of eleven other organizations classified as Commie fronts. Family man – a wife and two grown daughters. A highly paid screenwriter – 100 thou a year until he told HUAC to fuck off – now working for peanuts as a film splicer. Underwent analysis with Doc Lesnick out of a stated desire to 'explore Freudian thought' and allay his impulses to cheat on his wife with an onslaught of CP women 'out for my gelt – not my body.' A rabid, bad-tempered Marxist ideologue – a good man to bait on the witness stand – but he'd probably never snitch on his fellow Pinks. He sounded intelligent enough to make Ellis Loew seem like a fool, and his HUAC stint gave him an air of martyrdom. A maybe.

Mondo Lopez, Juan Duarte and Sammy Benavides, former Sleepy Lagoon Defense Committee bigshots, recruited out of the Sinarquistas – a zoot suit gang given to sporting Nazi regalia – by CP bosses. Now token ethnics in the UAES hierarchy, the three spent the '40s throwing it to condescending white lefty women – enraged over their airs, but grateful for the action; more enraged at being told by their 'puto' cell leader to 'explore' that rage by seeing a psychiatrist. Benavides, Duarte and Lopez were currently working at Variety International Pictures, half the time as stagehands, half the time playing Indians in cheapy cowboy pictures. They were also serving as picket bosses on Gower Gulch – the closest thing the UAES had to muscle – pitiful when compared to the Mickey Cohen goons the Teamsters were employing. Mal pegged them as pussy hounds who fell into clover, the Sleepy Lagoon job their only real political concern. The three probably had criminal records and connections stemming from their zoot suit days, a good approach for the team's troubleshooter – if Ellis Loew ever found one.

Now the brain trust got ugly.

Reynolds Loftis, movie character actor, snitched to HUAC by his former homo lover Chaz Minear, a Hollywood script hack. Loftis did not suspect that Minear ratted him, and in no way reciprocated the finking. Both men were still with the UAES, still friendly at their meetings and at other political functions they attended. Minear, guilt-crazed over his fink duty, had said to Doc Lesnick: 'If you knew who he left me for, you'd understand why I did it.' Mal had scanned both Loftis' and Minear's files for more mention of 'he' and came up empty; there was a large gap in Lesnick's Loftis transcripts – from the years '42 to '44 – and Minear's pages bore no other mention of the third edge of the triangle. Mal recalled Loftis from westerns he'd taken Stefan to: a tall, lanky, silver-haired man, handsome like your idealized U.S. senator. And a Communist, and a subversive, and a hostile HUAC witness and self-described switch-hitter. A potential friendly witness par excellence – next to Chaz Minear, the Red with the most closeted skclctons.

And finally the Red Queen.

Claire De Haven did not possess a file, and several of the men had described her as too smart, strong and good to need a psychiatrist. She also screwed half her CP cell and all the SLDC bigwigs, including Benavides, Lopez and Duarte, who worshiped her. Chaz Minear was in her thrall, despite his homosexuality; Reynolds Loftis spoke of her as the 'only woman I've evcr rcally loved.' Mal picked up on her smarts secondhand: Claire moved behind the scenes, tended not to shout slogans and retained the political and legal connections of her late father, a stolid right-wing counsel to the LA business establishment. Minear speculated to Doc Lesnick that her old man's political juice kept her from being subpoenaed by HUAC in '47 – and not one other witness mentioned her name. Claire De Haven screwed like a rabbit, but didn't come off as a slut; she inspired the loyalty of homosexual screenwriters, switch-hitter actors, Mexican stage-hands and Commies of all stripes.

Mal turned off the light, reminding himself to write Doc Lesnick a memo: all the files ended in the summer of '49 – five months ago. Why? Walking out to the elevator, he wondered what Claire De Haven looked like, where he could get a picture, if he could get his decoy to operate her out of her lust – politics and sex to nail the woman as a friendly witness, the Red Queen squeezed like a Chinatown whore, captain's bars dancing his way at the end of a stag movie.

CHAPTER NINE

Bagman time.

His first stop was Variety International, where Herman Gerstein gave him a five-minute lecture on the evils of Communism and handed him a fat envelope stuffed with C-notes; stop two was a short stroll through the Teamster and UAES picket lines over to Hollywood Prestige National Pictures, where Wally Voldrich, the head of Security, kicked loose with a doughnut box full of fifties dusted with powdered sugar and chocolate sprinkles. Howard's ten thou was already in his pocket; Mickey C.'s contribution to the Friends of the American Way in Motion Pictures would be his last pickup of the morning.

Buzz took Sunset out to Santa Monica Canyon, to the bungalow hideaway where Mickey palled with his stooges, entertained poon and hid out from his wife. The money in his pocket had him feeling brash: if Mal Considine was around when he dropped the bag with Ellis Loew, he'd rattle his cage to see what the four years since Laura had done to his balls. If it felt right, he'd tell Howard he'd sign on to fight Communism – Leotis Dineen was pressing him for a grand and a half, and he was a bad jigaboo to fuck with.

Cohen's bungalow was a bamboo job surrounded by

specially landscaped tropical foliage, camouflage for his triggermen when the Mick and Jack Dragna were skirmishing. Buzz parked in the driveway behind a white Packard ragtop, wondering where Mickey's bulletproofed Caddy was and who'd be around to hand him his envelope. He walked up to the door and rang the buzzer; a woman's deep-South voice drifted out a window screen. 'Come in.'

Buzz opened the door and saw Audrey Anders sitting at a living room table, hitting the keys of an adding machine. No makeup, dungarees and one of Mickey's monogrammed dress shirts didn't dent her beauty at all; she actually looked better than she did New Year's morning, pink party dress and high heels, kicking Tommy Sifakis in the balls. 'Hello, Miss Anders.'

Audrey pointed to a Chinese lacquered coffee table; a roll of bills secured by a rubber band was resting smack in the middle. 'Mickey said to tell you mazel tov, which I guess means he's glad you're in with this grand jury thing.'

Buzz sat down in an easy chair and put his feet up, his signal that he meant to stay and look awhile. 'Mickey takin' advantage of that master's degree of yours?'

Audrey tapped out a transaction, checked the paper the machine expelled and wrote on a pad, all very slowly. She said, 'You believe the program notes at the El Rancho Burlesque?'

'No, I just made you for the brains.'

'The brains to keep books for a lending operation?'

'Loan shark's more the word, but I meant brains in general.'

Audrey pointed to Buzz's feet. 'Planning to stay awhile?'

'Not long. You really got a master's degree?'

'Jesus, we keep asking each other these questions. No, I do not have a master's degree, but I do have a certificate in accounting from a second-rate teachers college in Jackson, Mississippi. Satisfied?'

Buzz didn't know if the woman wanted him out the

103

door pronto or if she welcomed the interruption – totalling shark vig on a fine winter day was his idea of hunger. He played his only ace, his one opening to see what she thought of him. 'Lucy Whitehall okay?'

Audrey lit a cigarette and blew two perfect smoke rings. 'Yes. Sol Gelfman has her tucked away at his place in Palm Springs, and Mickey had some friend of his on the Sheriff's Department issue something called a restraining order. If Tommy bothers Lucy, the police will arrest him. She told me she's grateful for what you did. I didn't tell her you did it for money.'

Buzz ignored the jibe and smiled. 'Tell Lucy hi for me. Tell her she's so pretty I might've done it for free.'

Audrey laughed. 'In a pig's eye you would. Meeks, what is between you and Mickey?'

'I'll answer that one with a question. Why you wanta know?'

Audrey blew two more rings and ground out her cigarette. 'Because he talked about you for an hour straight last night. Because he said he can't figure out if you're the stupidest smart man or the smartest stupid man he ever met, and he can't figure out why you blow all your money with colored bookies when you could bet with him for no vig. He said that only stupid men love danger, but you love danger and you're not stupid. He said he can't figure out whether you're brave or crazy. Does any of this make sense to you?'

Buzz saw the words inscribed on his tombstone, all crimped together so they'd fit. He answered straight, not caring who Audrey told. 'Miss Anders, I take risks Mickey's afraid to, so I make him feel safe. He's a little guy and I'm a little guy, and maybe I'm just a tad better with my hands and that baton of mine. Mickey's got more to lose than me, so he runs scared more than me. And if I'm crazy, it means he's smart. You know what surprises me about this talk we're havin', Miss Anders?'

The question interrupted Audrey starting to smile – a big beam that showed off two slightly crooked teeth and a cold sore on her lower lip. 'No, what?'

'That Mickey thinks enough of you to talk to you about stuff like that. That surely does surprise me.'

Audrey's smile fizzled out. 'He loves me.'

'You mean he appreciates the favors you do him. Like when I was a cop, I skimmed that good old white powder and sold it to Mickey, not Jack D. We got to be as friendly as anybody and Mickey can be 'cause of that. I'm just surprised he plays it that close with a woman is all.'

Audrey lit another cigarette; Buzz saw it as cover for bad thoughts, good banter flushed down the toilet. He said, 'I'm sorry. I didn't mean to be so personal.'

Audrey's eyes ignited. 'Oh yes you did, Meeks. You *surely* did.'

Buzz got up and walked around the room, checking out the strange chink furnishings, wondering who'd picked them out, Mickey's wife or this ex-stripper/book-keeper who was making him feel jumpy, like a gun would go off if he said the wrong thing. He tried small talk. 'Nice stuff. Hate to see Jack D. put bullet holes in it.'

Audrey's voice was shaky. 'Mickey and Jack are talking about burying the hatchet. Jack wants to go in on a deal with him. Maybe dope, maybe a casino in Vegas. Meeks, I love Mickey and he loves me.'

Buzz heard the last words as bang, bang, bang, bang. He picked up the cash roll, stuffed it in his pocket and said, 'Yeah, he loves takin' you to the Troc and the Mocambo, cause he knows every man there is droolin' for you and afraid of him. Then it's an hour at your place and back to the wife. It's real nice the two of you talk every once in awhile, but as far as I'm concerned you're gettin' short shrift from a Jewboy who ain't got the brains to know what he's got.'

Audrey's jaw dropped; her cigarette fell into her lap. She picked it up and stubbed it out. 'Are you *this* crazy or *that* stupid?'

Bang, bang, bang, bang – cannon loud. Buzz said, 'Maybe I just trust you,' walked over and kissed Audrey

Anders full on the lips, one hand holding her head, cradling it. She didn't open her mouth and she didn't embrace him back and she didn't push him away. When Buzz snapped that it was all he was going to get, he broke the clinch and floated to the car with quicksand under his feet.

It was bang, bang, bang, bang on the drive downtown, ricochets, old dumb moves kicked around to see how they stood up next to this doozie.

In '33 he'd charged six picket bulls outside MGM, caught nail-studded baseball bats upside his arms, took the boys out with his baton and caught tetanus – stupid, but the audaciousness helped get him his LAPD appointment.

Early in '42 he worked with the Alien Squad, rounding up Japs and relocating them to the horse paddocks at Santa Anita Racetrack. He grabbed a wiseacre kid named Bob Takahashi just as he was en route to get his ashes hauled for the first time, felt sorry for him and took him on a six-day toot in Tijuana – booze, whores, the dog track and a teary farewell at the border – bad Bob hightailing it south, a slant-eyed stranger in a round-eyed land. Very stupid – but he covered his absent ass by shaking down a suspicious-looking car outside San Diego, busting four grasshoppers transporting a pound of premium maryjane. The punks had a total of nineteen outstanding LA City warrants between them; he got a commendation letter and four felony notches on his gun. Another shit play turned into clover.

But the granddaddy was his brother Fud. Three days out of the Texas State Pen, Fud shows up at the door of then Detective-Sergeant Turner Meeks, informs him that he just stuck up a liquor store in Hermosa Beach, pistol-whipped the proprietor and intended to pay Buzz back the six yards he owed him with the proceeds. Just as Fud was digging through his blood-soaked paper bag, there was a knock at the door. Buzz looked through the spy hole, saw two blue uniforms, tagged blood as thicker

106

than water and fired his own service revolver into the living room wall four times. The bluesuits started knocking down the door; Buzz hustled Fud to the cellar, locked him in, smashed the window leading to the back porch and trampled his landlady's prize petunias. When the patrolmen made it inside, Buzz told them he was LAPD and the perpetrator was a hophead he'd sent to Big Q – Davis Haskins – in reality a recent overdose in Billings, Montana; he'd picked up the info working an extradition job. The blues fanned out, called for backup and surrounded the neighborhood until dawn; Davis Haskins made the front page of the *Mirror* and *Daily News*; Buzz shat bricks for a week and kept Fud docile in the cellar with whiskey, baloney sandwiches and smut mags swiped from the Central Vice squadroom. And he walked on the caper, white trash chutzpah carrying him through, no one informing the police powers that be that a dead man robbed the Happy Time Liquor Store, drove a stolen La Salle up to the front door of Sergeant Turner 'Buzz' Meeks, then shot out his living room wall and escaped on foot. When Fud bought it a year later at Guadalcanal, his squad leader sent Buzz a letter; baby brother's last words were something like, 'Tell Turner thanks for the fur books and sandwiches.'

Stupid, crazy, sentimental, lunatic dumb.

But kissing Audrey Anders was worse.

Buzz parked in the City Hall lot, transferred all the cash to his doughnut box and took it upstairs to Ellis Loew's office. Going in the door, he saw Loew, Big Dudley Smith and Mal Considine sitting around a table, all of them talking at once, garbled stuff about cop decoys. No one glanced up; Buzz eyeballed Considine four years after he gave him the cuckold's horns. The man still looked more like a lawyer than a cop; his blond hair was going gray; there was something nervous and raggedy-assed about him.

Buzz rapped on the door and tossed the box onto the chair holding it open. The three looked over; he fixed his eyes on Considine. Ellis Loew nodded, all business;

Dudley Smith said, 'Hello, Turner, old colleague,' all blarney; Considine eyed him back, all curiosity, like he was examining a reptile specimen he'd never seen before.

They held the look. Buzz said, 'Hello, Mal.'

Mal Considine said, 'Nice tie, Meeks. Who'd you roll for it?'

Buzz laughed. 'How's the ex, Lieutenant? She still wearin' crotchless panties?'

Considine stared, his mouth twitching. Buzz stared back, his mouth dry.

Mexican standoff.

50–50, Considine or Dragna.

Maybe he'd hold off just a tad, cut the Red Menace just a bit more slack before he signed on.

CHAPTER TEN

It was two nights of bad dreams and a day's worth of dead ends that had him making the run to Malibu Canyon.

Driving northbound on Pacific Coast Highway, Danny chalked it up as an elimination job: talk to the men on the list of fighting dog breeders he'd gotten from Sheriff's Central Vice, make nice with them and get educated confirmations or denials on Doc Layman's animal-aided killing/blood bait thesis. No such beast existed in the County Homicide files or with City R&I; if the breeders, men who would know if anyone did, laughed the theory off as nonsense, then maybe tonight he could sleep without the company of snapping hounds, entrails and screechy jazz.

It started this way:

After the Moonglow Lounge and Janice Modine's pass, he'd gotten an idea – build his own file on the Goines snuff, write down every shred of information, glom carbons of the autopsy and print reports, stick Dietrich with lackluster summaries and concentrate on *his* paperwork, *his* case – the 187 he'd follow up even if he didn't nail the bastard before the skipper pulled the plug. He drove to the Hollywood Ranch Market then, grabbed a stack of cardboard cartons, bought manila folders, colored side tabs, yellow legal pads, typing and carbon paper and drove home with them – allowing himself two extra shots of I. W. Harper as a reward for his dedication. The booze put him out on the couch – and it got hairy.

Goines' mutilations in wraparound Technicolor. Guts and big bruised penises, so close up that at first he couldn't tell what they were. Dogs rooting in the gore, him right there, Man Camera filming it until he joined the brood and started biting.

Two nights of it.

With a day of shit in between.

He put the first night's dream off as scare stuff caused by a frustrating case and no food in his system. In the morning he got double bacon, eggs, hash browns, toast and sweet rolls at the Wilshire Derby, drove downtown to the Sheriff's Central Bureau and scanned Homicide files. No animal-aided murders were on record; the only homosexual slashings even remotely similar to Marty Goines' were open-and-shut jobs – lovers' spats where the perpetrator was captured, still serving time or executed by the State of California.

Shitwork was next.

He called Karen Hiltscher at the Station and sweet-talked her into making phone queries of other musician's locals that might have sent Marty Goines out on gigs, and LA area jazz clubs that might have hired his trombone independently. He told her to ring the other LASD station houses and solicit run-throughs of their burglary files: paper scans for jazz musician/burglars who might prove to be known associates of Goines. The girl reluctantly agreed; he blew kisses into the phone, promised to call for results later and drove back to Local 3126.

There, the counterwoman gave him another look at the Horn of Plenty's employment record, and Danny copied down club and roadhouse addresses going back to Mad Marty's first gig in '36. He spent the rest of the day driving by jazz spots that were now laundromats and hamburger joints; jazz spots that had changed hands a half dozen times; jazz spots that had retained the same owner for years. And he got the same response across the board: a shrug at Goines' mugshot strip, the words 'Marty who?', a deadpan on the topics of jazzbo burglars and the longshot of a burglar kid with his face bandaged up.

At dusk, he called Karen for her results. Goose egg: more 'Marty who?', the burglar files yielding eleven names – seven negroes, two Mexicans, two white men whose jail records revealed AB+ and O– blood. Pure undiluted shit.

He remembered his promise to Janice Modine then, called the San Dimas Substation and talked to the boss of the Auto Theft Detail. John Lembeck was still in custody there, being sweated over a series of GTAs. Danny told the man his snitch story, stressing the angle that Lembeck was dead meat if he made it to the County jail. The squad boss agreed to roll him up for release; Danny could tell Jungle John was in for a severe thumping first – but not half as bad as he was going to give him.

Then it was back to his apartment, four shots of I.W. and work on the file, side tabs labeled and stuck to folders – 'Interviews,' 'Eliminations,' 'Chronology,' 'Canvassing,' 'Physical Evidence,' 'Background.' One thought burned throughout the writing of a detailed summary: where was Marty Goines living between the time of his release from Lexington State and his death? The thought led to a phone call – the night switchboard at the hospital for a list of other men released to California around the same time as Goines. The answer, after holding the line long distance for twenty minutes – *none*.

Exhaustion, writer's cramp and no sleep followed.

110

Four bonus shots and a sheet-thrashing roll on the bed got him unconsciousness and the dogs again, the Man Camera with teeth – his – biting at a whole morgueful of O+ stiffs lined up on gurneys. Morning and another big breakfast convinced him to make the elimination; he called Central Vice, got the list of breeders and was warned to go easy: the dog farms in Malibu Canyon were run by cracker strongarms, cousins from the Tennessee sticks. They bred their pit bulls there, which was not against the law; they only fought them in South LA, and none of the men had been convicted of dog fighting since the war.

Danny turned off Pacific Coast Highway at the Canyon Road and climbed inland through scrub-covered hills laced with little streams and valleys. The road was a narrow two-laner, the left side featuring kiddie camps, stables and occasional nightclubs, the right a wood retaining wall and a long drop into green-brown bush forest. Signs pointing into the scrub indicated clearings and houses and people; Danny saw the roofs of villas, Tudor steeples, the chimneys of extravagant log cabins. Gradually, the quality of the real estate declined – no ocean view, no sea breeze, the scrub thicker and thicker, no dwellings at all. When he hit the top of Malibu Ridge and started rolling downhill, he knew the dog farms had to be nearby – his vista was now dotted with tar-papered shacks and the heat was zooming up as the shade-producing foliage thinned out.

The Vice officer he'd talked to had the three farms tagged as a mile in on a dirt access road marked by a sign: PIT PUPS – AUTO PARTS. Danny found the sign just as the two-lane leveled off into a long, flat stretch, the San Fernando Valley in the distance. He swung onto it and wracked his Chevy's undercarriage for three-quarters of a mile, sharecropper-like shacks on both sides of him. Then he saw them – three cinderblock huts encircled by a barbed-wire fence; three dirt yards littered with axles, drive shafts and cylinder blocks; three individually penned broods of squat, muscular dogs.

111

Danny pulled up to the fence, pinned his badge to his jacket front and tapped the horn – a little courtesy to the hut dwellers. The dogs barked at the noise; Danny walked over to the nearest stretch of wire and looked at them.

They weren't the dogs of his dreams – black and sleek with flashing white teeth – they were brindle and tan and speckled terriers, barrel-chested, jaw-heavy and all muscle. They didn't have the outsized genitalia of his dogs; their barks weren't death snaps; they weren't ugly – they were just animals bred for a mean utility. Danny eyed the ones penned up closest to him, wondering what they'd do if he gave them a pat on the head, then told them he was glad they didn't look like some other dogs he knew.

'Rape-o, Hacksaw and Night Train. Them dogs won sixteen altogether. Southern California record for one man's stable.'

Danny turned to face the voice. A very fat man in overalls was standing in the doorway of the shack just off to his left; he was wearing thick glasses and probably couldn't see too well. Danny unpinned his badge and slipped it in his pocket, thinking the man was garrulous and ripe for an insurance agent ploy. 'Can I talk to you for a second about your dogs?'

The man ambled to the fence, squinting and blinking. He said, 'Booth Conklin. You in the market for a good pit hound?'

Danny looked into Booth Conklin's eyes, one a free-floating waller, the other cloudy and pocked with catar-acts. 'Dan Upshaw. You could start me off with some information on them.'

Conklin said, 'I kin do better than that,' waddled to a speckled dog's pen and flipped the latch. The beast made a dash, hit the fence with his front paws and started licking the wire. Danny knelt and scratched his snout, a slick pink tongue sliding over his fingers. He said, 'Good boy, good fellow,' putting off Doc Layman's theories as long longshots then and there.

112

Booth Conklin waddled back, holding a long piece of wood. 'First lesson with pits is don't talk baby talk to 'em or they won't respect you. Rape-o here's a leg pumper, just wants to get your trousers wet. My cousin Wallace named him Rape-o 'cause he'll mount anything with bad intentions. Down, Rape-o, down!'

The pit bull kept nuzzling Danny's fingers; Booth Conklin whacked him in the ass with his stick. Rape-o let out a shrill yowl, cowered away and started rubbing his backside in the dirt, all fours up and treading air. Danny felt his fists clenching; Conklin stuck the stick in Rape-o's mouth. The dog clamped down his jaws; Conklin lifted him up and held him out at arm's length. Danny gasped at the feat of strength.

Conklin spoke calmly, like holding seventy pounds of dog at the end of a stick was everyday stuff. 'Pits dish it out, so they gotta be able to take it. I won't sell you no dog if you gonna coddle it.'

Rape-o was hanging stock-still, groans vibrating from his throat. Every muscle was perfectly outlined; Danny thought that the animal was perfect mean beauty. He said, 'I live in an apartment, so I can't have a dog.'

'You just come out to look and jaw?'

Rape-o's groans were getting deeper and more pleasured; his balls constricted and he popped an erection. Danny looked away. 'Questions more than anything else.'

Conklin squinted, his eyes slits behind coke bottle glasses. 'You ain't a policeman, are you?'

'No, I'm an insurance investigator. I'm working a death claim and I thought you could help me with some questions.'

Conklin said, 'I'm the helpful type, ain't I, Rape-o,' moving the stick up and down, wrist flicks while the dog humped the air. Rape-o yowled, yipped and whimpered; Danny knew what was happening and fixed on the fat man's coke bottles. Rape-o let out a final yowl/yip/groan, let go and fell to the dirt. Conklin laughed. 'You ain't got the sense of humor for pits, I can tell. Ask your questions, boy. I got a cousin who's an insurance man, so I'm prone to the breed.'

Rape-o slinked over to the fence and tried to rub his snout up against Danny's knee; Danny took a step backward. 'It's a murder claim. We know the victim was killed by a man, but the coroner thinks he may have let a dog or coyote or wolf at him after he was dead. What do you think of the idea?'

Conklin stuck a toothpick in his mouth and worked his words around it. 'Mister, I know the canine family real good, and coyotes and wolves is out – 'less the killer captured and starved them and left the dead guy out for them to pick clean someplace amenable. What kind of damage on your victim?'

Danny watched Rape-o curl up in the dirt and go to sleep, sated, his muscles slack. 'Localized. Teeth marks on the stomach, the intestines bitten and sucked on. It had to have happened someplace inside, because the body was clean when the police found it.'

Conklin snickered. 'Then you rule out coyotes and wolves – they'd go crazy and eat the fucker whole, and you can't exactly keep them inside the house. You thinkin' pits? Dogs?'

'If anything, yes.'

'You sure them teeth marks ain't human?'

'No, we're not sure.'

Booth Conklin pointed to his pit pens. 'Mister, I run these three farms for my cousins, and I know how to get what I want from dogs, and if I was crazy enough to want one of my pups to eat a man's guts, I imagine I could think up a way for him to do it. I'll tell you though, I've got a real taste for blood sport, and I couldn't imagine any human being doin' what you just told me.'

Danny said, 'If you wanted to, how would you do it?'

Conklin petted Rape-o's hindquarters; the dog lazily wagged its tail. 'I'd starve him and pen him and let bitch dogs in heat parade around in front of his cage and make him crazy. I'd muzzle him and bind his legs and put a

114

restrainer around his dick so he couldn't get himself off. I'd get me a rubber glove and tweak his dick till he just about got there, then I'd clamp his balls so he couldn't shoot. I'd get me some doggie menstrual blood and spray it in his eyes and nose for a week or so, till he came to think of it as food and love. Then, when I had me a dead man, I'd spread a big puddle of pussy blood right where I wanted him to bite. And, mister? I'd have a gun handy in case that tormented old dog decided to eat *me*. That answer satisfy you?'

Danny thought: No animals, it just isn't *right*. But – have Doc Layman do organ taps on Goines, his body parts near the mutilations, tests for a second, nonhuman, blood type. He threw Booth Conklin a long-shot question. 'What kind of people buy dogs from you?'

'Boys who love blood sport, and I ain't talkin' 'bout your crazy shit either.'

'Isn't dog fighting against the law?'

'You know who to grease, then there ain't no law. You sure you ain't a policeman?'

Danny shook his head. 'Amalgamated Insurance. Look, do you remember selling a dog to a tall, gray-haired man, middle-aged, within the past six months or so?'

Conklin gave Rape-o a gentle kick; the dog stirred, got up and trotted back to his pen. 'Mister, my customers are young studs in pickup trucks and niggers lookin' to have the toughest dog on the block.'

'Do any of your customers stand out as different than that? Unusual?'

Booth Conklin laughed so hard he almost swallowed his toothpick. 'Back durin' the war, these movie types saw my sign, came by and said they wanted to make a little home movie, two dogs dressed up with masks and costumes fightin' to the death. I sold them boys two twenty-dollar dogs for a C-note apiece.'

'Did they make their movie?'

'I ain't seen it advertised at Grauman's Chinese, so how should I know? There's this sanitarium over on the beach side of the Canyon, dryout place for all the Hollywood types. I figured they were visitin' there and headin' to the Valley when they saw my sign.'

'Were any of the men tall and gray-haired?'

Conklin shrugged. 'I don't really remember. One guy had a funny European accent, that I do recall. Besides, my eyes ain't the best in the world. You about done with your questions, son?'

Ninety-five percent against on the blood bait theory; maybe a quash on his nightmares; useless dope on Hollywood lunacy. Danny said, 'Thanks, Mr. Conklin. You were a big help.'

'My pleasure, son. Come back sometime. Rape-o likes you.'

Danny drove to the Station, sent out for a hamburger, fries and milk even though he wasn't hungry, ate half the meal and called Doc Layman at the City Morgue.

'Norton Layman speaking.'

'It's Danny Upshaw, Doctor.'

'Just the man I was going to call. Your news first or mine?'

Danny flashed: Rape-o chewing on Marty Goines' midsection. He threw the remains of his burger in the wastebasket and said, 'Mine. I'm sure the teethmarks are human. I just talked to a man who breeds fighting dogs, and he said your blood bait theory is feasible, but it would take a lot of planning, and I think the killing wasn't *that* premeditated. He said dog menstrual blood would be the best bait, and I was thinking you could tap the cadaver's organs next to his wounds, see if you got any foreign blood.'

Layman sighed. 'Danny, the City of Los Angeles cremated Martin Mitchell Goines this morning. Autopsy completed, no claim on the body within forty-eight hours, ashes to ashes. I have some good news, though.'

Danny thought, 'Shit'; said 'Shoot.'

'The slash wounds on the victim's back interested me,

116

and I remembered Gordon Kienzle's wound book. Do you know it?'

'No.'

'Well, Kienzle is a pathologist who started out as an emergency room MD. He was fascinated with nonfatal assaults, and he put together a book of photos and specifications on man-inflicted woundings. I consulted it, and the cuts on Martin Mitchell Goines' back are identical to the sample wounds listed under 'Zoot Stick,' a two-by-four with a razor blade or blades attached at the end. Now, the zoot stick dates back to '42 and '43. It was popular with anti-Mexican gangs and Riot Squad cops, who used it to slash the zoot suits certain Latin elements were sporting.'

Check the City/County Homicide files for zoot stick killings. Danny said, 'It's a good lead, Doc. Thanks.'

'Don't thank me yet. I checked the files before I decided to call you. There are no zoot stick homicides on record. A friend of mine on the LAPD Riot Squad said 99 percent of your white-on-Mexican assaults weren't reported and the Mexicans never took the damn sticks to each other, it was considered dirty pool or whatever. But it *is* a lead.'

Robe wad suffocating, hands or sash strangling, teeth biting, and now a zoot stick cutting. *Why the different forms of brutality?* Danny said, 'See you in class, Doctor,' hung up and walked back to his car just to be moving. Jungle John Lembeck was leaning against the hood, his face bruised, one eye purple and closed. He said, 'They got real rough with me, Mr. Upshaw. I wouldn't have told Janice to ditz you, except they were hurting me so bad. I'm stand-up, Mr. Upshaw. So if you want payback, I'll understand.'

Danny balled his right fist and got ready to swing it – but a flash of Booth Conklin and his pit hound stopped him.

CHAPTER ELEVEN

The cigars were Havanas, and their aroma made Mal wish he hadn't quit smoking; Herman Gerstein's pep talk and Dudley Smith's accompaniment – smiles, nods, little chuckles – made him wish that he was back at the LAPD Academy interviewing recruits for the role of idealistic young leftist. His one day of it had yielded no one near appropriate, and starting their interrogations without a decoy at the ready felt like a mistake. But Ellis Loew and Dudley, fired up by Lesnick's psychiatric dirt, were trigger-happy – and here they were getting ready to brace Mondo Lopez, Sammy Benavides and Juan Duarte, UAESers playing Indians on the set of *Tomahawk Massacre*. And now Gerstein's schtick was making him itchy, too.

The Variety International boss was pacing behind his desk, waving his Havana; Mal kept thinking of Buzz Meeks sliming back into his life at *the* worst possible moment.

'. . . and I can tell you this, gentlemen: through passive resistance and other Commie shit the UAES is gonna force the Teamsters into kicking some ass, which is gonna make the UAES look good and us look bad. Commies like to get hurt. They'll eat any amount of shit, smile like it's filet mignon and ask for seconds, turn the other cheek, then bite *you* on the ass. Like those pachucos down on Set 23. Zoot suit punks who got themselves a union card, a license to give shit and think their own shit don't stink. Am I right or is Eleanor Roosevelt a dyke?'

Dudley Smith laughed uproariously. 'And a grand quiff diver she is. Dark meat, too, I've heard. And we all know about the late Franklin's bent for little black terriers. Mr. Gerstein, Lieutenant Considine and I would like to thank you for your contributions to our endeavor and your hospitality this morning.'

Mal took the cue and stood up; Herman Gerstein reached into a humidor and grabbed a handful of cigars. Dudley got to his feet; Gerstein came at them like a fullback, pumping hands, stuffing Havanas in all their available pockets, showing them the door with hard back slaps. When it closed behind him, Dudley said, 'No flair for language. You can take the Jew out of the gutter, but you can't take the gutter out of the Jew. Are you ready to interrogate, Captain?'

Mal looked down at the UAES picket line, caught a back view of a woman in slacks and wondered if she was Claire De Haven. 'Okay, *Lieutenant*.'

'Ah, Malcolm, what a grand wit you have!'

They took Herman Gerstein's private elevator down to ground level and two rows of sound stages separated by a center walkway. The buildings were tan stucco, silo tall and humpbacked at the top, with sandwich boards propped up by the front doors – the name, director and shooting schedule of the movie crayoned on white plastic. Actors riding bicycles – cowboys, Indians, baseball players, Revolutionary War soldiers – whizzed by; motorized carts hauled camera equipment; technicians hobnobbed by a snack cart where a Roman centurion dished out doughnuts and coffee. The enclosed sets extended for nearly a quarter mile, black numbers above the doors marking them. Mal walked ahead of Dudley Smith, running Benavides/Lopez/Duarte file dirt through his head, hoping an on-the-job bracing wasn't too much, too quick.

Dudley caught up outside Set 23. Mal rang the buzzer; a woman in a saloon girl outfit opened the door and popped her gum at them. Mal displayed his badge and identification. 'We're with the District Attorney's Office, and we want to speak to Mondo Lopez, Juan Duarte and Sammy Benavides.'

The saloon girl gave her gum a last pop and spoke with a thick Brooklyn accent. 'They're on a take. They're the hotheaded young Indians who want to attack the fort, but the wise old chief don't want them to. They'll be finished in a few minutes, and you can – '

Dudley cut in. 'We don't require a plot synopsis. If you'll tell them it's the police, they'll adjust their busy schedule to accommodate us. And please do it now.'

The girl swallowed her gum and walked in front of them. Dudley smiled; Mal thought: he's a spellbinder – don't let him run the show.

The sound stage was cavernous: wire-strewn walls, lights and cameras on dollies, anemic-looking horses tethered to equipment poles and people standing around doing nothing. Right in the middle was an olive drab teepee, obviously fashioned from army surplus material, Indian symbols painted on the sides – candy apple red lacquer – like it was some brave's customized hot rod. Cameras and tripod lights were fixed on the teepee and the four actors squatting in front of it – an old pseudo-Indian white man and three pseudo-Indian Mexicans in their late twenties.

The saloon girl stopped them a few feet behind the cameras, whispering, 'There. The Latin lover types.' The old chief intoned words of peace; the three young braves delivered lines about the white eyes speaking with forked tongue, their voices pure Mex. Someone yelled, 'Cut!' and the scene became a blur of moving bodies.

Mal elbowed into it, catching the three pulling cigarettes and lighters out of their buckskins. He made them make him as a cop; Dudley Smith walked over; the braves gave each other spooked looks.

Dudley flashed his shield. 'Police. Am I talking to Mondo Lopez, Juan Duarte and Samuel Benavides?'

The tallest brave slipped a rubber band off his pony tail and shaped his hair into a pachuco do – duck's ass back, pompadour front. He said, 'I'm Lopez.'

Mal opened up his end strong. 'Care to introduce your friends, Mr. Lopez? We don't have all day.'

The other two squared their shoulders and stepped

forward, the move half bravado, half kowtow to authority. Mal tagged the short, muscular one as Duarte, former Sinarquista squad leader, zoot suits and swastika armbands until the CP brought him around; his lanky pal as Benavides – Mr. Tight Lips to Doc Lesnick, his file a complete bore except for one session devoted to an account of how twelve-year-old Sammy molested his nine-year-old sister, a razor blade to her throat. Both men did a sullen foot dance; Muscles said, 'I'm Benavides.'

Mal pointed to a side door, then touched his tie clip – LAPD semaphore for *Let Me Run It*. 'My name's Considine, and this is Lieutenant Smith. We're with the DA's Office, and we'd like to ask you a few questions. It's just routine, and we'll have you back at work in a few minutes.'

Juan Duarte said, 'We got a choice?'

Dudley chuckled; Mal put a hand on his arm. 'Yes. Here or the Hall of Justice jail.'

Lopez cocked his head toward the exit; Benavides and Duarte fell in next to him, lit cigarettes and walked outside. Actors and technicians gawked at the Indian-paleface migration. Mal schemed a razzle-dazzle, himself abrasive at first, then making nice, Dudley asking the hard questions, him playing savior at the end – the big push to glom them as friendly witnesses.

The three halted their march just out the door, leaning against the wall, nonchalant. Mal let the men smoke in silence, then said, 'Boy, have you guys got it made.'

Three sets of eyes on the ground, three phony Indians in a cloud of cigarette smoke. Mal rattled the leader's cage. 'Can I ask you a question, Mr. Lopez?'

Mondo Lopez looked up. 'Sure, Officer.'

'Mr. Lopez, you must be taking home close to a C-note a week. Is that true?'

Mondo Lopez said, 'Eighty-one and change. Why?'

Mal smiled. 'Well, you're making almost half as much as I am, and I'm a college graduate and a ranking police

121

officer with sixteen years' experience. All of you quit high school, isn't that true?'

A quick look passed among the three. Lopez smirked, Benavides shrugged and Duarte took a long drag on his cigarette. Mal saw them sighting in on his ploy way too soon and tried for sugar. 'Look, I'll tell you why I brought it up. You guys have beat the odds. You ran with the First Street Flats and the Sinarquistas, did some Juvie time and stayed clean. That's impressive, and we're not here to roust you for anything you yourselves did.'

Juan Duarte ground out his cigarette. 'You mean this is about our friends?'

Mal dredged the files for ammo, grabbing the fact that all three tried to join the service after Pearl Harbor. 'Look, I've checked your Selective Service records. You quit the Sinarquistas and the Flats and you tried to fight the Japs, you were on the right side with Sleepy Lagoon. When you were wrong you copped to it. That's the sign of a good man in my book.'

Sammy Benavides said, 'Is a stool pigeon a good man in your book, Mr. Po – '

Duarte silenced him with a sharp elbow. 'Who you trying to tell us is wrong now? Who you *want* to be wrong?'

Finally a good opening. 'How about the Party, gentlemen? How about Uncle Joe Stalin getting under the sheets with Hitler? How about slave labor camps in Siberia and all the stuff the Party has pulled in America while they condoned the stuff going on over in Russia? Gentlemen, I've been a cop for sixteen years and I've never asked a man to snitch his friends. But I'll ask *any* man to snitch his *enemies*, especially if they also happen to be mine.'

Mal caught his breath, thinking of Summations 115 at Stanford Law; Dudley Smith stood easy at his side. Mondo Lopez eyed the blacktop, then his *Tomahawk Massacre* co-stars. Then all three starting clapping.

Dudley flushed; Mal could see his red face going

122

toward purple. Lopez brought a flat palm slowly down, killing the applause. 'How about you tell us what this is all about?'

Mal thrashed for file dirt and came up empty. 'This is a preliminary investigation into Communist influence in Hollywood. And we're not asking you to snitch your friends, just *our* enemies.'

Benavides pointed west, toward the front office and two picket lines. 'And this has got nothing to do with Gerstein wanting our union out and the Teamsters in?'

'No, this is a preliminary investigation that has nothing to do with whatever current labor troubles your union is involved in. This is – '

Duarte interrupted. 'Why *us*? Why me and Sammy and Mondo?'

'Because you're reformed criminals and you'd make damn good witnesses.'

'Because you thought we'd be jail-wise and bleed easy?'

'No, because you've been zooters and Reds, and we figured that maybe you had the brains to know it was *all* shit.'

Benavides kicked in, a leery eye on Dudley. 'You know the HUAC Committee pulled this snitch routine, and good people got hurt. Now it's happening again, and you want us to fink?'

Mal thought of Benavides as a kiddie raper talking decency; he could *feel* Dudley thinking the same thing, going crazy with it. 'Look, I *know* corruption. The HUAC chairman is in Danbury for bribery, HUAC itself was reckless. And I'll admit the LAPD screwed up on the Sleepy Lagoon thing. But you can't tell – '

Mondo Lopez shouted, 'Screwed up! Pendejo, it was a fucking pogrom against my people by your people! You're sweet-talking the wrong people on the wrong case to get the wrong fuck – '

Dudley stepped in front of the three, his suitcoat open, .45 automatic, sap and brass knuckles in plain view. His bulk cast the Mexicans in one big shadow and

123

his brogue went up octaves, but didn't crack. 'Your seventeen filthy compatriots murdered José Diaz in cold blood and beat the gas chamber because traitors and perverts and deluded weaklings banded up to save them. And I will brook no disrespect for a brother officer in my presence. Do you understand?'

Complete silence, the UAES men still in Dudley's shadow, stagehands eyeballing the action from the walkway. Mal stepped up to speak for himself, taller than Dudley but half his breadth. Scared. Pendejo. He got ready to give signals, then Mondo Lopez hit back. 'Those seventeen got fucked by the puto LAPD and the puto City court system. And that ees la fucking verdad.'

Dudley moved forward so that all there was between him and Lopez was the arc of a short kidney punch. Benavides backed away, shaking; Duarte mumbled that the SLDC got anonymous letters making a white guy for José Diaz, but nobody believed it; Benavides pulled him out of harm's way. Mal grabbed Dudley's arm; the big man flung him back and lowered his brogue to baritone range. 'Did you enjoy perverting justice with the SLDC, Mondo? Did you enjoy the favors of Claire De Haven – filthy rich capitalista, tight with the City Council, a real love for that undersized spic cock?'

Benavides and Duarte had their backs to the wall and were sliding away from the scene an inch at a time. Mal stood frozen; Lopez glared at Dudley; Dudley laughed. 'Perhaps that was unfair of me, lad. We all know Claire spread her favors thin, but I doubt she would have stooped to your level. Your SLDC friend Chaz Minear, now that's another story. Was he there for the prime Mex butthole?'

Benavides moved toward Dudley; Mal snapped out of his freeze, grabbed him and pushed him into the wall, seeing razor blades held to a little girl's throat. Benavides shouted, 'That puto bought boys at a puto escort service, he didn't do us!' Mal pressed harder, sweat-saturated suit against soaked buckskins, hard muscles straining at the body of a thin man almost forty.

Benavides suddenly went slack; Mal took his hands off him and got a file flash: Sammy railing against queers to Doc Lesnick, a weak point they could have played smart.

Sammy Benavides slid down the wall and watched the Smith-Lopez eyeball duel. Mal tried to make his hands give signals, but couldn't. Juan Duarte was standing by the walkway, scoping the business long-distance. Dudley broke the standoff with a pivot and a lilting brogue aside. 'I hope you learned a lesson today, Captain. You can't play sob sister with scum. You should have joined me on the Hat Squad. You would have learned then in grand fashion.'

Round one blown to hell.

Mal drove home, thinking of captain's bars snatched away from him, smothered in Dudley Smith's huge fists. And he had been partly at fault, going too easy when the Mexicans came on too smart, thinking he could reason with them, wheedle and draw them into logical traps. He'd thought of submitting a memo to Ellis Loew – lay off Sleepy Lagoon, it's too sympathetic – then he tossed it into the pot for empathy, hit a nerve with the Mexes and upset Dudley's bee in the bonnet on the case. And Dudley had stood up for him before he himself did, which made it hard to fault him for losing his temper; which meant that maybe direct UAES approaches were dead and they should concentrate solely on decoy infiltration and sub-rosa interrogations. His specialty – which didn't lessen the sting of Dudley's Hat Squad crack, and which increased the need for Buzz Meeks to join the grand jury team.

All debits, but on the plus side Dudley's ranting didn't put out information restricted to Lesnick's files, leaving that avenue of manipulation still open. What was troubling was a cop as smart as the Irishman taking a non-direct attack so personally, then hitting his 'brother officer' below the belt.

Pendejo.

Scared.

And Dudley Smith knows it.

At home, Mal took advantage of the empty house, dumping his sweaty clothes, showering, changing to a sport shirt and khakis and settling into the den to write a long memo to Loew – heavily stressing that there should be no further direct questioning of UAES members until their decoy was planted – a decoy now being a necessity. He was a page in when he realized that it had to be partly a gloss job – there was no way to accurately describe what happened at Variety International without portraying himself as a weakling or a fool. So he did gloss it, and filled up another page with warnings on the Loew choice for trouble-shooter – Buzz Meeks – the man who held the possible distinction of being the single most crooked cop in the history of the Los Angeles Police Department – heroin skimmer, shakedown artist, bagman and now glorified pimp for Howard Hughes. After that page, he knew it was futile; if Meeks wanted in he *was* in – Hughes was the heaviest contributor to the grand jury bankroll and Meeks' bossman – what he said would go. After two pages he knew *why* the tack wasn't worth pursuing: Meeks was absolutely the best man for the job. And the best man for the job was afraid of him, just like he was afraid of Dudley Smith. Even though there was no reason for the fear.

Mal threw the Meeks memo in the wastebasket and started thinking decoy. The LAPD Academy was already out – straight arrow youths with no spark for impersonation. The Sheriff's Academy was unlikely – the Brenda Allen mess and the LASD sheltering Mickey Cohen made it unlikely that they would lend the City a smart young recruit. Their best bet was a rank-and-file City officer, smart, good-looking, adaptable and ambitious, mid to late twenties, a malleable young man without a hard-edged cop quality.

Where?

Hollywood Division was out – half the men had been

126

implicated over Brenda Allen, had had their pictures in the paper, were running scared and angry and wild – there was even a rumor floating around that three men on the Hollywood Detective Squad had been behind last August's shootout at Sherry's – a botched snuff attempt on Mickey Cohen that wounded three and killed a Cohen utility trigger. *Out*.

And Central was packed with unqualified rookies who made the Department because of their war records; 77th Street, Newton and University featured outsized crackers hired on to keep the Negro citizenry in line. Hollenbeck might be a good place to look – but East LA was Mex, Benavides, Lopez and Duarte still had ties there, and that might blow their decoy's cover. The various detective divisions were a possible stalking ground – if they could find a man who didn't come off as irredeemably jaded.

Mal grabbed his LAPD station directory and started scanning it, one eye on the wall clock as it inched toward 3:00 and Stefan's home-from-school time. He was about to start calling CO's for preliminary screening talks when he heard footsteps in the hall; he swiveled in his chair, dropped his arms and got ready to let his son dogpile him.

It was Celeste. She looked at Mal's open arms until he dropped them; she said, 'I told Stefan to stay late after school in order that I should talk to you.'

'Yes?'

'The look on your face does not make this easy.'

'Spill it, goddamn you.'

Celeste clutched her beaded opera purse, a favored relic of Prague, 1935. 'I am going to divorce you. I have met a nice man, a man who is cultured and will make Stefan and me a better home.'

Mal thought: perfect calm, she knows her effects. He said, 'I won't let you. Don't hurt my boy or I'll hurt you.'

'You cannot. To the mother the child belongs.'

Maim her, let her know he *is* the law. 'Is he rich,

127

Celeste? If you have to fuck to survive, you should fuck rich men. Right, Fräulein? Or powerful men, like Kempflerr.'

'You always return to that because it is so ugly and because it excites you so.'

Match point; Mal felt his sense of gamesmanship go blooey. 'I saved your wretched rich-girl ass. I killed the man who made you a whore. I gave you a home.'

Celeste smiled, her standard parting of thin lips over perfect teeth. 'You killed Kempflerr to prove yourself not a coward. You wanted to be like a real policeman, and you were willing to destroy yourself to do it. Only your dumb luck saved you. And you keep your secrets so badly.'

Mal stood up on punch-drunk legs. 'I killed someone who deserved to die.'

Celeste fondled her purse, fingers over beadwork embroidery. Mal saw it as stage business, the buildup to a punch line. 'No comeback for that one?'

Celeste put on her deepest iceberg smile. 'Herr Kempflerr was very kind to me, and I only made up his nasty sexuality to excite you. He was a gentle lover, and when the war was almost over, he sabotaged the ovens and saved thousands of lives. You are lucky that military governor liked you, Malcolm. Kempflerr was going to help the Americans look for other Nazis. And I only married you because I felt very bad about the lies I seduced you with.'

Mal tried to say 'No,' but couldn't form the word; Celeste broadened her smile. Mal saw it as a target and ran to her. He grabbed her neck, held her to the doorway and aimed hard right hands at her mouth, teeth splintering up through her lips, cutting his knuckles. He hit her and hit her and hit her; he would have gone on hitting her, but 'Mutti!' and tiny fists pummeling his legs made him stop and run out of the house, afraid of a little boy – his own.

CHAPTER TWELVE

The phone wouldn't quit ringing.

First it was Leotis Dineen, calling to tell him that Art Aragon knocked out Lupe Pimentel in the second round, raising his debt to twenty-one hundred even, with a vig payment due tomorrow. Next was the real estate man up in Ventura County. His glad tidings: the top offer for Buzz's dry-rotted, shadeless, rock-laden, non-irrigable, poorly located and generally misanthropic farmland was fourteen dollars an acre, the offerer, the pastor of First Pentecostal Divine Eminence Church, who wanted to turn it into a cemetery for the sanctified pets of members of his congregation. Buzz said twenty per, minimum; ten minutes later the phone rang again. No salutation, just, 'I didn't tell Mickey, because you're not worth going to the gas chamber for.' He suggested a romantic drink somewhere; Audrey Anders replied, 'Fuck you.'

Skating on the stupidest stupid move of his life made him feel cocky, despite Dineen's implied warning: my money or your kneecaps. Buzz thought of cash shake-downs – him against fences and hotel crawlers he'd leaned on as a cop, then nixed the notion – he'd gotten older and flabbier, while they'd probably gotten meaner and better armed. There was just himself against 50–50 Mal Considine, who held a mean stare but otherwise looked pretty withered. He picked up the phone and dialed his boss's private number at the Bel-Air Hotel.

'Yes? Who is this?'

'Me. Howard, I want in on that grand jury turkey shoot. That job still open?'

CHAPTER THIRTEEN

Danny was trying hard to stay under the speed limit, hauling into Hollywood—City jurisdiction—with the speedometer needle straddling forty. A few minutes ago a Lexington State administrator had called the station; a letter from Marty Goines, postmarked four days before, had just arrived at the hospital. It was addressed to a patient there and contained nothing but innocuous stuff about jazz—and the word that Goines had moved into an above-garage flop at 2307 North Tamarind. It was a scalding hot lead; if the address had been County ground, he'd have grabbed a black-and-white and rolled red lights and siren.

2307 was a half mile north of the Boulevard, in the middle of a long block of wood-framed Tudors. Danny parked curbside and saw that the cold afternoon had kept the locals indoors—no one was out taking the air. He grabbed his evidence kit, trotted up to the door of the front house and rang the bell.

Ten seconds, no answer. Danny walked back to the garage, saw a shacklike built-on atop it and took rickety steps up to the door. He tapped the pane three times—silence—got out his pocket knife and stuck it into the lock/door jamb juncture. A few seconds of prying, and snap! Danny scanned for witnesses, saw none, pushed the door open and closed it behind him.

The smell hit him first: metallic, acidic. Danny slow-motioned his evidence kit to the floor, drew his gun and fingered the wall for a light switch. His thumb flicked one on abruptly, before he'd clamped down his nerves to look. He saw a one-room dive turned slaughterhouse.

Blood on the walls. Huge, unmistakable streaks, exemplary textbook spit marks: the killer expelling big mouthfuls, spritzing the red out through his teeth, drawing little patterns on cheap floral wallpaper. Four whole walls of it—dips and curlicues and one design that looked like an elaborate letter W. Blood matting a threadbare throw rug, blood in large caked pools on the linoleum floor, blood saturating a light-colored sofa oozing stuffing, blood splashed across a stack of news-papers next to a table holding a hot plate, saucepan and single can of soup. Much too much blood to come from one ravaged human being.

Danny hyperventilated; he saw two doorless doorways off the left wall. He holstered his .45, jammed his hands in his pockets so as not to leave prints and checked the closest one out.

The bathroom.

White walls covered with vertical and horizontal blood lines, perfectly straight, intersecting at right angles, the killer getting the knack. A bathtub, the sides and bottom caked with a pinkish-brown matter that looked like blood mixed with soapsuds. A stack of men's clothing— shirts, trousers, a herringbone sports coat–folded atop the toilet seat.

Danny turned on the sink faucet with a knuckle, low-ered his head, splashed and drank. Looking up, he caught his face in the mirror; for a second he didn't think it was him. He walked back to the main room, took rubber gloves from his evidence kit, slipped them on, returned to the bathroom and sifted through the clothing, dropping it on the floor.

Three pairs of pants. Three skivvy shirts. Three rolled-up pairs of socks. One sweater, one windbreaker, one sports jacket.

Three victims.

One other doorway.

Danny backed out of the bathroom and pivoted into a small kitchenette, expecting a gigantic rush of crimson. What he got was perfect tidiness: scrub brush, Ajax and a soap bar lined up on a rack above a clean sink; clean dishes in a plastic drainer; a 1949 calendar tacked to the wall, the first eleven months ripped off, no notations on

131

the page for December. A telephone on a nightstand placed against the side wall and a battered Frigidaire next to the sink.

No blood, no horror artwork. Danny felt his stomach settle and his pulse take over, jolts like wires frazzling. Two other stiffs dumped someplace; a B&E on LAPD turf—Hollywood Division, where the Brenda Allen mess was the worst, where they hated the Sheriff's Department the most. His violation of Captain Dietrich's direct order: no strongarm, no prima donna in the City. No way to report what he found. An outside chance of the killer bringing number four here.

Danny gulped from the sink, swathed his face, let his gloved hands and jacket sleeves get sopping. He thought of tossing the pad for a bottle; his stomach heaved; he picked up the phone and dialed the station.

Karen Hiltscher answered. 'West Hollywood Sheriff's. May I help you?'

Danny's voice wasn't his. 'It's me, Karen.'

'Danny? You sound strange.'

Just listen. I'm someplace where I should't be and I need something, and I need you to call me back here when you've got it. And nobody can know. *Nobody.* Do you understand?'

'Yes. Danny, please don't be so rough.'

'*Just listen.* I want your verbal on every dead body report filed city and countywide over the past forty-eight hours, and I want you to call me back here with it, *quick.* Ring twice, hang up and call again. Got it?'

'Yes, Sweetie, are you all–'

'Dammit, *just listen.* I'm at Hollywood–4619, it's *wrong* and I could get in big trouble for being here, so don't tell anybody. *Do you fucking understand?*'

Karen whispered, 'Yes, sweetie,' and let her end of the line go dead. Danny hung up, wiped sweat off his neck and thought of ice water. He saw the Frigidaire, reached over and opened the door, bolted for the sink when he caught what was inside.

Two eyeballs coated with clear jelly in an ashtray. A

severed human finger on top of a package of green beans.

Danny vomited until his chest ached and his stomach retched itself empty; he turned on the faucet and doused himself until water seeped inside his rubber gloves and he snapped that a sopping wet cop couldn't forensic a crime scene that Vollmer or Maslick would have killed for. He turned the water off and shook himself half dry, hands braced against the sink ledge. The phone rang; he heard it as a gunshot, pulled his piece and aimed it at nothing.

Another ring, silence, a third ring. Danny picked up the receiver. 'Yes? Karen?'

The girl had on her singsong pout. 'Three DOAs. Two female Caucasians, one male Negro. The females were a pill suicide and a car wreck and the Negro was a wino who died of exposure, and you owe me the Coconut Grove for being so nasty.'

Eight walls of blood spritz and a would-be lady cop who wanted to go dancing. Danny laughed and opened the icebox door for more comic relief. The finger was long, white and thin, and the eyeballs were brown and starting to shrivel. 'Anywhere, sweetie, anywhere.'

'Danny, are you sure you're —'

'Karen, listen real close. I'm staying here to see who shows up. Are you working a double shift tonight?'

'Until eight tomorrow.'

'Then do this. I want the City and County air monitored for male Caucasian DBs. Stay at your switchboard, keep the City and County boxes on low and listen for homicide squeals with male Caucasian victims. Call me here the same way you just did if you get any. Have you got that?'

'Yes, Danny.'

'And sweetie, nobody can know. Not Dietrich, not anyone on the squad, *not anyone*.'

A long sigh, Karen's version of Katharine Hepburn exhausted. 'Yes, Deputy Upshaw,' then a soft click.

Danny hung up and forensiced the pad.

He scraped dirt and dust samples off the floor in all three rooms, placing them in individually marked glassine envelopes; he got out his Rolleiflex evidence camera and shot wide angles and close-ups of the blood patterns. He scraped, tagged and tubed bathtub blood, couch and chair blood, wall blood, rug blood and floor blood; he took fiber samples from the three sets of clothes and wrote down the brand names on the labels.

Dusk came on. Danny kept the lights off, working with a pen flash held in his teeth. He dusted for latent prints, exhausting rolls of touch, grab and press surfaces, getting a rubber glove set – most likely the killer – and a full right- and partial left-hand unknown – which did not match the Marty Goines print abstract. Knowing Goines latents *should* appear, he kept going and was rewarded – a left spread off the kitchen sink ledge. Reconstructing the killer showering himself free of blood, he rolled every touch surface in the bathroom – bringing up one-, two-, three-finger and full hand span, surgical rubber tips, the hands of a large man, widely spaced where he braced himself into the shower /tub wall.

Midnight.

Danny took the severed finger out of the icebox, rolled it in ink, then on paper. A matchup to the middle right digit on the unknown set. The cut point was jagged, just above the knuckle, cauterized by scorching – charred black flesh scabbing it up. Danny checked the hot plate in the living room. Paydirt: fried skin stuck to the coils; the killer wanted to preserve the finger, a shock to whoever discovered the carnage.

Or was he planning to return with another victim?

And was he keeping the pad under surveillance to know when that option was blown?

12:45.

Danny gave the place a last toss. The one closet was empty; there was nothing secreted under the rugs; a penlight wall scan gave him another notch on his reconstruction: approximately two thirds of the blood caking was texturally uniform – victims two and three were almost certainly killed at the same time. Checking out the floor on his knees got him a last piece of evidence: a glob of hardened white paste residue, neutral in smell. He tagged and bagged it, tagged and bagged Marty Goines' eyeballs, sat down on the nonblooded edge of the sofa, gun out and resting on his knee – and waited.

Exhaustion crept in. Danny closed his eyes and saw blood patterns superimposed on the lids, white on red, the colors reversed like photographic negatives. His hands were numb from hours of working in rubber gloves; he imagined the metallic smell of the room as the smell of good whiskey, started tasting it, shut down the thought and ran theories in his head so the taste would stay away.

2307 Tamarind was a thirty-minute drive to the Strip tops – the killer had his maximum time of two hours to play with Marty Goines' corpse and decorate the pad. The killer was monstrously, *suicidally* bold to kill two other men – probably at the same time – in the same place. The killer probably had the subconscious desire to be captured that many psychopaths evinced; he was an exhibitionist and was probably distressed that the Goines snuff had received virtually no publicity. The other two bodies had probably been dumped someplace where they would be found, which meant that last night or yesterday was when murders two and three occurred. Questions: were the patterns on the wall significant in design or just blood spat in rage? What did the letter W mean? *Were the three victims randomly chosen on the basis of homosexuality or dope addiction, or were they previously known to the killer?*

More exhaustion, his brain wires frazzling from too much information, too few connecting threads. Danny took to looking at his luminous wristwatch dial to stay awake; 3:11 had just passed when he heard the outside lock being picked.

He got up and padded to the curtains beside the light switch, the door a foot away, his gun arm extended and braced with his left hand. The locking mechanism gave with a sharp ka-thack; the door opened; Danny hit the switch.

A fortyish fat man was frozen to the light. Danny took a step forward; the man pivoted into the muzzle of a .45 revolver. His hands jerked toward his pockets; Danny toed the door shut and barrel-lashed him across the face, knocking him into wallpaper zigzagged with blood. The fat man let out a yelp, saw the wall gore for real and hit his knees, hands clasped, ready to beg.

Danny squatted beside him, gun aimed at the trickle of blood on his cheek. The fat man mumbled Hail Marys; Danny fished out his cuffs, slid his .45 out of trouble, worked the ratchets and slapped them around prayer-pressed wrists. The bracelet teeth snapped; the man looked at Danny like *he* was Jesus. 'Cop? You're a cop?'

Danny gave him the once-over. Convict pallor, prison shoes, secondhand clothes and grateful that a policeman caught him breaking and entering, a parole violation and a dime minimum. The man looked at the walls, brought his eyes down, saw that he was kneeling two inches from a pool of blood with a dead cockroach basted in the middle. 'Goddammit, tell me you're—'

Danny grabbed his throat and squeezed it. 'Sheriff's. Keep your voice down and play straight with me and I'll let you walk out of here.' With his free hand, he gave Fats a pocket and waistband frisk, pulling out wallet, keys, a switchblade and a flat leather case, compact but heavy, with a zippered closure.

He eased off his throat hold and examined the wallet, dropping cards and papers to the floor. There was an expired California driver's license for Leo Theodore Bordoni, DOB 6/10/09; a County Parole identification card made out to the same name; a plasma bank donor slip stating that Leo Bordoni, type AB+, could sell his plasma again on January 18, 1950. The cards were racetrack stuff – voided betting stubs, receipts, match-

136

book covers with the names of hot horses and race numbers jotted on the back.

Danny let go of Leo Theodore Bordoni's neck, the fat man's reward for a parlay – reaction to the gore, blood type and physical description – that eliminated him as a killing suspect. Bordoni gurgled and wiped blood off his face; Danny unzipped the leather case and saw a set of bonaroos: pick gouger, baby glass cutter, chisel pry and window snap, all laid out on green velvet. He said, 'B&E, possession of burglar's tools, parole violation. How many falls have you taken, Leo?'

Bordoni massaged his neck. 'Three. Where's Marty?'

Danny pointed to the walls. 'Where do you think?'

'Oh fucking God.'

'That's right. Old Marty that nobody knows much about, except maybe you. You know about Governor Warren's habitual offender law?'

'Uh . . . no.'

Danny picked up his .45 and holstered it, helped Bordoni to his feet and shoved him into the one chair not soaked red/brown. 'The law says any fourth fall costs you twenty to life. No plea bargains, no appeals, nada. You boost a fucking pack of cigarettes, it's a double dime. So you tell me everything there is to know about you and Marty Goines, or you hang twenty up at Quentin.'

Bordoni flicked his eyes around the room. Danny walked to the curtains, looked out at dark yards and houses and thought of his killer leaving him, clued to a trap by the light burning. He flipped the wall switch; Bordoni let out a long breath. 'Really bad for Marty? That the truth?'

Danny could see neon signs on Hollywood Boulevard, miles away. 'The worst, so tell me.'

Bordoni talked while Danny looked out at neon and dwindling headlights. 'I came out of Quentin two weeks ago, seven out of seven for heists. I knew Marty when he did his turn for reef, and we were buddies. Marty knew I had a parole date, and he knew my sister's

137

number in Frisco. He'd send me these letters every once in a while after he got out, phony name, no return address, 'cause he was an absconder and he didn't want the censors to get a handle on him.

'So Marty calls me at my sister's five days or so ago, maybe the thirtieth, maybe the thirty-first. He says he's playing horn for peanuts and hates it, he took the cure, he's gonna stay off horseback and pull jobs – burglaries. He says he just got together with an old partner and they needed a third man for a housebreak gang. I told him I'd be down in a week or so, and he gave me this address and told me to let myself in. That's me and Marty.'

Darkness made the room pulsate. Danny said, 'What was the partner's name? Where did Goines know him from?'

'Marty didn't say.'

'Did he describe him? Was he a partner of Marty's when he was pulling jobs back in '43 and '44?'

Bordoni said, 'Mister, it was a two-minute conversation, and I didn't even know Marty pulled jobs back then.'

'Did he mention an old running partner with a burned or scarred face? He'd be mid to late twenties by now.'

'No. Marty was always close-mouthed. I was his only pal at Q, and I was surprised when he said he had an old partner. Marty wasn't really the partner type.'

Danny shifted gears. 'When Goines sent you letters, where were they postmarked and what did they say?'

Bordoni sighed like he was bored; Danny thought of giving him a peek at his old pal's eyeballs. 'Spill, Leo.'

'They were from all over the country, and they were just jive – jazz, stuff, wish you were here, the horses, baseball.'

'Did Marty mention other musicians he was playing with?'

Bordoni laughed. 'No, and I think he was ashamed to. He was gigging all these Podunk clubs, and all he said was 'I'm the best trombone they've ever seen,'' meaning Marty knew he wasn't much but these cats he was gigging with were really from hunger.'

'Did he mention anybody at all, other than this old partner you were going to team up with?'

'Nix. Like I told you, it was a two-minute conversation.'

The Miller High Life sign atop the Taft Building blipped off, jarring Danny. 'Leo, was Marty Goines a homosexual?'

'Marty! Are you crazy! He wouldn't even pork nancy boys up at Q!'

'Anybody up there ever makes advances to him?'

'Marty would have died before he let some brunser bust his cherry!'

Danny hit the light switch, hauled Bordoni up by his cuff chain and twisted his head so that it was level with a long slash of wall blood. 'That's your friend. That's why you were never here and you never met me. That's heat yu don't want, so you just stay frosty and think of this thing as a nightmare.'

Bordoni bobbed his head; Danny let him go and unlocked the cuffs. Bordoni gathered his stuff up off the floor, taking extra care with his tool case. At the door, he said, 'This is personal with you, right?'

Buddy Jastrow long gone, four shots a night not enough, his textbooks and classes not real. Danny said, 'It's all I've got.'

Alone again, Danny stared out the window, watching movie marquees blink off, turning the Boulevard into just another long, dark street. He added 'possible burglary partner' to 'tall gray-haired,' 'middle-aged,' 'homosexual,' and 'heroin-wise'; he put off Bordoni's protestations that Marty wasn't fruit as sincere but wrong – and wondered how long he could stick inside the room

139

without going crazy, without risking the landlord or someone from the front house dropping by.

Looking for house lights that might be *Him* looking back was childish; eye prowling for sinister shapes was a kid's game – the kind of game he played by himself as a schoolboy. Danny yawned, sat down in the chair and tried to sleep.

He got something near sleep, an exhaustion shortcut where he wasn't quite out, couldn't quite form thoughts and saw pictures that he wasn't making himself. Street signs, trucks, a saxophone man running scales on his instrument, flower patterns, a dog at the end of a stick. The dog made him twitch; he tried to open his eyes, felt them gummed and eased back to wherever he was going. Autopsy instruments hot from an autoclave, Janice Modine, a '39 Olds rocking on its suspension, a look inside, Tim pumping Roxy Beausoleil, an ether-soaked rag up to her nose so she'd giggle and pretend it was nice.

Danny jerked out of it, eyes opening to light through a part in the curtains. He swallowed dry phlegm, caught a reprise of his last image, got up and went to the kitchen for a drink of sink water. He was on a big gulping handful when the phone rang.

A second ring, stop, a third ring. Danny picked it up. 'Karen?'

The girl was almost breathless. 'City radio. See the maintenance man, Griffith Park, the hiking trail up from the observatory parking lot. Two dead men, LAPD rolling. Sweetie, did you *know* this was going to happen?'

Danny said, 'Just pretend it didn't happen,' slammed the phone down, grabbed his evidence kit and walked out of the upholstered slaughterhouse. He forced himself not to run to his car, eyes circuiting for onlookers, seeing none. Griffith Park was a mile away. He stripped off his rubber gloves, felt his hand tingle and gunned it there.

*

140

Two LAPD black-and-whites beat him.

Danny parked beside them at the foot of the hiking trail, the last stretch of asphalt before the stretch of mountain that formed the park's northern perimeter. No other cars were in the lot; he could see four bluesuits up ahead where the trail cut into woods, a longtime haven for winos and lovebirds without the price of a room.

Danny marked the time – 6:14 A.M. – got his badge out and walked up. The cops wheeled around, hands to holsters, shakes and queasy looks. Danny pointed to his tin. 'West Hollywood Sheriff's. I'm working a dumped body case, and I heard what you got over the air at the station.'

Two cops nodded; two turned away, like a County detective was lower than dirt. Danny swallowed dry; West Hollywood Substation was a half hour away, but the dummies didn't blink at the time glitch. They separated to give him a view; Danny got a mid-shot of hell.

Two dead men, nude, lying sideways on a little bed of dirt surrounded by low thornbushes. Rigor lock, coats of dust and leaf debris said they had been there at least twenty-four hours; the condition of the bodies said that they died at 2307 North Tamarind. Danny pulled a bush section back, knelt and zoomed his Man Camera in nightmare-close.

The men had been placed in a 69 position – head to groin, head to groin, genitals flopped towards each other's mouths. Their hands had been placed on each other's knees; the larger man was missing a right index finger. All four eyes were intact and wide open; the victims had been slashed like Marty Goines all over their backs – and their faces. Danny examined the pressed-together front sides; he could see blood and entrail residue.

He stood up. The patrolmen were smoking cigarettes, shuffling their feet, destroying the chance for a successful grid search. One by one they looked at him; the oldest of the four said, 'Those guys like yours?'

141

Danny said, 'Almost exactly,' thinking of the real camera in his evidence kit, snapshots for his file before the City bulls closed off *their* end of *his* case. 'Who found them?'

The old-timer cop answered him. 'Maintenance man saw a wino running down the hill screaming, so he went up and looked. He called us, came back up and got sick. We sent him home, and when the squad gets here they'll send you home, too.'

The other cops laughed. Danny let it pass and jogged down the trail to get the camera. He was almost to his Chevy when a plainclothes car and Coroner's wagon pulled into the lot and jammed up next to the black-and-whites.

A big, beef-faced man got out of the unmarked and looked right at him. Danny recognized him from newspaper pics: Detective Sergeant Gene Niles, squad whip at Hollywood Division, in up to his ears over Brenda Allen, no indictment, but a quashed lieutenancy and stalemated career – rumor having it that he took no cash, just trade goodies from Brenda's girls. The man's clothes said otherwise: smart navy blazer and razor-creased gray flannels, custom stuff no honest cop could afford.

Two Coroner's men hauled out collapsible gurneys; Danny saw Niles smell cop on him and head over, looking more and more curious and pissed; strange meat on his turf, too young to be working the Homicide Bureau downtown.

He met him halfway, a new story brewing, plausible stuff to satisfy a savvy cop. Face to face, he said, 'I'm with the Sheriff's.''

Niles laughed. 'You a little bit confused about your jurisdiction, Deputy?'

The 'Deputy' was all scorn, like a synonym for 'cancer.' Danny said, 'I'm working a homicide just like the two you've got up the hill.'

Niles bored in with his eyes. 'You sleep in those clothes, Deputy?'

Danny squeezed his hands into fists. 'I was on a stake-out.'

'You ever hear of carrying a razor on all-nighters, *Deputy*?'

'You ever hear of professional courtesy, *Niles*?'

Sergeant Gene Niles looked at his watch. 'A man who reads the papers. Let's try this. How'd you get up here twenty-two minutes after we logged the squeal at the station?'

Danny knew brass balls was the only way to cover his lie. 'I was down at the doughnut joint on Western, and there was a black-and-white with the radio on. How come it took *you* so long? You stop for a manicure?'

'A year ago I'd have reamed you for that.'

'A year ago you were going places. Do you want to hear about my homicide or do you want to sulk?'

Niles picked a piece of lint off his blazer. 'The dispatcher said it looks like a queer job. I hate queer jobs, so if you've got another queer job, I don't want to hear about it. Roll, *Deputy*. And get yourself some decent threads. Mickey Kike's got a haberdashery, and I know he gives all his prat boys a discount.'

Danny headed back to his Chevy seeing red. He drove down the park road to Los Feliz and Vermont and a pay phone, called Doc Layman and told him two Marty Goines companion stiffs were en route, grab them for autopsy no matter what. A minute later Niles' car and the Coroner's wagon went by southbound, no lights or sirens, flunkies killing a fine winter morning. Danny gave them a five-minute lead, took shortcuts downtown and parked in the shade of a warehouse across the street from the City Morgue loading dock. Fourteen minutes passed before the caravan appeared; Niles made a big show of shepherding the sheet-covered gurneys to the ramp; Norton Layman came out to help. Danny heard him berating Niles for separating the bodies.

He settled into his car to wait for Layman's findings; stretching out on the front seat, he closed his eyes and tried to sleep, knowing Doc would be four hours or more on the examinations. Sleep wouldn't come; a hot day started sizzling, warming up the car, making the upholstery sticky. Danny would begin to drop off, then start remembering his lies, what he could or couldn't tell whom. He could brazen his lie to the patrolmen, acting sheepish over being at the doughnut stand at 6:00 A.M., implying he'd been with a woman; he had to coddle Karen Hiltscher into keeping his stint at 2307 Tamarind under wraps. He couldn't let anyone see the contents of his evidence kit; he had to clue in LAPD to the letter that hipped him to Marty Goines' pad, post-dating the occurrence, making it seem like nothing big, letting them discover the gore for themselves. Leo Bordoni was a wild card, but he was probably con-wise enough to stay quiet; he had to fabricate a story to account for his whereabouts yesterday – a phony summary report to Dietrich was his best bet. And the big fear and big questions: if LAPD canvassed Tamarind, would a local report the tan 1947 Chevrolet parked outside 2307 overnight? Should he take advantage of his private lead, rape the neighborhood for witnesses himself, then report the letter, hoping that the worst they could get him for was *not* calling the dope in? If LAPD decided to ease off on their two homicides – Niles as catching officer hating 'queer jobs' – would they canvass at *all? He* had taken the call from Lexington State Hospital himself, via Karen Hiltscher's switchboard. If it all got tricky, would she blab fast to save herself? Would LASD/LAPD rivalry reduce the mess to something that only he cared about?

Heat reflecting off the windshield and too many brain wires short-circuiting on angles lulled Danny to sleep. Cramps and glare woke him up sweaty and itchy; his foot hit the horn and black dreamlessness became sound waves bouncing off four bloody walls. He looked at his watch, saw 12:10 and at least four hours unconscious; the Doc might be done with his dead men. Danny got out of the car, stretched his cramps and walked across the street to the morgue.

Layman was standing near the ramp, eating lunch off an examination slab, a body sheet for a tablecloth. He saw Danny, swallowed a bite of sandwich and said, 'You look bad.'

'That bad?'

'You look scared, too.'

Danny yawned; it made his gums ache. 'I've seen the bodies, and I don't think LAPD cares. That's scary.'

Layman wiped his mouth with a sheet corner. 'Here's a few more scares for you, then. Times of death – twenty-six to thirty hours ago. Both men were anally raped – O+ secretor semen. The wounds on their backs were pure zoot stick, identical in size and fiber content to Martin Mitchell Goines. The missing-finger man died from a throat gash made by a sharp, serrated knife. No cause of death on the other man, but I'd be willing to bet barbiturate OD. On our missing-finger friend I found a vomit-coated, punctured capsule, right up under the tongue. I tested some powder in it and got a home compound – sodium secobarbital, one part, one part strychnine. The secobarbital would hit first, inducing unconsciousness, the strychnine would kill. I think missing finger got indigestion, puked up part of his Mickey Finn and fought to live – that that was when he lost his digit – fighting with the knife man. Once I test the blood on both men and pump their stomachs, I'll know for sure. The missing finger man was bigger – a larger bloodstream, so the compound didn't kill him like it did our other friend.'

Danny thought of 2307, vomit traces lost in the blood. 'What about the stomach bites?'

Layman said, 'Not human, but human. I found O+ saliva and human gastric juices on the wounds, and the bites were too frenzied and overlapping to make casts from. But – I got three individual tooth cuts – too large to ascribe to any known human dental abstract and too shredded at the bottom to identify on any single-tooth forensic index. I also took a glob of dental mortar paste out of one of the wounds. He wears dentures, Danny.

Most likely on top of his own teeth. They might be steel, they might be some other synthetic material, they might be teeth fashioned from animal caracasses. And he's rigged up a way to mutilate with them *and* swallow. They're not human, and I know this doesn't sound professional, but I don't think this son of a bitch is either.'

CHAPTER FOURTEEN

Ellis Loew performed the ceremony in his office, Mal and Dudley Smith official witnesses. Buzz Meeks stood by the conference table, right hand raised; Loew recited the oath: 'Do you, Turner Meeks, hereby swear to loyally and conscientiously perform the duties of Special Investigator, Grand Jury Division of the District Attorney's Office for the City of Los Angeles, upholding the laws of this municipality, protecting the rights and property of its citizens, so help you God?'

Buzz Meeks said, 'Sure.' Loew handed him an ID holder replete with license photostat and DA's Bureau shield. Mal wondered how much Howard Hughes was paying the bastard, guessing at least three grand.

Dudley joined Meeks and Loew in a back-slapping circle; Mal credited an old rumor still holding: Meeks thought he was behind the shooting that got him his pension, Jack D. blowing it, then forgetting his grudge when the okie was no longer LAPD. Let him think it – anything to keep his new colleague as far away as two cops working the same job could be.

And Dudley. And maybe Loew now, too.

Mal watched the three share a toast, Glenlivet in crystal glasses. He took his notepad down to the far end of the table, Meeks and Dudley trading one-liners, Ellis shooting him a scowl that said, 'Let's work.' Loew's half nod acknowledged that their bad blood was just temporary. Mal thought: he should owe me, now I owe him. He picked up his pen to doodle, his knuckles throbbed, he knew Loew was right.

After the thing with Celeste, he'd driven around directionless until his hand started swelling, the pain brutal, blunting all his frantic plans to make it up to his son. He hauled to Central Receiving, flashed his badge and got special treatment: an injection of something that sent him higher than ten kites, teeth fragments pulled out of his fingers, cleansing and suturing and bandaging. He called the house and talked to Stefan, rambling about why he did it, how Celeste had hurt him worse, how she wanted to separate the two of them forever. The boy had seemed shocked, dumbfounded, stuttering details about Celeste's bloodied face – but he'd ended the conversation calling him 'Dad' and saying, 'I love you.'

And that little injection of hope made him think like a policeman. He called Ellis Loew, told him what happened, that lawyers and a custody battle were coming, don't let Celeste file charges and gain an advantage. Loew took the reins, driving to the house and shepherding Celeste to Hollywood Presbyterian, where her lawyer was waiting. The man took photographs of her bruised and bloody face; Loew convinced him not to let Celeste file criminal charges on a ranking DA's Bureau investigator, threatening reprisals if he did, promising not to intercede in the custody case if he agreed. The attorney did agree; Celeste's broken nose was set and two dental surgeons worked on her nearly destroyed gums and bridgework. Loew, enraged, called the pay phone where he was waiting and said, 'You're on your own with the kid. Never ask me for another favor.'

He drove back to the house then, finding Stefan asleep, breathing Celeste's old country sedative – schnapps and hot milk. He kissed the boy's cheek, moved a suitcase full of clothes and Lesnick's files to a motel on Olympic and Normandie, made arrangements for a woman cop he knew to check on Stefan once a day,

147

slept off the painkiller on a strange bed and woke up thinking of Franz Kempflerr.

He couldn't stop thinking about him, and he couldn't put together any rationalizations that said Celeste was a liar. He did put together a series of phone calls that got him a lawyer: Jake Kellerman, a pragmatist who said continuances were the smart money, postpone the custody trial until Captain Considine was a grand jury hero. Kellerman advised him to stay away from Celeste and Stefan, said he'd call him for a strategy meeting soon – and left him with a Demerol hangover, aching knuckles and the certainty he should take the day off and stay away from his boss.

He still couldn't shake Kempflerr.

Going over Lesnick's files was just a distraction. He was getting a case on Claire De Haven, every notation on her tweaked him; he knew direct questioning was out for now, that finding an operative should be his main priority. Still, putting together the woman's past was enticing, and when he hit a piece of information he'd overlooked – Mondo Lopez bragging to the shrink about a dress he'd shoplifted for Claire's thirty-third birthday in May of '43, making her exactly *his* age – he took the woman and the Nazi down to the main public library for research.

He scanned microfilm for hours, banishing the German, bringing the woman into focus.

Buchenwald liberated, the Nuremberg trials, the biggest Nazis stating they just followed orders. The incredible mechanized brutality. Sleepy Lagoon a just cause championed by bad people. A hunch that Claire De Haven made the society pages as a debutante; confirmation in summer 1929: nineteen-year-old Claire at the Las Madrinas Ball – blurred black and white that only hinted at who she was.

With Kempflerr eclipsed by Göring, Ribbentrop, Dönitz and Keitel, the woman came on that much stronger. He called the DMV and got her driver's license stats, drove to Beverly Hills and kept her Spanish manse

under surveillance. Two hours in, Claire left the house
– her picture a prophecy of beauty fulfilled. She was
trim, auburn-haired with just a few streaks of gray, and
wore a face that was natural beauty and the best that
money could buy – but *strong*. He followed her Cadillac
down to the Villa Frascati; she met Reynolds Loftis
there for lunch – the Mr. Dignity type he'd seen in a
dozen movies. He had a drink at the bar and watched
the two: the switch-hitter actor and the Red Queen held
hands and kissed across the table every few minutes;
they were undoubtedly lovers. He remembered Loftis
to Lesnick: 'Claire is the only woman I've ever loved' –
and felt jealous.

Glasses and ashtrays hit the table; Mal glanced up from
his doodling – swastikas and hangman's nooses – and
saw his fellow Red chasers looking at him. Dudley slid
a clean glass and the bottle down. Mal slid it back and
said, 'Lieutenant, you blew it for us with the Mexicans.
This is for the record. I say no direct interrogations until
Meeks gets us some hard criminal stuff that we can use,
like indictment threats. I say we hit lefties outside UAES
exclusively, turn them as friendly witnesses, get them to
inform and plant a decoy as soon as we find one. I say
we cover ourselves on the Mexicans by planting some
lines in the political columns. Ed Satterlee's pals with
Victor Reisel and Walter Winchell, they hate Commies,
the UAES probably reads them. Something like this:
'LA City grand jury team slated to investigate Red
influence in Hollywood scotched due to lack of funds
and political infighting.' Every Pinko in the UAES
knows what happened at Variety International the other
day, and I say we put a lid on it and lull them to sleep.'
    All eyes were on the Irishman; Mal wondered how
he'd field the gauntlet – two witnesses to irrefutable
logic. Dudley said, 'I can only apologize for my actions,
Malcolm. You were circumspect, I was bull-headed, and
I was wrong. But I think we should squeeze Claire De
Haven before we pull back and go sub rosa. She's the

fulcrum to snitch the whole brain trust, she's a virgin as far as grand juries go, breaking her would demoralize all those sad excuses for men in love with her. She's never been braced by the police, and I think she damn well might fold.'

Mal laughed. 'You're underestimating her. And I suppose you want to be the one to do the bracing?'

'No, lad, I think you should be the one. Of all of us here, you're the only one who comes off as even remotely idealistic. A kid gloves cop you are, kid gloves with a cruel streak. You'll nail her with that great right hook I've heard you've got.'

Ellis Loew mouthed the words, 'Not me,' hard eyes on Mal's end of the table. Buzz Meeks sipped Scotch. Mal winced, wondering exactly how much Dudley knew. 'It's a sucker play, Lieutenant. You screwed up once, now you're asking me to compound it. Ellis, a direct approach is bullshit. Tell him that.'

Loew said, 'Mal, control your language, because I agree with Dudley. Claire De Haven is a promiscuous woman, women like that are unbalanced, and I think we should risk the approach. In the meantime, Ed Satterlee is trying to co-opt a man for us, a man he knew in the seminary who's infiltrated Communist cells in Cleveland. He's a pro, but he doesn't work cheap. Even if the approach with De Haven fails and the UAES is alerted to us, he'll be able to get next to them so subtly that they'll never know it in a million years. And I'm sure we can get the money for our decoy from Mr. Hughes. Right, Buzz?'

Buzz Meeks winked at Mal. 'Ellis, if this babe is a roundheels, I wouldn't be sendin' in a seminary boy to work her. Howard himself might do the trick. He likes poon, so maybe you could send him in in disguise.'

Loew rolled his eyes; Dudley Smith laughed, like he'd heard a real knee-slapper at the Elks Club smoker. Meeks winked again, testing the water – were you the one who got me shot to shit back in '46? Mal thought of his custody juice riding with a cracker buffoon, hat-

chet cop and hard-on lawyer. It wasn't until Loew
banged the table to dismiss them that he realized he
would be meeting the Red Queen face to face, his own
pawn to operate.

CHAPTER FIFTEEN

Danny spent the next morning at his apartment, updat-
ing *his* file, all new stuff on the two new victims tied in
to *his* case.

Twenty-four hours in, he had this:

No ID on victims two and three; Doc Layman, as a
City pathologist, was privy to Hollywood Squad summary reports and would be calling when and if the bodies
got names. He had already called to say that Sergeant
Gene Niles was heading the LAPD investigation,
deemed it lowball and was short-shrifting it so that he
could return to a fur warehouse robbery that promised
some newspaper ink to make up for the Brenda Allen
smear that cost him his wife and kids. Uniformed cops
were rousting winos in Griffith Park and getting
nowhere; Niles himself had rubber-hosed two Sterno
jockeys with child molester jackets. Layman's seventeen-
page autopsy report – which *did* tag the smaller of the
two men as dying of a barbiturate OD – was ignored by
Niles and the handful of uniformed flunkies detached to
work under him. The Doc was convinced that a 'Reverse
Black Dahlia Syndrome' was in effect – the three stiffs
found so far had received a total of four inner section
newspaper columns, city editors shying away because
Marty Goines was trash and the whole thing was queer
shit that you couldn't print without the Legion for
Decency and Concerned Catholic Mothers on your ass.

Captain Dietrich had heard him out yesterday, facts,
theories, omissions, lies and his giant lie – the doughnut
stand whopper to cover him on 2307 Tamarind, still

unreported. He'd nodded along, then said he'd *try* to get the interagency ball rolling with LAPD. Sheriff's dicks were out of the question – the three other men on the station squad were deluged and the County Detective Bureau would deem the Goines job too Mickey Mouse and messy now that City cops were involved. He had a pal working Hollywood daywatch – a lieutenant named Poulson who'd stayed tight with Mickey C. despite Brenda A. He'd talk to the man about the two departments putting a Homicide team together, and again stated that he thought it would come down to the quality of the victims. If two and three were hopheads, ex-cons or queers – forget it. If they were squarejohns – maybe. And unless the case got some juice, with an LAPD/LASD team formed, he was off it in ten days, Martin Mitchell Goines, DOD 1/1/50 tossed into the open file.

On his evidence gathered at 2307 Tamarind:

With two exceptions, just repeat stuff, what Hans Maslick called 'double negatives to prove positives.' He had gotten an unknown set of prints that matched with the taller dead man's missing finger; Layman had also rolled both stiffs. The white paste residue he bagged was obviously the denture adhesive that led Doc to his 99 percent sure denture theory. Leo Bordoni did not touch print-sustaining surfaces while he was in the room; the three sets of clothes had to be left behind in case the killer was captured and specifically confessed to leaving them folded atop the toilet. The dust and dirt trace elements were useless until he got a suspect to run comparisons on – leaving him only two jumps on LAPD and the killer: his photos of the blood streaks and his chance to canvass Tamarind Street solo if the City bulls soft-pedaled their investigation. Nightmares and big jeopardy.

After leaving the morgue yesterday, he drove to a camera shop and paid quadruple the normal fee to have his rolls of film developed immediately. The man at the counter looked askance at his raggedy state but took his money; he waited while the job was done. The camera man handed the prints and negatives over an hour later, commenting, 'Them walls what you call modern art?' He'd laughed and laughed and laughed himself home – his chuckles dying out when he tacked the photos to a corkboard evidence display he'd erected beside his file boxes.

Blood in glossy black and white was jarring, unnatural, the pictures things he could never let anyone see, even if he busted the combined homicides wide open. Thinking of them as his alone was comforting; he spent hours just staring, seeing designs within designs. Drip marks became strange body appendages; spray streaks were knives cutting at them. The eye circuits got so illogical that he turned to his case history text: blood spray marks exemplified. The cases elaborated were all German and Eastern European, psychopaths enacting vampire fantasies, spraying their victim's blood on convenient objects, asserting their lunacy by creating pictures of little or no significance. Nothing resembling the formation of the letter W; nothing pertaining to dentures.

Dentures.

His one hard lead to come out of victims two and three.

Not human.

They could be steel teeth, they could be plastic teeth, they could be teeth ripped out of animal carcasses. The next investigatory step was a complete paper chase: men capable of making dentures cross-probed against 'tall, middle-aged,' 'gray-haired,' 'O+ blood' and time frame opportunity.

Needles in a haystack.

Yesterday, he had taken his first step, checking dental lab listings in the seventeen separate LA City/County Yellow Pages. There were a total of 349, plus, in consideration of a possible animal carcass angle, 93 taxidermists' shops. A phone call to a lab picked at random and a long talk with a cooperative foreman got him this information: the 349 number was low; LA was the big league for the denture industry. Some labs didn't advertise in the Yellow Pages; some dentists had denture makers working in their offices. If a man worked on human dentures he could apply the same skills to animal or plastic teeth. *He* didn't know of any labs that specialized in animal choppers, good luck Deputy Upshaw, you've got your work cut out for you.

It was a ride to the Station then. Karen Hiltscher was just swinging back on duty; he brought candy and flowers to chill down her curiosity over Tamarind and any poutiness for the largest deluge of shitwork he'd ever tossed her way: *all* individual station and Sheriff's Bureau files checked for men with dental lab work histories, plus eliminations against blood type and physical description; calls started to his list of dental labs for breakdowns of male workers with the same physical stats. The girl took the goodies while a group of muster room loungers guffawed; she seemed hurt and miffed, didn't mention 2307 and agreed in a Bette Davis bitch pout to make the queries in her 'spare time.' He didn't press; she knew she had gained the upper hand on him.

Danny finished up his file work, thinking of Tamarind Street as virgin canvassing territory, wondering if the burglary partner Leo Bordoni mentioned applied to the case, if he was or wasn't connected to the burn-faced boy from Marty Goines' past. His paperwork now totaled fifty-odd pages; he'd spent fifteen of the past twenty-four hours writing. He'd resisted the impulse to scour around Tamarind, wait, look, talk up the locals, jump the gun on LAPD. If Niles had gotten a lead on the place, Doc Layman would have called him; most likely the street was just existing, business as usual, while its residents forgot minor occurrences that might crack his case. Phone the Lexington Hospital lead to Dietrich, making like he just got the call at home, then brief Karen on the lie? Or do it after, no risk on the skipper handing the job to his LAPD pal, the interagency gig *he* asked for?

154

No contest. Danny drove to Hollywood, to Tamarind Street.

The block *was* business as usual, warmer than two days ago, foot traffic on the sidewalk, people sitting on front porches, mowing lawns and trimming shrubs. Danny parked and canvassed, straight zero into mid-afternoon: no strange occurrences in the neighborhood, no strange vehicles, no info on Marty Goines, nothing unusual going on at 2307 Tamarind, garage apartment rear. No loiterers, no strange noises, zero – and nobody mentioned his tan Chevy parked streetside. He was starting to feel cocky about his maneuvering when an old lady walking a miniature schnauzer responded to his lead question with a yes.

Three nights ago, around 10:00, she'd been strolling Wursti and saw a tall man with beautiful silver hair walking back toward the garage at 2307, a 'weaving drunk' on either side of him. No, she had not seen any of the three men before; no, no strange noises from the garage apartment followed; no, she didn't know the woman who owned the front house; no, the men did not talk to each other, and she doubted she would be able to ID the silver-haired man if she saw him again.

Danny let the woman go, went back to his car, hunkered down to keep a fix on 2307. Instincts hit him hard: Yes, the killer staked out the pad to see if cops showed up. Yes, he had the Griffith Park dump site already planned. Goines' name never made the papers, he was simply a vagrant, the killer knew his murder spot wasn't compromised by Goines' publicity. The only known Goines associates who knew of Mad Marty's demise were the jazzmen he had questioned, which eliminated jazzbos as suspects – with Goines ID'd by the law, no smart killer would bring future victims to the man's apartment. *Which meant that if no heat appeared in force on Tamarind Street, the killer might bring other victims here. Hold the lead safe from LAPD, stay staked out, pray the killer didn't witness his or Bordoni's break-in*

155

and today's canvassing, sit tight and he just might waltz right into your life with number four on his arm.

Danny held, eyes on the house, rear-view adjusted to frame the driveway. Time stretched; a wrong-looking man strolled by, then two old ladies pushing shopping carts and a gaggle of boys wearing Hollywood High letter jackets. A siren whirred, getting closer; Danny thought of code three trouble down on the Boulevard.

Then everything went very fast.

An old lady opened the 2307 front house door; an unmarked prowler jammed into the driveway. Sergeant Gene Niles got out, looked across the street and saw him – a sitting duck in the car he'd had at Griffith Park yesterday morning. Niles started to head over; the old woman intercepted him, pointing toward the garage apartment. Niles stopped; the woman grabbed at his coat sleeves; Danny flailed for lies. Niles let himself be led down the driveway. Danny got bad heebie-jeebies – and drove to the Station to lay some cover.

Dietrich was standing by the squadroom entrance, wolfing a cigarette; Danny took his arm and steered him to the privacy of his own office. Dietrich went with it, swinging around as Danny shut the door. 'Lieutenant Poulson just called me. Gene Niles just called him, because he caught a call from Martin Goines' landlady. Blood and bloody clothes all over Goines' apartment, a mile from Griffith Park. Our one and LAPD's two were obviously snuffed there, you were seen staking the place out and rabbited. Why? Make it good so I don't have to suspend you.'

Danny had his answer down pat. 'A man from Lexington State called me at home this morning and told me he'd gotten a letter from Marty Goines, addressed to another patient. The return address was 2307 North Tamarind. I thought about that talk we had, greasing things with Poulson, us being cooperative even though Niles was pulling a snit. But I didn't trust LAPD to

156

canvass properly, so I did it myself. I was taking a breather in my car when Niles saw me.'

Dietrich picked up an ashtray and stubbed out his smoke. 'And you didn't call me? On a lead that hot?'

'I jumped the gun, sir. I'm sorry.'

Dietrich said, 'I'm not sure I buy your story. Why didn't you talk to the landlady before you canvassed? Poulson said Niles told him the woman was cherry – she was the one who discovered the mess.'

Danny shrugged, trying to belittle the question. 'I knocked early on, but the old girl probably didn't hear it.'

'Poulson said she sounded like an alert old dame. Danny, were you in the neighborhood knocking off a matinee?'

The question didn't register. 'What do you mean, a movie?'

'No, pussy. Your bimbo's got a place near that dough-nut stand where you heard the squeal yesterday, and Tamarind is near there. Were you shacking on County time?'

Dietrich's tone had softened; Danny got his lies straight. 'I canvassed, then I shacked. I was resting in my car when Niles showed up.'

Dietrich smiled/grimaced; the phone on his desk rang. He picked it up, said, 'Yes, Norton, he's here,' listened and added, 'One question. Have you got jackets on the two men?'

A long stretch of silence. Danny fidgeted by the door; Karen Hiltscher nudged it open, dropped a sheaf of papers on the Captain's desk and walked out, eyes low-ered. Danny thought: don't let the skipper tell her I've got a woman; don't let her tell him she fielded the call from Lex. Dietrich said, 'Hold on, Norton. I want to talk to him first,' placed a hand over the receiver and spoke to Danny. 'There's an ID on LAPD's two bodies. They're trash, so I'm telling you now: no interagency investigation, and you've got five more days on Goines before I yank you off. The Sun-Fax Market was held up this morning and if we don't clear it by then, I want you on that. I'm letting you slide for not reporting Goines' address, but I'm warning you: stay out of LAPD's way. Tom Poulson is a close friend, we've stayed friends despite Mickey and Brenda, and I don't want you fucking it up. Now here, Norton Layman wants to talk to you.'

Danny grabbed the phone. 'Yeah, Doc.'

'It's your friendly City pipeline. Got a pencil?'

Danny fished pad and pen from his pockets. 'Shoot.'

'The taller man is George William Wiltsie, DOB 9/14/13. Two male prostitution arrests, booted out of the Navy in '43 for moral turpitude. The other man is address-verified as Wiltsie's known associate, maybe his brunser. Duane no middle name Lindenaur, DOB 12/5/16. One arrest for extortion – June, 1941. The beef did not go to court – the complainant dropped charges. There's no employment listed for Wiltsie; Lindenaur worked as a dialogue rewrite man at Variety International Pictures. Both men lived at 11768 Ventura Boulevard, the Leafy Glade Motel. LAPD is rolling there now, so stay clear. Does this make you happy?'

Danny counted lies. 'I don't know, Doc.'

From his cubicle, Danny called R & I and the DMV and got complete records readouts on victims two and three. George Wiltsie was arrested for soliciting indecent acts at cocktail lounges in '40 and '41; the DA dropped charges both times for lack of evidence, and the man possessed a lengthy list of traffic violations. Duane Lindenaur was DMV-clean, and had only the one dropped extortion beef Doc Layman mentioned. Danny had the R & I clerk break down the victims' arrests by location; Wiltsie's rousts were in City jurisdiction, Lindenaur's was in the southeastern part of the County patrolled by Firestone Division. A request for a check of Lindenaur's package got him the arresting officer's name – Sergeant Frank Skakel.

Danny called Sheriff's Personnel and learned that

Skakel was still working Firestone swingwatch. He buzzed him there, got the switchboard and was put through to the squadroom.

'Skakel. Speak.'

'Sergeant, this is Deputy Upshaw, West Hollywood.'

'Yeah, Deputy.'

'I'm working a homicide tied in to two City 187's, and you arrested one of the victims back in '41. Duane Lindenaur. Do you remember him?'

Skakel said, 'Yeah. He was working a queer squeeze on a rich lawyer named Hartshorn. I always remember the money jobs. Lindenaur got bumped, huh?'

'Yes. Do you remember the case?'

'Pretty well. The complainant's name was Charles Hartshorn. He liked boys, but he was married and he had a daughter he doted on. Lindenaur met Hartshorn through some fruit introduction service, perved with him and threatened to snitch Hartshorn's queerness to the daughter. Hartshorn called us in, we rousted Lindenaur, then Hartshorn got cold feet about testifying in court and dropped the charges.'

'Sergeant, was Hartshorn tall and gray-haired?'

Skakel laughed. 'No. Short and bald as a beagle. What's with the job? You got leads?'

'Lindenaur's on the City end, and there's no real leads yet. What was your take on Hartshorn?'

'He's no killer, Upshaw. He's rich, he's got influence and he won't give you the time of day. Besides, pansy jobs ain't worth it, and Lindenaur was a punk. I say c'est la vie, let sleeping queers lie.'

Back to the City, kid gloves this time, nothing to spawn more lies and trouble. Danny drove to Variety International Pictures, hoping Gene Niles would spend a decent amount of time at the Leafy Glade Motel. With the Goines end stalemated, victims two and three were the hot stuff, and Lindenaur as a studio scribe/extortionist felt hotter than Wiltsie as a male whore.

Rival union factions were picketing by the front gate;

159

Danny parked across the street, put an 'Official Police Vehicle' board on the windshield, ducked his head and weaved through a maze of bodies waving banners. The gate guard was reading a scandal tabloid featuring a lurid column on *his* three killings – gory details leaked by a 'reliable source' at the LA morgue. Danny scanned half a page while he got out his badge, the guard engrossed, chewing a cigar. The two cases were now connected in print – if only by the LA *Tattler* – and that meant the possibility of more ink, radio and television news, phony confessions, phony leads and scads of bullshit.

Danny rapped on the wall; the cigar chewer put down his paper and looked at the badge held up. 'Yeah? Who you here for?'

'I want to talk to the people who worked with Duane Lindenaur.'

The guard didn't flinch at the name; Lindenaur's monicker hadn't yet made the tabloid. He checked a sheet on a clipboard, said, 'Set 23, the office next to the *Tomahawk Massacre* interior,' hit a button and pointed. The gate opened; Danny threaded his way down a long stretch of blacktop filled with costumed players. The door to Set 23 was wide open; just inside it, three Mexican men were wiping war paint off their faces. They gave Danny bored looks; he saw a door marked REWRITE, went over and knocked on it.

A voice called, 'It's open'; Danny walked in. A lanky young man in tweeds and horn rims was stuffing pages in a briefcase. He said, 'Are you the guy replacing Duane? He hasn't showed up in three days and the director needs additional dialogue quicksville.'

Danny went in fast. 'Duane's dead, his friend George Wiltsie too. Murdered.'

The young man dropped his briefcase; his hands twitched up and adjusted his glasses. 'Mm-mm-murdered?'

'That's right.'

'And y-y-you're a policeman?'

'Deputy Sheriff. Did you know Lindenaur well?'

160

The youth picked up his briefcase and slumped into a chair. 'N-no, not well. Just here at work, just superficially.'

'Did you see him outside the studio?'

'No.'

'Did you know George Wiltsie?'

'No. I knew he and Duane lived together, because Duane told me.'

Danny swallowed. 'Were they lovers?'

'I wouldn't dream of speculating on their relationship. All I know is that Duane was quiet, that he was a good rewrite man and that he worked cheap, which is a big plus at this slave labor camp.'

A footstep scraped outside the door. Danny turned and saw a shadow retreating. Looking out, he caught a back view of a man fast-walking over to a bank of cameras and lighting fixtures. He followed; the man stood there, hands in his pockets, the classic 'I've got nothing to hide' routine.

Danny braced him, disappointed that he was young and mid-sized, no burn scars on his face, at best a conduit for second-hand dope. 'What were you doing listening outside that door?'

The man was closer to a boy – skinny, acned, a high voice with a trace of a lisp. 'I work here. I'm a set dresser.'

'So that gives you the right to eavesdrop on official police business?'

The kid primped his hair. Danny said, 'I asked you a question.'

'No, that doesn't give me–'

'Then why did you?'

'I heard you say Duaney and George were dead, and I knew them. Do you know–'

'No, I don't know who killed them, or I wouldn't be here. How well did *you* know them?'

The boy played with his pompadour. 'I shared lunch with Duaney – Duane – and I knew George to say hi to when he picked Duane up.'

'I guess the three of you had a lot in common, right?'

'Yes.'

'Did you associate with Lindenaur and Wiltsie outside of here?'

'No.'

'But you talked, because the three of you had so goddamn much in common. Is that right?'

The boy eyed the floor, one foot drawing lazy figure eights. 'Yes, sir.'

'Then you tell me about what they had going and who else they had going, because if anyone around here would know, you would. Isn't that right?'

The boy braced himself against a spotlight, his back to Danny. 'They'd been together for a long time, but they liked to party with other guys. Georgie was rough trade, and he mostly lived off Duane, but sometimes he turned tricks for this fancy escort service. I don't know anything else, so can I please go now?'

Danny thought of his call to Firestone Station – Lindenaur meeting the man he blackmailed through a 'fruit introduction service.' 'No. What was the name of the escort service?'

'I don't know.'

'Who else did Wiltsie and Lindenaur party with? Give me some names.'

'I don't know and I don't have any names!'

'Don't whine. What about a tall, gray-haired man, middle-aged. Did either Lindenaur or Wiltsie mention a man like that?'

'No.'

'Is there a man working here who fits that description?'

'There's a million men in LA who fit that description, so will you please–'

Danny clamped the boy's wrist, saw what he was doing and let go. 'Don't raise your voice to me, just answer. Lindenaur, Wiltsie, a tall, gray-haired man.'

The kid turned and rubbed his wrist. 'I don't know of

any men like that, but Duane liked older guys, and he told me he dug gray hair. Now are you satisfied?'

Danny couldn't meet his stare. 'Did Duane and George like jazz?'

'I don't know, we never discussed music.'

'Did they ever talk about burglary or a man in his late twenties with burn scars on his face?'

'No.'

'Were either of them hipped on animals?'

'No, just other guys.'

Danny said, 'Get out of here,' then moved himself, the kid still staring. The blacktop was deserted now, dusk coming on. He walked to the front gate; a voice from the guard hut stopped him. 'Say, Officer. You got a minute?'

Danny halted. A bald man in a polo shirt and golf slacks stepped out and extended his hand. 'I'm Herman Gerstein. I run this place.'

City turf. Danny gave Gerstein a shake. 'My name's Upshaw. I'm a Sheriff's detective.'

Gerstein said, 'I heard you were looking for the guys some script hack works with. That true?'

'Duane Lindenaur. He was murdered.'

'That's too bad. I don't like it when my people check out without telling me. What's the matter, Upshaw? You ain't laughing.'

'It wasn't funny.'

Gerstein cleared his throat. 'To each his own, and I don't have to beg for laughs, I've got comedians for that. Before you go, I want to inform you of something. I'm cooperating with a grand jury investigation into Commie influence in Hollywood, and I don't like the idea of extraneous cops asking questions around here. You dig? National security outranks a dead script hack.'

Danny threw out a tweak on general principles. 'A dead queer script hack.'

Gerstein looked him over. 'Now that really ain't funny, because I would never let a known homo work at my shop under any conditions. *Ever.* Is that clear?'

'Vividly.'

Gerstein whipped three long cigars out of his slacks and stuck them in Danny's shirt pocket. 'Develop a sense of humor and you might go places. And if you have to come on the lot again, see me first. You understand?'

Danny dropped the cigars on the ground, stepped on them and walked out the gate.

A check of the local papers and more phone work were next.

Danny drove to Hollywood and Vine, bought all four LA dailies, parked in a no-parking zone and read. The *Times* and *Daily News* had nothing on his case: the *Mirror* and *Herald* gave it a back page brush-off, 'Mangled Bodies Found in Griffith Park,' and 'Dead Derelicts Discovered at Dawn' their respective taglines. Sanitized descriptions of the mutilations followed; Gene Niles blasted his horn about the job's random nature. There was no mention of ID on the victims and nothing pertaining to the death of Marty Goines.

A pay phone stood next to the newsstand. Danny called Karen Hiltscher and got what he expected – her dental lab queries were going very slowly, ten negatives since he gave her the job; her calls to other LASD stations and the Detective Bureau for checks on burglars with dental tech backgrounds got a total zero – no such men existed. Trial calls to two taxidermists yielded the fact that all stuffed animals wore plastic teeth; real animal teeth did not show up in dentures, only in the mouths of creatures still on the hoof. Danny urged Karen to keep plugging, said his goodbyes accompanied by kissy sounds and dialed the Moonglow Lounge.

Janice Modine was not waitressing that night, but John Lembeck was drinking at the bar. Danny made nice with the man he'd spared a beating; the car thief/pimp made nice back. Danny knew he was good for some free information and asked him for scoop on homosexual pimps and escort services. Lembeck said the only queer service he knew of was ritzy, hush-hush

164

and run by a man named Felix Gordean, a legit talent agent with an office on the Strip and a suite at the Chateau Marmont. Gordean wasn't fruit himself, but provided boys to the Hollywood elite and old money LA.

Danny admonished Lembeck to stay frosty and took his Gordean dope to R & I and the DMV night line. Two calls, two squeaky-clean records and three plush addresses: 9817 Sunset for his office, the Chateau Marmont down the Strip at 7941 for his apartment, a beach house in Malibu: 16822 Pacific Coast Highway.

With one dime and one nickel left in his pocket, Danny played a hunch. He called Firestone Station, got Sergeant Frank Skakel and asked him the name of the 'fruit introduction service' where extortionist Duane Lindenaur met extortionee Charles Hartshorn. Skakel grumbled and said he'd ring Danny at his pay phone; ten minutes later he called back and said he'd dug up the original complaint report. Lindenaur met Hartshorn at a party thrown by a man who owned an escort service – Felix Gordean. Skakel ended with *his* admonition: while he was digging through the files, a buddy on the squad give him some lowdown: Gordean was paying heavy operation kickbacks to Sheriff's Central Vice.

Danny drove to the Chateau Marmont, an apartment house-hotel done up like a swank Renaissance fortress. The main building was festooned with turrets and parapets, and there was an inner courtyard of similarly adorned bungalows connected by pathways – high, perfectly trimmed hedges surrounding them. Gaslights at the end of wrought-iron poles illuminated address plates; Danny followed a winding string of numbers to 7941, heard dance music wafting behind the hedge and started for the path to the door. Then a gust of wind scudded clouds across the sky and moonlight caught two men in evening clothes kissing, swaying together in the dark porch enclosure.

Danny watched; the moon was eclipsed by more cloud cover; the door opened and admitted the men – laugh-

ter, a jump crescendo and a few seconds' worth of bright-
ness easing them inside. Danny went pins and needles,
squeezed between the hedge and the front wall and
scissor-walked over to a large picture window covered
by velvet drapes. There was a narrow space where the
two furls of purple were drawn apart, with a strip of
light giving access to tuxedos swirling across parquet,
wall tapestries, the sparkle of glasses hoisted. Danny
pressed his face to the window and looked in.

That close, he got distortion blur, Man Camera mal-
functions. He pulled back so that his eyes could capture
a larger frame, saw tuxedos entwined in movement,
cheek-to-cheek tangos, all male. The faces were up
against each other so that they couldn't be distinguished
individually; Danny zoomed out, in, out, in, until he
was pressed into the window glass with the pins and
needles localized between his legs, his eyes honing for
mid-shots, close-ups, faces.

More blur, blips of arms, legs, a cart being pushed
and a man in white carrying a punch bowl. Out, in, out,
better focus, no faces, then Tim and Coleman the alto
together, swaying to hard jazz. The pins and needles
hurting; Tim gone, replaced by a blond ingenu. Then
shadows killing his vision, his lens cleared by a step
backward – and a perfectly framed view of two fat, ugly
wallflowers tongue-kissing, all oily skin and razor burn
and hair pomade glistening.

Danny bolted home, seeing San Berdoo '39 and Tim
giving him the fisheye when he wouldn't take seconds
on Roxie. He found his spare I. W. Harper, knocked
down his standard four shots and saw it worse, Tim
reproachful, saying, yeah it was just horseplay, but *you*
really liked it. Two more shots, the Chateau Marmont
in Technicolor, all pretty ones that he knew had Timmy's
body.

He went straight to the bottle then, quality sourmash
burning like rotgut, Man-Cameraing women, women,
women. Karen Hiltscher, Janice Modine, strippers he'd
questioned about a stickup at the Club Largo, tits and

cunt on display in the dressing room, inured to men looking at their stuff. Rita Hayworth, Ava Gardner, the hat check girl at Dave's Blue Room, his mother stepping out of the bathtub before she got fat and became a Jehovah's Witness. All ugly and wrong, just like the two wallflowers at the Marmont.

Danny drank standing up until his legs went. Going down, he managed to throw the bottle at the wall. It hit a pinup of the blood patterns at 2307 Tamarind.

CHAPTER SIXTEEN

Mal got his lies straight on the doorstep and rang the bell. Heels over hardwood echoed inside the house; he pulled his vest down to cover his slack waistband – too many meals forgotten. The door opened and the Red Queen was standing there, perfectly coiffed, elegantly dressed in silk and tweed – at 9:30 in the morning.

'Yes? Are you a salesman? There's a Beverley Hills ordinance against soliciting, you know.'

Mal knew she knew otherwise. 'I'm with the District Attorney's Office.'

'Beverley Hills?'

'The City of Los Angeles.'

Claire De Haven smiled – movie star quality. 'My accumulation of jaywalking tickets?'

Cop-quality dissembling – Mal knew she had him pegged as the nice guy in the Lopez/Duarte/Benavides questioning. 'The City needs your help.'

The woman chuckled – elegantly – and held the door open. 'Come in and tell me about it, Mr . . . ?'

'Considine.'

Claire repeated the name and stood aside; Mal walked into a large living room furnished in a floral motif: gardenia-patterned divans, tufted orchid chairs, little tables and bookstands inlaid with wooden daisies. The walls were solid movie posters – anti-Nazi pictures popular in the late '30s and early '40s. Mal strolled up to a garish job ballyhooing *Dawn of the Righteous* – a noble Russki facing off a drooling blackshirt brandishing a Luger. Sunshine haloed the good guy; the German was shadowed in darkness. With Claire De Haven watching him, he counterpunched. 'Subtle.'

Claire laughed. 'Artful. Are you an attorney, Mr. Considine?'

Mal turned around. The Red Queen was holding a glass filled with clear liquid and ice. He couldn't smell gin and bet vodka – more elegant, no booze breath. 'No, I'm an investigator with the Grand Jury Division. May I sit down?'

Claire pointed to two chairs facing each other across a chess table. 'I'm warming to this. Would you like coffee or a drink?'

Mal said, 'No,' and sat down. The chair was upholstered in leather; the orchids were embroidered silk. Claire De Haven took the opposite seat and crossed her legs. 'You're crazy to think I'd ever inform. I won't, my friends won't, and we'll have the best legal talent money can buy.'

Mal played off the three Mexicans. 'Miss De Haven, this is a mop-up interview at best. My partner and I approached your friends at Variety International the wrong way, our boss is very angry and our funding has been cut. When we got our initial paperwork on the UAES – old HUAC stuff – we didn't find your name mentioned, and all your friends seemed . . . well . . . rather doctrinaire. I decided to play a hunch and present my case to you, hoping you'd keep an open mind and find aspects of what I'm going to tell you reasonable.'

Claire De Haven smiled and sipped her drink. 'You speak very well for a policeman.'

Mal thought: and you blast vodka in the morning and fuck pachuco hoodlums. 'I went to Stanford, and I was a major with the MPs in Europe. I was involved in processing evidence to convict Nazi war criminals, so you see

I'm not entirely unsympathetic to those posters on your walls.'

'You display empathy well, too. And now you've been employed by the studios, because it's easier to see Red than pay decent wages. You'll divide, conquer, get people to inform and bring in specialists. And you'll cause nothing but grief.'

From banter to cool outrage in a half second flat. Mal tried to look hangdog, thinking he could take the woman if he gave her a tough fight, but let her win. 'Miss De Haven, why doesn't the UAES strike in order to achieve its contract demands?'

Claire took a slow drink. 'The Teamsters would get in and stay in on a temporary payroll stipulation.'

A good opening; a last chance to play nice guy before they pulled back, planted newspaper dope and went decoy. 'I'm glad you mentioned the Teamsters, because they worry me. Should this grand jury succeed – and I doubt that it will – a racketeering force against the Teamsters would be a logical next step. They are very heavily infiltrated with criminal elements, much the way the American left is infiltrated by Communists.'

Claire De Haven sat still, not taking the bait. She looked at Mal, eyes lingering on the automatic strapped to his belt. 'You're an intelligent man, so state your case. Thesis sentence style, like you learned in your freshman comp class at Stanford.'

Mal thought of Celeste – juice for some indignation. 'Miss De Haven, I saw Buchenwald, and I know what Stalin is doing is just as bad. We want to get to the bottom of *totalitarian* Communist influence in the movie industry and inside the UAES, *end it*, prevent the Teamsters from kicking the shit out of you on the picket line and establish through the testimony some sort of demarcation line between *hard* Communist propaganda aggression and legitimate leftist political activity.' A pause, a shrug, hands raised in mock frustration. 'Miss De Haven, I'm a policeman. I collect evidence to put robbers and killers away. I don't like this job, but I think it needs to be done and I'm damn well going to do it as best I can. Can't you see my point?'

Claire took cigarettes and a lighter from the table and lit up. She smoked while Mal darted his eyes around the room, mock chagrin at blowing his calm. Finally she said, 'You're either a very good actor or in a way over your head with some very bad men. Which is it? I honestly don't know.'

'Don't patronize me.'

'I'm sorry.'

'No, you're not.'

'All right, I'm not.'

Mal got up and paced the room, advance man for his decoy. He noticed a bookcase lined with picture frames, examined a shelf of them and saw a string of handsome young men. About half were Latin lover types – but Lopez, Duarte and Benavides were absent. He remembered Lopez' comment to Lesnick: Claire was the only gringa he'd met who'd suck him, and he felt guilty about it because only whores did that, and she was his Communista madonna. On a shelf by itself was a picture of Reynolds Loftis, his Anglo-Saxon rectitude incongruous. Mal turned and looked at Claire. 'Your conquests, Miss De Haven?'

'My past and future. Wild oats lumped together and my fiancé all by himself.'

Chaz Minear had gotten explicit on Loftis – what they did, the feel of his weight downstairs. Mal wondered how much the woman knew about them, if she even guessed Minear finked her future husband to HUAC. 'He's a lucky man.'

'Thank you.'

'Isn't he an actor? I think I took my son to a movie he was in.'

Claire stubbed out her cigarette, lit another one and smoothed her skirt. 'Yes, Reynolds is an actor. When did you and your son see the movie?'

Mal sat down, juggling blacklist dates. 'Right after the war, I think. Why?'

'A point that I'd like to make, as long as we're talking in a civil manner. I doubt that you're as sensitive as you portray yourself, but if you are I'd like to illustrate an example of the hurt men like you cause.'

Mal hooked a thumb back at Loftis' picture. 'With your fiancé?'

'Yes. You see, you probably saw the movie at a revival house. Reynolds was a *very* successful character actor in the '30s, but the California State Un-American Activities Committee hurt him when he refused to testify back in '40. Many studios wouldn't touch him because of his politics, and the only work he could get was on Poverty Row – toadying to an awful man named Herman Gerstein.'

Mal played dumb. 'It could have been worse. People were blacklisted outright by HUAC in '47. Your fiancé could have been.'

Claire shouted, 'He *was* blacklisted, and I bet you know it!'

Mal jerked back in his chair; he thought he'd had her convinced he wasn't wise to Loftis. Claire lowered her voice. Maybe you knew it. Reynolds Loftis, Mr. Considine. Surely you know that he's in the UAES.'

Mal shrugged, smokescreening a lie. 'When you said Reynolds, I guessed that it was Loftis. I knew he was an actor, but I've never seen his photograph. Look, I'll tell you why I was surprised. An old lefty told my partner and me that Loftis was a homosexual. Now you tell me he's your fiancé.'

Claire's eyes narrowed; for a half second she looked like a shrew in waiting. 'Who told you that?'

Mal shrugged again. 'Some guy who used to hang out and chase girls at the Sleepy Lagoon Committee picnics. I forget his name.'

Shrew in waiting to nervous wreck; Claire's hands shaking, her legs twiching, grazing the table. Mal homed in on her eyes and thought he saw them pinning, like she was mixing pharmacy stuff with her vodka. Seconds dragged; Claire became calm again. 'I'm sorry. Hearing Reynolds described as that upset me.'

Mal thought: no it didn't – it was Sleepy Lagoon. 'I'm sorry, I shouldn't have said it.'

'Then why did you?'

'Because he's a lucky man.'

The Red Queen smiled. 'And not just because of me. Will you let me finish that point I wanted to make?'

'Sure.'

Claire said, 'In '47 someone informed on Reynolds to the House Committee – hearsay and innuendo – and he *was* blacklisted outright. He went to Europe and found work acting in experimental art films directed by a Belgian man he'd met in LA during the war. The actors all wore masks, the films created quite a stir, and Reynolds eked out a living acting in them. He even won the French version of the Oscar in '48, and got mainstream work in Europe. Now the *real* Hollywood studios are offereing him real work for real money, which will end if Reynolds is hauled before another committee or grand jury or kangaroo court or whatever you people call them.'

Mal stood up and looked at the door. Claire said, 'Reynolds will never name names, I'll never name names. Don't ruin the good life he's starting to have again. Don't ruin me.'

She even begged with elegance. Mal made a gesture that took in leather upholstery, brocade curtains and a small fortune in embroidered silk. 'How can you preach the Commie line and justify all this?'

The Red Queen smiled, beggar to muse. 'The good work I do allows me a dispensation for nice things.'

A stellar exit line.

Mal walked back to his car and found a note stuck under the wiper blades: 'Captain – greetings! Herman Gerstein called Ellis with a complaint: a Sheriff's dick is making waves at Variety International (pansy homicide). Ellis spoke to his CO (Capt. Al Deitrich) about it – and we're supposed to tell the lad to desist. West Hollywood Substation when you finish with C.D.H., please – D.S.'

Mal drove to the station, pissed at a stupid errand when he should be orchestrating the team's next move: radio and newspaper spots to convince UAES the grand jury was kaput. He saw Dudley Smith's Ford in the lot, left his car next to it and walked in the front door. Dudley was standing by the dispatching alcove, talking to a Sheriff's captain in uniform. A girl behind the switchboard was flagrantly eavesdropping, toying with the headset on her neck.

Dudley saw him and hooked a finger; Mal went over and offered the brass his hand. 'Mal Considine, Captain.'

The man gave him a bonecrusher shake. 'Al Dietrich. Good to meet a couple of City boys who come off as human beings, and I was just telling Lieutenant Smith here not to judge Deputy Upshaw too harshly. He's got a lot of newfangled ideas about procedure and the like, and he's a bit of a hothead, but basically he's a damn good cop. Twenty-seven years old and already a detective must tell you something, right?'

Dudley boomed tenor laughter. 'Smarts and naivete are a potent combination in young men. Malcolm, our friend is working on a County homo snuff tied to two City jobs. He seems to be obsessed as only a young idealist cop can be. Shall we give the lad a gentle lesson in police etiquette and priorities?'

Mal said, 'A brief one,' and turned to Dietrich. 'Captain, where's Upshaw now?'

'In an interrogation room down the hall. Two of my men captured a robbery suspect this morning, and Danny's sweating him. Come on, I'll show you – but let him finish up first.'

Deitrich led them through the muster room to a short corridor inset with cubicles fronted by one-way glass. Static was crackling out of a wall speaker above the last window on the left. The captain said, 'Take a listen, the kid is good. And try to let him down easy, he's got a bad temper and I like him.'

173

Mal strode ahead of Dudley to the one-way. Looking in, he saw a hood he'd rousted before the war. Vincent Scoppettone, a Jack Dragna trigger, was sitting at a table bolted to the floor, his hands cuffed to a welded-down chair. Deputy Upshaw had his back to the window and was drawing water from a wall cooler. Scoppettone squirmed in his chair, his County denims sweat-soaked at the legs and armpits.

Dudley caught up. 'Ah, grand. Vinnie the guinea. I heard that lad found out a quail of his was distributing her favors elsewhere and stuck a .12 gauge up her love canal. It must have been messy, albeit quick. Do you know the difference between an Italian grandmother and an elephant? Twenty pounds and a black dress. Isn't that grand?'

Mal ignored him. Scoppettone's voice came over the speaker, synched a fraction of a second behind his lips. 'Eyeball witnesses don't mean shit. They got to be alive to testify. Understand?'

Deputy Upshaw turned around, holding a cup of water. Mal saw a medium-sized young man, even-featured with hard brown eyes, a dark brown crew cut and razor nicks on heavily shadowed pale skin. He looked lithe and muscular – and there was something about him reminiscent of Claire De Haven's picture-pretty boys. His voice was an even baritone. 'Down the hatch, Vincent. Communion. Confession. Requiescat en pace.'

Scoppettone gulped water, sputtered and licked his lips. 'You a Catholic?'

Upshaw sat down in the opposite chair. 'I'm nothing. My mother's a Jehovah's Witness and my father's dead, which is what you're gonna be when Jack D. finds out you're clouting markets on your own. And as far as the eyeball witnesses go, they'll testify. You'll be no bail downtown and Jack'll give you the go-by. You're in dutch with Jack or you wouldn't be pulling heists in the first place. Spill, Vincent. Feed me on your other jobs and the captain here will recommend honor farm.'

Scoppettone coughed; water dribbled off his chin. 'Without them witnesses, you got no case.'

Upshaw leaned over the table; Mal wondered how much the speaker was distorting his voice. 'You're ixnay with Jack, Vinnie. At best, he lets you go on the Sun-Fax, at worst he has you whacked when you hit the penitentiary. And that'll be Folsom. You're a known mob associate, and that's where they go. And the Sun-Fax is in Cohen territory. Mickey buys the gift baskets he greases judges with there, and he'll make damn sure one of those judges hears your case. In my opinion, you are just too stupid to live. Only a stupid shit would knock off a joint in Cohen territory. Are you looking to start a fucking war? You think Jack wants Mickey coming after him over a chump-change stickup?'

Dudley nudged Mal. 'That lad is very, very good.'

Mal said, 'In spades.' He pushed Dudley's elbow aside and concentrated on Upshaw and his verbal style – wondering if he could run Commie argot as well as he did gangsterese. Vincent Scoppettone coughed again; static hit the speaker, then died out into words. 'There ain't gonna be no war. Jack and Mickey been talkin' about a truce, maybe going in on a piece of business together.'

Upshaw said, 'You feel like talking about that?'

'You think I'm stupid?'

Upshaw laughed. Mal caught the phoniness, that Scoppettone didn't interest him – that it was just a job. But it was a Class A phony laugh – and the kid knew how to squeeze his own tension into it.

'Vinnie, I already told you I think you're stupid. You've got panic city written all over you, and I think you're on the outs with Jack bad. Let me guess: you did something to piss Jack off, you got scared, you thought you'd hightail. You needed a stake, you heisted the Sun-Fax. Am I right?'

Scoppettone was sweating heavy now – it ws rolling off his face. Upshaw said, 'You know what else I think? One heist wouldn't have done it. I think there's other jobs we can make you for. I think I'm gonna check robbery

175

reports all over the City and County, maybe Ventura County, maybe Orange and San Diego. I'll bet if I wire your mugs around I'll come up with some other eyeball witnesses. Am I right?'

Scoppettone tried laughter – a long string of squeaky ha ha ha's. Upshaw joined in and mimicked them until his prisoner shut up. Mal snapped: he's wound tight as a steel spring on something else and shooting it to Vinnie because he's the one here – *and he probably doesn't know he's doing it*.

Squirming his arms, Scoppettone said, 'Let's talk deal-sky. I got something sweet.'

'Tell me.'

'Heroin. Heroin very large. That truce I told you about, Jack and Mickey partners. Quality Mex brown, twenty-five pounds. All for niggertown, cut-rate to lowball the independents down there. The God's truth. If I'm lyin', I'm flyin'.'

Upshaw aped Vinnie's tone. 'Then you've got wings stashed under your mattress, because the Mick and Dragna as partners is horseshit. Sherry's was six months ago, Cohen lost a man and doesn't forget stuff like that.'

'That wasn't Jack, that was LAPD. Shooters out of Hollywood Station, a snuff kitty half the fuckin' division kicked in for 'cause of fuckin' Brenda. Mickey Kike knows Jack didn't do it.'

Upshaw yawned – broadly. 'I'm bored, Vinnie. Niggers geezing heroin and Jack and Mickey as partners is a fucking snore. By the way, you read the papers?'

Scoppettone shook his head, spraying sweat. 'What?'

Upshaw pulled a rolled-up newspaper from his hip pocket. 'This was in last Tuesday's *Herald*. "Yesterday evening tragedy occurred at a convivial cocktail lounge in the Silverlake District. A gunman entered the friendly Moonmist Lounge, carrying a large-caliber pistol. He forced the bartender and three patrons to lie on the floor, ransacked the cash register and stole jewelry, wallets and purses belonging to his four victims. The bartender tried to apprehend the robber, and he pistol-whipped him senseless. The bartender died of head injuries this morning at Queen of Angels Hospital. The surviving robbery victims described the assailant as 'an Italian-looking white man, late thirties, five-ten, one hundred and ninety pounds.'" ' Vinnie, that's you.'

Scoppettone shrieked, 'That ain't me!' Mal craned his neck and squinted at the print on Upshaw's newspaper, glomming a full page on last week's fight card at the Olympic. He thought: pull out the stops, bluff him down, hit him once, don't get carried away and you're my boy –

'*That ain't fucking me!*'.

Upshaw leaned over the table, hard in Scoppettone's face. 'I don't fucking care. You're standing in a lineup tonight, and the three squarejohns from the Moonmist Lounge are gonna look you over. Three white bread types who think all wops are Al Capone. See, I don't want you for the Sun-Fax, Vinnie, I want you for keeps.'

'I didn't do it!'

'Prove it!'

'I can't prove it!'

'Then you'll take the fucking fall!'

Scoppettone was putting his whole body into his head, the only part of him not lashed down. He shook it; he twisted it; he thrust his chin back and forth like a ram trying to batter a defence. Mal got a flash: the kid had him nailed for a backup heist that night; the whole performance was orchestrated for the newspaper punch line. He elbowed Dudley and said, 'Our's'; Dudley gave him the thumbs-up. Vinnie Scoppettone tried to jerk his chair off the floor; Danny Upshaw grabbed a handful of his hair and slapped his face – forehand, backhand, forehand, backhand – until he went limp and blubbered, 'Deal. Deal. Deal.'

Upshaw whispered in Scoppettone's ear; Vinnie drooled an answer. Mal stood on his tiptoes for a better shot at the speaker and heard only static. Dudley lit a cigarette and smiled; Upshaw hit a button under the table. Two uniformed deputies and a woman holding a steno pad double-timed down the corridor. They opened the interrogation room door and swooped on their live one; Danny Upshaw walked out and said, 'Oh shit.'

Mal studied the reaction. 'Good work, Deputy. You were damn good.'

Upshaw looked at him, then Dudley. 'You're City, right?'

Mal said, 'Right, DA's Bureau. My name's Considine, this is Lieutenant Smith.'

'And it's about?'

Dudley said, 'Lad, we were going to reprimand you for rattling Mr. Herman Gerstein's cage, but that's water under the bridge now. Now we're going to offer you a job.'

'*What?*'

Mal took Upshaw's arm and steered him a few feet away. 'It's a decoy plant for a grand jury investigation into Communist activity in the movie studios. A very well-placed DA is running the show, and he'll be able to square a temporary transfer with Captain Dietrich. The job is a career maker, and I think you should say yes.'

'No.'

'You can transfer to the Bureau clean after the investigation. You'll be a lieutenant before you're thirty.'

'No. I don't want it.'

'What *do* you want?'

'I want to supervise the triple homicide case I'm working – for the County *and* the City.'

Mal thought of Ellis Loew balking, other City hotshots he could grease for the favor. 'I think I can manage it.'

Dudley came over, clapped Upshaw on the back and winked. 'There's a woman you'll have to get next to, lad. You might have to fuck the pants off of her.'

Deputy Danny Upshaw said, 'I welcome the opportunity.'

2

Upshaw, Considine, Meeks

CHAPTER SEVENTEEN

He was a cop again, bought and paid for, in with major leaguers playing for keeps. Howard's bonus had him out of hock with Leotis Dineen, and if the grand jury succeeded in booting the UAES from the studios he'd be minor-league rich. He had a set of keys to Ellis Loew's house and the use of the City clerks who'd be typing and filing there. He had a 'target list' of Pinkos untouched by previous grand juries. And he had the *big* list: UAES top dogs to glom criminal dirt on, no direct approaches now that they were deep in subterfuge, with newspaper pieces planted that said their investigation was dead. An hour ago he'd had his secretary place query calls to his local Fed contact, City/County DMV/R&I and the criminal records bureaus of California, Nevada, Arizona and Oregon States, requesting arrest report information on Claire De Haven, Morton Ziffkin, Chaz Minear, Reynolds Loftis and three unholy-sounding pachucos: Mondo Lopez, Sammy Benavides and Juan Duarte, asterisks after their names denoting them 'known youth gang members.' The gang squad boss at Hollenbeck Station had been his only call back; he said that the three were bad apples – members of a zooter mob in the early '40s before they cleaned up and 'got political.' East LA would be his first stop – once his secretary logged in the rest of her responses to his call-outs.

Buzz looked around his office for something to kill time with, saw the morning *Mirror* on the doormat and picked it up. He flipped through to the editorial page and got bingo! under Victor Reisel's by-line, less than twenty-four hours after cuckold Mal told Loew his plan.

The title was 'Reds 1 – City of Los Angeles 0. 3 Outs, No Witnesses on Base.' Buzz read:

It all came down to money – the great equalizer and common denominator. A grand jury was in the works, an important grand jury that would have been as far-reaching as the 1947 House Un-American Activities Committee hearings. Once again, Communist encroachment in the motion picture industry was to be delved into – this time within the context of labor trouble in the City of the Angels.

The United Alliance of Extras and Stagehands is currently under contract with a number of Hollywood studios. The union is rife with Communists and fellow travelers. The UAES is making exorbitant contract renegotiation demands, and a Teamster local which would like the opportunity to reach an amicable accord with the studios and step in to work UAES's job for reasonable wages and benefits is picketing against them. *Money*. The UAES implicitly advocates the end of the capitalist system and wants more of it. The non ideologically involved Teamsters want to prove their on-the-job mettle by working for wages that anticapitalists spurn. Hollywood, show biz: it's a crazy world.

Crazy Item #1: The glut of pro-Russian movies made during the early 1940's were largely scripted by members of the so-called UAES Brain trust.

Crazy Item #2: UAES Brain trust members belong to a total of 41 organizations that have been classified as Commie fronts by the State Attorney General's Office.

Crazy Item #3: The UAES wants more of that filthy capitalist lucre; the Teamsters want jobs for their people; a number of patriotic men in the LA District Attorney's Office had been slated to gather evidence for a prospective grand jury to delve into just *how* deep those green-loving UAESers' influence in the movie biz went. Let's face it: Hollywood is an unsurpassed tool for disseminating propaganda, and the Commies are the subtlest, most cruelly intelligent foe America has ever faced. Given access to the motion picture medium and its pervasiveness in our daily life, there is no end to the cancerous seeds of treason that well-placed movie Reds could plant

– subtle satires and attacks on America, subliminally planted so that the public and right-thinking movie people would have no idea they were being brainwashed. The DA's men had made approaches to several subversives, and were attempting to get them to admit to the error of their ways and appear as witnesses when money – the great equalizer and common denominator – reared its head to give aid and comfort to the enemy.

Lieutenant Malcolm Considine, of the DA's Bureau of Investigations, said: 'The City had promised us budget money, then withdrew. We're understaffed and now unfunded, with a backlog of criminal matters clogging up potential grand jury docket time. We might be able to begin gathering evidence again in fiscal '51 or '52, but how many inroads will the Communists have made into our culture by then?'

How many indeed. Lieutenant Dudley Smith of the Los Angeles Police Department, Lieutenant Considine's sadly short-lived partner in the DA Bureau's sadly short-lived investigation, said, 'Yes, it all came down to money. The City has precious little, and it would be immoral and illegal to seek outside funding. The Reds do not balk at exploiting the capitalist system, while we live by its rules, accepting the few inherent frailties in an otherwise just and humane philosophy. That's the difference between them and us. They live by the law of the jungle, we are too peace-loving to stoop to it.'

Reds – 1, the City of Los Angeles and the movie-going public – 0.

It's a crazy world.

Buzz put the paper down, thinking of crazy Dud circa '38 – brass-knuckling a nigger hophead half to death for drooling on a cashmere overcoat Ben Siegel greased him with. He hit the intercom. 'Sweetheart, any results on those calls yet?'

'Still waiting, Mr. Meeks.'

'I'm going out to East LA. Leave my messages on my desk, would you, please?'

'Yes, sir.'

The morning was cool, with rain threatening. Buzz took
Olympic straight out, Hughes Aircraft to Boyle Heights
with a minimum of red lights, no pretty scenery, time
to think. The .38 he'd strapped on made his rolls of flab
hang funny; his ID buzzer and the *Racing Form*
weighted his pockets wrong, bum ballast that had him
picking at his crotch to even things out. Benavides,
Lopez and Duarte were either White Fence, 1st Flats or
Apaches; the Mexes in the Heights were good people,
anxious to suck up right and be good Americans. He'd
get good information from them – and the idea bored
him.

He knew why: he hadn't been with a woman in years
who wasn't a whore or a starlet looking to get next to
Howard. Audrey Anders had him running on her time,
brainstorming on her so hard that even this sweetheart
of a deal with the DA's Office came a cropper. Betting
with Leotis Dineen was plain stupid; chasing Audrey
was stupid that meant something – a reason for him to
quit gorging on porterhouse, au gratins and peach pie
and lose a shitload of pounds so that his beaucoup wardrobe fit right – even though they'd never be able to go
out in public together.

Downtown came and went; the woman stayed. Buzz
tried concentrating on the job, turning north on Soto,
heading into the terraced hillsides that formed Boyle
Heights. The Jews had ceded the neighborhood to the
Mexicans before the war; Brooklyn Avenue had gone
from reeking of pastrami and chicken stock to reeking
of cornmeal and deep-fried pork. The synagogue across
from Hollenbeck Park was now a Catholic church; the
old men with beanies who played chess under the pepper
trees were replaced by pachucos in slit-bottom khakis –
strutting, primping, walking the road camp walk, talking
the jailhouse talk. Buzz circled the park, eyeing and
tagging them: unemployed, mid-twenties, probably
pushing fifty-cent reefers and collecting protection off

184

the hebe merchants too poor to move to the new kosher canyon at Beverly and Fairfax. White Fence or 1st Flats or Apaches, with tattoos between their left thumbs and forefingers spelling it out. Dangerous when fired up on mescal, maryjane, goofballs and pussy; restless when bored.

Buzz parked and stuck his billy club down the back of his pants, throwing the fit off even worse. He approached a group of four young Mexicans; two saw him coming and took off, obviously to drop hot shit in the grass somewhere, reconnoiter and see what the fat puto cop wanted. The other two stood there watching a cockroach fight: two bugs in a shoebox placed on a blench, gladiators brawling for the right to devour a dead bug soaked in maple syrup. Buzz checked out the action while the pachucos pretended not to notice him; he saw a pile of dimes and quarters on the ground and dropped a five spot on it. 'Finsky on the fucker with the spot on his back.'

The Mexicans did double-takes; Buzz did a quick sizeup: White Fence tattoos on two sinewy right fore-arms; both vatos lean and mean at the welterweight limit; one dirty T-shirt, one clean. Four brown eyes sizing *him* up. 'I mean it. That fucker's got style. He's a dancemaster like Billy Conn.'

Both pachucos pointed to the shoebox; Clean T-shirt said, 'Billy muerto.' Buzz looked down and saw the spotted bug belly up, stuck to the cardboard in a pool of amber goo. Dirty Shirt giggled, scooped up the change and five-spot; Clean Shirt took an ice cream stick, lifted the winner out of the box and put him on the bark of a pepper tree next to the bench. The bug hung there licking his feelers; Buzz said, 'Double or nothin' on a trick I learned back in Oklahoma.'

Clean Shirt said, 'This some goddamn cop trick?'

Buzz fished out his baton and dangled it by the thong. 'Sort of. I got a few questions about some boys who used to live around here, and maybe you can help me. I pull off the trick, you talk to me. No snitch stuff, just a few questions. I don't do the trick, you stroll. Comprende?'

The clean shirt vato started to walk away; Dirty Shirt stopped him and pointed to Buzz's stick. 'What's that thing got to do with it?'

Buzz smiled and took three steps backward, eyes on the tree. 'Son, you set that roach's ass on fire and I'll show you.'

Clean Shirt whipped out a lighter, flicked it on and held the flame under the victor bug. The bug scampered up the tree; Buzz got a bead and overhanded his baton. It hit and clattered to the ground; Dirty Shirt picked it up and fingered pulp off the tip. 'That's him. Holy fuck.'

Clean Shirt made the sign of the cross, pachuco version, his right hand stroking his balls; Dirty Shirt crossed the standard way. Buzz tossed his stick in the air, bounced it off the inside crook of his elbow, caught it and twirled it behind his back, let it hit the pavement, then brought it to parade rest with a jerk of the thong. The Mexicans were slack-jawed now; Buzz braced them while their mouths were still open. 'Mondo Lopez, Juan Duarte and Sammy Benavides. They used to gangsterize around here. Spill nice and I'll show you some more tricks.'

Dirty Shirt spat a string of obscenities in Spanish; Clean Shirt translated. 'Javier hates 1st Flats like a dog. Like a fucking evil dog.'

Buzz was wondering if Audrey Anders would go for his stick routine. 'So those boys ran with the Flats?'

Javier spat on the pavement – an eloquent lunger. 'Traitors, man. Back maybe '43, '44, the Fence and Flats had a peace council. Lopez and Duarte was supposed to be in on it, but they joined the fuckin' Sinarquista Nazi putos, then the fuckin' Commie Sleepy Lagoon putos, when they shoulda been fightin' with us. The fuckin' Apaches cleaned the Flats' and Fences' fuckin' clock, man. I lost my cousin Caldo.'

Buzz unclipped two more fivers. 'What else have you got? Feel free to get ugly.'

186

'Benavides was ugly, man! He raped his own fuckin' little sister!'

Buzz handed out the money. 'Easy now. Give me some more on that, whatever else you got and some leads on family. *Easy*.'

Clean Shirt said, 'It's just a rumour on Benavides, and Duarte's got a queer cousin, so maybe he's queer, too. Queerness runs in families, I read it in *Argosy* magazine.'

Buzz tucked his billy club back in his pants. 'What about families? Who's got family still around here?'

Javier answered. 'Lopez' mother died, and I think maybe he got some cousins in Bakersfield. 'Cept for the maricón, mosta Duarte's people moved back to Mexico, and I know that puto Benavides got parents livin' on 4th and Evergreen.'

'A house? An apartment?'

Clean Shirt piped in: 'Little shack with all these statues in front.' He twirled a finger and pointed to his head. 'The mother is crazy. Loca grande.'

Buzz sighed. 'That's all I get for fifteen scoots and my show?'

Javier said, 'Every vato in the Heights hates those cabróns, ask them.'

Clean Shirt said, 'We could make up some shit, you could pay us for that.'

Buzz said, 'Try to stay alive,' and drove to 4th and Evergreen.

The lawn was a shrine.

Jesus statues were lined up facing the street; there was a stable made out of kid's Lincoln Logs behind them, a dog turd reposing in baby J.C.'s manger. Buzz walked up to the porch and rang the bell; he saw the Virgin Mary on an end table. The front of her flowing white gown bore an inscription: 'Fuck me.' Buzz made a snap deduction – Mr. and Mrs. Benavides couldn't see too well.

An old woman opened the door. 'Quién?'

Buzz said, 'Police, ma'am. And I don't speak Spanish.'

The ginch fingered a string of beads around her neck. 'I speak Inglés. Is about Sammy?'

'Yes, ma'am. How'd you know that?'

The old girl pointed to the wall above a chipped brick fireplace. A devil had been drawn there – red suit, horns and trident. Buzz walked over and scoped him out. A photo of a Mex kid was glued where his face should be, and a line of Jesus statues was looking up from the ledge, giving him the evil eye. The woman said, 'My son Sammy. Communisto. Devil incarnate.'

Buzz smiled. 'It looks like you're well protected, ma'am. You've got Jesus on the job.'

Mama Benavides grabbed a sheaf of papers off the mantel and handed them over. The top sheet was a State Justice Department publicity job – California-based Commie fronts in alphabetical order. The Sleepy Lagoon Defense Committee was check-marked, with a line in brackets next to it: 'Write P.O. Box 465, Sacramento, 14, California, for membership list.' The old woman snatched the pages, flipped through them and stabbed a finger at a column of names. Benavides, Samuel Tomás Ignacio, and De Haven, Claire Katherine, were starred in ink. 'There. Is the truth, anti-Christ Communista y Communisto!'

The ginch had tears in her eyes. Buzz said, 'Well, Sammy's got his rough edges, but I wouldn't exactly call him the devil.'

'Is true! Yo soy la madre del diablo! You arrest him! Communisto!'

Buzz pointed to Claire De Haven's notation. 'Mrs. Benavides, what have you got on this woman here? Give me some good scoop and I'll beat that boogie man up with my stick.'

'Communista! Drug addict! Sammy took her to clinica for cure, and she–'

Buzz saw a prime opening. 'Where is that clinic, ma'am? Tell me slow.'

'By ocean. Devil doctor! Communista whore!'

Satan's mother started bawling for real. Buzz blew East LA and headed for Malibu – a sea breeze, a doctor who owed him, no cockroach fights, no fuck me madonnas.

Pacific Sanitarium was in Malibu Canyon, a booze and dope dry-out farm nestled in foothills a half mile from the beach. The main building, lab and maintenance shacks were surrounded by electrified barbed wire; the price for kicking hooch, horse and drugstore hop was twelve hundred dollars a week; detoxification heroin was processed on the premises – per a gentleman's agreement between Dr. Terence Lux, the clinic's bossman, and the Los Angeles County Board of Supervisors – the agreement based on the proviso that LA politicos in need of the place could boil out for free. Buzz drove up to the gate thinking of all the referrals he'd given Lux: RKO juicers and hopheads spared jail jolts and bum publicity because Dr. Terry, plastic surgeon to the stars, had given them shelter and him a 10 percent kickback. One still rankled: a girl who'd OD'd when Howard booted her out of his A list fuck pad and back to selling it in hotel bars. He almost burned the three hundred Lux shot him for the business.

Buzz beeped his horn; the gate watchman's voice came over the squawk box: 'Yes, sir?'

Buzz spoke to the receiver by the fence. 'Turner Meeks to see Dr. Lux.'

The guard said, 'One moment, sir'; Buzz waited. Then: 'Sir, follow the road all the way down the left fork to the end. Dr. Lux is in the hatchery.'

The gate opened; Buzz cruised past the clinic and maintenance buildings and turned onto a road veering off into a scrub-covered miniature canyon. There was a shack at the end: low wire walls and a tin roof. Chickens squawked inside it; some of the birds were shrieking bloody murder.

Buzz parked, got out and peered through the wire.

Two men in hipboots and khaki smocks were slaughtering chickens, hacking them with razor-bladed two-by-four's – the zoot sticks Riot Squad bulls used to pack back in the early '40s, emasculating Mex hoodlums by slashing their threads. The stick wielders were good: single neck shots, on to the next one. The few remaining birds were trying to run and fly away; their panic had them scudding into the walls, the roof and the zoot men. Buzz thought: no chicken marsala at the Derby tonight, and heard a voice behind him.

'Two birds with one stone. A bad pun, good business.'

Buzz turned. Terry Lux was standing there – all rangy gray handsomeness, like a dictionary definition of 'physician'. 'Hello, Doc.'

'You know I prefer Doctor or Terry, but I've always made allowances for your homespun style. Is this business?'

'Not exactly. What's *that*? You doin' your own catering?'

Lux pointed to the slaughterhouse, silent now, the stick men tossing dead chickens in sacks. 'Two birds, one stone. Years ago I read a study that asserted a heavy chicken diet is beneficial to people with low blood sugar, which most alcoholics and drug addicts have. Stone one. Stone two is my special cure for narcotics users. My technicians drain out all their existing contaminated blood and rotate in fresh, healthy blood filled with vitamins, minerals and animal hormones. So, I have a hatchery and a slaughterhouse. It's all very cost-effective and beneficial to my patients. What is it, Buzz? If it isn't business, then it's a favor. How can I help you?'

The smell of blood and feathers was making him gag. Buzz noticed a pulley system linking the maintenance huts to the clinic, a tram car stationed on a landing dock about ten yards in back of the chicken shack. 'Let's go up to your office. I've got some questions about a woman who I'm pretty damn sure was a patient of yours.'

Lux frowned and cleaned his nails with a scalpel. 'I never divulge confidential patient information. You know that. It's a prime reason why Mr. Hughes and yourself use my services exclusively.'

'Just a few questions, Terry.'

'I suppose money instead is out of the question?'

'I don't need money. I need information.'

'And if I don't proffer this information you'll take your business elsewhere?'

Buzz nodded toward the tram car. 'No tickee, no washee. Be nice to me, Terry. I'm in with the city of Los Angeles these days, and I just might get the urge to spill about that dope you manufacture here.'

Lux scratched his neck with the scalpel. 'For medical purposes only, and politically approved.'

'Doc, you tellin' me you don't trade the skim to Mickey C. for *his* referrals? The City hates Mickey, you know.'

Lux bowed in the direction of the car; Buzz walked ahead and got in. The doctor hit a switch; sparks burst from the cables; they moved slowly up and docked on an overhang adjacent to a portico with a spectacular ocean view. Lux led Buzz down a series of antiseptic white hallways to a small room crammed with filing cabinets. Medical posters lined the walls: a picture primer for plastic surgeons, facial reconstruction in the style of Thomas Hart Benton. Buzz said, 'Claire Katherine De Haven. She's some kind of Commie.'

Lux opened a cabinet, leafed through folders, plucked one and read from the top page: 'Claire Katherine De Haven, date of birth May 5, 1910. Chronic controlled alcoholic, sporadically addicted to phenobarbital, occasional Benzedrine use, occasional heroin skin-popper. She took my special cure I told you about three times – in '39, '43, and '47. That's it.'

Buzz said, 'Nix, I want more. That file of yours list any details? Any good dirt?'

Lux held up the folder. 'It's mostly medical charts and financial accounting. You can read them if you like.'

'No thanks. You remember her good, Terry. I can tell. So feed me.'

Lux put the file back and slid the cabinet shut. 'She seduced a few of her fellow patients while she was here the first time. It caused an upheaval, so in '43 I kept her isolated. She was on remorseful both times, and on her second go-round I gave her a little psychiatric counseling.'

'You a headshrinker?'

Lux laughed. 'No, but I enjoy getting people to tell me things. In '43 De Haven told me she wanted to reform because some Mexican boyfriend of hers got beat up in the zoot suit riots and she wanted to work more efficaciously for the People's Revolt. In '47 the Red hearings back east sent her around the twist – some pal of hers got his you-know-what in the wringer. HUAC was good for business, Buzz. Lots of remorse, ODs, suicide attempts. Commies with money are the best Commies, don't you agree?'

Buzz ran the rest of the target list through his head. 'Who got his dick in the wringer, some bimbo of Claire's?'

'I don't remember.'

'Morton Ziffkin?'

'No.'

'One of her spics? Benavides, Lopez, Duarte?'

'No, it wasn't a Mex.'

'Chaz Minear, Reynolds Loftis?'

Bingo on 'Loftis' – Lux's face muscles tensing, coming together around a phony smile. 'No, not them.'

Buzz said, 'Horseshit. You give on that. *Now*.'

Lux shrugged – phony. 'I had a case on Claire, and so did Loftis. I was jealous. When you mentioned him, that brought it all back.'

Buzz laughed – his patented shitkicker job. 'Horse pucky. You've only got a case on money, so you fuckin' give me better than that.'

The doctor got out his scalpel and tapped it against his leg. 'Okay, let's try this. Loftis used to buy heroin for Claire, and I didn't like it – I wanted her beholden to me. Satisfied?'

A good morning's work: the woman as a hophead/-Mex fucker, Benavides a maybe kiddie raper, Loftis copping H for a fellow Red. 'Who'd he glom from?'

'I don't know. *Really*.'

'You got anything else good?'

'No. You have any fine young Howard rejects to spice up the ward?'

'See you in church, Doc.'

A stack of messages was waiting back at the office, partial results from his secretary's phone queries. Buzz leafed through them.

Traffic ticket rebop predominated, along with some stale bread on the spics: unlawful assembly, nonfelony assault and battery resulting in Mickey Mouse juvie time. No sex shit on Samuel Tomás Ignacio Benavides, the 'devil incarnate'; no political dirt on any of the three ex-White Fencers. Buzz turned to the last message slip – his secretary's call back from the Santa Monica PD.

Mr. Meeks –
3/44 – R. Loftis & another man – Charles (Eddington) Hartshorn, D.O.B. 9/6/1897, routinely questioned during vice Squad raid of S.M. deviant bar (Knight in Armor – 1684 S. Lincoln, S.M.) This from F.I. card check DMV/ R&I on Hartshorn: no crim. rec., traffic rec. clean, attorney. Address – 419 S. Rimpau, L.A. – hope this helps – Lois.

419 South Rimpau was Hancock Park, pheasant under glass acres, old LA money; Reynolds Loftis had a case on Claire De Haven – and now it looked like he addressed the ball from both sides of the plate. Buzz ran an electric shaver over his face, squirted cologne at his armpits and brushed a chunk of pie crust off his necktie. Filthy rich always made him nervous; filthy rich and fruit was a combo he'd never worked before.

Audrey Anders stuck with him on the ride over; he pretended his Old Spice was her Chanel #5 in just the right places. 419 South Rimpau was a Spanish mansion fronted by a huge expanse of grass dotted with rose gardens; Buzz parked and rang the bell, hoping for a single-o play: no witnesses if it got ugly.

A peephole opened, then the door. A peaches-and-cream blonde about twenty-five had her hand on the knob, wholesome pulchritude in a tartan skirt and pink button-down shirt. 'Hello. Are you the insurance man here to see Daddy?'

Buzz pulled his jacket over the butt of his .38. 'Yes, I am. In private, please. No man likes to discuss such grave matters in the presence of his family.'

The girl nodded, led Buzz through the foyer to a book-lined study and left him there with the door ajar. He noticed a liquor sideboard and thought about a quick one – a mid-afternoon bracer might give him some extra charm. Then 'Phil, what's this in-private stuff?' took it out of his hands.

A short pudgy man, bald with a fringe, had pushed the door open. Buzz held out his badge; the man said, 'What is this?'

'DA's Bureau, Mr. Hartshorn. I just wanted to keep your family out of it.'

Charles Hartshorn closed the door and leaned against it. 'Is this about Duane Lindenaur?'

Buzz drew a blank on the name, then remembered it from yesterday's late-edition *Tattler*: Lindenaur was a victim in the homo killings Dudley Smith told him about – the job the Sheriff's dick they just co-opted was set to run. 'No, sir. I'm with the Grand Jury Division, and we're investigating the Santa Monica Police. We need to know if they abused you when they raided the Knight in Armor back in '44.'

Veins throbbed in Hartshorn's forehead; his voice was boardroom-lawyer cold. 'I don't believe you. Duane Lindenaur attempted to extort money from me nine years ago – spurious allegations that he threatened to leak to my family. I dealt with the man legally then, and a few days ago I read that he had been murdered. I've

194

been expecting the police at my door, and now you show up. Am I a suspect in Lindenaur's death?'

Buzz said, 'I don't know and I don't care. This is about the Santa Monica Police.'

'No, it is not. This pertains to the spurious allegations Duane Lindenaur made against me and the non sequitur of my happening to be in a cocktail lounge frequented by certain not respectable people when a police raid occurred. I have an alibi for the newspapers' estimated time of Duane Lindenaur's and the other man's deaths, and I want you to corroborate it without involving my family. If you so much as breathe a word to my wife and daughter, I will have your badge and your head. Do you understand?'

The lawyer's tone had gotten calmer; his face was one massive contortion. Buzz tried diplomacy again. 'Reynolds Loftis, Mr. Hartshorn. He was rousted with you. Tell me what you know about him, and I'll tell the Sheriff's detective who's workin' the Lindenaur case to leave you alone, that you're alibied up. That sound nice to you?'

Hartshorn folded his arms over his chest. 'I don't know any Reynolds Loftis and I don't make deals with grubby little policemen who reek of cheap cologne. Leave my home now.'

Hartshorn's 'Reynolds' was all wrong. Buzz moved to the sideboard, filled a glass with whiskey and walked up to the lawyer with it. 'For your nerves, Charlie. I don't want you kickin' off a heart attack on me.'

'*Get out of my home, you grubby little worm.*'

Buzz dropped the glass, grabbed Hartshorn's neck and slammed him against the wall. 'You're humpin' the wrong boy, counselor. *The* last boy around here you want to fuck with. Now here's the drill: you and Reynolds Loftis or I go into the living room and tell your little girl that daddy sucks cock at the Westlake Park men's room and takes it up the ass on Selma and Las Palmas. And you breathe a word to anybody that I

195

leaned on you, and I'll have you in Confidential Magazine porkin' nigger drag queens. *Do you understand?*'

Hartshorn was beet red and spilling tears. Buzz let go of his neck, saw the imprint of a big ham hand and made that hand a fist. Hartshorn tremble-walked to the sideboard and picked up the whiskey decanter. Buzz swung at the wall, pulling the punch at the last second. 'Spill on Loftis, goddamnit. Make it easy so I can get the fuck out of here.'

Glass on glass chimed, followed by hard breathing and silence. Buzz stared at the wall. Hartshorn spoke, his voice dead hollow. 'Reynolds and I were just a . . . fling. We met at a party a Belgian man, a movie director, threw. The man was very au courant, and he threw lots of parties at clubs for our . . . his kind. It never got serious with Reynolds because there was a screenwriter he had been seeing, and some third man they were disturbed over. I was the odd man . . . so it never . . .'

Buzz turned and saw Hartshorn slumped in a chair, warming his hands on a whiskey glass. 'What else you got?'

'Nothing. I never saw Reynolds after that time at the Knight in Armor. Who are you going to – '

'Nobody, Charlie. Nobody's gonna know. I'll just say I got word that Loftis is . . .'

'Oh God, is this the witch hunts again?'

Buzz exited to the sound of the sad bastard weeping.

Rain had hit while he was applying the strongarm – hard needle sheets of it, the kind of deluge that threatened to melt the foothills into the ocean and sieve out half the LA Basin. Buzz laid three to one that Hartshorn would keep his mouth shut; two to one that more cop work would drive him batshit; even money that dinner at the Nickodell and the evening at home writing up a report on the day's dirt was the ticket. He could smell the queer's sweat on himself, going stale with his own sweat; he felt a beaucoup case of the sucker punch blues coming on. Halfway to the office, he cracked the window

196

for air and a rain bracer, changed directions and drove to his place.

Home was the Longview Apartments at Beverly and Mariposa, four rooms on the sixth floor, southern exposure, the pad furnished with leftovers from RKO movie sets. Buzz pulled into the garage, ditched his car and took the elevator up. And sitting by his door was Audrey Anders in a rain-spattered, sequin-spangled, gold lamé gown, a wet mink coat in her lap. She was using it as an ashtray; when she saw Buzz, she said, 'Last year's model. Mickey'll get me a new one,' and stubbed her cigarette out on the collar.

Buzz helped Audrey to her feet, holding her hands just a beat too long. 'Did I really get this lucky?'

'Don't count your chickens. Lavonne Cohen took a trip with her mah-jongg club and Mickey thinks it's open season on me. Tonight was supposed to be the Mocambo, the Grove and late drinks with the Gersteins. I pulled a snit and escaped.'

'I thought you and Mickey were in love.'

'Love has its flip side. Did you know you're the only Turner Meeks in the Central White Pages?'

Buzz unlocked the door. Audrey walked in, dropped her mink on the floor and scoped the living room. The furnishings included leather couches and easy chairs from *London Holiday* and zebra head wall mounts from *Jungle Bwana;* the swinging doors leading to the bedroom were scavenged off the saloon set of *Rage on the Rio Grande*. The carpeting was lime green and purple striped – the bedspread one the Amazon huntress lolly-gagged on in *Song of the Pampas*. Audrey said, 'Meeks, did you *pay* for this?'

'Gifts from a rich uncle. You want a drink?'

'I don't drink.'

'Why not?'

'My father, sister and two brothers are drunks, so I thought I'd give it a pass.'

Buzz was thinking she looked good – but not as good

as she did with no makeup and Mickey's shirt hanging to her knees. 'And you became a stripper?'

Audrey sat down, kicked off her shoes and warmed her feet on the mink. 'Yes, and don't ask me to do the tassel trick for you, because I won't. Meeks, what *is* the matter with you? I thought you'd be glad to see me.'

He could still smell the queer. 'I coldcocked a guy today. It was shitty.'

Audrey wriggled her toes, making the coat jump. 'So? That's what you do for a living.'

'The guys I usually do it to give me more of a fight.'

'So you're telling me it's all a game?'

He'd told Howard once that the only women worth having were the ones who had your number. 'There's gotta be somethin' we're better at than buttin' heads and askin' each other questions.'

The Va Va Voom Girl kicked the mink up in her lap. 'Is the bedroom this outré?'

Buzz laughed. '*Casbah Nocturne* and *Paradise Is Pink*. That tell you anything?'

'That's another question. Ask *me* something provocative.'

Buzz took off his jacket, unhooked his holster and threw it on a chair. 'Okay. Does Mickey keep a tail on you?'

Audrey shook her head. 'No. I made him stop it. It made me feel cheap.'

'Where's your car?'

'Three blocks away.'

All green lights to make his best stupid move an epic. 'You got it all figured out.'

Audrey said, 'I didn't think you'd say no.' She waved her mink coat. 'And I brought a towel for the morning.'

Buzz thought, RIP Turner Prescott Meeks, 1906–1950. He took a deep breath, sucked in his flab, pushed through the saloon doors and started peeling. Audrey came in and laughed at the bed – pink satin spread, pink canopy, pink embroidered gargoyles as foot posts. She got naked with a single flick of a clasp; Buzz felt his legs buckling as her breasts bobbed free. Audrey came to him and slipped off his tie, undid his shirt buttons, loosened his belt. He pried his shoes and socks off standing up; his shirt hit the floor via a bad case of the shivers. Audrey laughed and traced the goosebumps on his arms, then ran her hands over the parts of himself he couldn't stand: his melon gut, his side rolls, the knife scars running up into his chest hair. When she started licking him there he knew she was okay on it; he picked her up to show her how strong he was – his legs almost blowing it – and put her down on the bed. He got out of his trousers and boxers under his own steam and lay down beside her – and in a half second she was all arms and legs around him, face to face and mouth open, pushing up against him like he was everything she'd ever wanted.

He kissed her – soft, hard, soft; he rubbed his nose into her neck and smelled Ivory Soap – not the perfume he'd played pretend with. He took her breasts in his hands and pinched the nipples, remembering everything every cop had told him about the headliner at the Burbank Burlesque. Audrey made different noises for each part of her he touched; he kissed and tongued between her legs and got one big noise. The big noise got bigger and bigger; her legs and arms went spastic. Her going so crazy got him almost there, and he went inside her so he could be part of it. Audrey's hips pushing off the covers made him burst going in; he held on and she held him, and he gave her all his strength to smother their aftershocks. Half his weight, she was still able to push him up as she kept coming – and he grabbed her head and buried his head in her hair until he went limp and she quit fighting him.

Pink satin sheets and sweat bound them together. Buzz rolled over on his side, hooking a finger around Audrey's wrist so they'd keep on touching while he got his breath. Eight years without a cigarette and he was panting like a track dog – and she was lying there all still and calm, a vein on the back of her arm tapping his

199

finger the only thing that said she was still racing inside. His chest heaved; he tried to think of something to say; Audrey made finger tracks of his knife scars. She said, 'This could get complicated.'

Buzz got his wind. 'That mean you're thinkin' angles already?'

Audrey made like her nails were animals' claws and pretended to scratch him. 'I just like to know where I stand.'

The moment was slipping away from him – like it wasn't worth the danger. Buzz grabbed Audrey's hands. 'So that means we're lookin' at a next time?'

'You didn't have to ask. I'd have told you in a minute or so.'

'I like to know where I stand, too.'

Audrey laughed and pulled her hands away. 'You stand guilty, Meeks. You got me thinking the other day. So whatever happens, it's your fault.'

Buzz said, 'Sweetie, don't underestimate Mickey. He's sugar and spice with women and kids, but he kills people.'

'He knows I'll leave him sooner or later.'

'No, he doesn't. He figures you're an ex-stripper, a shiksa, you're thirty-somethin' and you've got no place to go. You give him a little bit of grief, maybe it gets his dick hard. But you stroll, that's somethin' else.'

She couldn't meet his eyes. Buzz said, 'Sweetie, where would you go?'

Audrey pulled a pillow down and hugged it, giving him both baby browns. 'I've got some money saved. A bunch. I'm going to buy some grove property in the Valley and bankroll rentals on a shopping center. They're the coming thing, Meeks. Another ten thousand and I can get in on the ground floor with thirty-five acres.'

Like his acreage: fourteen dollars per on the sure thing that should have made him rich. 'Where'd you get the money?'

'I saved it.'

200

'From Mickey's handouts?'

Audrey surprised him by chucking the pillow away and poking his chest. 'Are you jealous, *sweetie*?'

Buzz grabbed her finger and gave it a little love bite. 'Maybe just a tad.'

'Well, don't be. Mickey's all wrapped up in his union business and his drug thing with Jack Dragna, and I know how to play this game. Don't you worry.'

'Sweetie, you better. Because it is surely for keeps.'

'Meeks, I wish you'd quit talking about Mickey. You'll have me looking under the bed in a minute.'

Buzz thought of the .38 in the other room and the fruit lawyer with the bruised neck and tear-mottled cheeks. 'I'm glad bein' with you is dangerous. It feels good.'

CHAPTER EIGHTEEN

Acting Supervisor Upshaw.

Task Force Boss.

Skipper.

Danny stood in the empty Hollywood Station muster room, waiting to address *his* three men on *his* homicide case – running the titles down in *the* single place where the Brenda Allen job caused the most grief. A cartoon tacked to the notice board spelled it out: Mickey Cohen wearing a Jew skullcap with a dollar sign affixed to the top, dangling two uniformed Sheriff's deputies on puppet strings. A balloon elaborated his thoughts: *Boy, did I give it to the LAPD! It's good I got the County cops to wipe my ass for me!* Danny saw little holes all over Mickey's face; LA's number-one hoodlum had been used as a dartboard.

There was a lectern and blackboard at the front of the room; Danny found chalk and wrote 'Deputy D. Upshaw, LASD,' in boldface letters. He positioned himself behind the stand like Doc Layman with his forensics class and forced himself to think of his other assignment so he wouldn't get antsy when it came time to lay down the law to *his* men, three detectives older and much more experienced than he. That job was coming on like a snooze and a snore, maybe a little shot of elixir to keep bad thoughts down and business on; it was why he was standing triumphant in a spot where the County police were loathed more than baby rapers. The deal was like pinching yourself to make sure the great things that were happening weren't just a dream – and he pinched himself for the ten millionth time since Lieutenant Mal Considine made his offer.

Dudley Smith had called him at home yesterday afternoon, interrupting a long day of nursing watered-down highballs and working on his file. The Irishman told him to meet him and Considine at West Hollywood Station; the fix was in via Ellis Loew, with the temporary detachment order approved by both Chief Worton and Sheriff Biscailuz. He'd brushed his teeth, gargled and forced down a sandwich before he met them – anticipating one question and building a lie to field it. Since they'd already told him he would be planted around Variety International Pictures and they knew he'd incurred bossman Gerstein's wrath there, he had to convince them that only the gate guard, the rewrite man and Gerstein saw him in his cop capacity. It was Considine's *first* question – and a residue of bourbon calm helped him brazen it out. Smith bought it whole, Considine secondhand, when he ran his prerehearsed spiel on how he would completely alter his haircut and clothes to fit the role of Commie idealist. Smith gave him a stack of UAES paperwork to take home and study and made him scan a batch of psychiatric reports in their presence; then it was hard brass tacks.

His job was to approach UAES's suspected weak link – a promiscuous woman named Claire De Haven – gain entrance to the union's strategy meetings and find out what they were planning. Why haven't they called a strike? Do the meetings involve the actual advocacy of armed revolt? Is there planned subversion of motion picture content? Did the UAES brain trust fall for Considine's sub-rosa move – planting newspaper and radio pieces that said the grand jury investigation had gone down – and just how strongly is UAES connected to the Communist Party?

Career maker.

'You'll be a lieutenant before you're thirty.'

'There's a woman you'll have to get next to, lad. You might have to fuck the pants off of her.'

A bludgeon to smash his nightmares.

He felt cocky when he left the briefing, taking the nonpsychiatric reports under his arm, promising to report for a second confab this afternoon at City Hall. He went back to his apartment, called a dozen dental labs that Karen Hiltscher hadn't tapped and got zilch, read a dozen homosexual homicide histories without drinking or thinking of the Chateau Marmont. He then started feeling *very* cocky, took his 2307 Tamarind blood scrapings to the USC chemistry building and bribed a forensics classmate into typing them, hoping he could combine the wall spray pictures with the victims' names, reconstruct and get another fix on his man. The classmate didn't even blink at the bloodwork and did his tests; Danny took home data and put it together with the photographs.

Three victims, three different blood types – the risk of showing illegally obtained evidence was worth it. The Marty Goines AB+ blood matched the sloppiest of the wall sprays; he was the first victim, and the killer had not yet perfected his interior decorating technique. George Wiltsie and Duane Lindenaur, types O− and B+, had their blood spat out *separately*, Wiltsie in designs less intricate, less polished. Conclusions reinforced and conclusions gained: Marty Goines was a spur-of-the-moment victim, and the killer went at him in a total rage. Although filled with suicidal bravado – as witnessed by his bringing victims two and three to Goines' apartment

– he had to have had an ace reason for choosing Mad Marty, which could be one of three:

He knew the man and wanted to kill him out of hatred – a well-defined personal motive;

He knew the man and found him a satisfactory victim based on convenience and/or blood lust;

He did not know Marty Goines previously, but was intimately acquainted with the darktown jazz strip, and trusted himself to find a victim there.

Have *his* men recanvass the area.

On Wiltsie/Lindenaur:

The killer bit and gnawed and swallowed and sprayed Wiltsie's blood first, because he was the one who most attracted him. The relative refinement of the Lindenaur blood designs denoted the killer's satisfaction and satiation; Wiltsie, a known male prostitute, was his primary sex fix.

Tonight, double-agency sanctioned, he'd brace talent agent/procurer Felix Gordean, connected circumstantially to Wiltsie's squeeze Duane Lindenaur – and try for a handle on who the men were.

Danny checked the clock: 8:53; the other officers should be arriving at 9:00. He decided to stick behind the lectern, got out his notepad and went over the assignments he'd laid out. A moment later, he heard a discreet throat-clearing and looked up.

A stocky blond man, thirty-fivish, was walking toward him. Danny remembered something Dudley Smith said: a Homicide Bureau 'protégé' of his would be on the 'team' to grease things and make sure the other men 'fell in line.' He pasted on a smile and stuck out his hand; the man gave him a hard shake. 'Mike Breuning. You're Danny Upshaw?'

'Yes. Is it Sergeant?'

'I'm a sergeant, but call me Mike. Dudley sends regards and regrets – the station boss here says Gene Niles has to work the case with us. He was the catching officer, and the Bureau can't spare any other men. C'est la vie, I always say.'

Danny winced, remembering his lies to Niles. 'Who's the fourth man?'

'One of your guys, Jack Shortell, a squadroom sergeant from the San Dimas Substation. Look, Upshaw, I'm sorry about Niles. I know he hates the Sheriff's and he thinks the City end of the job should be shitcanned, but Dudley said to tell you, "Remember, you're the boss." Dudley likes you, by the way. He thinks you're a comer.'

His take on Smith was that he enjoyed hurting people. 'That's great. Tell the Lieutenant thanks for me.'

'Call him Dudley, and thank him yourself – you guys are partners on that Commie thing now. Look, here's the others.'

Danny looked. Gene Niles was walking to the front of the room, giving a tall man with wire-frame glasses a wide berth, like all Sheriff's personnel were disease carriers. He sat down in the first row of chairs and got out a notepad and pen – no amenities, no acknowledgment of rank. The tall man came up and gave Breuning and Danny quick shakes. He said, 'I'm Jack Shortell.'

He was at least fifty years old. Danny pointed to his name on the blackboard. 'A pleasure, Sergeant.'

'All mine, Deputy. Your first big job?'

'Yes.'

'I've worked half a dozen, so don't be too proud to yelp if you get stuck.'

'I won't be.'

Breuning and Shortell sat down a string of chairs over from Niles; Danny pointed to a table in front of the blackboard – three stacks of LAPD/LASD paper on the Goines/Wiltsie/Lindenaur snuffs. Nothing speculative from his personal file; nothing on the lead of Felix Gordean; nothing on Duane Lindenaur as a former extortionist. The men got out cigarettes and matches and fired up; Danny put the lectern between him and them and grabbed his first command.

'Most of what we've got is in there, gentlemen. Autopsy reports, log sheets, my summary reports as catching officer on the first victim. LAPD didn't see fit to forensic the apartment where the victims were killed, so there's some potential leads blown. Of the officers working the two separate jobs, I've been the only one to turn up hard leads. I wrote out a separate chronology on what I got, and included carbons in with your official stuff. I'll run through the key points for you now.'

Danny paused and looked straight at Gene Niles, who'd been staring hot pokers at him since he tweaked LAPD for fumbling the forensic ball. Niles would not move his eyes; Danny braced his legs into the lectern for some more frost. 'On the night of January one, I canvassed South Central Avenue, the vicinity where the car that was used to transport Martin Goines' body was stolen from. Eyewitnesses placed Goines with a tall, gray-haired, middle-aged man, and we know from the autopsy reports that the killer has O+ blood – typed from his semen. Goines was killed by a heroin overjolt, Wiltsie and Lindenaur were poisoned by a secobarbital/ strychnine compound. All three men were mutilated in the same manner – cuts from an implement known as a zoot stick, bites with the dentures the killer was wearing all over their abdominal areas. The dentures could not possibly be duplicates of human teeth. He could be wearing plastic teeth or duplicates of animal teeth or steel teeth – but not human ones.'

Danny took his eyes off Niles and scoped all three of his men. Breuning was smoking nervously; Shortell was taking notes; Big Gene was burning cigarette holes in the desktop. Danny looked at him exclusively and dropped his first lie. 'So we've got a tall, gray-haired, middle-aged white man with O+ blood who can cop horse and barbs, knows some chemistry and can hotwire cars. When he slammed the horse into Goines, he stuffed a towel into his mouth, which means that he knew the bastard's heart arteries would pop and he'd vomit blood. So maybe he's got medical knowledge. I'm betting he knows how to make dentures, and yesterday I got a tip from a snitch of mine: Goines was putting together a burglary gang. When you read my summary reports you'll see that I questioned a vagrant named Chester Brown, a jazz musician. He knew Marty Goines back in the early '40s and stated that he was a burglar then. Brown mentioned a youth with a burned face who was Goines' KA, but I don't think he fits in the picture. So add "burglar possible" to our scenario, and I'll tell you what we're going to do.

'Sergeant Shortell, you'll be making phone queries on the dental work lead. I've got a very long list of dental labs, and I want you to call them and get to whoever keeps employment records. You've got solid elimination stuff to go with: blood type, physical description, the dates of the killings. Also ask about dental workers who aroused *any* kind of suspicion at their workplace, and if your instincts tell you someone is suspicious but you've got no blood type, call for jail records or Selective Service records or hospital records – or call any place else you can think of where you can get the information.'

Shortell had nodded along, writing it down; Danny gave him a nod and zeroed in on Niles and Breuning. 'Sergeant Breuning and Sergeant Niles, you are to check every City, County and individual municipality Vice and sex crime file for biting aberrations and eliminate potential suspects against our man's blood type and description. I want the files of every registered sex offender in the LA area gone through. I want a more thorough background check on Wiltsie and Lindenaur, and Wiltsie's male prostitution jacket pulled for KAs with our guy's stats. I want you to cross-check the sex information against the burglary files of middle-aged white men city- and countywide, and look for arrest reports on youth burglars with burn marks going back to '43. For every possible you get, I want a set of mugshots.

'There's an approach that I've let lie because of jurisdictional problems, and that's where the mugs come in. I want every known heroin and goofball pusher to see those pictures – hard muscle shakedowns, especially in jigtown. I want you to shake down *your* snitches for information, call every Vice Squad commander in every

207

division, City and County, and tell them to have their officers check with their snitches for fruit bar scuttlebutt. Who's tall, gray, middle-aged and has a biting fetish? and I want you to call County and State Parole for dope on violent loony bin parolees. I want Griffith Park, South Central and the area where Goines' body was dumped thoroughly recanvassed.'

Breuning groaned; Niles spoke for the first time. 'You want a lot, Upshaw. You know that?'

Danny leaned over the lectern. 'It's an important case, and you'll share credit for the collar.'

Niles snorted. 'It's homo horseshit, we'll never get him, and if we did, so what? Do you care how many queers he cuts? I don't.'

Danny flinched at 'homo' and 'queers'; holding a stare on Niles made his eyes flicker, and he realized that he hadn't used the word 'homosexual' in his profile of the killer. 'I'm a policeman, so I care. And the job is good for our careers.'

'For *your* career, sonny. You've got some deal with some Jew DA downtown.'

'Niles, shitcan it!'

Danny looked around to see who shouted, felt his throat vibrating and saw that he'd gripped the lectern with blue-white fingers. Niles evil-eyed him; Danny couldn't match the stare. He thought of the rest of his pitch and delivered it, a trace of a flutter in his voice. 'Our last approach is pretty obscure. All three men were slashed by zoot sticks, which Doc Layman says Riot Squad cops used to use. There are no zoot stick homicides on record, and most zoot stick assaults were by Caucasians on Mexicans and not reported. Again, check with your informants on this and make your eliminations against blood type and description.'

Jack Shortell was still scribbling; Mike Breuning was looking up at him strangely, eyes narrowed to slits. Danny turned back to Niles. 'Got that, Sergeant?'

Niles had another cigarette going; he was scorching

his desk with the tip. 'You're really in tight with the Jews, huh, Upshaw? What's Mickey Kike paying you?'

'More than Brenda paid you.'

Shortell laughed; Breuning's strange look broke into a smile. Niles threw his cigarette on the floor and stamped it out. 'Why didn't you report your lead on Marty Goines' pad, hotshot? What the fuck was happening there?'

Danny's hands snapped a piece of wood off the lectern. He said, 'Dismissed,' with some other man's voice.

Considine and Smith were waiting for him in Ellis Loew's office; big Dudley was hanging up a phone with the words, 'Thank you, lad.' Danny sat down at Loew's conference table, sensing the 'lad' was flunky Mike Breuning with a report on his briefing.

Considine was busy writing on a yellow legal pad; Smith came over and gave him the glad hand. 'How was your first morning as Homicide brass, lad?'

Danny knew he knew – verbatim. 'It went well, Lieutenant.'

'Call me Dudley. You'll be outranking me in a few years, and you should get used to patronizing men much your senior.'

'Okay, Dudley.'

Smith laughed. 'Lad, you're a heartbreaker. Isn't he a heartbreaker, Malcolm?'

Considine slid his chair next to Danny. 'Let's hope Claire De Haven thinks so. How are you, Deputy?'

Danny said, 'I'm fine, Lieutenant,' picking up something wrong between his superiors – contempt or plain tension working two ways – Dudley Smith in the catbird seat.

'Good. The briefing went well, then?'

'Yes.'

'Have you read that paperwork we gave you?'

'I've got it practically memorized.'

Considine tapped his pad. 'Excellent. We'll start now, then.'

Dudley Smith sat at the far end of the table; Danny geared his brain to listen and *think* before speaking. Considine said, 'Here's some rules for you to follow.

'One, you drive your civilian car everywhere, on your decoy job *and* your homicide job. We're building an identity for you, and we'll have a script ready by late tonight. You're going to be a lefty who's been living in New York for years, so we've got New York plates for your car, and we've got a whole personal background for you to memorize. When you go by your various station houses to check reports or whatever, park on the street at least two blocks away, and when you leave here, go downstairs to the barbershop. Al, Mayor Bowron's barber, is going to get rid of that crew cut of yours and cut your hair so that you look less like a cop. I need your trouser, shirt, jacket, sweater and shoe sizes, and I want you to meet me at midnight at West Hollywood Station. I'll have your new Commie wardrobe and script ready, and we'll finalize your approach. Got it?'

Danny nodded, pulled a sheet of paper off Considine's pad and wrote down his clothing sizes. Dudley Smith said, 'You wear those clothes everywhere, lad. On your queer job, too. We don't want your new Pinko friends seeing you on the street looking like a dapper young copper. Malcolm, give our fair Daniel some De Haven lines to parry. Let's see how he fields them.'

Considine spoke directly to Danny. 'Deputy, I've met Claire De Haven, and I think that for a woman she's a tough piece of work. She's promiscuous, she may be an alcoholic and she may take drugs. We've got another man checking out her background and the background of some other Reds, so we'll know more on her soon. I spoke to the woman once, and I got the impression that she thrives on banter and one-upmanship. I think that it sexually excites her, and I know she's attracted to men of your general appearance. So we're going to try a little exercise now. I'll feed you lines that I think would be typical of Claire De Haven, you try to top them. Ready?'

Danny shut his eyes for better concentration. 'Go.'

' "But some people call us Communists. Doesn't that bother you?" '

'That old scarlet letter routine doesn't wash with me.'

'Good. Let's follow up on that. "Oh, really? Fascist politicians have ruined many politically enlightened people by slandering us as subversives." '

Danny grabbed a line from a musical he saw with Karen Hiltscher. 'I've always had a thing for redheads, baby.'

Considine laughed. 'Good, but don't call De Haven "baby," she'd consider it patronizing. Here's a good one. "I find it hard to believe that you'd leave the Teamsters for us." '

Easy. 'Mickey Cohen's comedy routines would drive anybody out.'

'Good, Deputy, but in your decoy role you'd never get close to Cohen, so you wouldn't know that about him.'

Danny got a brainstorm: the dirty joke sheets and pulp novels his fellow jailers passed around when he worked the main County lockup. 'Give me some sex banter, Lieutenant.'

Considine flipped to the next note page. ' "But I'm thirteen years older than you." '

Danny made his tone satirical. 'A grain of sand in our sea of passion.'

Dudley Smith howled; Considine chuckled and said, 'You just walk into my life when I'm engaged to be married. I don't know that I trust you.'

'Claire, there's only one reason *to* trust me. And that's that around you I don't trust myself.'

'Great delivery, Deputy. Here's a curveball: "Are you here for me or the cause?" '

Extra easy: the hero of a paperback he'd read working night watch. 'I want it all. That's all I know, that's all I want to know.'

Considine slid the notebook away. 'Let's improvise on that. "How can you look at things so simplistically?" '

His mental gears were click-click-clicking now; Danny

211

quit digging for lines and flew solo. 'Claire, there's the fascists and us, and there's you and me. Why do *you* always complicate things?'

Considine, coming on like a femme fatale. ' "You know I'm capable of eating you whole." '

'I love your teeth.'

' "I love your eyes." '

'Claire, are we fighting the fascists or auditing Physiology 101?'

' "When you're forty, I'll be fifty three. Will you still want me then?" '

Danny, aping Considine's vamp contralto. 'We'll be dancing jigs together in Moscow, sweetheart.'

'Not so satirical on the political stuff, I'm not sure I trust her sense of humour on that. Let's get dirty. "It's so *good* with you." '

'The others were just girls, Claire. You're my first woman.'

' "How many times have you used that line?" '

Aw-shucks laughter – à la a pussy hound deputy he knew. 'Every time I sleep with a woman over thirty-five.'

' "Have there been many?" '

'Just a few thousand.'

' "The cause needs men like you." '

'If there were more women like you around, there'd be millions of us.'

' "What's that supposed to mean?" '

'That I really like you, Claire.'

' "Why?" '

'You drink like one of the boys, you know Marx chapter and verse, and you've got great legs.'

Dudley Smith started clapping; Danny opened his eyes and felt them misting. Mal Considine smiled. 'She does have great legs. Go get your haircut, Deputy. I'll see you at midnight.'

Mayor Bowron's barber shaped Danny's outgrown crew cut into a modified pompadour that changed the whole set of his face. Before, he looked like what he was: a dark-haired, dark-eyed Anglo-Saxon, a policeman who wore suits or sports jacket/slacks combos everywhere. Now he looked slightly Bohemian, slightly Latin, more of a dude. The new hairstyle offset his clothes rakishly; any cop who didn't know him and spotted the gun bulge under his left armpit would shake him down on the spot, figuring him for some kind of outlaw muscle. The look and his banter improvisations made him feel cocky, like the Chateau Marmont was a fluke that nailing Claire De Haven would disprove once and for all. Danny drove back to Hollywood Station to prepare for his second pass at the Marmont and his first shot at Felix Gordean.

He went straight to the squadroom. Mickey Cohen was vilified on the walls: cartoons of him stuffing cash in Sheriff Biscailuz' pockets, cracking a whip at a team of sled dogs in LASD uniforms, poking innocent citizens in the ass with a switchblade sticking out of his prayer cap. Danny fielded an assortment of fisheyes, found the records alcove and hit the sex offender files – shaking hands with the beast – fuel for his Gordean interrogation.

There were six cabinets full of them: musty folders stuffed with occurrence reports, mugshots clipped to the first inner page. The filing was not alphabetical, and there was no logic to the penal code placements – homosexual occurrences were lumped with straight exhibitionism and child molestation; misdemeanants and felons brushed against each other. Danny scanned the first two files in the top cabinet and snapped why the system was so sloppy: the men on the squad wanted this wretched data out of sight and out of mind. Knowing he *had* to look, he dug in.

Most of the stuff was homo.

The Broadway Departemnt Store on Hollywood and Vine had a fourth-floor men's room known as 'Cocksucker's Paradise.' Enterprising deviants had bored holes through the walls of the toilet stalls, enabling the occupants of adjoining shitters to get together for oral copulation. If you parked on a Griffith Park roadway with a blue handkerchief tied to your radio aerial, you were a queer. The corner of Selma and Las Palmas was where ex-cons with a penchant for anal rape and young boys congregated. The Latin inscription on the Pall Mall cigarette pack – 'In Hoc Signo Vinces' – translated as 'With this sign we shall conquer' – was a tentative means of homo identification – a sure thing when coupled with wearing a green shirt on a Thursday. The muscular Mex transvestite who blew sailors behind Grauman's Chinese was known as 'Donkey Dan' or 'Donkey Danielle' because he/she possessed a thirteen-inch dick. The E-Z Cab Company was run by homos, and they would deliver you a boy, queer smut films, extra KY Jelly, bennies, or your favourite liquor twenty-four hours a day.

Danny kept reading, weak in the knees and stomach, learning. When he saw a 1900–1910 birthdate or 6' and up on a male Caucasian's yellow sheet, he checked the mugstrip; every man he locked eyes with looked too ugly and pathetic to be *his* man – and prowling the ensuing arrest reports for blood types always proved him right. Thomas (NMI) Milnes, 6'2", 11/4/07, exposed himself to little boys and begged the arresting officers to rubber-hose him for it; Cletus Wardell Hanson, 6'1", 4/29/04, carried a power drill with him to pave the way for new blow job territory, restaurant men's rooms his speciality. In stir, he put his ass on the line: day room gang bangs, a pack of cigarettes per man. Willis (NMI) Burdette, 6'5", 12/1/1900, was a syphilitic street whore, beaten brainless by a half dozen johns he'd passed the disease to. Darryl 'Lavender Blue' Wishnick, 6', 3/10/03, orchestrated orgies in the hills surrounding the Hollywood Sign and liked to pork pretty boys dressed in the attire of the United States armed forces.

Four hours in, four cabinets down. Danny felt his stomach settling around hunger pangs and the desire for a drink he usually got in the mid-afternoon. That was comforting; so was the new hairstyle he kept running his fingers through, and the new embellishments on his new identity that he'd mention to Considine tonight: nothing at his apartment should seem settled – he was just in from New York; he should leave his piece, cuffs and ID buzzer at home when he played Commie. Everything in the first four drawers was wrong for his man, not applicable to his bad moments outside Felix Gordean's window. Then he hit cabinet five.

This set of files was in some kind of order – 'No Arraignments,' 'Charges Dropped' or 'Check Agst. Future Arrests' stamped on the front of each folder. Danny read through the first handful and got straight male-on-male sex that went to arrest but not to court: coitus interruptus in parked cars; male shack jobs snitched by shocked landladies; a toilet assignation where the theater proprietor blew the whistle, then punked out for fear of bad publicity. Straight sex recounted in straight copese: abbreviations, technical terms for the acts, a few humorous asides by waggish Vice officers.

Danny felt shakes coming on. The files carried twin yellow sheets – two mugshot strips, both sex participants in black and white. He eyed the pages for birthdates and physical stats, but kept returning to the mugs, superimposing them against each other, playing with the faces – making them prettier, less conwise. After a half dozen files, he fell into sync: a look at the photos, a scan of the arrest report, back to the mugs and the action visualized with prettified versions of the two plug-uglies clipped to the first page. Mouths on mouths; mouths to crotches; sodomy, fellatio, soixante-neuf, a Man Camera smut job, a little voice going, 'It's for the investigation' when some detail hit him so large that his stomach queased to the point where he thought his bowels would go. *No* middle-aged tall guy's stats to make him stop and think; just the pictures, rapid fire, like nickelodeon flickers.

Bedspreads wet from fucking.

A naked blond man catching his breath, veins pumping in his legs.

Zoom-in shots of awful insertions.

'It's for the investigation.'

Danny broke the string of images – making the pretty ones all gray, all forty-fivish, all his killer. Knowing the killer only had sex to hurt helped put the brakes on his fantasies; Danny got his legs back and saw that he'd twisted a lank of his new hairdo clean off his scalp. He slammed the cabinet shut; he recalled queer vernacular and interposed it into the questions he'd ask Felix Gordean – himself as a smart young detective who came prepared, who'd talk on the level of anyone – even if it was wrong sex to a queer pimp.

Cop to voyeur and back again.

Danny drove home, showered and checked his closet for the best suit to go with his new hair, settling on a black worsted Karen Hiltscher had bought him – too stylish, too tapered and skinny in the lapels. When he put it on, he saw that it made him look dangerous – and the narrow shoulders outlined his .45 revolver. After two shots and a mouthwash chaser, he drove to the Chateau Marmont.

The night was damp and chilly, hinting of rain; music echoed through the Marmont's inner courtyard – string swells, boogie jumps and odd ballad tremolos. Danny took the footpath to 7941, chafing from the fit of Karen's suit. 7941 was brightly lit, the velvet curtain he'd peered through open wide; the dance floor of three nights before gleamed behind a large picture window. Danny fidgeted with his jacket and rang the bell.

Chimes sounded; the door opened. A small man with a short dark beard and perfectly layered thin hair stood there. He was wearing a tuxedo with a tartan cummerbund, dangling a brandy snifter against his leg. Danny smelled the same fifty-year-old Napoleon he bought himself once a year as his reward for spending Christmas with his mother. The man said, 'Yes? Are you with the Sheriff's?'

Danny saw that he'd unbuttoned his coat, leaving his gun exposed. 'Yes. Are you Felix Gordean?'

'Yes, and I don't appreciate bureaucratic faux pas. Come in.'

Gordean stood aside; Danny walked in and ran eye circuits of the room where he'd glimpsed men dancing and kissing. Gordean moved to a bookcase, reached behind the top shelf and returned with an envelope. Danny caught an address: 1611 South Bonnie Brae, the Sheriff's Central Vice operations front, where recalcitrant bookies got strong-armed, recalcitrant hookers got serviced, protections kickbacks got tallied. Gordean said, 'I always mail it in. Tell Lieutenant Matthews I don't appreciate in-person calls with their implied threat of additional charges.'

Danny let Gordean's hand hover in front of him – buffed nails, an emerald ring and probably close to a grand in cash. 'I'm not a bagman, I'm a detective working a triple homicide.'

Gordean smiled and held the envelope down at his side. 'Then let me initiate you regarding my relationship with your Department, Mr. – '

'It's Deputy Upshaw.'

'Mr. Upshaw, I cooperate fully with the Sheriff's Department in exchange for certain courtesies, chief among them your contacting me by telephone when you require information. Do you understand?'

Danny got a strange sensation: Gordean's frost was making him frosty. 'Yes, but as long as I'm here . . .'

'As long as you're here, tell me how I can assist you. I've never been questioned on a triple homicide before, and frankly I'm curious.'

Danny speedballed his three victims' names. 'Martin Goines, George Wiltsie and Duane Lindenaur. Dead. Raped and hacked to death.'

Gordean's reaction was more frost. 'I've never heard of a Martin Goines. I brokered introductions for George Wiltsie throughout the years, and I think George mentioned Duane Lindenaur to me.'

Danny felt like he was treading on an iceberg; he knew going in for shock value wouldn't play. 'Duane

Lindenaur was an extortionist, Mr. Gordean. He met and attempted to exort money from a man named Charles Hartshorn – who allegedly met at a party you threw.'

Gordean smoothed his tuxedo lapels. 'I know Hartshorn, but I don't recall actually meeting Lindenaur. And I throw a lot of parties. When was this alleged one?'

'In '40 or '41.'

'That's a long time ago. You're staring at me very acutely, Mr. Upshaw. Is there a reason for that?'

Danny touched his own lapels, caught what he was doing and stopped. 'I usually get at least a "my God" or a twitch when I tell someone that an acquaintance of theirs has been murdered. You didn't bat an eye.'

'And you find that dismaying?'

'No.'

'Curious?'

'Yes.'

'Am I an actual suspect in these killings?'

'No, you don't fit my description of the killer.'

'Do you require alibis for me to further assert my innocence?'

Danny snapped that he was being sized up by an expert. 'All right. New Year's Eve and the night of January fourth. Where were you?'

Not a second's hesitation. 'I was here, hosting well-attended parties. If you require verification, please have Lieutenant Matthews do it for you – we're old friends.'

Danny saw flashes of *his* party: black-on-black tangos framed in velvet. He flinched and stuffed his hands in his pockets; Gordean's eyes flicked at the show of nerves. Danny said, 'Tell me about George Wiltsie.'

Gordean walked to a liquor cabinet, filled two glasses and returned with them. Danny smelled the good stuff and jammed his hands down deeper so he wouldn't grab. 'Tell me about George Wilt – '

'George Wiltsie was a masculine image that a number of men found enticing. I paid him to attend my parties, dress well and act civilized. He made liaisons here, and

I received fees from those men. I imagine that Duane Lindenaur was his lover. That's all I know about George Wiltsie.'

Danny took the glass Gordean was offering – something to do with his hands. 'Who did you fix Wiltsie up with?'

'I don't recall.'

'You *what?*'

'I host parties, guests come and meet the young men I provide, money is discreetly sent to me. Many of my clients are married men with families, and keeping a blank memory is an extra service I provide them.'

The glass was shaking in Danny's hand. 'Do you expect me to believe that?'

Gordean sipped brandy. 'No, but I expect you to accept that answer as all you are going to get.'

'I want to see the books for your service, and I want to see a client list.'

'No. I write nothing down. It might be considered pandering, you see.'

'Then name names.'

'No, and don't ask again.'

Danny forced himself to barely touch his lips to the glass; barely taste the brandy. He swirled the liquid and sniffed it, two fingers circling the stem – and stopped when he saw he was imitating Gordean. 'Mr. Gor – '

'Mr. Upshaw, we've reached an impasse. So let me suggest a compromise. You said that I don't fit your killer's description. Very well, describe your killer to me, and I will try to recall if George Wiltsie went with a man like that. If he did, I will forward the information to Lieutenant Matthews, and he can do with it what he likes. Will that satisfy you?'

Danny bolted his drink – thirty-dollar private stock guzzled. The brandy burned going down; the fire put a rasp on his voice. 'I've got the LAPD with me on this case, and the DA's Bureau. They might not like you hiding behind a crooked Vice cop.'

Gordean smiled – very slightly. 'I won't tell Lieutenant Matthews you said that, nor will I tell Al Dietrich the next time I send him and Sheriff Biscailuz passes to play golf at my club. And I have *good* friends with both the LAPD and the Bureau. Another drink, Mr. Upshaw?'

Danny counted to himself – one, two, three, four – the kibosh on a hothead play. Gordean took his glass, moved to the bar, poured a refill and came back wearing a new smile – older brother looking to put younger brother at ease. 'You know the game, Deputy. For God's sake quit coming on like an indignant boy scout.'

Danny ignored the brandy and sighted in on Gordean's eyes for signs of fear. 'White, forty-five to fifty, slender. Over six feet tall, with an impressive head of silver hair.'

No fear; a thoughtful scrunching up of the forehead. Gordean said, 'I recall a tall, dark-haired man from the Mexican Consulate going with George, but he was fifty-ish during the war. I remember several rather rotund men finding George attractive, and I know that he went regularly with a very tall man with red hair. Does that help you?'

'No. What about men in general of that description? Are there any who frequent your parties or regularly use your service?'

Another thoughtful look. Gordean said, 'It's the impressive head of hair that tears it. The only tall, middle-aged men I deal with are quite balding. I'm sorry.'

Danny thought, no you're not – but you're probably telling the truth. He said, 'What did Wiltsie tell you about Lindenaur?'

'Just that they were living together.'

'Did you know that Lindenaur attempted to extort money from Charles Hartshorn?'

'No.'

'Have you heard of either Wiltsie or Lindenaur pulling other extortion deals?'

'No, I have not.'

'What about blackmail in general? Men like your clients are certainly susceptible to it.'

Felix Gordean laughed. 'My clients come to my parties and use my service because I insulate them from things like that.'

Danny laughed. 'You didn't insulate Charles Hartshorn too well.'

'Charles was never lucky – in love or politics. He's also not a killer. Question him if you don't believe me, but be courteous, Charles has a low threshold for abuse and he has much legal power.'

Gordean was holding out the glass of brandy; Danny took it and knocked the full measure back. 'What about enemies of Wiltsie and Lindenaur, known associates, guys they ran with?'

'I don't know anything about that sort of thing.'

'Why not?'

'I try to keep things separate and circumscribed.'

'Why?'

'To avoid situations like this.'

Danny felt the brandy coming on, kicking in with the shots he'd had at home. 'Mr. Gordean, are you a homosexual?'

'No, Deputy. Are you?'

Danny flushed, raised his glass and found it empty. He resurrected a crack from his briefing with Considine. 'That old scarlet letter routine doesn't wash with me.'

Gordean said, 'I don't quite understand the reference, Deputy.'

'It means that I'm a professional, and I can't be shocked.'

'Then you shouldn't blush so easily – your color betrays you as a naif.'

The empty glass felt like a missile to heave; Danny hit back on 'naif' instead. 'We're talking about three people dead. Cut up with a fucking zoot stick, eyes poked out, intestines chewed on. We're talking about blackmail and burglary and jazz and guys with burned-

221

up faces, and you think you can hurt me by calling *me* naif? You think you – '

Danny stopped when he saw Gordean's jaw tensing. The man stared down at the floor; Danny wondered if he'd stabbed a nerve or just hit him on simple revulsion. 'What is it? Tell me.'

Gordean looked up. 'I'm sorry. I have a low threshold for brash young policemen and descriptions of violence, and I shouldn't have called – '

'Then help me. Show me your client list.'

'No. I told you I don't keep a list.'

'Then tell me what bothered you so much.'

'I did tell you.'

'And I don't feature you as that sensitive. So tell me.'

Gordean said, 'When you mentioned jazz, it made me think of a client, a horn player that I used to broker introductions to rough trade to. He impressed me as volatile then, but he's not tall or middle-aged.'

'And that's *all*?'

'Cy Vandrich, Deputy. Your tactics have gotten you more than I would normally have been willing to part with, so be grateful.'

'And that's *all?*'

Gordean's eyes were blank, giving nothing up. 'No. Direct all your future inquiries through Lieutenant Matthews and learn to sip fine brandy – you'll enjoy it more.'

Danny tossed his crystal snifter on a Louis XIV chair and walked out.

An hour and a half to kill before his meeting with Considine; more liquor out of the question. Danny drove to Coffee Bob's and forced down a hamburger and pie, wondering how much of the Gordean questioning slipped between the cracks: his own nerves, the pimp's police connections and savoir faire. The food calmed him down, but didn't answer his questions; he hit a pay phone and got dope on Cy Vandrich.

There was only one listed with DMV/R&I: Cyril 'Cy' Vandrich, WM, DOB 7/24/18, six arrests for petty theft, employment listed as 'transient' and 'musician.' Currently on his sixth ninety-day observation jolt at the Camarillo loony bin. A follow-up call to the bin revealed that Vandrich kept pulling crazy man stunts when he got rousted for shoplifting; that the Misdemeanor Court judge kept recommending Camarillo. The desk woman told Danny that Vandrich was in custody there on the two killing nights; that he made himself useful teaching music to the nuts. Danny said that he might come up to question the man; the woman said that Vandrich might or might not be in control of his faculties – no one at the bin had ever been able to figure him out – whether he was malingering or seriously crazy. Danny hung up and drove to West Hollywood Station to meet Mal Considine.

The man was waiting for him in his cubicle, eyeing the Buddy Jastrow mug blowup. Danny cleared his throat; Considine wheeled around and gave him a closer once-over. 'I like the suit. It doesn't quite fit, but it looks like something a young lefty might affect. Did you buy it for your assignment?'

'No, Lieutenant.'

'Call me Mal. I want you to get out of the habit of using rank. *Ted.*'

Danny sat down behind his desk and pointed Considine to the spare chair. 'Ted?'

Considine took the seat and stretched his legs. 'As of today, you're Ted Krugman. Dudley went by your apartment house and talked to the manager, and when you get home tonight you'll find T. Krugman on your mailbox. Your phone number is now listed under Theodore Krugman, so we're damn lucky you kept it unlisted before. There's a paper bag waiting for you with the manager – your new wardrobe, some fake ID and New York plates for your car. You like it?'

Danny thought of Dudley Smith inside his apartment, maybe discovering his private file. 'Sure, Lieut – Mal.'

Considine laughed. 'No, you don't – it's all happening too fast. You're Homicide brass, you're a Commie

223

decoy, you're a big-time comer. You're *made*, kid. I hope you know that.'

Danny caught glee wafting off the DA's man; he decided to hide his file boxes and blood spray pics behind the rolled-up carpet in his hall closet. 'I do, but I don't want to get fat on it. When do I make my approach?'

'Day after tomorrow. I think we've got the UAES lulled with our newspaper and radio plants, and Dudley and I are going to concentrate on lefties outside the union – KAs of the brain trusters – vulnerable types that we should be able to get to snitch. We're going over INS records for deportation levers on them, and Ed Satterlee is trying to get us some hot SLDC pictures from a rival clearance group. Call it a two-front war. Dudley and I on outside evidence, you inside.'

Danny saw Considine as all frayed nerves; he saw that *his* suit fit him like a tent, the jacket sleeves riding up over soiled shirtcuffs and long, skinny arms. 'How do I get inside?'

Considine pointed to a folder atop the cubicle's Out basket. 'It's all in there. You're Ted Krugman, DOB 6/16/23, a Pinko New York stagehand. In reality you were killed in a car wreck on Long Island two months ago. The local Feds hushed it up and sold the identity to Ed Satterlee. All your past history and KAs are in there. There's surveillance pictures of the Commie KAs, and there's twenty-odd pages of Marxist claptrap, a little history lesson for you to memorize.

'So, day after tomorrow, around two, you go to the Gower Street picket line, portraying a Pinko who's lost his faith. You tell the Teamster picket boss that the day labor joint downtown sent you out, muscle for a buck an hour. The man knows who you are, and he'll set you up to picket with two other guys. After an hour or so, you'll get into political arguments with those guys – per the script I've written out for you. A third argument will result in a fistfight with a real bruiser – a PT instructor at the LAPD Academy. He'll pull his punches, but you fight for real. You're going to take a few lumps, but what the hell. Another Teamster man will shout obscenities about you to the UAES picket boss, who'll hopefully approach you and lead you to Claire De Haven, UAES's member screener. We've done a lot of homework, and we can't directly place Krugman with any UAESers. You look vaguely like him and at worst you'll be secondhand heard of. It's all in that folder, kid. Pictures of the men you'll be pulling this off with, everything.'

A clean day to work the homicides; a full night to become Ted Krugman. Danny said, 'Tell me about Claire De Haven.'

Considine countered, 'Have you got a girlfriend?'

Danny started to say no, then remembered the bogus paramour who helped him brazen out Tamarind. 'Nothing serious. Why?'

'Well, I don't know how susceptible you are to women in general, but De Haven's a presence. Buzz Meeks just filed a report that makes her as a longtime hophead – H and drugstore – but she's still formidable – and she's damn good at getting what she wants out of men. So I want to make sure you seduce her, not the opposite. Does that answer your question?'

'No.'

'Do you want a physical description?'

'No.'

'The odds that you'll have to lay her?'

'No.'

'Do you want her sexual background?'

Danny threw his question out before he could back down. 'No. I want to know why a ranking policeman has a crush on a Commie socialite.'

Considine blushed pink – the way Felix Gordean told him *he* blushed; Danny tried reading his face and caught: *got me*. Call-me-Mal laughed, slid off his wedding band and tossed it in the wastebasket. He said, 'Man to man?'

Danny said, 'No, brass to brass.'

Considine made the sign of the cross on his vestfront. 'Ashes to ashes, and not bad for a minister's son. Let's just say I'm susceptible to dangerous women, and my wife is divorcing me, so I can't chase around and give her ammo to use in court. I want custody of my son, and I will not give her one shred of evidence to spoil my case. And I don't usually offer my confessions to junior officers.'

Danny thought: this man is so far out on a limb that you can say anything to him and he'll stick around – because at 1:00 A.M. he's got no place fucking else to go. 'And *that's* why you're getting such a kick out of operating De Haven?'

Considine smiled and tapped the top desk drawer. 'Why am I betting there's a bottle in here?'

Danny felt himself blush. 'Because you're smart?'

The hand kept tapping. 'No, because your nerves are right up there with mine, and because you always stink of Lavoris. Brass to rookie, here's a lesson: cops who smell of mouthwash are juicers. And juicer cops who can keep it on a tight leash are usually pretty good cops.'

'Pretty good cops' flashed a green light. Danny nudged Considine's hand away, opened the drawer and pulled out a pint and two paper cups. He poured quadruple shots and offered; Considine accepted with a bow; they hoisted drinks. Danny said, 'To both our cases'; Considine toasted, 'To Stefan Heisteke Considine.' Danny drank, warmed head to toe, drank: Considine sipped and hooked a thumb over his back at Harlan 'Buddy' Jastrow. 'Upshaw, who is this guy? And why are you so bent out of shape on your goddamn homo killings?'

Danny locked eyes with Jastrow. 'Buddy's the guy I used to want to get, the guy who used to be the worst, the hardest nut to crack because he was just plain nowhere. Now there's this other thing, and it's just plain terror. It's incredibly brutal, and I think it might be random, but I don't quite go with that. I think I'm dealing with revenge. I think all the killer's methods are reenactments, all the mutilations are symbolic of him trying to get his past straight in his mind. I keep thinking it all out, and I keep coming back to revenge on old wrongs. Not everyday childhood trauma shit, but big, big stuff.'

Danny paused, drank and sighted in on the mugboard around Jastrow's neck: Kern County Jail, 3/4/38. 'Sometimes I think that if I know who this guy is and why he does it, then I'll know something so big that I'll be able to figure out all the everyday stuff like cake. I can get on with making rank and handling meat and potatoes stuff, because everything I ever sensed about what people are capable of came together on one job, and I nailed *why*. *Why*. Fucking *why*.'

Considine's, 'And why you do what you do yourself,' was very soft. Danny looked away from Jastrow and killed his drink. 'Yeah, and that. And why you're so hopped on Claire De Haven and me. And don't say out of patriotism.'

Considine laughed. 'Kid, would you buy patriotism if I told you the grand jury guarantees me a captaincy, Chief DA's Investigator and the prestige to keep my son?'

'Yeah, but there's still De Haven and – '

'Yeah, and me. Let's just put it this way. I have to know why, too, only I like going at it once removed. Satisfied?'

'No.'

'I didn't think you would be.'

'Do you *know* why?'

Considine sipped bourbon. 'It wasn't hard to figure out.'

'I used to steal cars, Lieut – Mal. I was the ace car thief of San Berdoo County right before the war. Turnabout?'

Lieutenant Mal Considine stuck out a long leg and hooked the wastebasket over to his chair. He rummaged in it, found his wedding band and slipped it on. 'I've got a confab with my lawyer for the custody case tomorrow, and I'm sure he'll want me to keep wearing this fucking thing.'

Danny leaned forward. 'Turnabout, Captain?'

Considine stood up and stretched. 'My brother used

227

to blackmail me, threaten to rat me to the old man every time I said something snotty about religion. Since ten strokes with a switch was the old man's punishment for blasphemy, old Desmond pretty much got his way, which was usually me breaking into houses to steal stuff he wanted. So let's put it this way: I saw a lot of things that were pretty swell, and some things that were pretty spooky, and I liked it. So it was either become a burglar or a spy, and policeman seemed like a good compromise. And sending in the spies appealed to me more than doing it myself, sort of like Desmond in the catbird seat.'

Danny stood up. 'I'm going to nail De Haven for you. Trust me on that.'

'I don't doubt it, Ted.'

'In vino veritas, right?'

'Sure, and one more thing. I'll be Chief of Police or something else that large before too long, and I'm taking you with me.'

CHAPTER NINETEEN

Mal woke up thinking of Danny Upshaw.

Rolling out of bed, he looked at the four walls of Room 11, the Shangri-Lodge Motel. One framed magazine cover per wall – Norman Rockwell testimonials to happy family life. A stack of his soiled suits by the door – and no Stefan to run them to the dry cleaners. The memo corkboard he'd erected, one query tag standing out: locate Doc Lesnick. The fink/shrink could not be reached either at home or at his office and the 1942–1944 gaps in Reynolds Loftis' file had to be explained; he needed a general psych overview of the brain trusters now that their decoy was about to be in place, and all the files ended in the late summer of last year – why?

And the curtains were cheesecloth gauze; the rug was

as threadbare as a tortilla; the bathroom door was scrawled over with names and phone numbers – 'Sinful Cindy, DU–4927, 38–24–38, loves to fuck and suck' – worth a jingle – if he ever ran Vice raids again. And Dudley Smith was due in twenty minutes good guy/bad guy as today's ticket: two Pinko screenwriters who avoided HUAC subpoenas because they always wrote under pseudonyms and blew the country when the shit hit the fan in '47. They had been located by Ed Satterlee operatives – private eyes on the Red Crosscurrents payroll – and both men knew the UAES bigshots intimately back in the late '30s, early '40s.

And getting so chummy with an underling was strange. A couple of shared drinks and they were spilling their guts to each other – bad chain of command policy – ambitious policemen should keep it zipped while they climbed the ladder.

Mal showered, shaved and dressed, running book – De Haven versus Upshaw, even money as his best bet. At 8:30 exactly a car horn honked; he walked outside and saw Dudley leaning against his Ford. 'Good morning, Malcolm! Isn't it a grand day!'

The drove west on Wilshire, Mal silent, Dudley talking politics. '. . . I've been juxtaposing the Communist way of life against ours, and I keep coming back to family as the backbone of American life. Do you believe that, Malcolm?'

Mal knew that Loew had filled him in on Celeste – and that as far as partners went, he could have worse – like Buzz Meeks. 'It has its place.'

'I'd be a bit more emphatic on that, given the trouble you're taking to get your son back. Is it going well with your lawyer?'

Mal thought of his afternoon appointment with Jake Kellerman. 'He's going to try to get me continuances until the grand jury is in session and making hay. I have the preliminary in a couple of days, and we'll start putting the stall in then.'

Dudley lit a cigarette and steered with one pinky. 'Yes, a crusading captain might convince the judge that water is thicker than blood. You know, lad, that I've a wife and five daughters. They serve well to keep the reins on certain unruly aspects of my nature. If he can keep them in perspective, a family is an essential thing for a man to have.'

Mal rolled down his window. 'I have no perspective where my son is concerned. But if I can keep you in perspective until the grand jury convenes, then I'll be in *grand* shape.'

Dudley Smith exhaled laughter and smoke. 'I'm fond of you, Malcolm – even though you don't reciprocate. And speaking of family, I've a little errand to run – my niece needs a talking-to. Would you mind a small detour to Westwood?'

'A brief detour, Lieutenant?'

'Very, Lieutenant.'

Mal nodded; Dudley turned north on Glendon and headed up toward the UCLA campus, parking in a meter space on Sorority Row. Setting the brake, he said, 'Mary Margaret, my sister Brigid's girl. Twenty-nine years old and on her third masters degree because she's afraid to go out and meet the world. Sad, isn't it?'

Mal sighed. 'Tragic.'

'The very thing I was thinking, but without your emphasis on sarcasm. And speaking of youths, what's your opinion of our young colleague Upshaw?'

'I think he's smart and going places. Why?'

'Well, lad, friends of mine say that he has no sense of his own place, and he impresses me as weak and ambitious, which I view as a dangerous combination in a policeman.'

Mal's first thought of rising: He shouldn't have confided in the kid, because half his juice was front just waiting to crack. 'Dudley, what do you want?'

'Communism vanquished. And why don't you enjoy the sight of comely young coeds while I speak to my niece?'

Mal followed Dudley up the steps of a Spanish manse fronted by a lawn display: Greek symbols sunk into the grass on wood stakes. The door was open; the lounge area buzzed: girls smoking, talking and gesturing at text-books. Dudley pointed upstairs and said, 'Toot sweet'; Mal saw a stack of magazines on an end table and sat down to read, fielding curious looks from the coeds. He thumbed through a *Collier's*, a *Newsweek* and two *Life*'s – stopping when he heard Dudley's brogue, enraged, echoing down the second-floor hallway.

It got louder and scarier, punctuated by pleas in a whimpering soprano. The girls looked at Mal; he grabbed another magazine and tried to read. Dudley's laughter took over – spookier than the bellows. The coeds were staring now; Mal dropped his *Weekly Sportsman* and walked upstairs to listen.

The hallway was long and lined with narrow wooden doors; Mal followed Ha! Ha! Ha! to a door with 'Conroy' nameplated on the front. It was ajar a few inches; he looked in on a back wall lined with photos of Latino prizefighters. Dudley and the soprano were out of sight; Mal eavesdropped.

'. . . bull banks and piñatas and spic bantomweights. It's a fixation, lassie. Your mother may lack the stomach to set you straight, but I don't.'

The soprano, groveling, 'But Ricardo is a lovely boy, Uncle Dud. And I – '

A huge hand flashed across Mal's strip of vision, a slap turned to a caress, a head of curly red hair jerking into, then out of sight. 'You're not to say you love him, lassie. Not in my presence. Your parents are weak, and they expect me to have a say regarding the men in your life. I will always exercise that say, lassie. Just remember the trouble I spared you before and you'll be grateful.'

A plump girl/woman backed into view, hands on her face, sobbing. Dudley Smith's arms went around her; her hands turned to fists to keep him from completing the embrace. Dudley murmured sweet nothings; Mal walked back to the car and waited. His partner showed up five minutes later. 'Knock, knock, who's there? Dudley Smith, so Reds beware! Lad, shall we go impress Mr. Nathan Eisler with the righteousness of our cause?'

Eisler's last known address was 11681 Presidio, a short run from the UCLA campus. Dudley hummed show tunes as he drove; Mal kept seeing his hand about to hit, the niece cowering from her genial uncle's touch. 11681 was a small pink prefab at the end of a long prefab block; Dudley double-parked, Mal jammed facts from Satterlee's report:

Nathan Eisler. Forty-nine years old. A German Jew who fled Hitler and company in '34; CP member '36 to '40, then member of a half dozen Commie front organizations. Co-scenarist on a string of pro-Russki turkeys, his writing partner Chaz Minear; poker buddies with Morton Ziffkin and Reynolds Loftis. Wrote under pseudonyms to guard his professional privacy; slipped through the HUAC investigators' hands; currently living under the alias Michael Kaukenen, the name of the hero of *Storm Over Leningrad*. Currently scripting RKO B westerns, under yet another monicker, the work fronted by a politically acceptable hack writer who glommed a 35 percent cut. Best pals with Lenny Rolff, fellow writer expatriate, today's second interrogee.

Former lover of Claire De Haven.

They took a toy-littered walkway up to the porch; Mal looked through a screen door into the perfect prefab living room: plastic furniture, linoleum floor, spangly pink wallpaper. Children squealed inside; Dudley winked and rang the buzzer.

A tall, unshaven man walked up to the screen, flanked by a toddler boy and girl. Dudley smiled; Mal watched the little boy pop a thumb in his mouth, and spoke first. 'Mr. Kaukenen, we're with the District Attorney's Office and we'd like to talk to you. Alone, please.'

The kids pressed themselves into the man's legs; Mal saw scared slant eyes – two little half-breeds spooked by two big boogeymen. Eisler/Kaukenen called out,

'Michiko!'; a Japanese woman materialized and whisked the children away. Dudley opened the door uninvited; Eisler said, 'You are three years late.'

Mal walked in behind Dudley, amazed at how cheap the place looked – a white trash flop – the home of a man who made three grand a week during the Depression. He heard the kids bawling behind wafer-thin walls; he wondered if Eisler had to put up with the same foreign language shit he did – then popped that he probably dug it on general Commie principles. Dudley said, 'This is a charming house, Mr. Kaukenen. The color motif especially.'

Eisler/Kaukenen ignored the comment and pointed them to a door of the living room. Mal walked in and saw a small square space that looked warm and habit-able: floor-to-ceiling books, chairs around an ornate coffee table and a large desk dominated by a class A typewriter. He took the seat furthest from the squeal of little voices; Dudley sat across from him. Eisler shut the door and said, 'I am Nathan Eisler, as if you did not already know.'

Mal thought: no nice guy, no 'I loved your picture *Branding Iron*.' 'Then you know why we're here.'

Eisler locked the door and took the remaining chair. 'The bitch is in heat again, despite reports that she had a miscarriage.'

Dudley said, 'You are to tell no one that we questioned you. There will be dire repercussions should you disobey us on that.'

'Such as what, Herr – '

Mal cut in. 'Mort Ziffkin, Chaz Minear, Reynolds Loftis and Claire De Haven. We're interested in their activities, not yours. If you cooperate fully with us, we might be able to let you testify by deposition. No open court, probably very little publicity. You slid on HUAC, you'll slide on this one.' He stopped and thought of Stefan, gone with his crazy mother and her new para-mour. 'But we want hard facts. Names, dates, places and admissions. You cooperate, you slide. You don't,

233

it's a subpoena and open court questioning by a DA I can only describe as a nightmare. Your choice.'

Eisler inched his chair away from them. Eyes lowered, he said, 'I have not seen those people in years.'

Mal said, 'We know, and it's their *past* activities that we're interested in.'

'And they are the only people that you want to know about?'

Mal lied, thinking of Lenny Rolff. 'Yes. Just them.'

'And what are these repercussions you speak of?'

Mal drummed the table. 'Open court badgering. Your picture in the – '

Dudley interrupted, 'Mr. Eisler, if you do not cooperate, I will inform Howard Hughes that you are authoring RKO films currently being credited to another man. That man, your conduit to gainful employment as a writer, will be terminated. I will also inform the INS that you refused to cooperate with a sanctioned municipal body investigating treason, and urge that their Investigations Bureau delve into *your* seditious activities with an eye toward your deportation as an enemy alien and the deportation of your wife and children as potential enemy aliens. You are a German and your wife is Japanese, and since those two nations were responsible for our recent world conflict, I would think that the INS would enjoy seeing the two of you returned to your respective homelands.'

Nathan Eisler had hunched himself up, elbows to knees, clasped hands to chin, head down. Tears rolled off his face. Dudley cracked his knuckles and said, 'A simple yes or no answer will suffice.'

Eisler nodded; Dudley said, 'Grand.' Mal got out his pen and notepad. 'I know the answer, but tell me anyway. Are you now or have you ever been a member of the Communist Party, U.S.A.?'

Eisler bobbed his head; Mal said, 'Yes or no answers, this is for the record.'

A weak 'Yes.'

'Good. Where was your Party unit or cell located?'

'I – I went to meetings in Beverly Hills, West Los Angeles and Hollywood. We – we met at the homes of different members.'

Mal wrote the information down – verbatim shorthand. 'During what years were you a Party member?'

'April '36 until Stalin proved him – '

Dudley cut in. 'Don't justify yourself, just answer.'

Eisler pulled a Kleenex from his shirt pocket and wiped his nose. 'Until early in '40.'

Mal said, 'Here are some names. You tell me which of these people were known to you as Communist Party members. Claire De Haven, Reynolds Loftis, Chaz Minear, Morton Ziffkin, Armando Lopez, Samuel Benavides and Juan Duarte.'

Eisler said, 'All of them.' Mal heard the kids tromping through the living room and raised his voice. 'You and Chaz Minear wrote the scripts for *Dawn of the Righteous, Eastern Front, Storm Over Leningrad* and *The Heroes of Yakustok*. All those films espoused nationalistic Russian sentiment. Were you told by Communist Party higher-ups to insert pro-Russian propaganda in them?'

Eisler said, 'That is a naive question'; Dudley slapped the coffee table. 'Don't comment, just answer.'

Eisler moved his chair closer to Mal. 'No. No, I was not told that.'

Mal flashed Dudley two fingers of his necktie – *he's mine*. 'Mr. Eisler, do you deny that those films contain pro-Russian propaganda?'

'No.'

'Did you and Chaz Minear arrive at the decision to disseminate that propaganda yourselves?'

Eisler squirmed in his chair. 'Chaz was responsible for the philosophizing, while I held that the story line spoke most eloquently for the points he wanted to make.'

Mal said, 'We have copies of those scripts, with the obvious propaganda passages annotated. We'll be back to have you initial the dialogue you attribute to Minear's disseminating of the Party line.'

No response. Mal said, 'Mr. Eisler, would you say that you have a good memory?'

'Yes, I would say that.'

'And did you and Minear work together in the same room on your scripts?'

'Yes.'

'And were there times when he said things along the lines of "This is great propaganda" or "This is for the Party"?'

Eisler kept squirming, shifting his arms and legs. 'Yes, but he was just being satirical, poking fun. He did not – '

Dudley shouted, 'Don't interpret, just answer!'

Eisler shouted back, 'Yes! Yes! Yes! Goddamn you, yes!'

Mal gave Dudley the cut-off sign; he gave Eisler his most soothing voice. 'Mr. Eisler, did you keep a journal during the time you worked with Chaz Minear?'

The man was wringing his hands, Kleenex shredding between fingers pumped blue-white. 'Yes.'

'Did it contain entries pertaining to your Communist Party activities and your script work with Chaz Minear?'

'Oh God, yes.'

Mal thought of the report from Satterlee's PIs: Eisler coupling with Claire De Haven circa '38-'39. 'And entries pertaining to your personal life?'

'Oh, Gott in himm . . . yes, yes!'

'And do you still have that journal?'

Silence, then, 'I don't know.'

Mal slapped the table. 'Yes, you do, and you'll have to let us see it. Only the germane political entries will be placed in the official transcript.'

Nathan Eisler sobbed quietly. Dudley said, 'You will give us that journal, or we will subpoena it and uniformed officers will tear your quaint little abode apart, gravely upsetting your quaint little family, I fear.'

Eisler gave a sharp little yes nod; Dudley eased back in his chair, the legs creaking under his weight. Mal saw a Kleenex box on the windowsill, grabbed it and placed it on Eisler's lap. Eisler cradled the box; Mal said, 'We'll take the journal with us, and we'll put Minear aside for now. Here's a general question. Have you ever heard any of the people we're interested in advocate the armed overthrow of the United States government?'

Two negatives shakes, Eisler with his head back down, his tears drying. Mal said, 'Not in the way of a formal pronouncement, but that sentiment stated.'

'Every one of us said it in anger, and it always meant nothing.'

'The grand jury will decide what you meant. Be specific. Who said it, and when.'

Eisler wiped his face. 'Claire would say. "The end justifies the means" at meetings and Reynolds would say that he was not a violent man, but he would take up a shillelagh if it came to us versus the bosses. The Mexican boys said it a million different times in a million contexts, especially around the time of Sleepy Lagoon. Mort Ziffkin shouted it for the world to hear. He was a courageous man.'

Mal caught up on his shorthand, thinking of UAES and the studios. 'What about the UAES? How did it tie in to the Party and the front groups you and the others belonged to?'

'The UAES was founded while I was out of the country. The three Mexican boys had found work as stagehands and recruited members, as did Claire De Haven. Her father had served as counsel to vested movie interests and she said she intended to exploit and . . . and . . .'

Mal's head was buzzing. 'And *what?* Tell me.'

Eisler went back to his finger-clenching; Mal said '*Tell me.* "Exploit" *and what?*'

'Seduce! She grew up around movie people and she knew actors and technicians who had been coveting her since she was a girl! She seduced them as founding members and got them to recruit for her! She said it was her penance for not getting subpeonaed by HUAC!'

Big time triple bingo.

237

Mal willed his voice as controlled as Dudley's. 'Who specifically did she seduce?'

Eisler picked and plucked and tore at the tissue box. 'I don't know, I don't know, I honestly do not know.'

'A lot of men, a few men, how many?'

'I do not know. I suspect only a few influential actors and technicians who she knew could help her union.'

'Who else helped her recruit? Minear, Loftis?'

'Reynolds was in Europe then, Chaz I don't know.'

'What was discussed at the first UAES meetings? Was there some kind of charter or overview they worked on?'

The Kleenex box was now a pile of ripped cardboard; Eisler brushed it off his lap. 'I have never attended their meetings.'

'We know, but we need to know who besides the initial founders were there and what was discussed.'

'I don't know!'

Mal threw an outside curve. 'Are you still hot for Claire, Eisler? Are you protecting her? You know she's marrying Reynolds Loftis. How's that make you feel?'

Eisler threw his head back and laughed. 'Our affair was brief, and I suspect that handsome Reynolds will always prefer young boys.'

'Chaz Minear's no young boy.'

'And he and Reynolds did not last.'

'Nice people you know, comrade.'

Eisler's laughter turned low, guttural – and supremely Germanic. 'I prefer them to you, obersturmbahnführer.'

Mal held his temper by looking at Dudley; Mr. Bad Guy returned him the cut-off sign. 'We'll overlook that comment out of deference to your cooperation, and you may call this your initial interview. My colleague and I will go over your answers, check them against our records and send back a long list of other questions, detailed specifics pertaining to your Communist front activities and the activities of the UAES members we discussed. A City Marshal will monitor that transaction, and a court reporter will take your deposition. After that interview, providing you answer a few more questions now and allow us to take your journal, you will be given friendly witness status and full immunity from prosecution.'

Eisler got up, walked on rubber legs to his desk and unlocked a lower drawer. He poked through it, pulled out a leather-bound diary, brought it back and laid it on the table. 'Ask your few questions and leave.'

Dudley moved a flat palm slowly down: *Go easy*. Mal said, 'We have a second interview this afternoon, and I think you can help us with it.'

Eisler stammered, 'Wh-what, wh-who?'

Dudley, in a whisper. 'Leonard Hyman Rolff.'

Their interrogee rasped the single word, 'No.' Dudley looked at Mal; Mal placed his left hand over his right fist: *no hitting*. Dudley said, '*Yes*, and we will brook no argument, no discussion. I want you to think of something shameful and incriminating indigenous to your old friend Lenny, something that other people know, so that we can put the blame of informing on them. *You will inform*, so I advise you to think of something effective, something that will loosen Mr. Rolff's tongue and spare you a return visit from myself – without my colleague who serves so well to restrain me.'

Nathan Eisler had gone slab white. He sat stock-still, looking way past tears or shock or indignation. Mal thought that he seemed familiar; a few seconds of staring gave him his connection: the Buchenwald Jews who'd beat the gas chamber only to sink to an early grave via viral anemia. The memory made him get up and prowl the bookshelves; the dead silence kept going. He was scanning a shelf devoted to Marxist economics when Dudley's whisper came back. 'The repercussions, comrade. Refugee camps for your half-breed whelps. Mr. Rolff will receive his chance for friendly witness status, so if he's an obstreperous sort, you'll be doing him a favor by supplying us with information to convince him to inform. Think of Michiko forced to keep body and soul together back in Japan, all the tempting offers she'll receive.'

Mal tried to look back, but couldn't make himself; he fixed on *Das Kapital – A Concordance, Marx's Theories of Commerce and Repression* and *The Proletariat Speak Out*. Quiet sank in behind him; heavy fingers tapped the table. Then Nathan Eisler's monotone: 'Young girls. Prostitutes. Lenny is afraid his wife will find out he frequents them.'

Dudley sighed. 'Not good enough. Try harder.'

'He keeps pornographic pictures of the ones – '

'Too bland, comrade.'

'He cheats on his income tax.'

Dudley ha! ha! ha!'d. 'So do I, so does my friend Malcolm and so would our grand savior Jesus Christ should he return and settle in America. You know more than you are telling us, so please rectify that situation before I lose my temper and revoke your friendly witness status.'

Mal heard the kids giggling outside, the little girl squealing in Japanese. He said, 'Goddamn you, talk.'

Eisler coughed, took an audible breath, coughed again. 'Lenny will not inform as easily as I. He has not so much to lose.'

Mal turned, saw a death's head and turned away; Dudley cracked his knuckles. Eisler said, 'I will always try to think I did this for Lenny and I will always know I am lying.' His next deep breath wheezed; he let it out fast, straight into his snitch. 'I was traveling with Lenny and his wife Judith in Europe in '48. Paul Doinelle was making his masked series with Reynolds Loftis and hosted a party to seek financial backing for his next film. He wanted to solicit Lenny and brought a young prostitute for him to enjoy. Judith did not attend the party, and Lenny caught gonorrhea from the prostitute. Judith became ill and returned to America, and Lenny had an affair with her younger sister Sarah in Paris. He gave her the gonorrhea. Sarah told Judith she had the disease, but not that Lenny gave it to her. Lenny would not make love to Judith for many weeks after he returned to America and took a cure, employing various excuses. He has always been afraid Judith would logically connect the two events and realize what had occurred. Lenny confided in me and Reynolds and our friend David Yorkin, who I am sure you know from your wonderful list of front organizations. Since you are so concerned with Reynolds, perhaps you could make him the informant.'

Dudley said, 'God bless you, comrade.'

Mal grabbed Eisler's journal, hoping for enough treason to make two silver bars and his boy worth the price. 'Let's go nail Lenny.'

They found him alone, typing at a card table in his back yard, clack-clack-clack leading them around the side of the house to a fat man in a Hawaiian shirt and chinos pecking on an ancient Underwood. Mal saw him look up and knew from his eyes that this guy was no pushover.

Dudley badged him. 'Mr. Leonard Rolff?'

The man put on glasses and examined the shield. 'Yes. You're policemen?'

Mal said, 'We're with the District Attorney's Office.'

'But you're policemen?'

'We're DA's Bureau Investigators.'

'Yes, you are policemen as opposed to lawyers. And your names and ranks?'

Mal thought of their newspaper ink – and knew he had no recourse. 'I'm Lieutenant Considine, this is Lieutenant Smith.'

Rolff grinned. 'Recently portrayed as regretting the demise of the would-be City grand jury, which I now take it is a going concern once again. The answer is no, gentlemen.'

Mal played dumb. 'No what, Mr. Rolff?'

Rolff looked at Dudley, like he knew he was the one he had to impress. '*No*, I will not inform on members of the UAES. *No*, I will not answer questions pertaining to my political past or the pasts of friends and acquaintances. If subpoenaed, I will be a hostile witness and stand on the Fifth Amendment, and I am prepared to go to prison for contempt of court. You cannot make me name names.'

Dudley smiled at Rolff. 'I respect men of principle, however deluded. Gentlemen, would you excuse me a moment? I left something in the car.'

The smile was a chiller. Dudley walked out; Mal ran interference. 'You may not believe this, but we're actually on the side of the legitimate, non-Communist American left.'

Rolff pointed to the sheet of paper in his typewriter. 'Should you fail as a policeman you have a second career as a comedian. Just like me. The fascists took away my career as a screenwriter; now I write historical romance novels under the nom de plume Erica St. Jane. And my publisher knows my politics and doesn't care. So does the employer of my wife, who has full tenure at Cal State. You cannot hurt either of us.'

Out of the mouths of babes.

Mal watched Lenny Rolff resume work on page 399 of *Wake of the Lost Doubloons*. Typewriter clack filled the air; he looked at the writer's modest stone house and mused that at least he saved more of his money than Eisler and had the brains not to marry a Jap. More clack-clack-clack; Page 399 became pages 400 and 401 – Rolff really churned it out. Then Dudley's brogue, the most theatrical he had ever heard it. 'Bless me father, for I have sinned. My last confession was never, because I am Jewish. I will currently rectify that situation, Monsignors Smith and Considine my confessors.'

Mal turned and saw Dudley holding a stack of photographs; Rolff finished typing a paragraph and looked up. Dudley pushed a snapshot in his face; Rolff said, 'No,' calmly. Mal walked around the table and scoped the picture close up.

It was fuzzy black and white, a teenage girl naked with her legs spread. Dudley read from the flip side. 'To

Lenny. You were the best. Love from Maggie at Minnie Robert's Casbah, January 19, 1946.'

Mal held his breath; Rolff stood, gave Dudley an eye-to-eye deadpan and a steady voice. '*No*. My wife and I have forgiven each other our minor indiscretions. Do you think I would leave the pictures in my desk otherwise? *No. Thief. Fascist parasite. Irish pig*.'

Dudley tossed the photos on the grass; Mal shot him the no hitting sign; Rolff cleared his throat and spat in Dudley's face. Mal gasped; Dudley smiled, grabbed a manuscript sheet and wiped the spittle off. '*Yes*, because fair Judith does not know about fair Sarah and the clap you gave her, and I just played a hunch on where you took your cure. Terry Lux keeps meticulous records, and he has promised to cooperate with me should you decide not to.'

Rolff, still voice steady. 'Who told you?'

Dudley, making motions: *verbatim transcription*. 'Reynolds Loftis, under much less duress than you were just subjected to.'

Mal thought through the gamble: if Rolff approached Loftis, all their covert questionings were compromised; the UAES might put the kibosh on new members – terrified of infiltration, blowing Danny Upshaw's approach. He got out pen and pad, grabbed a chair and sat down; Dudley called his own bluff. 'Yes or no, Mr. Rolff. Give me your answer.'

Veins pulsed all over Leonard Rolff's face. He said, 'Yes.'

Dudley said, 'Grand'; Mal wrote *L. Rolff, 1/8/50* at the top of a clean sheet. Their interrogee squared his glasses. 'Open court testimony?'

Mal took the cue. 'Most likely deposition. We'll start with – '

Dudley, his voice raised for the first time. 'Let me have this witness, counselor. Would you mind?'

Mal shook his head and turned his chair around, steno pad braced on the top slat. Dudley said, 'You know why we're here, so let's get to it. Communist influence in the motion picture business. Names, dates, places and seditious words spoken. Since I'm sure he's much on your mind, we'll start with Reynolds Loftis. Have you ever heard him advocate the armed overthrow of the United States government?'

'No, but – '

'Feel free to volunteer information, unless I state otherwise. Have you some grand tidbits on Loftis?'

Rolff's tone seethed. 'He tailored his policeman roles to make the police look bad. He said he was doing his part to undermine the American system of jurisprudence.' A pause, then, 'If I testify in court, will he get the chance to tell about Sarah and me?'

Mal answered, half truth/half lies. 'It's very unlikely he'll stand as a witness, and if he tries to volunteer that information the judge won't let him get two seconds in. You're covered.'

'But outside of court – '

Dudley said, 'Outside of court you're on your own, and you'll have to rely on the fact that repeating the story makes Loftis appear loathsome.'

Rolff said, 'If Loftis told you that, then he must have been cooperative in general. Why do you need information to use against him?'

Dudley, not missing a trick. 'Loftis informed on you months ago, when we thought our investigation was going to be centred outside the UAES. Frankly, what with the recent labor troubles, the UAES presents a much nicer target. And frankly, you and the others were too ineffectual to bother with.'

Mal looked over and saw that Rolff bought it: his squared shoulders had relaxed and his hands had quit clenching. His follow-up question was dead on target: 'How do I know you won't do the same thing with me?'

Mal said, 'This grand jury is officially on, and you'll be given immunity from prosecution, something we never offered Loftis. What Lieutenant Smith said about the labor trouble is true. It's now or never, and we're here to make hay now.'

Rolff stared at him. 'You acknowledge your opportunism so openly that it gives you an awful credibility.'

Dudley ha' ha'd. 'There is one difference between our factions – we're right, you're wrong. Now, concerning Reynolds Loftis. He deliberately portrayed American policemen as misanthropic, correct?'

Mal went back to transcribing; Rolff said, 'Yes.'

'Can you recall when he said that?'

'At a party somewhere, I think.'

'Oh? A party for *the* Party?'

'No. No, I think it was a party back during the war, a summertime party.'

'Were any of these people also present and making seditious comments: Claire De Haven, Chaz Minear, Mort Ziffkin, Sammy Benavides, Juan Duarte and Mondo Lopez?'

'I think Claire and Mort were there, but Sammy and Juan and Mondo were busy with SLDC around that time, so they weren't.'

Mal said, 'So this was summer of '43, around the time the Sleepy Lagoon Defense Committee was going strongest?'

'Yes. Yes, I think so.'

Dudley said, 'Think, comrade. Minear was Loftis' bedmate. Was he there and acting vociferous?'

Mal caught up on his note-taking, shorthanding Dudley's flair down to simple questions; Rolff ended a long pause. 'What I remember about that party is that it was my last social contact with the people you mentioned until I became friendly with Reynolds again in Europe a few years ago. I recall that Chaz and Reynolds had been spatting and that Reynolds did not bring him to that party. After the party I saw Reynolds out by his car talking to a young man with a bandaged face. I also recall that my circle of political friends had become involved in the Sleepy Lagoon defense and were angry when I took a job in New York that precluded my joining them.'

Dudley said, 'Let's talk about Sleepy Lagoon.' Mal

245

thought of his memo to Loew: nothing on the case should hit the grand jury – it was political poison that made the Pinkos look good. Rolff said, 'I thought you wanted me to talk about Reynolds.'

'Digress a little. Sleepy Lagoon. Quite an event, wasn't it?'

'The boys your police department arrested were innocent. Concerned apolitical citizens joined the Southern California left and secured their release. *That* made it quite an event, yes.'

'That's your interpretation, comrade. Mine differs, but that's what makes for horse races.'

Rolff sighed. 'What do you want to know?'

'Give me your recollections of the time.'

'I was in Europe for the trial and appeals and release of the boys. I remember the actual murder from the previous summer – '42, I think. I remember the police investigation and the arrest of the boys and Claire De Haven becoming outraged and holding fund-raisers. I remember thinking that she was currying favor with her many Latin suitors, that that was one reason she was so carried away with the cause.'

Mal butted in, thinking of culling facts from Dudley's bum tangent, wondering *why* the tangent. 'At these fund-raisers, were there CP bigshots present?'

'Yes.'

'We're going to be getting some SLDC surveillance pictures. You'll be required to help identify the people in them.'

'Then there's more of this?'

Dudley lit a cigarette and motioned Mal to quit writing. 'This is a preliminary interview. A City marshal and court reporter will be by in a few days with a long list of specific questions on specific people. Lieutenant Considine and I will prepare the questions, and if we're satisfied with your answers we'll mail you an official immunity waiver.'

'Are you finished now, then?'

'Not quite. Let's return to Sleepy Lagoon for a moment.'

'But I told you I was in New York then. I was gone for most of the protests.'

'But you did know many of the SLDC principals. Duarte, Benavides and Lopez, for instance.'

'Yes. And?'

'And they were the ones who most loudly contended that the poor persecuted Mex boys got the railroad, were they not?'

'Yes. Sleepy Lagoon sparked the zoot suit riots, *your* police department running amok. A number of Mexicans were practically beaten to death, and Sammy and Juan and Mondo were anxious to express their solidarity through the Committee.'

Mal swiveled his chair around and watched. Dudley was on a big fishing expedition, soaking up a *big* dose of rhetoric in the process – not the man's style. Rolff said, 'If that sounds doctrinaire to you, I'm sorry. It's simply the truth.'

Dudley made a little pooh-pooh noise. 'It always surprised me that the Commies and your so-called concerned citizens never proferred a suitable killer or killers of their own to take the fall on José Diaz. You people are masters of the scapegoat. Lopez, Duarte and Benavides were gang members who probably knew plenty of white punks to put the onus on. Was that ever discussed?'

'No. What you say is incomprehensible.'

Dudley shot Mal a little wink. 'My colleague and I know otherwise. Let's try this. Did the three Mexes or any other SLDC members proffer sincerely believed theories as to who killed José Diaz?'

Gritting his teeth, Rolff said, 'No.'

'What about the CP itself? Did it advance any potential scapegoats?'

'I *told* you no, I *told* you I was in New York for the bulk of the SLDC time.'

Dudley, straightening his necktie knot with one finger

pointed to the street: 'Malcolm, any last questions for Mr. Rolff?'

Mal said, 'No.'

'Oh? Nothing on our fair Claire?'

Rolff stood up and was running a hand inside his collar like he couldn't wait to ditch his inquisitors and take a bath; Mal knocked his chair over getting to his feet. He dug for cracks to throw and came up empty. 'No.'

Dudley stayed seated, smiling. 'Mr Rolff, I need the names of five fellow travelers, people who are well acquainted with the UAES brain trust.'

Rolff said, 'No. Unequivocally *no*.'

Dudley said, 'I'll settle for the names now, whatever intimate personal recollections you can supply us with in a few days, after a colleague of ours conducts background checks. The names, please.'

Rolff dug his feet in the grass, balled fists at his sides. 'Tell Judith about Sarah and me. She won't believe you.'

Dudley took a piece of paper from his inside jacket pocket. 'May 11, 1948. "My Dearest Lenny. I miss you and want you in me despite what you carried with you. I keep thinking that of course you didn't know you had it and you met that prostitute before we became involved. The treatments hurt, but they still make me think of you, and if not for the fear of Judith finding out about us, I would be talking about you my every waking moment." Armbuster 304's are the cheapest wall safes in the world, comrade. A man in your position should not be so frugal.'

Lenny Rolff hit the grass on his knees. Dudley knelt beside him and coaxed out a barely audible string of names. The last name, sobbed, was 'Nate Eisler.' Mal double-timed it to the car, looking back once. Dudley was watching his friendly witness hurl typewriter and manuscript, table and chairs helter-skelter.

Dudley drove Mal back to his motel, no talk the whole time, Mal keeping the radio glued to a classical station:

bombastic stuff played loud. Dudley's goodbye was, 'You've more stomach for this work than I expected'; Mal went inside and spent an hour in the shower, until the hot water for the entire dump was used up and the manager came knocking on the door to complain. Mal calmed him down with his badge and a ten-spot, put on his last clean suit and drove downtown to see his lawyer.

Jake Kellerman's office was in the Oviatt Tower at Sixth and Olive. Mal arrived five minutes early, scanning the bare-bones reception room, wondering if Jake sacrificed a secretary for rental freight in one of LA's ritziest buildings. Their first confab had been overview; this one had to be meat and potatoes.

Kellerman opened his inner office door at 3:00 on the dot; Mal walked in and sat down in a plain brown leather chair. Kellerman shook his hand, then stood behind a plain brown wooden desk. He said, 'Preliminary day after tomorrow, Civil Court 32. Greenberg's on vacation, and we've got some goyishe stiff named Hardesty. I'm sorry about that, Mal. I wanted to get you a Jew who'd be impressed by your MP work overseas.'

Mal shrugged, thinking of Eisler and Rolff; Kellerman smiled. 'Care to enlighten me on a rumor?'

'Sure.'

'I heard you coldcocked some Nazi bastard in Poland.'

'That's true.'

'You killed him?'

The bare little office was getting stuffy. 'Yes.'

Kellerman said, 'Mazel tov,' checked his court calendar and some papers on the desk. 'At preliminary I'll start stalling for continuances and try to work out an angle to get you switched to Greenberg's docket. He'll fucking love you. How's the grand jury gig going?'

'It's going well.'

'Then why are you looking so glum? Look, is there any chance you'll get your promotion before the grand jury convenes?'

Mal said, 'No. Jake, what's your strategy past the continuances?'

Kellerman hooked two thumbs in his vest pockets. 'Mal, it's a hatchet job on Celeste. She deserted the boy – '

'She didn't desert him, the fucking Nazis picked up her and her husband and threw him in fucking Buchenwald.'

'Ssh. Easy, pal. You told me the boy was molested as a direct result of being deserted by his mother. She peddled it inside to stay alive. Your MP battalion has got her liberation interview pictures – she looks like Betty Grable compared to the other women who came out alive. I'll kill her in court with that – Greenberg or no Greenberg.'

Mal took off his jacket and loosened his tie. 'Jake, I don't want Stefan to hear that stuff. I want you to get a writ barring him from hearing testimony. An exclusion order. You can do it.'

Kellerman laughed. 'No wonder you dropped out of law school. Writs excluding minor children from over-hearing testimony in custody cases cannot be legally sanctioned unless the counsel of both parents approve it – which Celeste's lawyer will never go for. If I break her down in court – and I will – he'll want Stefan there on the off-chance he runs to mommy, not daddy. It's out of our hands.'

Mal saw Stefan Heisteke, Prague '45, coming off a three-year jag of canned dog food and rape. 'You swing it, or you find stuff that happened after the war to hit Celeste with.'

'Like her dutifully schooling Stefan in Czech? Mal, she doesn't drink or sleep around or hit the boy. You don't wrest custody from the natural mother because the woman lives in the past.'

Mal got up, his head throbbing. 'Then you make me the biggest fucking hero since Lucky Lindy. You make me look so fucking good I make motherhood look like shit.'

Jake Kellerman pointed to the door. 'Go get me a big load of Commies and I'll do my best.'

Mal rolled to the Pacific Dining Car. The general idea was a feast to pamper himself away from Eisler, Rolff and Dudley Smith – the purging that an hour of scalding hot water didn't accomplish. But as soon as his food arrived he lost interest, grabbed Eisler's diary and flipped to 1938–1939, the writer's time with Claire De Haven.

No explicitness, just analysis.

The woman hated her father, screwed Mexicans to earn his wrath, had a crush on her father and got her white lefty consorts to dress stuffed-shirt traditional like him – so she could tear off their clothes and make a game out of humiliating paternal surrogates. She hated her father's money and political connections, raped his bank accounts to lavish gifts on men whose politics the old man despised; she went to tether's end on booze, opiates and sex, found causes to do penance with and fashioned herself into an exemplary leftist Joan of Arc: organizing, planning, recruiting, financing with her own money and donations often secured with her own body. The woman's political efficacy was so formidable that she was never dismissed as a camp follower or dilettante; at worst, only her psyche and motives were viewed as spurious. Eisler's fascination with Claire continued after their affair ended; he remained her friend throughout her liaisons with pachuco thugs, dryouts at Terry Lux's clinic, her big penance number over Sleepy Lagoon: A Mex boyfriend beat up in the zoot riots, a boilout at Doc Terry's and then a full social season, stone cold sober, with the SLDC. Impressive. Dudley Smith's lunatic fixation aside, the seventeen kids accused of snuffing José Diaz were by all accounts innocent. And Claire Katherine De Haven – Commie rich girl slut – was a major force behind getting them sprung.

Mal leafed through the journal; the De Haven entries dwindled as he hit '44 and '45. He picked at his food and backtracked through a glut of pages that made Eisler look intelligent, analytical, a do-goodnik led down the primrose path by Pinko college professors and the spectre of Hitler looming over Germany. So far, zero hard evidence – if the diary were introduced to the grand jury it would actually make Eisler appear oddly heroic. Remembering the man as a Reynolds Loftis friend/Chaz Minear co-worker, Mal scanned pages for them.

Minear came off as weak, the nance of the two, the clinging vine. Mal read through accounts of Chaz and Eisler scripting *Eastern Front* and *Storm Over Leningrad* together circa 1942–1943, Eisler pissed at Minear's sloppy work habits, pissed at his mooning over Loftis, pissed at himself for despising his friends' homosexuality – tolerable in Reynolds because at least he wasn't a swish. You could see Minear's impotent rage building back in the Sleepy Lagoon days – his crying on Eisler's shoulder over some fling Loftis was having – 'My God, Nate, he's just a boy, and he's been disfigured' – then refusing to go any further on the topic. Hindsight: in '47, Chaz Minear hit back at his faithless lover – the snitch to HUAC that got Reynolds Loftis blacklisted. Mal made a mental note: if Danny Upshaw couldn't infiltrate the UAES braintrust, then Chaz Minear, homosexual weak sister, might be ripe for overt bracing – exposure of his snitch duty the lever to get him to snitch again.

The rest of the diary was a bore: meetings, committees, gatherings and names for Buzz Meeks to check out along with the names Dudley coerced from Lenny Rolff. Mal killed it off while his steak got cold and his salad wilted in the bowl; he realized that he liked Nathan Eisler. And that with the journal checked out and dinner attempted, he had no place to go except back to the Shangri-Lodge Motel and nothing he wanted to do except talk to Stefan – a direct violation of Jake Keller-man's orders. All the motel had to offer was women's names scrawled on the bathroom door, and if he called Stefan he'd probably get Celeste, their first amenities since he reworked her face. Restless, he paid the check, drove up into the Pasadena foothills and parked in the middle of a totally dark box canyon: 'Cordite Alley,'

252

the spot where his generation of LAPD rookies got fried on kickback booze, shot the shit and target practiced, tall clumps of sagebrush to simulate bad guys.

The ground held a thick layer of spent shells; dousing his headbeams, Mal saw that the other cop generations had blasted the sagebrushes to smithereens and had gone to work on the scrub pines; the trees were stripped of bark and covered with entry holes. He got out of the car, drew his service revolver and squeezed off six rounds into the darkness; the echo hurt his ears and the cordite stink smelled good. He reloaded and emptied the .38 again; over the hill in South Pasadena skid other guns went off, like a chain of dogs barking at the moon. Mal reloaded, fired, reloaded and fired until his box of Remingtons was empty; he heard cheers, howls, shrieks and then nothing.

The canyon rustled with a warm wind. Mal leaned against the car and thought about Ad Vice, operations, turning down the Hat Squad, where you went in the door gun first and cops like Dudley Smith respected you. In Ad Vice he busted a string of Chinatown whorehouses deemed inoperable – sending in fresh-scrubbed recruits for blow jobs, followed five minutes later by door-kicking harness bulls and lab techs with cameras. The girls were all straight off the boat and living at home with mama-san and papa-san, who thought they were working double shifts at the Shun-Wong Shirt Factory; he had a cordon of muscle cops accompany him to the storefront office of Uncle Ace Kwan, LA's number-one boss chink pimp. He informed Uncle Ace that unless he took his whores over the line to the County, he would show the pictures to the papa-sans – many of them Tong-connected – and inform them that Kwan-san was getting fat off daughter-san's diet of Caucasian dick. Uncle Ace bowed, said yes, complied and always sent him a candied duck and thoughtful card at Christmastime, and he always thought about passing the greeting on to his brother – while he was still on speaking terms with him.

Him.

Desmond.

Big Des.

Desmond Confrey Considine, who coerced him into dark houses and made him a cop, an operator.

Three years older. Three inches taller. An athlete, good at faking piety to impress the Reverend. The Reverend caught him boosting a pack of gum at the local Pig and Whistle and flayed his ass so bad that Big Des popped a bunch of tendons trying to get free of his bonds and was sidelined for the rest of the football season, a first-string linebacker with a third-string brain and a first-class case of kleptomania that he was now terrified to run with: no legs and no balls, courtesy of Liam Considine, first-string Calvinist.

So Desmond recruited his gangly kid brother, figuring his whippet thinness would get him inside the places he was now afraid to B&E, get him the things he wanted: Joe Stinson's tennis racquet, Jimmy Harris's crystal radio set, Dan Klein's elk's teeth on a string and all the other good stuff he couldn't stand to see other kids enjoying. Little Malcolm, who couldn't stop blaspheming even though the Reverend told him that now that he was fourteen the penalty was a whipping – not the dinner of pine tar soap and castor oil he was used to. Little Mally would become his stealer, or the Reverend would get an earful of Jesus doing it with Rex the Wonder Dog and Mary Magdalene jumping Willy, the old coon who delivered ice to their block on a swayback nag – stuff the Reverend knew Des didn't have the imagination to come up with.

So *he* stole, afraid of Desmond, afraid of the Reverend, afraid to confide in Mother for fear she'd tell her husband and he'd kill Des, then go to the gallows and leave them to the mercy of the cheapshit Presbyterian Charity Board. Six feet and barely one-ten, he became the San Francsico Phantom, shinnying up drainpipes and popping window latches, stealing Desmond sporting junk that he was too afraid to use, books he was too stupid to read, clothes he was too big to wear. He knew that as long as Des kept the stuff he had the goods on him – but he kept playing the game.

Because Joe Stinson had a snazzy sister named Cloris, and he liked being alone in her room. Because Dan Klein had a parrot who'd eat crackers out of your mouth. Because Jimmy Harris' roundheels sister caught him raiding the pantry on his way out, took his cherry and said his thing was big. Because en route to swipe Bill Rice's *National Geographics* he found Biff's baby brother out of his crib, chewing on an electrical cord – and he put him back, fed him condensed milk and maybe saved his life, pretending it was his kid brother and he was saving him from Des and the Reverend. Because being the San Francisco Phantom was a respite from being a stick-thin, scaredy-cat school grind with a crackpot father, doormat mother and idiot brother.

Until October 1, 1924.

Desmond had sent him on a second run to Jimmy Harris' place; he sqeezed in through the woodbox opening, knowing round-heels Annie was there. She *was* there, but not alone: a cop with his blue serge trousers down to his ankles was on the living room carpet pumping her. *He* gasped, tripped and fell; the cop beat him silly, signet rings lacerating his face to shreds. He cleansed his wounds himself, tried to get up the guts to break into Biff Rice's place to see if the baby was okay, but couldn't get up the nerve; he went home, hid Desmond's burglary stash and told him the tables were turned: ripped tendons or not, the ringleader had to steal for the thief or he'd spill the beans to the Reverend. There was only one thing he wanted, and then they'd be quits – one of Annie Harris' negligees – and *he'd* tell him when to pull the job.

He staked the Harris house out, learning that Annie serviced Officer John Rokkas every Tuesday afternoon when the rest of the family worked at the Harris' produce stall in Oakland. On a cold November Tuesday, *he* picked the lock for Des; Des went in and came out twenty minutes later, beaten to a pulp. *He* stole

Desmond's booty and secreted it in a safe deposit box, establishing a parity of fear between the two Considine brothers. Desmond flunked out of Union Theological Seminary and became a big shot in the used-car racket. Mal went to Stanford, graduated and lollygagged through a year of law school, dreaming of back-alley adventure, prowling for loose women and never really enjoying the capture. When law school became excruciatingly boring, he joined the Los Angeles Police Department, not knowing how long he'd last as a cop – or if he even could last. Then he went home for Christmas, twenty-three years old and a rookie running scared in LA niggertown. He wore his uniform to Christmas dinner: Sam Browne belt, silver-plated whistle, .38 revolver. Car king Desmond, still bearing the scars of Officer John Rokkas' beating, was terrified of his new persona. *He* knew he'd be a policeman until the day he died.

Mal segued from his brother to Danny Upshaw, the black box canyon surrounding him, spent ammunition sliding under his feet. How good was he? What would he see? Would what he saw be worth today multiplied fifty times – Ellis Loew stalking grand jury chambers wrapped in the American flag?

'You've more stomach for this work than I expected.'

Dudley was right.

Mal picked up a handful of empty shells, hurled them at nothing and drove home to the Shangri-Lodge Motel.

CHAPTER TWENTY

Mickey Cohen's hideaway was SRO.

The Mick and Davey Goldman were working on a new nightclub routine, a .12 gauge pump substituting for a floor mike. Johnny Stompanato was playing rummy with Morris Jahelka, going over plans for the Cohen-

Dragna dope summit between hands. And Buzz was interviewing Mickey's Teamster goons, taking down picket line scuttlebutt, a last-minute precaution before Mal Considine sent in his operative.

So far, boring Commie jive:

The De Haven cooze and Mort Ziffkin traded clichés about overthrowing the 'studio autocracy'; Fritzie 'Ice-pack' Kupferman had a Teamster file clerk tagged as a UAES plant – they'd been spoon-feeding him only what they wanted him to hear for weeks now, letting him run the lunch truck across from the Variety International line. Mo Jahelka had a hinky feeling: UAES pickets weren't fighting back when shoved or verbally provoked – they seemed smug, like they were biding their time, even old lefty headbashers maintaining their frost. Moey seemed to think UAES had something up its sleeve. Buzz had padded the statements so Ellis Loew would think he was working harder than he was, feeling like a nice, tasty Christian in a lion's den, waiting for the lion to get hungry and notice him.

Johnny Stomp Lion.

Mickey Lion.

Johnny had been giving him the fisheye ever since he walked in the door, ten days since he kiboshed the squeeze on Lucy Whitehall and bought the guinea sharpster off with five Mickey C-notes. 'Hi, Buzz,' 'Hi, Johnny,' nothing else. He'd been with Audrey three times now, the one all-nighter at his place, two quick shots at Howard's fuck pad in the Hollywood Hills. If Mickey had any kind of surveillance on Audrey it was Johnny; if he got wise, it was mortgage his life to the fucker or kill him, no middle ground. If Mickey got wise, it was the Big Adios, when crossed, the little guy got vicious: he'd found the trigger who bumped Hooky Rothman, gave him two hollow points in the kneecaps, an evening of agony with a Fritzie Kupferman coup de grace: an icepick in the ear, Fritzie making like Toscanini conducting Beethoven, little dips and swirls with his baton before he speared the poor bastard's brain.

Mickey Lion, this bamboo bungalow his den.

Buzz put away his notepad, taking a last look at the four names Dudley Smith had called him with earlier: Reds to be back-ground-checked, more shitwork, probably more padding. Mickey Lion and Johnny Lion were schmoozing by the fireplace now, a picture of Audrey Lioness in pasties and panties on the wall above them. The Mick hooked a finger at him; he walked over.

The comedian had some schtick ready. 'A guy comes up and asks me, "Mickey, how's business?" I tell him, "Pal, it's like show business, there is no business." I make a pass at this ginch, she says, "I don't lay for every Tom, Dick and Harry." I say, "What about me? I'm Mickey!" '

Buzz laughed and pointed to the picture of Audrey, eyes hard on Johnny Stomp. 'You should put her in your routine. Beauty and the Beast. You'll bring the house down.'

Goose egg from Johnny; Mickey screwing up his face like he was actually considering the suggestion. Buzz tested the water again. 'Get some big jig to play sidekick, make like he's giving it to Audrey. Coons are always good for a laugh.'

More nothing. Mickey said, 'Shvartzes I don't need, shvartzes I don't trust. What do you get when you cross a nigger and a Jew?'

Buzz played dumb. 'I don't know. What?'

Mickey sprayed laughter. 'A janitor who owns the building!'

Johnny chuckled and excused himself; Buzz eyed the Va Va Voom Girl at twenty and made quick book: a hundred to one he knew less than nothing about them. Mickey said, 'You should laugh more. I don't trust guys who don't have no sense of humor.'

'You don't trust anybody, Mick.'

'Yeah? How's this for trust. February eighth at the haberdashery, my deal with Jack D. Twenty-five pounds of Mex brown, cash split, food and booze. All my men, all Jack's. Nobody heeled. *That* is trust.'

Buzz said, 'I don't believe it.'

'The deal?'

'The nobody heeled. Are you fuckin' insane?'

Mickey put his arm around Buzz's shoulders. 'Jack wants four neutral triggers. He's got two City bulls, I got this Sheriff's dick won the Golden Gloves last year, and I'm still one short. You want the job? Five hundred for the day?'

He'd spend the money on Audrey: tight cashmere sweaters, red and pink and green and white, a size too small to show off her uplift. 'Sure, Mick.'

Mickey's grip tightened. 'I got a storefront on the Southside. County juice, a little sharking, a little book. Half a dozen runners. Audrey's keeping the ledgers for me, and she says I'm getting eaten alive.'

'The runners?'

'Everything tallies, but the daily take-in's been short. I pay salary, the guys enforce their own stuff. Short of shaking down the guys, I got no way to know.'

Buzz slid free of Mickey's arm, thinking of lioness larceny: Audrey with a hot pencil and a wet brain. 'You want me to ask around on the QT? Get the squad boss at Firestone to shake down the locals, find out who's bettin' what?'

'Trust, Buzzchik. You nail who's doing me, I'll throw some bones your way.'

Buzz grabbed his coat. Mickey said. 'Hot date?'

'The hottest.'

'Anybody I know?'

'Rita Hayworth.'

'Yeah?'

'Yeah, trust me.'

'She red downstairs?'

'Black to the roots, Mick. There's no business like show business.'

His date was for 10:00 at Howard's spot near the Hollywood Bowl; Mickey and Johnny's no-take and the skim story had him running jumpy, his watch set to Audrey

259

standard time, which made killing an hour somewhere pure horseshit. Buzz drove to the lion woman's house, parked behind her Packard ragtop and rang the bell.

Audrey answered the door, slacks, sweater and no makeup. 'You said you didn't want to know where I lived.'

Buzz shuffled his feet, making like a swain on a prom date. 'I checked your driver's licence while you were asleep.'

'Meeks, that's not something you do to somebody you're sleeping with.'

'You're sleepin' with Mickey, ain't you?'

'Yes, but what does –'

Buzz slid past Audrey, into a bargain basement front room. 'Savin' money on furnishings to bankroll your shopping center?'

'Yes. Since you ask, I am.'

'Sweetie, you know what Mickey did to the ginzo killed Hooky Rothman?'

Audrey slammed the door and wrapped her arms around herself. 'He beat the man senseless and had Fritzie what's his name drive him over the state line and warn him never to come back. Meeks, what is this? I can't *stand* you this way.'

Buzz shoved her against the door, pinned her there and put his hands on her face, holding her still, his hands going gentle when he saw she wasn't going to fight him. 'You're skimmin' off Mickey 'cause you think he won't find out and he wouldn't hurt you if he did and now *I'm* the one that had to fuckin' protect you because you are so fuckin' dumb about the fuckin' guys you fuck and I'm in way over my fuckin' head with you so you get fuckin' smart because if Mickey hurts you I'll fuckin' kill him and all his fuckin' kike guinea pigshit – '

He stopped when Audrey started bawling and trying to get out words. He stroked her hair, bending down to listen better, turning to jelly when he heard, 'I love you, too.'

260

They made love on the bargain basement floor and in the bedroom and in the shower, Buzz pulling the curtain loose, Audrey admitting she cheapskated on the bathroom fixtures, too. He told her he'd check with an ex-Dragna paper man he knew and show her how to redoctor Mickey's books – or fix an angle to lay the onus off on some nonexistent welcher; she said she'd quit skimming, straighten up, fly right, and play the stock market like a squarejohn woman who didn't screw gangsters or Red Squad bagmen. He said, 'I love you' fifty times to make up for her saying it first; he got her sizes so he could blow all his kickback take on clothes for her; they went down on each other to seal a pact: nobody was supposed to mention Mickey unless absolutely necessary, nobody was to talk about their future or lack of it, two dates a week was their limit, Howard's fuck pads rotated, her place or his place as a treat once in a while, their cars stashed where the bad guys wouldn't see them. No outside dates, no trips together, no telling friends what they had going. Buzz asked Audrey to do the tassel trick for him; she did; she went on to model her stripper outfits, then all the clothes in her wardrobe. Buzz figured that if he spent his gambling output on threads he wanted to see her in, he'd never be bored staying inside with her: he could take the clothes off, make love to her, watch her dress again. He thought that if they stayed inside forever, he'd tell her everything about himself, all the shitty stuff included, but he'd lay it out slowly, so she'd got to know him, not get scared and run. He talked a blue streak; she talked a blue streak; he let slip about the Doberman pinscher he killed when he burglarized a lumber-yard in Tulsa in 1921, and she didn't care. Toward dawn, Audrey started falling asleep and he started thinking about Mickey and got scared. He thought about moving his car, but didn't want to upset the perfect way his lioness had her head tucked against his collarbone. The scare got worse, so he reached to the floor, grabbed his .38 and stuck it under the pillow.

CHAPTER TWENTY-ONE

The nut bin waiting room featured tables and plasticene couches in soothing colors: mint green, ice blue, pale yellow. Artwork by the nuts was tacked to the walls: finger paintings and draw-by-the-numbers jobs depicting Jesus Christ, Joe DiMaggio and Franklin D. Roosevelt. Danny sat waiting for Cyril 'Cy' Vandrich, dressed in Ted Krugman garb: dungarees, skivvy shirt, steel-toed motorcycle boots and a bombardier's leather jacket. He'd been up most of the night studying Mal Considine's scenario; he'd spent yesterday doing his own background checks on Duane Lindenaur and George Wiltsie, prowling their Valley hangouts and getting nothing but a queasy sense of the two as homo slime. Slipping into the Ted role had been a relief, and when he drove up to the Camarillo gate the guard had double-taked his get-up and New York plates and openly challenged him as a cop, checking his ID and badge, calling West Hollywood Station to get the okay. So far, Upshaw into Krugman was a success – the acid test this afternoon at the picket line.

An orderly ushered a thirtyish man in khakis into the room – a shortish guy, skinny with broad hips, deep-set gray eyes and a hepcat haircut – one greasy brown lock perfectly covering his forehead. The orderly said, 'Him,' and exited; Vandrich sighed, 'This is a humbug. I've got connections on the switchboard, the girl said this is about murders, and I'm not a murderer. Jazz musicians are Joe Lunchmeat to you clowns. You've been trying to crucify Bird for years, now you want me.'

Danny let it go, sizing up Vandrich sizing him up. 'Wrong. This is about Felix Gordean, Duane Lindenaur and George Wiltsie. I know you're not a killer.'

Vandrich slumped into a chair. 'Felix is a piece of

work, Duane what's his face I don't know from Adam and George Wiltsie padded his stuff so he'd look big to impress all the rich queens at Felix's parties. And why are you dressed up like rough trade? Think you'll get me to talk that way? That image is from hunger, and I outgrew it a long time ago.'

Danny thought: smart, hep, probably wise to the game. The rough trade crack washed over him; he fondled his jacket sleeves, loving the feel of the leather. 'You've got them all buffaloed, Cy. They don't know if you're crazy or not.'

Vandrich smiled; he shifted in his chair and cocked a hip toward Danny. 'You think I'm a malingerer?'

'I know you are, and I know that Misdemeanor Court judges get tired of giving the same old faces ninety days here when they could file on them for Petty Theft Habitual and get them some felony time. Quentin time. Up there they don't ask you for it, they take it.'

'And I'm sure you know a lot about that, with your tough leather goods and all.'

Danny laced his hands behind his head, the jacket's soft fur collar brushing him. 'I need to know what you know about George Wiltsie and Felix Gordean, and maybe what Gordean does or doesn't know about some things. Cooperate, you'll always pull ninetys. Dick me around, the judge gets a letter saying you withheld evidence in a triple homicide case.'

Vandrich giggled. 'Felix got murdered?'

'No. Wiltsie, Lindenaur and a trombone man named Marty Goines, who used to call himself the 'Horn of Plenty'. Have you heard of him?'

'No, but I'm a trumpeter and I used to be known as the 'Lips of Ecstasy.' That's a double entendre, in case you haven't guessed.'

Danny laughed off the vamp. 'Five seconds or I walk and nudge the judge.'

Vandrich smiled. 'I'll play, Mr. Policeman. And I'll even give you a free introductory observation. But first I've got a question. Did Felix tell you about me?'

'Yes.'

Vandrich did a little number, crossing his legs, making mincy hand motions. Danny saw it as the fuck going nance in order to knuckle to authority; he felt himself start to sweat, his lefty threads too hot, too much. 'Look, just tell me.'

Vandrich quieted down. 'I knew Felix during the war, when I was putting on a crazy act to get out of the service. I played that act *everywhere*. I was living off an inheritance then, living it *up*. I went to Felix's parties and I trucked with Georgie once, and Felix thought I was non compos mentis, so if he sent you to see me he was probably playing a game. There. That's my free introductory observation.'

And *his* Gordean instincts confirmed: the pimp couldn't draw breath without trying an angle – which meant that he *was* holding back. Danny said, 'You're good,' got out his notebook and turned to the list of questions he'd prepared.

'Burglary, Vandrich. Did you know George Wiltsie to be involved in it, or do you know of anyone connected to Felix Gordean who pulls burglaries?'

Vandrich shook his head. 'No. Like I said, George Wiltsie I trucked with once, talk wasn't his forte, so we stuck to business. He never mentioned that guy Lindenaur. I'm sorry he got killed, but I just take nice things from stores, I don't associate with burglars.'

Danny wrote down 'No.' 'The same thing on dentists and dental technicians, men capable of making dentures.'

Vandrich flashed perfect teeth. 'No. And I haven't been to a dentist since high school.'

'A young man, call him a boy – with a scarred, burned-up face in bandages. He was a burglar, and this would be back during the war.'

'No. Ugh. Awful.'

Two more. 'Nos.' Danny said, 'A zoot stick. That's a long wooden stick with a razor blade or razor blades

264

attached at the end. It's a weapon from the war days, for cutting up the zoot suits that Mexicans used to wear.'

Vandrich said, 'Double ugh and an ugh on pachucos in zoot suits in general.'

No, no, no, no – underlined. Danny put out his ace question. 'Tall, gray-haired men, mid-forties now. Nice silver hair, guys who know jazz spots, hep enough to buy dope. Homosexual men who went to Gordean's parties back when you did.'

Vandrich said, 'No'; Danny turned to fresh paper. 'This is where you shine, Cyril. Felix Gordean. Everything you know, everything you've heard, everything you've thought about him.'

Vandrich said, 'Felix Gordean is . . . a . . . piece of . . . work,' drawing the words out into a lisp. 'He doesn't truck with man, woman or beast, and his only kick is bringing guys out, getting them to admit what they are, then . . . procuring for them. He has a legitimate talent agency, and he meets lots of young men, really sensitive creative types . . . and . . . well . . . they're prone to bcing like . . .'

Danny wanted to scream QUEER, FAGGOT, FRUIT, HOMO, PEDERAST, BRUNSER, PUNK, COCKSUCKER and ram slime from the Hollywood Squad reports down Vandrich's throat, making him spit it out in the open where *he* could spit on it. He kneaded his jackct slceves and said, 'He gets his thrills getting guys to admit that they're homosexuals, right?'

'Uh, yes.'

'You can *say* it, Vandrich. Five minutes ago you were trying to flirt with me.'

'It . . . it's hard to say. It's so ugly and clinical and cold.'

'So Gordean brings these *homosexuals* out. Then what?'

'Then he enjoys showing them off at his parties and fixing them up. Getting them acting jobs, then taking their money for the introductions he arranges. Sometimes he has parties at his beach house and watches through these mirrors he has. He can look in, but the fellows in the bedroom can't look out.'

Danny remembered his first pass at the Marmont: peeping, his stuff pressed to the window, jazzing on it. 'So Gordean's a fucking queer voyeur, he likes watching homos fuck and suck. Let's try this: *Does he keep records for his introduction service*?'

Vandrich had pushed his chair into the wall. 'No. He didn't back then, at least. The word was that he had a great memory, and he was terrified of writing things down . . . afraid of the police. But . . .'

'But what?'

'B-but I h-heard he loves to keep it all in his head, and once I heard him say that his biggest dream was to have something on everybody he knew and a profitable way to use it.'

'Like blackmail?'

'Y-yes, I thought of that.'

'Do you think Gordean's capable of it?'

No lips, stutter or hesitation. 'Yes.'

Danny felt his soft fur collar sticky with sweat. 'Get out of here.'

Gordean holding back.

His talent agency a tool to fuel his voyeurism.

Blackmail.

No suspicious Gordean reactions on Duane Lindenaur, extortionist; Charles Hartshorn – 'Short and bald as a beagle' – eliminated as a suspect on his appearance, that fact buttressed by Sergeant Frank Skakel's assessment of his character and his take on Hartshorn's juice – the lawyer unapproachable for now. If Gordean himself was some sort of extortionist, it had to be coincidental to Lindenaur – both men moved in a world rife with blackmailees. The talent agency was the place to start.

Danny took PCH back to LA, all the windows down so he could keep his jacket on and buttoned full. Per Considine's orders, he parked three blocks from Hollywood Station and walked the rest of the way, heading into the muster room dead on time for the noon meeting he'd called.

His men were already there, sitting in the first row of chairs, Mike Breuning and Jack Shortell gabbing and smoking. Gene Niles was four seats over, picking at a pile of papers on his lap. Danny grabbed a chair and sat down facing them.

Shortell said, 'You still look like a cop.' Breuning nodded agreement. 'Yeah, but the Commies won't get it. If they were so smart they wouldn't be Commies, right?'

Danny laughed; Niles said, 'Let's get this over with, huh, Upshaw? I've got lots of work to do.'

Danny got out pad and pen. 'So do I. Sergeant Shortell, you first.'

Shortell said, 'Cut and dried. I've called ninety-one dental labs, run the descriptions by the people in charge and got a total of sixteen hinkers: strange-o's, guys with yellow sheets. I eliminated nine of them by blood type, four are currently in jail and the other three I talked to myself. No sparks, plus the guys had alibis for the times of death. I'll keep going, and I'll call you if anything bites me.'

Danny said, 'Just make sure it's a denture bite,' and turned to Breuning. 'Mike, what have you and Sergeant Niles got?'

Breuning consulted a big spiral notebook. 'What we've got is the old goose egg. On the biting MO, we checked LAPD, County and the muni files. We got a shine queer who bit his boyfriend's dick off, a fat blond guy with a kiddie raper jacket who bites little girls and two guys who match our description – both in Atascadero for aggravated assault. On the queer bar scuttlebutt, zero. Biters do not hang out at homo cocktail lounges and say, 'I bite. Want some?' The fruit detail cops I talked to laughed me out on that one. On the Vice and sex offender file eliminations, nothing. Burglarly, ditto. I cross-checked them, nothing duplicated.

Nothing on a kid with burn scars. There were six middle-aged gray-haired possibles – all either in custody on the nights of the killings or alibied – squarejohn witnesses. On the recanvassing – nada – it's too old now. Niggertown, Griffith Park, the area where Goines was dumped, nothing. Nobody saw anything, nobody gives a shit. On checking with snitches, forget it. This guy is a loner, I'd bet my pension he does not associate with criminal riff-raff. I personally leaned on the only three possibles I got from State and County Parole – two queers and a real sweetheart – this tall, gray preacher type who cornholed three Marines back during the war, used to lube his prong with toothpaste. All three were in for curfew at the Midnight Mission – alibied by no less than Sister Mary Eckert herself.'

Breuning stopped, out of breath, and lit a cigarette. He said, 'Gene and I muscled every southside H man we could find, which wasn't many – it's dry all over. Rumor has it that Jack D, and/or Mickey C. are getting ready to move a load of cut-rate. Nothing. We leaned on the jazz musician angle, nothing with our man's description. Ditto on goofballs. Nothing. And we leaned *hard*.'

Niles chuckled; Danny looked at his own absent doodling: a page of concentric zeros. 'Mike, what about the zoot stick angle? – the assault files and snitch calls?'

Breuning eyes narrowed. 'Another goose. And that's old Mex stuff, pretty far afield. I know Doc Layman tagged the back wounds as zoot stick, but don't you think he could be wrong? As far as I'm concerned, it just doesn't play.'

A Dudley Smith stooge patronizing Norton Layman, MD, PhD. Danny reached for some frost. 'No. Layman's the best, and he's right.'

'Then I don't think it's a real lead. I think our guy just read about the damn sticks or eyeballed one of the zoot riots and got a kick out of them. He's a fucking psycho, there's no reason to those guys.'

Something about Breuning's take on the sticks was

off; Danny shrugged to cover the thought. 'I think you're wrong. I think the zoot sticks are essential to the way the killer thinks. My instincts tell me he's revenging old wrongs, and the specific mutilations are a big part of it. So I want you and Niles to comb the station files in Mex neighborhoods and check old occurrence reports – '42, '43, around in there, the zoot riots, Sleepy Lagoon – back when the Mexes were taking heat.'

Breuning stared at Danny; Niles groaned and muttered, 'My instincts.' Danny said, 'Sergeant, if you've got comments, address them to me.'

Niles cracked a grin. 'Okay. One, I don't like the Los Angeles County Sheriff's Department and their good buddy Mickey Kike, and I've got a County pal who says you're not the goody two shoes you pretend to be. Two, I've been doing a little work on my own, and I talked to a couple of Quentin parolees who said no way was Marty Goines a queer – and I believe them. And three, I think you personally fucked me by not calling in Tamarind Street, and I don't like that.'

No Bordoni. No Bordoni. No fucking Bordoni. Danny, calm. 'I don't care what you like or what you think. *And who were the parolees?*'

Two hard stares locked; Niles glancing down at his notebook. 'Paul Arthur Koenig and Lester George Mazmanian. And four, I don't like you.'

The bluff called. Danny looked at Niles, spoke to LASD Sergeant Shortell. 'Jack, there's a poster on the notice board that shits on our Department. Rip it up.'

Shortell's voice, admiring. 'My pleasure, skipper.'

Ted Krugman.

Ted Krugman.

Theodore Michael Krugman.

Teddy Krugman, Red Commie Pinko Subversive Stagehand.

Friends with Jukey Rosensweig of Young Actors Against Fascism and Bill Wilhite, a cell boss with the Brooklyn CP; ex-lover of Donna Patrice Cantrell, leftist firebrand at Columbia University circa '43, jumper suicide in '47 – a dive off the George Washington Bridge when she got the news that her socialist father attempted suicide over his HUAC subpoena, turning himself into a permanent vegetable via ingestion of a scouring powder cocktail that scoured his brain down to sub-idiot quality. Ex-member of AFL-CIO, North Shore Long Island CP, Garment Workers' Defense Committe, Concerned Americans Against Bigotry, Friends of the Abraham Lincoln Brigade and the Fair Play for Paul Robeson League. Socialist summer camps as a kid, New York City College dropout, not drafted because of his subversive politics, liked to work as a theater grip because of all the politically enlightened people you met and pussy. Worked a long string of Broadway shows, plus a handful of B movies shot on location in Manhattan. Slogan shouter, brawler, hardcase. Loved to attend meetings and demonstrations, sign petitions and talk Commie rebop. Active in the New York leftist scene until' 48 – then nowhere.

Pictures.

Donna Patrice Cantrell was pretty but hard, a softer version of her dad the Ajax guzzler. Jukey Rosensweig was a big fat guy with bulging thyroid eyes and thick glasses; Bill Wilhite was white-bread handsome. His supporting cast of characters, caught in Fed surveillance snaps, were just faces attached to bodies wielding placards: names, dates and causes on the back, to shore him up with some more history.

Parked on Gower just north of Sunset, Danny ran through his script and photo kit. He had his co-star's faces down pat: the Teamster picket boss he was supposed to introduce himself to, the goons he'd be picketing and arguing with, the LAPD Academy muscleman he'd fight – and finally – if Considine's scenario played to perfection – Norman Kostenz, UAES picket boss, the man who'd take him to Claire De Haven. Deep-breathing, he locked his gun, badge, cuffs and Daniel Thomas Upshaw ID in the glove compartment, sliding

Theodore Michael Krugman license photostats into the sleeves in his wallet. Upshaw into Krugman completed; Danny walked over, ready to do it.

The scene was pandemonium divided into two snake-like strips of bodies: UAES, Teamsters, banners on sticks, shouts and catcalls, three feet of sidewalk separating the factions, a debris-filled gutter and studio walls bracketing the lines down a quarter-mile-long city block. Newsmen standing by their cars on the opposite side of Gower; lunch trucks dispensing coffee and doughnuts; a bunch of oldster cops stuffing their faces, watching newshounds shoot craps on a piece of cardboard laid across the hood of an LAPD black-and-white. Duelling bullhorns bombarding the street with squelch noise and static-layered repetitions of 'REDS OUT!' and 'FAIR PAY NOW!'

Danny found the Teamster picket boss, picture pure; the man winked on the sly and handed him a pine slab with UAES – UN-AMERICAN ESCAPED SUBVERSIVES printed on reinforced cardboard at the top. He went through a rigmarole of laying down the law and making him fill out a time card; Danny saw the guy working the Teamster lunch truck eyeball the transaction – obviously the UAES plant man mentioned in Considine's info package. The shouts got louder; the picket boss hustled Danny over to his marching buddies, Al and Jerry, picture perfect in their grubby work clothes. Tough-guy salutations per the script: three hard boys who brook no horsehit getting down to business. Then him – Ted Krugman – starring in his own Hollywood epic, surrounded by extras, one line of good guys, one of bad guys, all of them moving, separate lines going in opposite directions.

He marched, three abreast with Al and Jerry – pros who knew their stuff; signs came at him: FISCAL JUSTICE NOW!; END THE STUDIO AUTOCRACY!; NEGOTIATE FAIR WAGES! Teamster elbows dug into UAES rib cages; the bad guys winced, didn't elbow back, kept marching and yelling. It was Man Camera with something like Sound-

O-Vision thrown in; Danny kept imagining mixmasters, meat grinders, buzz saws and cycle engines working overtime, not letting you think or sight on a fixed image. He kept talking his pre-planned diatribe, feeding Jerry, right on the button with Considine's first cue: 'You're talkin' the fuckin' Moscow party line, pal. Who's fucking side are you on?'

Himself, coming back: 'The side that's paying me a fucking buck an hour to picket, *pal!*'

Jerry, grabbing his arm as UAESers stood aside and watched: 'That's not good enough – '

He broke free and kept walking and shouting per the scenario; per the scenario the picket boss came over and issued him a warning about team play, hauling Al and Jerry over, making them all shake hands like kids in a schoolyard, a bunch of anaemic lefties scoping it out. All three of them played it sullen; the picket boss hot-footed it to the lunch truck; Danny saw him talking to the coffee man – UAES's plant – hooking a thumb back at the little fracas he just refereed. Al said, 'Don't goldbrick, Krugman'; Jerry muttered anti-Red epithets; Danny launched his 'I'm one of the guys' spiel, real real Krugman stuff in case the bad guys had a close ear down, stuff Considine yanked out of an old NYPD Red Squad report: garment worker unions bashing heads insanely, the 'bosses' on both sides fucking over the rank and file. Him *pleading* with philistine Al and Jerry to see the *reason* behind what he was saying; them shaking their heads and picketing away from him, disgusted at working the same line as a rat fucker Commie traitor.

Danny marched, banner high, shouting, 'REDS OUT!,' meaning it, but savoring the curve he'd just pitched. His Man Camera started working, everything seemed contained and controlled like he'd just had his four shots and didn't want a fifth, like he was born for this and the queer shit at Gordean's pad didn't really send him. It felt like chaos in a vacuum, being shoved into a meat grinder and laughing as you got chopped up. Time passed; Al and Jerry brushed by him: once, twice, three times, side-mouthing ugly stuff, bringing the LAPD goon with them on their fourth go-round, a brick shithouse blocking his path, fingers on his chest, the hump *improvising* on Considine's script: 'This guy's a tough guy Commie? He looks like a weak sister to me.'

The wrong words, then, 'Make it good you County fuck,' whispered up close. Danny improvised, bending the shithouse's fingers back, snapping them at the bottom digit. The man shrieked and swung a bum left hook; Danny stepped inside with a counter one-two to the solar plexus. The LAPD man doubled over; Danny shot him a steel-toed right foot to the balls, crashing him into a group of UAES pickets.

Shouts all around; whistles blowing. Danny picked up a discarded pine slab and got ready to swing it at his co-star's head. Then blue uniforms surrounded him and billy clubs beat him to the ground and he was pummeled, lifted, pummeled, lifted, dumped and kicked at. He went stone cold out – then he tasted blood and sidewalk and felt hands lifting him up until he was face to face with Norman Kostenz, looking just like Mal Considine's surveillance pic, a friendly guy who was saying, 'Ted Krugman, huh? I think I've heard of you.'

The next hour went Speed-O-Vision fast.

Friendly Norm helped him clean himself up and took him to a bar on the Boulevard. Danny came out of his thumping quickly, thudding pains in the soft part of his back, loose teeth, side aches. The bluesuits had to have been in on Considine's plan – improvising in his favor – or they'd have cracked his head open for real. The script had called for them to break up a fistfight, separating the combatants, some minor roughhouse before cutting them loose. They'd obviously played off his improvisation, the kicks and gutter dump their aside for his wailing on one of their own. Now the question was how hard 'Call me Mal' would come down on him for the damage he'd done – he was an ex-LAPD man himself.

At the bar it was all questions, back to Ted Krugman, no time to think of repercussions.

Norm Kostenz took his photograph for a record of the assault and kissed his ass, a tough-guy worshiper; Danny moved into Ted, nursing a beer and double shot, making like he rarely boozed, that it was just to ease his aching, fascist-thumped bones. The liquor did help – it took the bite off his aches and got him moving his shoulders, working out the kinks that would come later. The juice downed, he started feeling good, proud of his performance; Kostenz ran a riff on how Jukey Rosensweig used to talk about him and Donna Cantrell. Danny put out a sob number on Donna, using it to segue into his missing years: Prof Cantrell a vegetable, his beloved Donna dead, the fascists responsible, but him too numbed by grief to organize, protest or generally fight back. Koztenz pressed on what he had been doing since Donna's suicide; Danny gave him an Upshaw/Krugman combo platter: real-life car thief stories under Red Ted's aegis, phony East Coast venues. Friendly Norm ate it up, vicarious kicks on a platter; he called for a second round of drinks and asked questions about the garment district wars, the Robeson League, stuff Jukey had told him about. Danny winged it, flying high: names and pictures from Considine's kit, long spiels extolling the virtues of various lefties, borrowing from the actual personalities of deputies and San Berdoo townies he'd known. Kostenz licked his plate and begged for more; Danny went sky high, all his aches lulled, spun tales out of thin air and Considine's facts: a long schtick about his loss of political faith, his rapacious womanizing with the Commie quail from Mal's surveillance pics, his long cross-country odyssey and how self-hatred and a desire to scope the scene brought him to the Teamster picket line, but now he knew he could never be fascist muscle – he wanted to work, fight, organize and help UAES end the bloodsucking tyranny of the studio bosses. Almost breathless, Norm Kostenz took it in, got up and said,

'Can you meet me and our member screener tomorrow? The El Coyote on Beverly at noon?'

Danny stood up, weaving, knowing it was more from his Academy Award acting than from booze and a beating. He said, 'I'll be there,' and saluted like Uncle Joe Stalin in a newsreel he'd seen.

Danny drove home, checked to make sure his files and pictures were secure in their hiding place, hot-showered and daubed linament on the bruises that were starting to form on his back. Naked, he performed intro lines to Claire De Haven in front of the bathroom mirror, then dressed from his lefty wardrobe: wool slacks with a skinny belt, T-shirt, his workboots and the leather jacket. Ted Krugman but a cop, he admired himself in the mirror, then drove to the Strip.

Dusk was falling, twilight darkening over low rain clouds. Danny parked on Sunset across from the Felix Gordean Agency, hunkered down in the seat with binoculars and fixed on the building.

It was a one-story gray French Provincial, louvered windows and an arched doorway, deco lettering in brass above the mailbox. An enclosed autoport was built on, the entrance illuminated by roof lights. Three cars were parked inside; Danny squinted and wrote down three Cal '49 license numbers: DB 6841, GX 1167, QS 3334.

Full darkness hit; Danny kept his eyes on the doorway. At 5:33, a twenty-fivish male Caucasian walked out, got into green Ford coupé GX 1167 and drove away. Danny wrote down a description of the car and the man, then went back to straight surveillance. At 5:47, a white prewar La Salle, Cal '49 TR 4191, pulled in; a handsome young Latin type wearing a suitcoat and pegged pants got out, rang the buzzer and entered the agency. Danny jotted his stats down, kept looking, saw two older, dark-haired men in business suits leave, walk to the carport and get into a DB 6841 and QS 3334, back out and go off in opposite directions on Sunset. The Latin type left ten minutes later; Danny filled in his descriptions of the men – none of whom matched his suspect.

Time dragged; Danny stayed glued, smelling linament, feeling his muscle aches return. At 6:14 a Rolls-Royce pulled into the carport; a man in a chauffeur's outfit got out, rang the agency buzzer, spoke into the intercom and walked across the street and out of sight. Lights went off inside – until only a single window was glowing.

Danny thought: Gordean's driver leaving his car, probably no more 'clients' coming in. He spotted a phone booth on the corner, walked over, gave the box a coin and called the DMV Police Line.

'Yes? Who's requesting?'

Danny eyed the one light still on. 'Deputy Upshaw, West Hollywood Squad, and make this fast.'

The operator said, 'We're a little bit backlogged on vehicle registrations, but – '

'This is the *police* line, not DMV Central. I'm a Homicide detective, so you kick loose for me.'

The man sounded chastised. 'We were helping regis – I'm sorry, Deputy. Give me your names.'

Danny said, 'I've got the numbers and the vehicle descriptions, *you* give *me* the names. Four California '49s: DB 6841, GX 1167, QS 3334 and TR 4191. Go fast.'

The operator said, 'Yessir.' The line buzzed; Danny watched the Felix Gordean Agency. Seconds stretched; the DMV man came back on the line. 'Got them, Deputy.'

Danny braced his notepad against the wall. 'Go.'

'DB 6841 is Donald Willis Wachtel, 1638 Franklin Street, Santa Monica. GX 1167 is Timothy James Costigan, 11692 Saticoy Street, Van Nuys. On QS 3334, we've got Alan Brian Marks with a K-S, 209 4th Avenue, Venice, and TR 4191 is Augie Luis – that's L-U-I-S – Duarte, 1890 North Vendome, Los Angeles. That's it.'

No sparks on the names – except the 'Duarte' seemed vaguely familiar. Danny hung up just as the light in the

276

window went off; he ran back to his car, got in behind the wheel and waited.

Felix Gordean walked out the door a few moments later. He checked the lock and flipped a switch that doused the carport lights, backed the Rolls out and hung a U-turn, then headed west on Sunset. Danny counted to five and pursued.

The Rolls was easy to track – Gordean drove cautiously and stuck to the middle lane. Danny let a car get in front of him and fixed on Gordean's radio aerial, a long strip of metal with an ornamental Union Jack at the top, oncoming headlight glare making it stand out like a marker.

They cruised west, out of the Strip and into Beverley Hills. At Linden the middle car hung a right turn and headed north; Danny closed the gap on Gordean, touching the Rolls' bumper with his headlights, then idling back. Beverly Hills became Holmby Hills and Westwood; traffic thinned out to almost nothing. Brentwood, Pacific Palisades, looming greenery dotted with Spanish houses and vacant lots – Sunset Boulevard winding through blackish green darkness. Danny caught the reflection of highbeams in back of him.

He let the throttle up; the beams came on that much stronger, then disappeared. He looked in the rear-view, saw low headlights three car lengths back and no one else on the road; he hit the gas and jammed forward until Gordean's Rolls was less than a short stone's throw from the snout of his Chevy. Another check of the rear-view; the back car right on his ass.

Tail.

Moving surveillance on *him*.

Three-car rolling stakeout.

Danny swallowed and glimpsed a string of vacant lots, dirt shouldered, off the right side of the street. He downshifted, swung a hard right turn, hit the shoulder and fishtailed across rock-strewn dirt, wracking the Chevy's undercarriage. He saw the tail car on Sunset, lights off and zooming; he cut hard left, went down to first gear,

277

back off dirt onto good hard blacktop. High beams on; second and third, the gas pedal floored. A brown post-war sedan losing ground as he gained on it; him right on the car's ass, mud smeared across its rear plate, the driver probably near blinded by his lights.

Just then the sedan turned hard right and hauled up a barely lit side street. Danny downshifted, hit the brakes and skidded into a full turnaround brody, stalling the car facing the flow of traffic. Headlights were coming straight at him; he sparked the ignition, popped the clutch and gas, banged over the curb and up the street, horns blasting down on Sunset.

Bungalows lined both sides of the street; a sign designated it 'La Paloma Dr, 1900 N.' Danny speeded up, the blacktop getting steeper, no other moving cars in sight. Bungalow lights gave him some illumination; La Paloma Drive became a summit and leveled off – and there was his brown sedan on the roadside, the driver's door open.

Danny pulled up behind it, hit his brights, unholstered his piece. He got out and walked over, gun arm first. He looked in the front seat and saw nothing but neat velveteen upholstery; he stepped back and saw a '48 Pontiac Super Chief, abandonded on a half-developed street surrounded by totally dark hills.

His heart was booming; his throat was dry; his legs were butter and his gun hand twitched. He listened and heard nothing but himself; he scanned for escape routes and saw a dozen driveways leading into back yards and the entire rear of the Santa Monica Mountains.

Danny thought: *think procedure, go slow, you're inter-agency Homicide brass*. The 'brass' calmed him; he tucked his .45 into his waistband, knelt and checked out the front seat.

Nothing on the seat covers; the registration strapped to the steering column – right where it should be. Danny undid the plastic strip without touching flat surfaces, held it up to the light of his highbeams and read:

Wardell John Hascomb, 9816 1/4 South Iola, Los

Angeles. Registration number Cal 416893-H; license number Cal JQ 1338.

LA South Central, darktown, the area where the killer stole the Marty Goines transport car.

HIM.

Danny got fresh shakes, drove back to Sunset and headed west until he spotted a filling station with a pay phone. With shaky hands, he slipped a nickel in the slot and dialed DMV Police Information.

'Yeah? Who's requesting?'

'D-Deputy Upshaw, West Hollywood Squad.'

'The guy from half an hour or so ago?'

'Goddamn – yes, and check the Hot Sheet for this: 1948 Pontiac Super Chief Sedan, Cal JQ 1338. If it's hot, I want the address it was stolen from.'

'Gotcha,' silence. Danny stood in the phone booth, warm one second, chilled the next. He took out his pad and pen, ready to write down what the operator gave him; he saw 'Augie Luis Duarte' and snapped why it seemed familiar: there was a Juan Duarte in the UAES info he studied – meaning nothing – Duarte was as common a Mex name as Garcia or Hernandez.

The operator came back. 'She's hot, clouted outside 9945 South Normandie this afternoon. The owner is one Wardell J. Hascomb, male Negro, 9816 South – '

'I've got that.'

'You know, Deputy, your partner was a whole lot nicer.'

'*What?*'

The operator sounded exasperated, like he was talking to a cretin. 'Deputy Jones from your squad. He called in for a repeat on those four names I gave you, said you lost your notes.'

Now the booth went freezing. No such deputy existed; someone – probably HIM – had been watching him stake Gordean's office, close enough to overhear his conversation with the clerk and glom the gist – that he was requesting vehicle registrations. Danny shivered and said, 'Describe his voice.'

279

'Your partner's? Too cultured for a County plain-clothes dick, I'll – '

Danny slammed the receiver down, gave the phone his last coin and dialed the direct squadroom line at Hollywood Station. A voice answered, 'Hollywood Detectives'; Danny said, 'Sergeant Shortell. Tell him it's urgent.'

'Okay,' a soft click, the old-timer cop yawning, 'Yes? Who's this?'

'Upshaw. Jack, the killer was tailing me in a hot roller.'

'What the – '

'Just listen. I spotted him, and he rabbited and abandoned the car. Write this down: '48 Pontiac Super, brown, La Paloma Drive off Sunset in the Palisades, where it flattens out at the hill. Print man to dust it, you to canvass. He took off on foot and it's all hills there, so I'm pretty sure he's gone, but do it anyway. And fast – I won't be there to watchdog.'

'Holy fuck.'

'In spades, and get me this – records checks on these four men – Donald Wachtel, 1638 Franklin, Santa Monica. Timothy Costigan, 11692 Saticoy, Van Nuys. Alan Marks, 209 4th Avenue, Venice, and Augie Duarte, 1890 Vendome, LA. Got it?'

Shortell said, 'You've got it'; Danny hung up and trawled for HIM. He cruised back to La Paloma and found the car exactly the way he left it; he hung his flashlight out the window and shone it at bungalows, alleyways, back yards and foothills. Squarejohn husbands and wives taking out the trash; dogs, cats and a spooked coyote transfixed by the glare in its eyes. No tall, middle-aged man with lovely silver hair calmly making his getaway from a count of Grand Theft Auto. Danny drove back to Sunset and took it slowly out to the beach, scanning both sides of the street; at Pacific Coast Highway, he dug in his memory for Felix Gordean's address, came up with 16822 PCH and rolled there.

It was on the beach side of the road, a white wood

Colonial built on pilings sunk into the sand, 'Felix Gordean, Esq,' in deco by the mailbox. Danny parked directly in front and rang the bell; chimes like the ones at the Marmont sounded; a pretty boy in a kimono answered. Danny badged him. 'Sheriff's. I'm here to see Felix Gordean.'

The boy lounged in the doorway. 'Felix is indisposed right now.'

Danny looked him over, his stomach queasing at blond hair straight from a peroxide bottle. The living room backdropping the boy was ultramodern, with one whole wall mirrored – tinted glass like the one-ways in police interrogation stalls. Vandrich on Gordean: he perved watching men with men. Danny said, 'Tell him it's Deputy Upshaw.'

'It's all right, Christopher. I'll talk to this officer.'

The pretty boy jumped at Gordean's voice; Danny walked in and saw the man, elegant in a silk robe, staring at the one-way. He kept staring; Danny said, 'Are you going to look at me?'

Gordean pivoted slowly. 'Hello, Deputy. Did you forget something the other night?'

Christopher went over and stood by Gordean, giving the mirror a look-see and a giggle. Danny said, 'Four names that I need rundowns on. Donald Wachtel, Alan Marks, Augie Duarte and Timothy Costigan.'

Gordean said, 'Those men are clients and friends of mine, and they were all at my office this afternoon. Have you been spying on me?'

Danny stepped toward the two, angling himself away from the mirror. 'Get specific. Who are they?'

Gordean shrugged and put his hands on his hips.'As I said, clients and friends.'

'Like I said, get specific.'

'Very well. Don Wachtel and Al Marks are radio actors, Tim Costigan used to be a crooner with the big bands and Augie Duarte is a budding actor who I've found commercial work for. In fact, maybe you've seen

281

him on television. I found him a job playing a fruit picker in a spot for the California Citrus Growers' Association.'

Pretty Boy was hugging himself, entranced by the mirror; Danny smelled fear on Gordean. 'Remember how I described my suspect the other night? Tall, gray-haired and forty-fivish?'

'Yes. So?'

'So have you seen anyone like that hanging out around your office?'

A deadpan from Gordean; Christopher turning from the mirror, his mouth opening. A brief hand squeeze, pimp to Pretty Boy; the kid's deadpan. Danny smiled, 'That's it. I'm sorry I bothered you.'

Two men walked into the living room. They were wearing red silk briefs; one man was removing a sequined mask. Both were young and overly muscular, with shaved legs and torsos slicked down with some kind of oil. They eyed the three standing there; the taller of them threw Danny a kissy face. His partner scowled, hooked his fingers inside his briefs, pulled him back to the hallway and out of sight. They trailed giggles; Danny felt like vomiting and went for the door.

Gordean spoke to his back. 'No questions about that, Deputy?'

Danny turned around. 'No.'

'Wouldn't you say it runs contrary to your life? I'm sure you've got a nice family. A wife or a girlfriend, a nice family who would find that shocking. Would you like to tell me about them over a glass of that nice Napoleon brandy you enjoy so much?'

For a split second Danny felt terrified; Gordean and Pretty Boy became paper silhouettes, villains to empty his gun into. He about-faced out the door, slamming it; he puked into the street, found a hose attached to the adjoining house, drank and doused his face with water. Steadied, he pulled his Chevy around to the opposite side of PCH and parked, lights off, to wait.

Pretty Boy left the house twenty minutes later, walking toward an overpass to the beach. Danny let him get

282

to the steps, cut him five seconds' more slack, then ran over. His motorcycle boots thunked on cement; the kid looked around and stopped. Danny slowed and walked up to him. Christopher said, 'Hello. Want to enjoy the view with – '

Danny hooked him to the gut, grabbed a handful of bottle blond hair and lashed slaps across his face until he felt his knuckles wet with blood. The moon lit up that face: no tears, eyes wide open and accepting. Danny let the boy kneel to the cement and looked down at him huddling into his kimono. 'You did see that man hanging around Gordean's office. Why didn't you talk?'

Christopher wiped blood from his nose. He said, 'Felix didn't want me to talk to you about it,' no whimper, no defiance, no nothing in his voice.

'Do you do everything Felix tells you to do?'

'Yes.'

'So you saw a man like that?'

Christopher got to his feet and leaned over the railing with his head bowed. 'The man had really beautiful hair, like movie star hair. I do file work at the agency, and I've seen him out at the bus stop on Sunset a lot the last few days.'

Danny worked the kinks out of his knuckles, rubbing them on his jacket sleeve. 'Who is he?'

'I don't know.'

'Have you seen him with a car?'

'No.'

'Have you seen anybody talking to him?'

'No.'

'But you told Felix about him?'

'Y-yes.'

'And how did he react?'

Christopher shrugged. 'I don't know. He didn't react much at all.'

Danny leaned over the railing, fists cocked. 'Yes, he fucking did, so you fucking tell me.'

'Felix wouldn't like me to tell.'

'No, but you tell me, or I'll hurt you.'

The boy pulled away, gulped and spoke fast, a fresh-turned snitch anxious to get it over with. 'At first he seemed scared, then he seemed to be thinking, and he told me I should point the man out from the window the next time I saw him.'

'Did you see him again?'

'No. No, I really didn't.'

Danny thought: and you never will, now that he knows I'm wise to his stakeout. He said, 'Does Gordean keep records for his introduction service?'

'No. No, he's afraid of it.'

Danny shot the boy an elbow. 'You people like playing games, so here's a good one. I tell you something, you put it together with Gordean, who I'm sure you know *real* well. And you look at me, so I can tell if you're lying.'

The kid turned, profile to full face, pretty to beaten and slack-featured. Danny tried to evil-eye him; trembly lips made him look at the ocean instead. 'Does Gordean know any jazz musicians, guys who hang at the jazz clubs down in darktown?'

'I don't think so, that's not Felix's style.'

'Think fast. Zoot stick. That's a stick with razor blades at the end, a weapon.'

'I don't know what you're talking about.'

'A man who looks like the one you say by the bus stop, a man who uses Gordean's service.'

'No. I'd never seen that man by the bus stop before, and I don't know any – '

'Dentists, dental workers, men who can make dentures.'

'No. Too chintzy for Felix. Oh God, this is so strange.'

'Heroin. Guys who push it, guys who like it, guys who can get it.'

'No, no, *no*. Felix hates needle fiends, he thinks they're vulgar. Can we please hurry up? I never stay out on my walks this long, and Felix might get worried.'

Danny got the urge to hit again; he stared harder at the water, imagining shark fins cutting the waves. '*Shut up and just answer*. Now the service. Felix gets his kicks bringing guys out, right?'

'Oh Jesus – yes.'

'Were any of those four men I mentioned queers that he brought out?'

'I – I don't know.'

'Queers in general?'

'Donald and Augie, yes. Tim Costigan and Al Marks are just clients.'

'Did Augie or Don ever turn tricks for the service?'

'Augie did, that's all I know.'

'Christopher! Did you fall in and drown!'

Danny shifted his gaze, wave churn to beach. Felix Gordean was standing on his back porch, a tiny figure lit by a string of paper lanterns. A glass door stood half open behind him; the two musclemen, barely visible, were entwined on the floor inside. Christopher said, 'Please, can I go now?'

Danny looked back at his sharks. 'Don't you tell Gordean about this.'

'What should I tell him about my nose?'

'Tell him a fucking shark bit you.'

'Christopher! Are you coming!'

Danny drove back to La Paloma Drive. An arclight was shining down on the abandoned Pontiac; Mike Breuning was sitting on the hood of an LAPD unmarked, watching a print man dust for latents. Danny killed his engine and beeped the horn; Breuning walked over and leaned in the window.'No prints except the shine the car belongs to – we eliminated him from a gun registration set he had on file at the station. No records on those four names you gave Shortell, and he's out canvassing now. What happened? Jack said you said the killer was tailing you.'

Danny got out of the car, pissed that Breuning was goldbricking. 'I was staking a place on the Strip – a talent agency run by a guy who queer-pimps on the side. I got some license numbers and called the DMV, and somebody called up impersonating a cop and got them too. I was tailed out here, and the guy rabbited when I spotted him. This car was stolen from darktown – right near where the Marty Goines transport car was grabbed. I've got an eyeball witness that places a man matching the killer's description hanging around outside the pimp's office, which means that those four men should be put under surveillance. *Now*.'

Breuning whistled; the print man called out, 'Nothing but the guy from the elimination set.' Danny said, 'You and Jack keep shaking down the citizens. I know it's a long shot, but do it anyway. When you finish, check cab company log sheets for pickups in the Palisades and Santa Monica Canyon and shake down the bus drivers working the Sunset line. He had to blow the area somehow. He might have stolen another car, so check with the desks at West LA Station, Samo PD and the Malibu Sheriff's. I'm going home for a minute, then I'll head down to the Southside and check around where the Pontiac was clouted.'

Breuning pulled out a notebook. 'Will do, but where do you expect to get the extra men for your stakes on those names? Gene and Jack and I have got work up the wazoo already, and Dudley told me he's got you busy on that Commie thing.'

Danny thought of Mal Considine. 'We'll get the men, don't worry.'

The arclight went off; the stretch of roadway went dark. Breuning said, 'Upshaw, what's with this name Augie Luis Duarte? The killer ain't Mex and none of his victims were, so why'd you call it in?'

Danny decided to spill on Gordean. 'It's part of a lead I've been following up on my own. The pimp is a man named Felix Gordean, and he runs a classy introduction service for homos. George Wiltsie worked for him, the killer was staking his office out, Duarte was one of the names I gave the DMV clerk, and he's an ex-Gordean whore. Satisfied?'

Breuning whistled again. 'Maybe Dudley can get us the extra men. He's good at that.'

Danny slid back in the car, catching a funny jolt – Dudley Smith's toady was stringing him along. He said, 'You and Jack go to work, and if you get anything hot, call me at home.' He U-turned and took La Paloma down to Sunset, thinking of a sandwich, a weak highball and jigtown canvassing. Sunset was rife with late-evening drivers; Danny turned east and joined a jetstream of lights. His mind went nicely blank; miles passed. Then, hitting the Strip, he got terrified like the half second at the beach house – this time around Man Camera short takes.

Cy Vandrich vamping him.

Breuning going strange over the zoot sticks, like one of the things was slashing at him.

Niles and his two parolees; his 'I got a County pal who says you're not the goody two shoes you pretend to be.'

'Make it good you County fuck' and an LAPD man bloody at his feet.

The chase, like a car thief gig reversed; it had to be him, it couldn't be him, it was too wrong to be him and too right not to be him.

Gordean making like a mind reader.

Strong-arming a pathetic homo.

The takes dissolved into a cold craving for a drink that saw him the rest of the way home. Danny opened the door and blinked at unexpected light in his living room; he saw the bottle on the coffee table and thought he was entering a hallucination. He drew his gun, snapped that it was a crazy-man stunt and put it back; he walked up to the table, saw a note propped against the jug and read:

Ted –

You were brilliant at the picket line today. I was camped out at a surveillance spot on De Longpre and saw the whole thing. By the way, I told the Academy man to call you a 'County fuck,' hoping it would give you an added incentive to kick ass. Your ability exceeded my expectations, and I now owe that officer a good deal more than a bottle of whiskey – you broke all his fingers and nicely enlarged his nuts. I wangled him a commendation, and he's mollified for now. More good news: Captain Will Bledsoe died this morning of a massive stroke, and DA McPherson has promoted me to Captain and appointed me Chief DA's Investigator. Good luck with the UAESers (I saw Kostenz approach you). Let's nail them good, and after the grand jury I'll recommend you for an interim LASD Sergeantcy and start pulling strings to get you to the Bureau. I need a good exec, and the lieutenant's bars that come with it will make you the youngest brass hat in City/County history. Meet me tomorrow night at midnight at the Pacific Dining Car – we'll celebrate and you can update me on your work.

Yours,
Mal.

Danny began sobbing, racking sobs that wouldn't go into tears. He kept sobbing, forgetting all about the liquor.

CHAPTER TWENTY-TWO

Chief DA's Investigator.

Two Silver Bars, an extra 3.5 grand a year, prestige for the custody battle. The command of twenty-four detectives culled from other police agencies on the basis of their brains and ability to collect evidence that would stand up in court. Substantial say-so in *the* decision process: when or when not to seek major felony indictments. The inside track for LAPD Chief of Detectives and Big Chief. Power: including rank over Dudley Smith and the noblesse oblige to make an afternoon of shitwork with Buzz Meeks tolerable.

Mal walked into the Los Angeles office of the U.S. Immigration and Naturalization Service. Ellis Loew had called early; he and Meeks were to meet at INS, 'Try to bury whatever hatchet exists between you,' and check the service's files on UAES sympathizers born outside the United States for deportation levers. Loew had phrased it like an order; captain or not, he had no choice. The DA had also requested a detailed memo on his non-UAES questionings and an update on the overall investigation – which he was late on – eyeballing Danny Upshaw's performance had cost him an afternoon – he'd been playing operator boss while Dudley was out shaking down the Pinkos Lenny Rolff ratted on.

Mal settled into the file room the records supervisor had arranged for them to use. He checked his watch and saw that he was early: Meeks wasn't due until 9:00; he had forty minutes to work before the fat man slimed in. Stacks of files had been arranged on a long metal table; Mal shoved them to the far corner, sat down and started writing.

Memo – 1/10/50
To: Ellis Loew
From: Mal Considine
Ellis –

My first memo as Chief DA's Investigator – if it wasn't confidential you could frame it.

First off, Upshaw made a successful approach yesterday. I didn't get a chance to tell you on the phone, but he was terrific. I observed, and saw the UAES member screener approach him. I left Upshaw a note instructing him to meet me late tonight at the Dining Car for a report, and I'm betting he'll have made contact with Claire De Haven by then. I'll call you tomorrow morning with a verbal report on what he has to say.

Two days ago, Dudley and I approached Nathan Eisler and Leonard Rolff, screenwriters not subpoenaed by HUAC. Both men corroborated UAES members Minear and Loftis as planning to subvert motion picture content with Communist doctrine and both have agreed to testify as friendly witnesses. Eisler yielded a diary which further confirms Claire De Haven as promiscuous – good news for Upshaw. Eisler stated that De Haven recruited initial UAES members by sexual means – good to have for open court should she have the audacity to seek to testify. Rolff informed on a total of 4 non-UAES leftists. Dudley questioned 2 of them yesterday and phoned me last night with the results: they agreed to appear as friendly witnesses, time-, date- and place-corroborated Ziffkin, De Haven, Loftis, Minear and the 3 Mexicans as making inflammatory statements supporting the overthrow of the U.S.A. by the U.S. Party and informed on a total of 19 other fellow travelers. I'm working on a detailed questionnaire to be submitted to all friendly witnesses, facts for you to use in your opening presentation, and I want low-key City Marshals to oversee the delivery and pickup of the paperwork. The reason for this is that Dudley is too frightening a presence – sooner or later his intimidation tactics will have to backfire. The chance for a successful grand jury depends on the UAES being kept in the dark. We've lulled them to sleep, so let's keep Dudley on a tight leash. If one of our friendlies balks and squeals on us to the brain trust, we're screwed.

Here's some random thoughts:

1. – This thing is becoming an avalanche and soon it's going to be an avalanche of paper. Get those clerks out to your house: I'll be submitting reports, questionnaires, and interview abstracts constructed from details in Eisler's diary. Dudley, Meeks and

Upshaw will be filing reports. I want all this info cross-filed for clarity's sake.

2. – You were worried on the Upshaw secrecy angle. Don't be. We checked and rechecked. 'Ted Krugman' was not directly known to any UAES members, he's secondhand known at best, but *known of*. Upshaw is a *very* smart officer, he knows how to run with the ball and I suspect he's enjoying his role-playing.

3. – Where's Dr. Lesnick? I need to talk to him, to run psych overview questions by him and to get his opinion on certain parts of Eisler's diary. Also, all his files end in Summer '49. Why? There's a gap ('42-'44) in the Loftis file, key to the time he was rabidly mouthing Commie sentiment and portraying cops as evil on screen to 'undermine the American system of jurisprudence.' I hope he didn't die on us – he looked almost dead ten days ago. Have Sgt. Bowman locate him and make sure he calls me, will you?

4. – When we've got our evidence together and collated, we'll need to spend a goodly amount of time deciding which of our friendlies to call to the stand. Some will be shaky and angry, thanks to Dudley and his browbeatings. As I said before, his methods have to backfire. Once we're satisfied with the number of witnesses we've turned, I want to take over the questionings and go solo on them, kid gloves – more for the sake of the investigation's security than anything else.

5. – Dudley has a bee in his bonnet over the Sleepy Lagoon case, and he keeps bringing it up in our questionings. By all accounts, the defendants were innocent, and I think we should gag testimony pertaining to the SLDC in court – unless it tangents us to viable testimony. The case made the LA left look good, and we can't afford to make the UAES members (many) who also belonged to SLDC out as martyrs. I outrank Dudley now, and I'm going to dress him down on this and generally have him play it softer with witnesses.

In light of the above and in keeping with my new rank and promotion, I'm asking you to promote me to commanding officer of this investigation.

Yours,
Captain M. E. Considine,
Chief DA's Investigator

Writing out his new title gave Mal the chills; he thought of buying a fancy pen to commemorate the occasion. He moved down to the file stacks, heard 'Think fast' and saw a little blue object lobbing toward him, Buzz Meeks the lobber. He caught it on reflex – a velvet jeweler's box. Meeks said, 'A peace offering, skipper. I'll be damned if I'm gonna spend the day with a guy who mighta had me shot without kissin' some ass.'

Mal opened the box and saw a pair of shiny silver captain's bars. He looked at Meeks; the fat man said, 'I'm not askin' for a handshake or a "Gee, thanks, old buddy," but I sure would like to know if it was you sent those torpedoes after me.'

Something about Meeks was off: his usual slimy charm was subdued and he had to know that whatever happened in '46 had no bearing on now. Mal snapped the box shut and tossed it back. 'Thanks, but no thanks.'

Meeks palmed the gift. 'My last shot at civility, skipper. When I moved on Laura, I didn't know she was a cop's wife.'

Mal smoothed his vest front; Meeks always made him feel like he needed steam cleaning. 'Take the files on the end. You know what Ellis wants.'

Meeks shrugged and complied, a pro. Mal dug into his first file, read through a long INS background check report, sensed a solid citizen type with bum politics spawned by the big European inflation and put the folder aside. Files two and three were more of the same; he kept stealing glances at Meeks grinding notes, wondering what the cracker wanted. Four, five, six, seven, eight, all Hitler refugee stuff, poison that made drifts to the far left seem justified. Meeks caught his eye and winked; Mal saw that he was happy or amused about something. Nine and ten dawdled over, then a rap on the file room door. 'Knock, knock, who's there? Dudley Smith, so Reds beware!'

Mal stood up; Dudley came over and gave him a barrage of hard back slaps. 'Six years my junior, and a captain you are. How grand! Lad, you have my most heartfelt congratulations.'

Mal saw himself trashing the Irishman, making him eat orders and kowtow. 'Congratulations accepted, Lieutenant.'

'And you've a wicked wit to match your new rank. Wouldn't you say so, Turner?'

Meeks rocked in his chair. 'Dudley, I can't get this boy to say much of anything.'

Dudley laughed. 'I suspect there's old fury between you two. What it derives from I don't know, although cherchez la femme might be a good bet. Malcolm, while I'm here let me ask you something about our friend Upshaw. Is he sticking his snout into our investigation past his decoy work? The other men on the homo job resent him and seem to think he's a meddler.'

'While I'm here' echoed; 'cherchez la femme' thundered Mal knew Dudley had the story on him and Meeks. 'You're as subtle as a freight train, Lieutenant. And what is it about you and Upshaw?'

Dudley ha' ha'd; Meeks said, 'Mike Breuning's ditzed on the kid, too. He called me last night and ran a list of names by me, four guys Upshaw wanted tails put on. He asked me if they were from the queer job or the grand jury. I told him I didn't know, that I never met the kid, all I got on him was third-hand.'

Mal cleared his throat, ticked at being talked around. 'What third hand, Meeks?'

The fat man smiled. 'I was workin' an angle on Reynolds Loftis, and I came up with a lead from Samo PD Vice. Loftis was rousted at a queer bar back in '44, pallin' with a lawyer named Charles Hartshorn, a big wheel downtown. I braced Hartshorn, and he thought at first I was a Homicide dick, 'cause he was acquainted with one of the dead homos from Upshaw's job. I knew the guy was no killer. I leaned on him hard, then bought myself off on him rattin' me by tellin' him I'd keep the County heat away.'

Mal remembered Meeks' memo to Ellis Loew: their first outside corroboration of Loftis' homosexuality. 'You're sure Hartshorn wasn't essential to Upshaw's case?'

'Boss, that guy's only crime is bein' a homo with money and a family.'

Dudley laughed. 'Which is preferable to being a homo with no money and no family. You're a family man, Malcolm. Wouldn't you say that's true?'

Mal's chain snapped. 'Dudley, what the fuck do you want? I'm running this job and Upshaw is working for me, so you just tell me why you're so interested in him.'

Dudley Smith did a master vaudeville take: a rebuked youth shuffling his feet, going hangdog with hunched shoulders and a pouting lower lip. 'Lad, you hurt my feelings. I just wanted to celebrate your good fortune and make it known that Upshaw has incurred the wrath of his fellow officers, men not used to taking orders from twenty-seven-year-old dilettantes.'

'The wrath of a Dragna bagman with a grudge on the Sheriff's and your protégé, you mean.'

'That's one interpretation, yes.'

'Lad, Upshaw is *my* protégé. And I'm a captain and you're a lieutenant. Don't forget what that means. Now please leave and let us work.'

Dudley saluted crisply and walked out; Mal saw that his hands were steady and his voice hadn't quivered; Meeks started applauding. Mal smiled, remembered who he was smiling at and stopped. 'Meeks, what do *you* want?'

Meeks rocked his chair. 'Steak lunch at the Dining Car, maybe a vacation up at Arrowhead.'

'And?'

'And I'm not hog-wild about this job and I don't like the idea of you makin' voodoo eyes at me till it's over and I liked you standin' up to Dudley Smith.'

Mal half smiled. 'Keep going.'

'You were scared of him and you dressed him anyway. I liked that.'

'I've got rank on him now. A week ago I'd have let it go.'

Meeks yawned, like it was all starting to bore him. 'Pal, bein' afraid of Dudley Smith means two things: that you're smart and you're sane. And I outranked him once and let him slide, because that is one smart fucker that never forgets. So, accolades, Captain Considine, and I still want that steak lunch.'

Mal thought of the two silver bars. 'Meeks, you're not the type to offer amends.'

Buzz stood up. 'Like I said, I'm not hog-wild about this job, but I need the money. So let's just say it's got me thinkin' about the amenities of life.'

'I'm not hog-wild about it either, but I need it.'

Meeks said, 'I'm sorry about Laura.'

Mal tried to remember his ex-wife naked, and couldn't. 'It wasn't me that had you shot. I heard it was Dragna triggers.'

Meeks tossed Mal the velvet box. 'Take it while I'm feelin' generous. I just bought my girl two C-notes' worth of sweaters.'

Mal pocketed the insignia and stuck out his hand; Meeks gave him a bonecrusher. 'Lunch, Skipper?'

'Sure, Sarge.'

They took the elevator down to ground level and walked out to the street. Two patrolmen were standing in front of a black-and-white sipping coffee; Mal picked a string of words out of their conversation: 'Mickey Cohen, bomb, bad.'

Meeks badged the two, hard. 'DA's Bureau. What'd you just say about Cohen?'

The younger cop, a peach-fuzz rookie type, said, 'Sir,

we just heard on the radio. Mickey Cohen's house just got bombed. It looks bad.'

Meeks took off running; Mal followed him to a mint green Caddy and got in – one look at the fat man's face telling him 'why?' was a useless question. Meeks hung a tire-screeching U-ey out into Westwood traffic and hauled west, through the Veterans Administration Compound, out onto San Vicente. Mal thought of Mickey Cohen's house on Moreno; Meeks kept the pedal down, zigzagging around cars and pedestrians, muttering, 'Fuck, fuck, fuck, fuck.' At Moreno, he turned right; Mal saw fire engines, prowl units and tall plumes of smoke up the block. Meeks skidded up to a crime scene rope and got out; Mal stood on his tiptoes and saw a nice Spanish house smoldering, LA's number-one hoodlum standing on the lawn, unsinged, ranting at a cadre of uniform brass. Rubberneckers were choking the street, the sidewalk and adjoining front lawns; Mal looked for Meeks and couldn't see him anywhere. He turned and gave his backside a shot – and there was his grand jury cohort, the most corrupt cop in LA history, engaged in pure suicide.

Buzz was just past the edge of the commotion, smothering a showstopper blonde with kisses. Mal recognized her from gossip column pics: Audrey Anders, the Va Va Voom Girl, Mickey Cohen's on-the-side woman. Buzz and Audrey kissed; Mal gawked from a distance, then turned around and checked the lovebirds' flank, scoping for witnesses, Cohen goons who'd squeal to their master. The whole crowd was contained behind the crime scene ropes, occupied with Mickey's tirade; Mal kept scanning anyway. He felt a hard tap on his shoulder; Buzz Meeks was there wiping lipstick off his face. 'Boss, I am in your power. Now we gonna go get that steak?'

CHAPTER TWENTY-THREE

'. . . And Norm says you can fight. He's a prizefighting fan, so it must be true. Now the question is, are you willing to fight in other ways – and for us.'

Danny looked across the table at Claire De Haven and Norman Kostenz. Five minutes into his audition; the woman all business so far, keeping friendly Norm businesslike with little taps that chilled his gushing about the picket line fracas. A handsome woman who had to keep touching things: her cigarettes and lighter, Kostenz when he gabbed too heavy or said something that pleased her. Five minutes in and he knew this about acting: a big part of the trick was sneaking what was really going on with you into your performance. He'd been up all night canvassing darktown straight off a weird jag of sobbing, coming up with nothing on the stolen Pontiac, but sensing HIM watching; the La Paloma Drive canvassing was a zero, ditto the bus line and cab company checks, and Mike Breuning had called to tell him he was trying to wangle four officers to tail the men on his surveillance list. He felt tired and edgy and knew it showed; he was running with *his* case, not this Commie shit, and if De Haven pressed for background verification he was going to play pissed and bring the conversation down to brass tacks: his resurgence of political faith and what UAES had for him to prove it with. 'Miss De Haven – '

'Claire.'

'Claire, I want to help. I want to get moving again. I'm rusty with everything but my fists, and I have to find a job pretty soon, but I want to help.'

Claire De Haven lit a cigarette and sent a hovering waitress packing with a wave of her lighter. 'I think for now you should embrace a philosophy of nonviolence.

I need someone to come with me when I go out courting contributors. You'd be good at helping me secure contributions from HUAC widows, I can tell.'

Danny took 'HUAC widows' as a cue and frowned, wounded by sudden memories of Donna Cantrell – hot love drowned in the Hudson River. Claire said, 'Is something wrong, Ted?'; Norm Kostenz touched her hand as if to say, 'Man stuff.' Danny winced, his muscle aches kicking in for real. 'No, you just reminded me of someone I used to know.'

Claire smiled. 'I reminded you or what I said did?'

Danny exaggerated a grimace. 'Both, Claire.'

'Care to elaborate?'

'Not quite yet.'

Claire called the waitress over and said, 'A pitcher of martinis'; the girl curtsied away, writing the order down. Danny said, 'No more action on the picket line, then?'

Kostenz said, 'The time isn't right, but pretty soon we'll lower the boom'; Claire shushed him – a mere flicker of her zealot's eyes. Danny horned in, Red Ted the pushy guy who'd step on anybody's toes. 'What "boom"? What are you talking about?'

Claire played with her lighter. 'Norm has a precipitate streak, and for a boxing fan he's read a lot of Gandhi. Ted, he's impatient and I'm impatient. There was a grand jury investigation forming up, sort of a baby HUAC, but now it looks like it went bust. That's still scary. And I listened to the radio on the ride over. There was another attempt on Mickey Cohen's life. Sooner or later, he'll go crazy and sic his goons on the picket line at us. We'll have to have cameras there to catch it.'

She hadn't really answered his question, and the passive resistance spiel sounded like subterfuge. Danny got ready to deliver a flirt line; the waitress returning stopped him. Claire said, 'Just two glasses, please'; Norm Kostenz said, 'I'm on the wagon,' and left with a wave. Claire poured two tall ones; Danny hoisted his glass and toasted, 'To the cause.' Claire said. 'To all things good.'

Danny drank, making an ugh face, a nonboozer notching points with a juicehead woman; Claire sipped and said, 'Car thief, revolutionary, ladies' man. I am suitably impressed.'

Cut her slack, let *her* move, reel her in. 'Don't be, because it's all phony.'

'Oh? Meaning?'

'Meaning I was a punk kid revolutionary and a scared car thief.'

'And the ladies' man?'

The hook baited. 'Let's just say I was trying to recapture an image.'

'Did you ever succeed?'

'No.'

'Because she's that special?'

Danny took a long drink, booze on top of no sleep making him misty. 'She was.'

'Was?'

Danny knew she'd gotten the story from Kostenz, but played along. 'Yeah, was. I'm a HUAC widower, Claire. The other women were just not . . .'

Claire said, 'Not her.'

'Right, not her. Not strong, not committed, not . . .'

'Not her.'

Danny laughed. 'Yeah, not her. Shit, I feel like a broken record.'

Claire laughed. 'I'd give you a snappy rejoinder about broken hearts, but you'd hit me.'

'I only beat up fascists.'

'No rough stuff with women?'

'Not my style.'

'It's mine occasionally.'

'I'm shocked.'

'I doubt that.'

Danny killed the drink. 'Claire, I want to work for the union, more than just lubing old biddies for money.'

'You'll get your chance. And they're not old biddies – unless you think women *my* age are old.'

A prime opening. 'How old are you? Thirty-one, thirty-two?'

Claire laughed the compliment out. 'Diplomat. How old are you?'

Danny reached for Ted Krugman's age, coming up wit it maybe a beat too slow. 'I'm twenty-six.'

'Well, I'm too old for boys and too young for gigolos. How's that for an answer?'

'Evasive.'

Claire laughed and fondled her ashtray. 'I'll be forty in May. So thanks for the subtraction.'

'It was sincere.'

'No, it wasn't.'

Hook her now, get to the station early. 'Claire, do I have political credibility with you?'

'Yes, you do.'

'Then let's try this on the other. I'd like to see you outside our work for the union.'

Claire's whole face softened; Danny got an urge to slap the bitch silly so she'd get mad and be a fit enemy. He said, 'I mean it,' Joe Clean Cut Sincere, Commie version.

Claire said, 'Ted, I'm engaged'; Danny said, 'I don't care.' Claire reached into her purse, pulled out a scented calling card and placed it on the table. 'We should at least get better acquainted. Some of us in the union are meeting at my house tonight. Why don't you come for the end of the meeting and say hello to everybody. Then, if you feel like it, we can take a drive and talk.'

Danny palmed the card and stood up. 'What time?'

'8:30.'

He'd be there early; pure cop, pure work. 'I look forward to it.'

Claire De Haven had gotten herself back together, her face set and dignified. 'So do I.'

Krugman back to Upshaw.

Danny drove to Hollywood Station, parked three blocks away and walked over. Mike Breuning met him

300

in the muster room doorway, grinning. 'You owe me one, Deputy.'

'What for?'

'Those guys on your list are now being tailed. Dudley authorized it, so you owe him one, too.'

Danny smiled. 'Fucking A. Who are they? Did you give them my number?'

'No. They're what you might wanta call Dudley's boys. You know, Homicide Bureau guys Dudley's brought up from rookies. They're smart guys, but they'll only report to Dud.'

'Breuning, this is my investigation.'

'Upshaw, I know. But you're damn lucky to have the men you've got, and Dudley's working the grand jury job too, so he wants to keep you happy. Have some goddamn gratitude. You've got no rank and you're running seven full-time men. When I was your age, I was rousting piss bums on skid row.'

Danny moved past Breuning into the muster room, knowing he was right, pissed anyway. Plainclothesmen and bluesuits were milling around, chuckling over something on the notice board. He looked over their shoulders and saw a new cartoon, worse than the one Jack Shortell ripped down.

Mickey Cohen, fangs, skullcap and a giant hard-on, pouring it up the ass of a guy in an LASD uniform. The deputy's pockets were spilling greenbacks; Cohen's speech balloon said: 'Smile, sweetie! Mickey C. gives it kosher!'

Danny shoved a line of blues aside and pulled the obscenity off the wall; he pivoted around, faced a full contingent of enemy cops and tore the piece of cardboard to shreds. The LAPD men gawked, simmered and plain stared; Gene Niles pushed through them and faced Danny down. He said, 'I talked to a guy named Leo Bordoni. He wouldn't blab outright, but I could tell he'd been questioned before. I think you rousted him, and I think it was inside Goines' pad. When I described the place it was like he'd already fucking been there.'

301

Except for Niles, the room was a blur. Danny said, 'Not now, Sergeant,' brass, the voice of authority.

'Up your ass, not now. I think you B&E'd in my jurisdiction. I know you didn't catch that squeal at the doughnut stand, and I've got a damn good lead where you did get it. If I can prove it, you're – '

'Niles not now.'

'Up your ass, not now. I had a good robbery case going until you came along with your crazy homo shit. You've got a queer fix, you're cuckoo on it and maybe you are a fucking queer!'

Danny lashed out, quick lefts and rights, short speed punches that caught Niles flush, ripped his face but didn't move his body back one inch. The enemy cops dispersed; Danny launched a hook to the gut; Niles feinted and came in with a hard uppercut, slamming Danny into the wall. He hung there, a stationary target, pretending to be gone; Niles telegraphed a huge right hand at his midsection. Danny slid away just before contact; Niles' fist hit the wall; he screeched into the sound of bones crunching. Danny sidestepped, swung Niles around and rolled sets at his stomach; Niles doubled over; Danny felt the enemy cops moving in. Somebody yelled, 'Stop it!'; strong arms bear-hugged and picked him up. Jack Shortell materialized, whispering, 'Easy, easy,' in the bear hugger's ear; the arms let go; another somebody yelled 'Watch Commander walking!' Danny went limp and let the old-timer cop lead him out a side exit.

Krugman to Upshaw to Krugman.

Shortell got Danny back to his car, extracting a promise that he'd try to sleep. Danny drove home, woozy one second, all jitters the next. Finally pure exhaustion hit him and he employed Ted-Claire repartee to stay awake. The banter saw him straight to bed, a pass on Mal Considine's bottle. With the Krugman leather jacket as his blanket, he fell asleep immediately.

And was joined by odd women and HIM.

The San Berdoo High senior hop, 1939. Glenn Miller and Tommy Dorsey on the PA system, Susan Leffert leading him out of the gym and into the boys' locker room, a Mason jar of schnapps as bait. Inside, she fumbles at his shirt buttons, licking his chest, biting the hair. He tries to drum up enthusiasm by staring at his body in the dressing mirror, but keeps thinking of Tim; that feels good, but hurts, and finally having it both ways is just bad. He tells Susan he met an older woman he wants to be loyal to, she reminds him of Suicide Donna who bought him his nice bombardier jacket, a real war hero number. Susan says, 'What war?'; the action fades because he knows something's off, Pearl Harbor is still two years away. Then this tall, faceless man, silver-haired, naked, is there, all around him in a circle, and squinting to see his face makes him go soft in Susan's mouth.

Then a whole corridor of mirrors, him chasing HIM, Karen Hiltscher, Roxy Beausoleil, Janice Modine and a bevy of Sunset Strip gash swooping down while he hurls excuses.

'I can't today, I have to study.'

'I don't dance, it makes me self-conscious.'

'Some other time, okay?'

'Sweetie, let's keep this light. We work together.'

'I don't want it.'

'No.'

'Claire, you're the only real woman I've met since Donna.'

'Claire, I want to fuck you so bad just like I used to fuck Donna and all the others. They all loved it because I loved doing it so much.'

He was gaining ground on HIM, gaining focus on the gray man's brick shithouse build. The apparition twirled around; he had no face, but Tim's body and bigger stuff than Demon Don Eversall, who used to hang out in the shower, trap water in his jumbo foreskin, hold his thing out and croon, 'Come drink from my cup of love.' Hard kissing; bodies mashed together, the two of them inside

303

each other, Claire walking out of the mirror, saying, 'That's impossible.'

Then a gunshot, then another and another.

Danny jolted awake. He heard a fourth ring, saw that he'd sweated the bed sopping, felt like he had to piss and threw off the jacket to find his trousers wet. He fumbled over to the phone and blurted, 'Yes?'

'Danny, it's Jack.'

'Yeah, Jack.'

'Son, I cleared you with the assistant watch commander, this lieutenant named Poulson. He's pals with Al Dietrich, and he's reasonable about our Department.'

Danny thought: and Dietrich's pals with Felix Gordean, who's got LAPD and DA's Bureau pals, and Niles is pals with God knows who on the Sheriff's. 'What about Niles?'

'He's been yanked from our job. I told Poulson he'd been riding you, that he provoked the fight. I think you'll be okay.' A pause, then, 'Are you okay? Did you sleep?'

The dream was coming back; Danny stifled a shot of HIM. 'Yeah, I slept. Jack, I don't want Mal Considine to hear about what happened.'

'He's your boss on the grand jury?'

'Right.'

'Well, I won't tell him, but somebody probably will.'

Mike Breuning and Dudley Smith replaced HIM. 'Jack, I have to do some work on the other job. I'll call you tomorrow.'

Shortell said, 'One more thing. We got minor league lucky on our hot car queries – an Olds was snatched two blocks from La Paloma. Abandoned at the Samo Pier, no prints, but I'm adding "car thief" to our records checks. And we're a hundred and forty-one down on the dental queries. It's going slow, but I have a hunch we'll get him.'

HIM.

Danny laughed, yesterday's wounds aching, new bone bruises firing up in his knuckles. 'Yeah, we'll get him.'

Danny segued back to Krugman with a shower and change of clothes, Red Ted the stud in Karen Hiltscher's sports jacket, pegged flannels and a silk shirt from Considine's disguise kit. He drove to Beverly Hills middle-lane slow, checking his rear-view every few seconds for cars riding his tail too close and a no-face man peering too intently, shining his headlights too bright because deep down he wanted to be caught, wanted everyone to know *WHY*. No likely suspects appeared in the mirror; twice his trawling almost got him into fender benders. He arrived at Claire De Haven's house forty-five minutes early; he saw Caddies and Lincolns in the driveway, muted lights glowing behind curtained windows and one narrow side dormer cracked for air, screened and shade covered – but open. The dormer faced a stone footpath and tall shrubs separating the De Haven property from the neighboring house; Danny walked over, squatted down and listened.

Words came at him, filtered through coughs and garbled interruptions. He picked out a man's shout: 'Cohen and his farshtunkener lackeys have to go nutso first'; Claire's 'It's all in knowing when to squeeze.' A soft, mid-Atlantic drawl: 'We have to give the studios an out to save face with, that's why knowing when is so important. It has to hit the fan just right.'

Danny kept checking his blind side for witnesses; he heard a long digression on the '52 presidential election – who'd run, who wouldn't – that degenerated into a childish shouting match, Claire finally dominating with her opinion of Stevenson and Taft, fascist minions of varying stripes. There was something about a movie director named Paul Doinelle and his 'Cocteau-like' classics; then an almost complete duet: the soft-voiced man chuckling over 'old flames,' a man with a stentorian Southern accent punch-lining, 'But I got Claire.' Danny recalled the psychiatric files: Reynolds Loftis and Chaz

305

Minear were lovers years ago; Considine told him that now Claire and Loftis were engaged to be married. He got stomach flip-flops and looked at his watch: 8:27, time to meet the enemy.

He walked around and rang the bell. Claire opened the door and said, 'Right on time'; Danny saw that her makeup and slacks suit tamped down her wrinkles and showed off her curves better than the powder job and dress at the restaurant. He said, 'You look lovely, Claire.'

Claire whispered, 'Save it for later,' took his arm and led him into the living room, subtle swank offset by framed movie posters: Pinko titles from the grand jury package. Three men were standing around holding drinks: a Semitic-looking guy in tweeds, a small, trim number wearing a tennis sweater and white ducks, and a dead ringer composite for HIM – a silver-maned man pushing fifty, topping six feet by at least two inches, as lanky as Mal Considine but ten times as handsome. Danny stared at his face, thinking something about the set of his eyes was familiar, then looked away – queer or ex-queer or whatever, he was just an image – a Commie, not a killer.

Claire made the introductions. 'Gentlemen, Ted Krugman. Ted, left to right we have Mort Ziffkin, Chaz Minear and Reynolds Loftis.'

Danny shook their hands, getting, 'Hey there, slugger,' from Ziffkin, 'A pleasure,' from Minear and a wry smile out of Loftis, an implicit aside: I allow my fiancée to dally with younger guys. He gave the tall man his strongest grip, snapping hard into Ted K. 'The pleasure's all mine, and I'm looking forward to working with you.'

Minear smiled; Ziffkin said, 'Attaboy''; Loftis said, 'You and Claire have a good strategy talk, but get her home early, you hear?' – a Southern accent, but no syrup and another aside: he was sleeping with De Haven tonight.

Danny laughed, knowing he'd just memorized Loftis' features; Claire sighed, 'Let's go, Ted. Strategy awaits.'

They walked outside. Danny thought of rolling tails and steered Claire to his car. She said, 'Where do you want to strategize'; *her* aside, her parody on Loftis playing cute. Danny opened the passenger door, getting an idea: prowl darktown with the protective coloration of a woman in tow. It was nearly two weeks since he'd gone strongarming down there, he probably wouldn't be recognized in his non-cop outfit and HE was near the Southside strip just yesterday. 'I like jazz. Do you?'

'I love it, and I know a great spot in Hollywood.'

'I know some places on South Central that really bop. What do you say?'

Claire hesitated, then said, 'Sure, sounds like fun.'

East on Wilshire, south on Normandie. Danny drove fast, thinking of his midnight meeting and ways to chill Considine on the Niles ruckus; he kept checking the rear-view mock casual, gifting Claire with a smile each time so she'd think he was thinking of her. Nothing strange appeared in the mirror; Reynolds Loftis' face stayed in his mind, a non-face to make *the* face jump out and bite him. Claire chain-smoked and drummed her nails on the dashboard.

The silence played right, two idealists deep in thought East on Slauson, south on Central, more mirror checks now that they were on HIS stomping ground. Danny pulled up in front of the Club Zombie; Claire said, 'Ted, what are you afraid of?'

The question caught him checking his waistband for the sap he always packed on niggertown assignments; he stopped and grabbed the wheel, Red Ted the persecuted Negro's buddy. 'The Teamsters, I guess. I'm rusty.'

Claire put a hand on his cheek. 'You're tired and lonely and driven. You want to please and do the right thing so badly that it just about breaks my heart.'

Danny leaned into the caress, a catch in his throat like when he saw Considine's bottle. Claire took her hand away and kissed the spot she'd touched. 'I am such a sucker for strays. Come on, strong silent type. We're going to listen to music and hold hands, and we're *not* going to talk about politics.'

The catch stuck; the kiss was still warm. Danny walked ahead of Claire to the door; the bouncer from New Year's Day was there and eyed him like he was just another white hepcat. Claire caught up just as the cold air got him back to normal: Krugman the Commie on a hot date, Upshaw the Homicide cop on overtime. He took her arm and led her inside.

The Zombie interior was just like two weeks before, with an even louder, more dissonant combo wailing on the bandstand. This time the clientele was all Negro: sea of black faces offset by colored lighting, a flickering canvas where a white/gray face would stand out and scream, 'Me!' Danny slipped the maitre d' a five-spot and requested a wall table with a floor view; the man led them to seats near the back exit, took their order for a double bonded and a dry martini, bowed and motioned for a waitress. Danny settled Claire into the chair closest to the bandstand; he grabbed the one facing the bar and audience.

Claire laced her fingers through Danny's and beat time on the table with her hands, a gentle beat, counterpoint to the screechy bebop that filled the room. The drinks arrived; Claire paid, a fiver to the high-yellow waitress, her free hand up to refuse the change. The girl sashayed off; Danny sipped bourbon – cheap house stuff that burned. Claire squeezed his hand; he squeezed back, grateful for loud music that made talk impossible. Looking out at the crowd, he sensed that HIM here was just as impossible – he'd know the police now had him pegged as a darktown car thief – he'd avoid South Central like the plague.

But the place felt right, safe and dark, Danny closed his eyes and listened to the music, Claire's hand on his still making a beat. The combo's rhythm was complex: drums shooting a melody to the sax, the sax winging it off on digressions, returning to simpler and simpler chords, then the main theme, then the trumpet and the bass taking flight, going crazy with more and more complicated riffs. Listening for the handoffs was hypnotic; half the sounds were ugly and strange, making him wish for the simple, pretty themes to come back. Danny listened, ignoring his drink, trying to figure the music out and predict where it was going. He felt like he was getting the synchronization when a crescendo came out of nowhere, the players quit playing, applause hit like thunder and bright lights came on.

Claire dropped his hand and started clapping; a mulatto lounge lizard sidled by the table, saying, 'Hello, sweet. I ain't seen you in a dog's age.' Claire averted her eyes; Danny stood up; the mulatto said, 'Forget old friends, see if I care,' and kept sidling.

Claire lit a cigarette, her lighter shaking. Danny said, 'Who was that?'

'Oh, a friend of a friend. I used to have a thing for jazz musicians.'

The mulatto had made his way up to the bandstand; Danny saw him slip something into the bass player's hand, a flash of green picked up at the same time. Considine on De Haven: she was a skin-popper and devotee of pharmacy hop.

Danny sat down; Claire stubbed out her cigarette and sparked another one. The lights were dimmed; the music started – a slow romantic ballad. Danny tried the beating time maneuver, but Claire's hand wouldn't move. Her eyes were darting around the room; he saw the exit door across from them open up, spotlighting Carlton W. Jeffries, the grasshopper he'd strong-armed for a snitch on H pushers. The doorway cast a strip of light all the way over to Claire De Haven making with rabbity eyes, a rich white girl with a snout for lowlife afraid that more embarrassment might ruin her date with an undercover cop out to get her indicted for treason. The door closed; Danny felt her fear jump on him and turn the nice, dark, safe place bad, full of crazy jungle niggers who'd eat him whole, revenging all the niggers he'd pushed around. He said, 'Claire, let's leave, okay?;'

Claire said, 'Yes, let's.'

The ride back was all Claire with the jitters, rambling on what she'd accomplished with what organizations – a litany that sounded harmless and probably contained not one shred of information that Considine and Loew would find interesting. Danny let it wash over him, thinking of his meeting, wondering what Leo Bordoni told Gene Niles, if Niles really had a County source to place him inside 2307, and if he could prove it, would anybody care? Should he grease Karen Hiltscher on general principles, her being the only *real* snitch possibility, even though her even knowing Niles was unlikely? And how should he lay off the blame for the fight? How to make Considine think his future exec beating up one of his own men was kosher, when that man might just have him by the balls?

Danny turned onto Claire's block, thinking of good exit lines; slowing down and stopping, he had two at the ready. He smiled and prepared to perform; Claire touched his cheek, softer than the first time. 'I'm sorry, Teddy. It was a lousy first date. Rain check?'

Danny said, 'Sure,' going all warm, the catch again.

'Tomorrow night, here? Just us, strategy and whatever the spirit moves us to?'

Her hand had reversed itself, knuckles lightly tracing his jawline. 'Sure . . . darling.'

She stopped then, eyes shut, lips parted. Danny moved into the kiss, wanting the soft hand, not the hungry mouth painted pinkish red. Just as they touched, he froze and almost pulled away. Claire's tongue slid across his teeth, probing. He thought of Reynolds Loftis, gave the woman his face and did it.

CHAPTER TWENTY-FOUR

Mal was watching Buzz Meeks eat, thinking that suicide love must be good for the appetite: the fat man had devoured a plate of stuffed shrimp, two double-thick pork chops with onion rings, and was now killing a huge piece of peach pie buried in ice cream. It was their second meal together, with INS file work and his run by Jake Kellerman's office in between; at lunch Meeks had wolfed a porterhouse, home fries and three orders of rice pudding. Mal picked at a plate of chicken salad and shook his head: Meeks said, 'A growin' boy's got to feed. What time's Upshaw due?'

Mal checked his watch. 'I told him midnight. Why, do you have plans?'

'A late one with my sweetie. Howard's usin' his spot up by the Bowl, so we're meetin' at her place. I told her I'd be there by one at the latest, and I mean to be punctual.'

'Meeks, are you taking precautions?'

Buzz said, 'We use the rhythm method. Her place when Howard's rhythm moves us.' He dug in his coat pockets and fished out an envelope. 'I forgot to tell you. When you were at your lawyer's, Ellis came by. I gave him your memo, and he read it and wrote you one. Apparently, your boy traded blows with some LAPD dick. Ellis said to read this and abide by it.'

Mal opened the envelope and pulled out a slip of paper covered with Ellis Loew's handwriting. He read:

M.C. –

I agree wholeheartedly with everything but your assessment of Dudley's methods. What you don't realize is that Dudley is so effective that his methods minimize the chance that potential witness will balk and inform on us to UAES. Also, I can't give you command of the investigation, not with the obvious dislike that exists between you and Dudley. It would ruffle the feathers of a man who up until yesterday shared your rank with many more years in grade. You're equals in this investigation and once we go to court you'll never have to work with him again.

Something has come up on Deputy Upshaw. A Sgt. Breuning (LAPD) called to tell me that Upshaw got into a fistfight with another City officer (Sgt. G. Niles) this afternoon, over a stupid remark Niles made about 'queers.' This is, in light of the interagency command we set up for Upshaw, intolerable. Breuning also stated that Upshaw demanded four officers for surveillance work, and that Dudley, wanting to keep him happy, found the men. This is also intolerable. Upshaw is a young, inexperienced officer who, however gifted, has no right to be making such demands. I want you to sternly inform him that we will tolerate no more fisticuffs or prima donna behavior.

Sgt. Bowman is now looking for Dr. Lesnick. I hope he didn't die on us, too – he's a valuable addition to our team.

E.L.

P.S. – Good luck in court tomorrow. Your promotion and current duties should help you secure a continuance. I think Jake Kellerman's strategy is sound.

Mal wadded the paper up and hurled it blindly; it bounced off the back of the booth, and landed on Meeks' butter plate. Buzz said, 'Whoa, partner'; Mal looked up and saw Danny Upshaw hovering. He said, 'Sit down, Deputy,' ticked until he noticed the kid's hands were shaking.

Danny slid into the booth next to Meeks. Buzz said, 'Turner Meeks' and gave him a shake; Danny nodded and turned to Mal. 'Congratulations, Captain. And thanks for the jug.'

Mal eyed his decoy, thinking that right now he looked not one iota cop. 'Thank you, and my pleasure. And before we get to business, what happened with Sergeant Niles?'

Danny gripped an empty water glass. 'He's got a crazy idea I B&E'd the place where the second and third victims were found. Essentially, he's miffed at taking orders from me. Jack Shortell told me the watch commander yanked him off the case, so I'm glad he's out of my hair.'

The answer sounded rehearsed. Mal said, 'That's all of it?'

'Yes.'

'And did you B&E?'

'No, of course not.'

Mal thought of the 'queer' remark, but let it pass. 'All right, then consider this a reprimand, from Ellis Loew *and* myself. No more of that, *period*. Don't let it happen again. Got that?'

Danny raised the glass, looking chagrined when he found it empty. 'Yes, Captain.'

'It's still "Mal". Do you want something to eat?'

'No thanks.'

'A drink?'

Danny pushed the glass away. 'No.'

Buzz said, 'Save your dukes for the Police Golden Gloves. I knew a guy made Sergeant beatin' up on guys his CO hated.'

Danny laughed; Mal wished that he'd order a shot for his nerves. 'Tell me about the approach. Have you met with De Haven?'

'Yeah, twice.'

'And?'

'And she's making a play for me.'

His operative was actually blushing. Mal said, 'Tell me about it.'

'There's not much to tell yet. We had a date tonight, we've got another one set for tomorrow night. I listened outside her house while a meeting was going on, and I

313

picked up some stuff. Pretty vague, but enough to tell me that they have some kind of extortion angle going against the studios and they're planning to time it with the Teamsters going crazy on the picket line. So tell Mickey to keep his guys in check. I could tell this angle is important to their strategy, and when I see De Haven tomorrow, I'm going to press her for details.'

Mal kicked the dope around, thinking that it played true to his take on the brain trusters: they were duplicitous, they talked a lot, they took their own sweet time acting and let outside events call the tune. 'Who have you met besides Kostenz and De Haven?'

'Loftis, Minear and Ziffkin, but just briefly.'

'How did they impress you?'

Danny made an open-handed gesture. 'They didn't really impress me at all. I only spoke to them for a minute or so.'

Buzz chuckled and loosened his belt. 'You were lucky old Reynolds didn't jump your bones instead of De Haven. Nice-lookin' young guy like you would probably get that old prowler stiffin' up a hard yard.'

Danny flushed again. Mal thought of him working two twenty-four-hour-a-day cases, jamming them into one twenty-four-hour day. He said, 'Tell me how your other job's going.'

Danny's eyes were darting, flicking over the neighboring booths, lingering on men at the bar before returning to Mal. He said, 'Slow but well, I think. I've got my own home file, all the evidence and all my impressions and that's a help. I've got a bunch of records checks going, and so far that's slow, but steady. Where I think I'm getting close is on the victims, putting them together. He's not a random psycho, I *know* that. If I get closer I might need a decoy to help draw him out. Would it be possible to get another man?'

Mal said, 'No'; he watched Danny's eyes follow two men walking past their booth. 'No, not after your stunt with Niles. You've got those four officers Dudley Smith swung you – '

314

'They're Dudley's men, not mine! They won't even report to me, and Mike Breuning's jerking my chain! For all I know he's bunked out on the whole job!'

Mal slapped the table, bringing Danny's eyes back to him. 'Look at me and listen. I want you to calm down and take things slow. You're doing all you can on both your assignments, and aside from Niles you're doing great. Now you've lost one man, but you've got your tailing officers, so just figure you've cut your goddamn losses, knuckle down and be a professional. *Be a policeman.*'

Danny's eyes, blurry, held on Mal. Buzz said, 'Deputy, you got any hard leads on your victims, any whatcha call common denominators?'

The operative spoke to his operator. 'A man named Felix Gordean. He's a homosexual procurer connected to one of the victims, and I *know* the killer's got some kind of fix on him. I haven't leaned on him too hard yet, because he's paying off County Central Vice and he says he's got influence with LAPD and the Bureau.'

Mal said, 'Well, I've never heard of him, and I'm top Bureau dog. Buzz, do you know this guy?'

'Sure do, boss. Large City juice, larger County. One lean and mean fruitfly, plays golf with Sheriff Eugene Biscailuz, puts a few shekels in Al Dietrich's pockets come Christmastime, too.'

As he said the words, Mal knew it was one of the finest moments of his life. 'Lean on him, Danny. I'll stand the heat, and if anyone gives you grief, you've got the Chief DA's Investigator for the City of Los Angeles in your corner.'

Danny stood up, looking heartbreaker grateful. Mal said, 'Go home and sleep, Ted. Have nightcap on me.' The decoy left, saluting his brother officers; Buzz breathed out slowly. 'That boy is upon a tall old tree limb lookin' down at a tall old boy with a saw, and you've got more balls than brains.'

It was just about the nicest thing anyone ever told

him. Mal said, 'Have another piece of pie, lad. I'm picking up the check.'

CHAPTER TWENTY-FIVE

The hall window scraping, three soft footsteps on the bedroom floor.

Buzz stirred, rolled away from Audrey, reached under the pillow and palmed his .38, camouflaging the movement with a sleep sigh. Two more footsteps, Audrey snoring, light through a crack in the curtains eclipsed. A shape coming around his side of the bed; the sound of a hammer being cocked; 'Mickey, you're dead.'

Buzz stiff-armed Audrey to the floor, away from the voice; a silencer snicked and muzzle flash lit up a big man in a dark overcoat. Audrey screamed; Buzz felt the mattress rip an inch from his legs. In one swipe, he grabbed his billy club off the nightstand and swung it at the man's knees; wood-encased steel cracked bone; the man stumbled toward the bed. Audrey shrieked, 'Meeks!'; a shot ripped the far wall; another half second of muzzle light gave Buzz a sighting. He grabbed the man's coat and pulled him to the bed, smothering his head with a pillow and shot him twice in the face point-blank.

The explosions were muffled; Audrey screeching was siren loud. Buzz moved around the bed and bear-hugged her, killing her tremors with his own shakes. He whispered, 'Go into the bathroom, keep the light off and your head down. This was for Mickey, and if there's a back-up man outside, he's comin'. Stay fuckin' down and stay fuckin' calm.'

Audrey retreated on her knees; Buzz went into the living room, parted the front curtains and looked out. There was a sedan parked directly across the street that wasn't there when he walked in; no other cars were

statione   through on what probably h

He   he drove a
gree   yesterday;
Mic   arked his car
the   surveillance
co   short fat okie
s

yed still, no tell-
t by; no cops or
s a single-o play,
ed on the overhead

bed was soaked in
blood;   olid   rated crimson. Buzz
lifted it off and propped up the dead man's head. It had
no face, there were no exit wounds, all the red was
leaking out his ears. He rifled his pockets – and the
wicked bad willies came on.

An LAPD badge and ID buzzer: Detective Sergeant
Eugene J. Niles, Hollywood Squad. An Automobile
Club card, vehicle dope in the lower left corner –
maroon '46 Ford Crown Victoria Sedan, Cal '49 JS 1497.
A California driver's license made out to Eugene Niles,
residence 3987 Melbourne Avenue, Hollywood. Car
keys and other keys and pieces of paper with Audrey's
address and an architectural floor plan for a house that
looked like Mickey's pad in Brentwood.

Old rumors, new facts, killer shakes.

The LAPD was behind the shootout at Sherry's; Jack
D. and Mickey had buried the hatchet; Niles worked
Hollywood Division, the eye of the Brenda Allen storm.
Buzz ran across the street on fear overdrive, saw that
the sedan was '46 Vicky JS 1497, unlocked the trunk
and ran back. He hauled out a big bed quilt, wrapped
Niles and his gun up in it, shoulder-slung him up and
over to the Vicky and locked him in the trunk, folding
him double next to the spare tire. Panting, sweat-soaked
and shaky, he walked back and braced Audrey.

317

She was sitting on the toilet, naked, smoking. A half dozen butts littered the floor; the bathroom was a tobacco cloud. She looked like the woman from Mars: tears had melted her makeup and her lipstick was still smudged from their lovemaking.

Buzz knelt in front of her. 'Honey, I'll take care of it. This was for Mickey, so I think we're okay. But I should stay away from you for a while, just in case this guy had partners – we don't want them figurin' out it was you and me instead of you and Mickey.'

Audrey dropped her cigarette on the floor and snuffed it with her bare feet, no pain registering. She said, 'All right,' a hoarse smoker's croak.

Buzz said, 'You strip the bed and burn it in the incinerator. There's bullets in the mattress and the wall, you dig 'em out and toss 'em. And you don't tell *nobody*.'

Audrey said, 'Tell me it'll be all right.' Buzz kissed the part in her hair, seeing the two of them strapped down in the gas chamber. 'Honey, this will surely be all right.'

Buzz drove Niles' car to the Hollywood Hills. He found gardening tools in the back seat, a level patch of hard-scrabble off the access road to the Hollywood Sign and buried Mickey Cohen's would-be assassin in a plot about 4 by 4 by 4, working with an earth spade and grub hoe. He packed the dirt hard and tight so coyotes wouldn't smell flesh rot and get hungry; he put branches atop the spot and pissed on it: an epitaph for a fellow bad cop who'd put him in the biggest trouble of his trouble-prone life. He buried Niles' gun under a thornbush, drove the car out to the Valley, wiped it down, yanked the distributor and left it in an abandoned garage atop Suicide Hill – a youth gang fuck turf near the Sepulveda VA Hospital. Undrivable, the Vicky would be spare parts inside twenty-four hours.

It was 4:30 A.M.

Buzz walked down to Victory Boulevard, caught a cab to Hollywood and Vermont, walked the remaining

318

half mile to Melbourne Avenue. He found a pay phone, glommed 'Eugene Niles' from the White Pages, dialed the number and let it ring twenty times – no answer. He located 3987 – the bottom left apartment of a pink stucco four-flat – and let himself in with Niles' keys, set to prowl for one thing: evidence that other men were in on the Mickey hit.

It was a typical bachelor flop: sitting/sleeping room with Murphy bed, bathroom, kitchenette. There was a desk facing a boarded-up window; Buzz went straight for it, handling everything he touched with his shirttails. Ten minutes in, he had solid circumstantial evidence:

A certificate from the U.S. Army Demolition School, Camp Polk, Louisiana, stating that Corporal Eugene Niles successfully completed explosives training in December 1931 – make the fucker for the bomb under Mickey's house.

Letters from Niles' ex-wife, condemning him for trucking with Brenda Allen's hookers. She'd read the grand jury transcript and knew her husband did his share of porking in the Hollywood Station felony tank – Niles' motive to want Mickey dead.

An address book that included the names and phone numbers of four ranking Jack Dragna strongarms, listings for three other Dragna bagmen – cops he knew when he was LAPD – and a weird listing: 'Karen Hiltscher, W. Hollywood Sheriff's,' with '!!!!' in bright red doodles. That aside, more verification of Niles hating Mickey before the truce with Jack D. All told, it looked like a poorly planned single-o play, Niles desperate when his bomb didn't blow the Mick to shit.

Buzz killed the lights and wiped both sides of the doorknob on his way out. He walked to Sunset and Vermont, dropped Niles' house and car keys down a sewer grate and started laughing, wildly, stitches in his side. He'd just saved the life of the most dangerous, most generous man he'd ever met, and there was no way in the world he could tell him. The laughter got worse, until he doubled over and had to sit down on a bus bench. He laughed until the punch line sucker-pun-ched him – then he froze.

Danny Upshaw beat up Gene Niles. The City cops hated the County cops. When Niles was tagged as missing, LAPD would be like flies over shit on a green kid already in shit up to his knees.

CHAPTER TWENTY-SIX

Danny was trying to get Felix Gordean alone.

He'd begun his stakeout in the Chateau Marmont parking lot; Gordean foiled him by driving to his office with Pretty Boy Christopher in tow. Rain had been pouring down the whole three hours he'd been eyeing the agency's front door; no cars had hit the carport, the street was flooded and he was parked in a tow-away zone with his ID, badge and .45 at home because he was really Red Ted Krugman. Ted's leather jacket and Considine's sanction kept him warm and dry with the window cracked; Danny decided that if Gordean didn't leave the office by 1:00, he'd lean on him then and there.

At 12:35, the door opened. Gordean walked out, popped an umbrella and skipped across Sunset. Danny turned on his wiper blades and watched him duck into Cyrano's, the doorman fussing over him like he was the joint's most popular customer. He gave Gordean thirty seconds to get seated, turned up his collar and ran over, ducking rain.

The doorman looked at him funny, but let him in; Danny blinked water, saw gilt and red velvet walls, a long oak bar and Felix Gordean sipping a martini at a side table. He threaded his way past a clutch of business-man types and sat down across from him; Gordean almost swallowed the toothpick he was nibbling.

Danny said, 'I want to know what you know. I want you to tell me everything about the men you've brought out, and I want a report on all your customers and clients. I want it now.'

Gordean toyed with the toothpick. 'Have Lieutenant Matthews call me. Perhaps he and I can effect a compromise.'

'Fuck Lieutenant Matthews. Are you going to tell me what I want to know? *Now?*'

'No, I am not.'

Danny smiled. 'You've got forty-eight hours to change your mind.'

'Or?'

'Or I'm taking everything I know about you to the papers.'

Gordean snapped his fingers; a waiter came over; Danny walked out of the restaurant and into the rain. He remembered his promise to call Jack Shortell, hit the phone booth across from the agency, dialed the Hollywood Station squadron and heard, 'Yes?,' Shortell himself speaking, his voice strained.

'It's Upshaw, Jack. What have you got on – '

'What we've got is another one. LAPD found him last night, on an embankment up from the LA River. Doc Layman's doing him now, so – '

Danny left the receiver dangling and Shortell shouting, 'Upshaw!'; he highballed it downtown, parked in front of the City Morgue loading dock and almost tripped over a stiff on a gurney running in. Jack Shortell was already there, sweating, his badge pinned to his coat front; he saw Danny, blocked the path to Layman's examination room and said, 'Brace yourself.'

Danny got his breath. 'For what?'

Shortell said, 'It's Augie Luis Duarte, one of the guys on your tailing list; The bluesuits who found him ID'd him from his driver's license. LAPD's had the stiff since 12:30 last night – the squad guy who caught didn't know about our team. Breuning was here and just left, and he was making noises that Duarte blew *his* tail last night. Danny, I know that's horseshit. I was calling around last night looking for you, to tell you our car thief and zoot

321

stick queries were bust. I talked to a clerk at Wilshire Station, and she told me Breuning was there all evening with Dudley Smith. I called back later, and the clerk said they were still there. Breuning said the other three men are still under surveillance, but I don't believe him.'

Danny's head boomed; morgue effluvia turned his stomach and stung his razor burns. He beelined for a door marked 'Norton Layman MD,' pushed it open and saw the country's premier forensic pathologist writing on a clipboard. A nude shape was slab-prone behind him; Layman stepped aside as if to say, 'Feast your eyes.'

Augie Duarte, the handsome Mex who'd walked out the Gordean Agency door two nights ago, was supine on a stainless steel tray. He was blood-free; bite wounds extruding intestinal tubes covered his stomach; bite marks ran up his torso in a pattern free of overlaps. His cheeks were slashed down to the gums and jawbone and his penis had been cut off, inserted into the deepest of the cuts and hooked around so that the head extended out his mouth, teeth clamped on the foreskin, rigor mortis holding the obscenity intact. Danny blurted, 'Oh God fuck no'; Layman said, 'The rain drained the body and kept the cuts fresh. I found a tooth chip in one of them and made a wet cast of it. It's unmistakably animal, and I had an attendant run it down to a forensic ortho-dontist at the Natural History Museum. It's being exam-ined now.'

Danny tore his eyes off the corpse; he walked out to the dock looking for Jack Shortell, gagging on the stench of formaldehyde, his lungs heavy for fresh air. A group of Mexicans with a bereaved-family look was standing by the loading ramp staring in; a pachuco type stared at him extra hard. Danny strained to see Shortell, then felt a hand on his shoulder.

It was Norton Layman. He said, 'I just talked to the man at the Museum, and he identified my specimen. The killer wears wolverine teeth.'

Danny saw a blood W on cheap wallpaper. He saw

W's in black and white, W's burned into Felix Gordean's face, W's all over the rosary-clutching wetbacks huddled together grieving. He saw W's until Jack Shortell walked up the dock and grabbed his arm and he heard himself say, 'Get Breuning. I don't trust myself on it.'

Then he saw plain blood.

CHAPTER TWENTY-SEVEN

A stakeout for his own son.

Mal sat on the steps outside Division 32, Los Angeles Civil Court. He was flanked by lawyers smoking; keeping his back to them kept light conversation away while he scanned for Stefan, Celeste and her shyster. When he saw them, it would be a quick men's room confab: don't believe the bad things you hear about me; when my man gets ugly about your mother, try not to listen.

Ten of the hour; no Stefan, Celeste and lawyer. Mal heard an animated burst of talk behind him.

'You know Charlie Hartshorn?'

'Sure. A nice guy, if a bit of a bleeding heart. He worked the Sleepy Lagoon defense for free.'

'Well, he's dead. Suicide. Hung himself at his house last night. Beautiful house, right off Wilshire and Rimpau. It was on the radio. I went to a party at that house once.'

'Poor Charlie. What a goddamn shame.'

Mal turned around; the two men were gone. He remembered Meeks telling him Reynolds Loftis was connected to Hartshorn via a queer-bar roust, but he didn't mention the man being associated with the Sleepy Lagoon Defense Committee at all. There was no mention of Hartshorn in any of the psychiatric or other grand jury files, and Meeks had also said that the lawyer had turned up – as a non-suspect – in Danny Upshaw's homicide investigation.

The Hartshorn coincidence simmered; Mal wondered how Meeks would take his suicide – he said he'd gut-shot the man with his queerness. Looking streetside, he saw Celeste, Stefan and a young guy with a briefcase get out of a cab; his boy glanced up, lit up and took off running.

Mal met him halfway down the steps, scooped him up laughing and pinwheeled him upside down and over. Stefan squealed; Celeste and briefcase double-timed; Mal whipped his son over his shoulder, quick-marched inside and turned hard into the men's room. Out of breath, he put Stefan down and said, 'Your dad's a captain,' dug in his pockets and pulled out one of the insignia Buzz gave him. 'You're a captain, too. Remember that. Remember that if your mother's lawyer starts talking me down.'

Stefan squeezed the silver bars; Mal saw that he had that bewildered fat-kid look he got when Celeste stuffed him with starchy Czech food. 'How have you been? How's your mother been treating you?'

Stefan spoke hesitantly, like he'd been force-fed old country talk since the breakup. 'Mutti . . . wants that we should move out. She said we . . . we must move away before she decides to marry Rich-Richard.'

Richard.

'I – I don't like Richard. He's nice to Mutti, but he's n-nasty to his d-d-dog.'

Mal put his arms around the boy. 'I won't let it happen. She's a crazy woman, and I won't let her take you away.'

'Malcolm – '

'*Dad*, Stefan.'

'Dad, please not to don't hit Mutti again. *Please*.'

Mal held Stefan tighter, trying to squeeze the bad words out and make him say, 'I love you.' The boy felt wrong, flabby, like he was too skinny wrong as a kid. 'Sssh. I'll never hit her again and I'll never let her take you away from me. Sssh.'

The door opened behind them; Mal heard the voice

of an old City bailiff who'd been working Division 32 forever. 'Lieutenant Considine, court's convening and I'm supposed to bring the boy into chambers.'

Mal gave Stefan a last hug. 'I'm a captain now. Stefan, you go with this man and I'll see you inside.'

Stefan hugged back – hard.

Court convened ten minutes later. Mal sat with Jake Kellerman at a table facing the judge's bench; Celeste, her attorney and Stefan were seated in chairs stationed diagonally across from the witness stand. The old bailiff intoned, 'Hear ye, hear ye, court is now in session, the Honorable Arthur F. Hardesty presiding.'

Mal stood up. Jake Kellerman whispered, 'In a second the old fart'll say, "Counsel will approach the bench." I'll hit him for a first continuance for a month from now, citing your grand jury duties. Then, we'll get another stay until the jury convenes and you're gold. *Then* we'll get you Greenberg.'

Mal gripped Kellerman's arm. 'Jake, make this happen.'

Kellerman whispered extra low, 'It will. Just pray a rumor I heard isn't true.'

Judge Arthur F. Hardesty banged his gavel. 'Counsel will approach the bench.'

Jake Kellerman and Celeste's lawyer approached, huddling around Hardesty; Mal strained to hear and picked up nothing but garbles – Jake sounding agitated. The huddle ended with a gavel slam; Kellerman walked back, fuming.

Hardesty said, 'Mr. Considine, your counsel's request for a one-month continuance has been denied. Despite your police duties, I'm sure you can find enough time to consult with Mr. Kellerman. All parties will meet here in my chambers ten days hence, Monday, January 22. Both contestants should be ready to testify. Mr. Kellerman, Mr. Castleberry, make sure your witnesses are informed of the date and bring whatever documents you wish to be considered as evidence. This preliminary is dismissed.'

The judge banged his gavel; Castleberry led Celeste and Stefan outside. The boy turned around and waved; Mal flashed him the V for victory sign, tried to smile and couldn't. His son was gone in a breath; Kellerman said, 'I heard Castleberry heard about your promotion and went batshit. I heard he leaked the hospital pictures to one of Hardesty's clerks, who told the judge. Mal, I'm sorry and I'm angry. I'm going to tell Ellis what Castleberry did and make sure that punk gets reamed for it.'

Mal stared at the spot where his son waved goodbye. 'Ream her. Pull out all the stops. If Stefan has to hear, he has to hear. Just fucking take her down.'

CHAPTER TWENTY-EIGHT

Looking around Ellis Loew's living room, Buzz set odds:

Twenty to one the grand jury handed down beaucoup UAES indictments; twenty to one the studios booted them on the treason clause prior to the official word, with the Teamsters signing to take their place inside twenty-four hours. If he convinced Mickey to make book on the proceedings, he could lay a bundle down and get well on top of Howard's bonus. Because the action in Loew's little command post said the Pinkos were buying one-way tickets for the Big Fungoo.

Except for tables and chairs set aside for clerks, all the furniture had been removed and dumped in the back yard. Filing cabinets filled with friendly witness depositions covered the fireplace; a corkboard was nailed to the front window, space for reports from the team's four investigators: M. Considine, D. Smith, T. Meeks and D. Upshaw. Captain Mal's stack of interrogation forms – questions tailored to individual lefties, delivered and notarized by City Marshals – was thick; Dudley's field summaries stacked out at five times their width – he had now turned fourteen hostiles into groveling snitch friendlies, picking up dirt on over a hundred snitchees in the process. His own reports comprised six pages: Sammy Benavides porking his sister, Claire De Haven skin-popping H and Reynolds Loftis as a homo bar hopper, the rest padding, all of it snoozeville compared to Mal's and Dudley's contributions. Danny Upshaw's stuff ran two pages – evesdrop speculation and necking with Pinko Claire – him and the kid were not exactly burning down barns in their effort to destroy the Communist Conspiracy. There were tables with 'In' and 'Out' baskets for the exchange of information, tables for the photographic evidence Crazy Ed Satterlee was accumulating, a huge cardboard box filled with cross-referenced names, dates, political organizations and documented admissions: Commies, pinkers and fellow travelers embracing Mother Russia and calling for the end of the U.S.A. by means fair and foul. And – across the broadest stretch of bare wall – Ed Satterlee's conspiracy graph, his grand jury thumbscrew.

In one horizontal column, the UAES brain trust; in another, the names of the Communist front organizations they belonged to; in a vertical column atop the graph the names of friendly witnesses and their 'accusation power' rated by stars, with lines running down to intersect with the brainers and the fronts. Each star was Satterlee's assessment of the number of days' testimony a friendly was worth, based on the sheer power of time, place and hearsay: which Pinko attended where, said what, and which recanted Red was there to listen – a brain-frying, mind-boggling, super-stupendous and absolutely amazing glut of information impossible to disprove.

And he kept seeing Danny Upshaw smack in the middle of it, treading shit, even though the kid was on the side of the angels.

Buzz walked out to the back porch. He'd been brainstorming escape routes under the guise of writing reports for hours; three phone calls had fixed Audrey's skimming spree. One was to Mickey, handing him a convoluted epic on how a bettor skimmed an unnamed runner who was screwing the bettor's sister and couldn't turn him in, but finally made him cough up the six grand he'd welched – the exact amount Audrey had grifted off the Mick. The second was to Petey Skouras, a tight-lipped runner who agreed to play the lovesick fool who finally made good to his boss for a cool grand – knowing Johnny Stompanato would come snouting around for the name Buzz wouldn't give on, find him acting hinky and pound a confession out of him – the returned cash his assurance that that was his only punishment. The third was to an indy shylock: seven thousand dollars at 20 percent, $8,400 due April 10 – his woman out of trouble, his gift for her grief: Gene Niles with his face blown off on her bed. Seven come eleven, thank God for the Commie gravy train. If they didn't succumb to the hots for each other, he and his lioness would probably survive.

The kid was still the wild card he didn't know how to play.

It was twelve hours since he'd prowled Niles' pad. Should he go back and make it look like Niles hightailed it? Should he have planted some incriminating shit? When the fucker was missed, would LAPD fix on him as a Dragna bad apple and let it lie? Would they make him for the bomb job and press Mickey? Would they assume a snuff and go hog-wild to find the killer?

Buzz saw Dudley Smith and Mike Breuning at the back edge of the yard, standing by Ellis Loew's couch, left out in the rain because the DA put business before comfort. A late sun was up; Dudley was laughing and pointing at it. Buzz watched dark clouds barrelling in from the ocean. He thought: fix it, fix it, fix it, be a fixer. Be what Captain Mal told the kid to be.

Be a policeman.

CHAPTER TWENTY-NINE

Danny unlocked his door and tapped the wall light. The blood W's he'd been seeing since the morgue became his front room, spare and tidy, but with something skewed. He eyed the room in grids until he got it: the rug was puckered near the coffee table – he always toed it smooth on his way out.

He tried to remember if he did it *this* morning. He recalled dressing as Ted Krugman, nude to leather jacket in front of the bathroom mirror; he remembered walking outside thinking of Felix Gordean, Mal Consadine's 'Lean on him, Danny' ringing in his ears. He did not remember his methodical rug number, probably because Teddy K. wasn't the meticulous type. Nothing else in the room looked askew; there was no way in the world HE would break into a policeman's apartment . . .

Danny thought of his file, ran for the hall closet and opened the door. It was there, pictures and paperwork intact, covered by wadded-up carpeting puckered just the right way. He checked the bathroom, kitchen and bedroom, saw the same old same old, sat down in a chair by the phone and skimmed the book he'd just bought.

The Weasel Family – Physiology and Habits, hot off a back shelf at Stanley Rose's Bookshop.

Chapter 6, page 59: The Wolverine.

A 40- to 50-pound member of the weasel family indigenous to Canada, the Pacific Northwest and the upper Midwest; pound for pound, the most vicious animal on earth. Utterly fearless and known for attacking animals many times its size; known to drive bears and cougars from their kills. A beast that cannot stand to watch other creatures enjoying a good feed – often blitzing them just to get at what remained of their food.

Equipped with a highly efficient digestive system: wolverines ate fast, digested fast, shit fast and were always hungry; they possessed a huge appetite to match their general nastiness. All the vicious little bastards wanted to do was kill, eat and occasionally fuck other members of their misanthropic breed.

W

W

W

W

W

W

W

W

The Wolverine.

Alter ego of a biting, gouging, raping, flesh-eating killer of immense hunger: sexual and emotional. A man who possessed total identification with an obscenely rapacious animal, an identity he has assumed to right old wrongs, animal mutilations the specific means, *his specific inner reconstruction of what was done to him*.

Danny turned to the pictures at the back of the book, ripped three wolverine shots out, dug through his file for the 2307 blood pics and made a collage above the bed. He tacked the awful weasel thing in the middle; he shone his floor lamp on the collection of images, stood back, looked and thought.

A fat, shuffle-footed creature with beady eyes and a thick brown coat to ward off the cold. A slinky tail, a short, pointed snout, sharp nails and long, sharp teeth bared at the camera. An ugly child who knew he was ugly and made up for it by hurting the people he blamed for making him that way. Snap flashes as the animal and 2307 merged: the killer was somehow disfigured or thought he was; since eyewitnesses tagged him as not facially marred, the disfigurement might be somewhere on his body. The killer thought he was ugly and tied it to sex, hence Augie Duarte slashed cheek to bone with his thing sticking out his mouth. A big snap, all instinct, but feeling gut solid: HE knew the burned-face burglar boy, who was too young to be the killer himself; HE drew inspiration or sex from his disfigurement – hence the facial slashing. Zoot stick assaults were being tapped at station houses citywide; car thief MO's were being collated; he told Jack Shortell to start calling wild-animal breeders, zoo suppliers, animal trappers and fur wholesalers. cross-reference them with dental tech and *go*. Burglar, jazz fiend, H copper, teeth maker, car thief, animal worshiper, queer, homo, pederast, brunser and devotee of male whores. It was there waiting for them, some fact in a police file, some nonplussed dental worker saying. 'Yeah, I remember that guy.'

Danny wrote down his new impressions, thinking of Mike Breuning bullshitting him on the Augie Duarte tail, the other tails probably horseshit. Breuning's only possible motive was humoring him – keeping him happy on the homicide case so he'd be a good Commie operative and keep Dudley Smith happy on his anti-Red crusade. Shortell had called the other three men, warned them of possible danger and was trying to set up interviews: the only cop he could trust now, Jack would be tapping into Dudley's 'boys' to see if the three Gordean 'friends' had ever been under surveillance at all. He himself had stuck outside Gordean's agency trawling for more license plates, more potential victims, more information and maybe Gordean alone for a little strongarm – but the carport had stayed empty, the pimp hadn't showed and there was no traffic at his front door – rain had probably kept the 'clients' and 'friends' away. And he'd had to break the stakeout for his date with Claire De Haven.

A thud echoed outside the door – the sound of the paperboy chucking the *Evening Herald*. Danny walked out and picked it up, scanning a headline on Truman and trade embargoes, opening to the second page on the off-chance there was an item on his case. Another scan told him the answer was no; a short column in the bottom right corner caught his attention.

Attorney Charles Hartshorn a Suicide – Served Both
the Society Elite and Society's Unfortunate

This morning Charles E. (Eddington) Hartshorn,
52, a prominent society lawyer who dabbled in social
causes was found dead in the living room of his Hancock Park home, an apparent self-asphyxiation suicide. Hartshorn's body was discovered by his daughter
Betsy, 24, who had just arrived home from a trip
and told Metro reporter Bevo Means: 'Daddy was
despondent. A man had been around talking to him
– Daddy was certain it had to do with a grand jury
investigation he'd heard about. People always bothered him because he did volunteer work for the Sleepy
Lagoon Defense Committee, and they found it strange
that a rich man wanted to help poor Mexicans.'

Lieutenant Walter Reddin of the LAPD's Wilshire
Station said, 'It was suicide by hanging, pure and
simple. There was no note, but no signs of a struggle.
Hartshorn simply found a rope and a ceiling beam
and did it, and it's a darn shame his daughter had to
find him.'

Hartshorn, a senior partner of Hartshorn, Welborn
and Hayes, is survived by daughter Betsy and wife
Margaret, 49. Funeral service notices are pending.

Danny put the paper down, stunned. Hartshorn was
Duane Lindenaur's extortionee in 1941; Felix Gordean
said that he attended his parties and was 'unlucky in
love and politics.' He never questioned the man for
three reasons: he did not fit the killer's description; the
extortion was nearly nine years prior; Sergeant Frank
Skakel, the investigating officer on the beef, had said
that Hartshorn would refuse to talk to the police regarding the incident – and he stressed old precedents. Hartshorn was just another name in the file, a tangent name
that led to Gordean. Nothing about the lawyer had
seemed wrong; aside from Gordean's offhand 'politics'
remark, there was nothing that tagged him as having a

yen for causes, and there were no notations in the grand jury file on him – despite the preponderance of Sleepy Lagoon information. *But he was questioned by a member of the grand jury team.*

Danny called Mal Considine's number at the DA's Bureau, got no answer and dialed Ellis Loew's house. Three rings, then, 'Yeah? Who's this?', Buzz Meeks' okie twang.

'It's Deputy Upshaw. Is Mal around?'

'He's not here, Deputy. This is Meeks. You need somethin'?'

The man sounded subdued. Danny said, 'Do you know if anybody questioned a lawyer named Charles Hartshorn?'

'Yeah, I did. Last week. Why?'

'I just read in the paper that he killed himself.'

A long silence, a long breath. Meeks said, 'Oh shit.'

Danny said, 'What do you mean?'

'Nothin', kid. This on your homicide case?'

'Yes. How did you know that?'

'Well, I braced Hartshorn, and he thought I had to be a Homicide cop, 'cause a guy who tried to shake him down on his queerness years ago just got bumped off. This was right around when you joined up with us, and I remembered somethin' about this dink Lindenaur from the papers. Kid, I was a cop for years, and this guy Hartshorn wasn't holdin' nothing' back 'cept the fact he likes boys, so I didn't tell you about him – I just figured he was no kind of suspect.'

'Meeks, you should have told me anyway.'

'Upshaw, you gave me some barter on the old queen. I owe you on that, 'cause I had to rough him up, and I bought out by tellin' him I'd keep the homicide dicks away. And kid, that poor sucker couldn't of killed a fly.'

'Shit! Why did you go talk to him in the first place? Because he was connected to the Sleepy Lagoon Committee?'

'No. I was trackin' corroboration dirt on the Commies and I got a note said Hartshorn was rousted with Reynolds Loftis at a fruit bar in Santa Monica in '44. I wanted to see if I could squeeze some more dirt on Loftis out of him.'

Danny put the phone to his chest so Meeks wouldn't hear him hyperventilating, wouldn't hear his brain banging around the facts he'd just been handed and the way they *might just really play*:

Reynolds Loftis was tall, gray-haired, middle-aged.

He was connected to Charles Hartshorn, a suicide, the blackmail victim of Duane Linenaur, homicide victim number three.

He was the homosexual lover of Chaz Minear circa early '40s; in the grand jury psychiatric files, Sammy Benavides had mentioned 'puto' Chaz buying sex via a 'queer date-a-boy gig' – a possible reference to Felix Gordean's introduction service, which employed snuff victims George Wiltsie and Augie Duarte.

Last night in darktown, Claire De Haven had been all nerves; the killer had picked up Goines on that block and a hop pusher at the Zombie had addressed her. She sloughed it off, but she was known to the grand jury team as a longtime hophead. Did she procure the junk load that killed Marty Goines?

Danny's hands twitched the receiver off his chest; he heard Meeks on the other end of the line – 'Kid, you there? You there, kid?' – and managed to hook the mouthpiece into his chin. 'Yeah, I'm here.'

'There something you ain't tellin' me?'

'Yes – no – fuck, I don't know.'

The line hung silent for good long seconds; Danny stared at his wolverine pinups; Meeks said, 'Deputy, are you tellin' me Loftis is a suspect for your killin's?'

Danny said, 'I'm telling you *maybe*. Maybe real strong. He fits the killer's description, and he . . . fits.'

Buzz Meeks said, 'Holy fuckin' dog.'

Danny hung up, thinking he'd kissed Reynolds Loftis in his mind – and he liked it.

Krugman into Upshaw into Krugman, pure Homicide cop.

Danny drove to Beverly Hills, no rear-view trawling. He Man Camera'd Reynolds Loftis wolverine slashing; the combination of 2307 pictures, Augie Duarte's body and Loftis' handsome face rooting in gore had him riding the clutch, shifting when he didn't need to just to keep the images a little bit at bay. Pulling up, he saw the house lights on bright – cheery, liked the people inside had nothing to hide; he walked up to the door and found a note under the knocker: 'Ted. Back in a few minutes. Make yourself at home – C.'

More nothing to hide. Danny opened the door, moved inside and saw a writing table wedged against a wall by the stairwell. A floor lamp was casting light on it; papers were strewn across the blotter, a leather-bound portfolio weighing them down, nothing to hide blinking neon. He walked over, picked it up and opened it; the top page bore clean typescript: 'MINUTES AND ATTEND-ANCE, UAES EXECUTIVE COMMITTEE, 1950 MEETINGS.'

Danny opened to the first page. More perfect type-script: the meeting/New Year's party on 12/31/49. Pres-ent – scrawled signatures – were C. De Haven, M. Ziffkin, R. Loftis, S. Benavides, M. Lopez, and one name crossed out, illegible. Topics of discussion were 'Picket Assignments.' 'Secretary's Report,' 'Treasurer's Report' and whether or not to hire private detectives to look into the criminal records of Teamster picketers. The soiree commenced at 11:00 P.M. and ended at 6:00 A.M.; Danny winced at the gist: the ledger could be construed as an alibi for Reynolds Loftis – he was here during the time Marty Goines was snatched and killed – and the minutes contained nothing at all subversive.

Too much nothing to hide.

Danny flipped forward, finding a meeting on 1/4/50, the same people in attendance during the time frame of the Wiltsie/Lindenaur killings, the same strange cross-out, the same boring topics discussed. And Loftis was with Claire last night when Augie Duarte probably got it – he'd have to check with Doc Layman on the estimated time of death. Perfect group alibis, no treason on the side, Loftis not HIM, unless the whole brain trust was behind the killings – which was ridiculous.

Danny stopped thinking, replaced the ledger, jammed his jumpy hands into his warm leather pockets. It was too much nothing to hide, because there was nothing to hide, because none of the brain trusters knew he was a Homicide cop, Loftis could have forged his name, a five-time corroborated alibi would stand up in court ironclad, even if the alibiers were Commie traitors, none of it meant anything, get your cases straight and identities straight and be a policeman.

The house was getting hot. Danny shucked his jacket, hung it on a coatrack, went into the living room and pretended to admire the poster for *Storm Over Leningrad*. It reminded him of the stupid turkeys Karen Hiltscher coerced him to; he was making a note to lube her on 2307 when he heard, 'Ted, how the hell are you?'

HIM

Danny turned around. Reynolds Loftis and Claire were doffing their coats in the foyer. She looked coiled; he looked handsome, like a cultured blood sport connoisseur. Danny said, 'Hi. Good to see you, but I've got some bad news.'

Claire said, 'Oh'; Loftis rubbed his hands together and blew on them. 'Hark, what bad news?'

Danny walked up to frame their reactions. 'It was in the papers. A lawyer named Charles Hartshorn killed himself. It said he worked with the SLDC, and it implied he was being hounded by some fascist DA's cops.'

Clean reactions: Claire giving her coat a brush, saying, 'We'd heard. Charlie was good friend to our cause'; Loftis tensing up just a tad – maybe because he and the lawyer had sex going. 'That grand jury went down, but it took Charlie with them. He was a frail man and a kind one, and men like that are easy pickings for the fascists.'

336

Danny flashed; he's talking about himself, he's weak, Claire's his strength. He moved into close-up range and hit bold. 'I read a tabloid sheet that said Hartshorn was questioned about a string of killings. Some crazy queer killing people he knew.'

Loftis turned his back, moving into a shamefully fake coughing attack; Claire played supporting actress, bending to him with her face averted, mumbling, 'Bad for your bronchitis.' Danny held his close-up and brain-screened what his eyes couldn't see: Claire giving her fiancé guts; Loftis the actor, knowing faces don't lie, keeping his hidden.

Danny walked into the kitchen and filled a glass with sink water, break to give the players time to recover. He walked back slowly and found them acting nonchalant, Claire smoking, Loftis leaning against the staircase, sheepish, a Southern gentleman who thought coughing déclassé. 'Poor Charlie. He liked Greek revelry once in a while, and I'm sure the powers that be would have loved to crucify him for that, too.'

Danny handed him the water. 'They'll crucify you for anything they can. It's a shame about Hartshorn, but personally, I like women.'

Loftis drank, grabbed his coat and winked. He said, 'So do I,' kissed Claire on the cheek and went out the door.

Danny said, 'We've got bad luck so far. Last night, your friend Charlie.'

Claire tossed her purse on the table holding the meeting ledger – too casual. Her tad too-studied glance said she'd arranged the still life for him – Loftis' alibi – *even though they couldn't know who he was*. The threads of who was who, knew who, knew what got tangled again; Danny quashed them with a lewd wink. 'Let's stay in, huh?'

Claire said, 'My idea, too. Care to see a movie?'

'You've got a television set?'

'No, silly. I've got a screening room.'

Danny smiled shyly, proletarian Ted wowed by Hollywood customs. Claire took his hand and led him through the kitchen to a room lined with bookcases, the front wall covered by a projection screen. A long leather couch faced the screen; a projector was mounted on a tripod a few feet behind it, a reel of film already fed in. Danny sat down; Claire hit switches, doused the lights and snuggled into him, legs curled under a swell of skirt. Light took over the screen, the movie started.

A test pattern; a black-and-white fade-in; a zoftig blonde and a Mexican with a duck's ass haircut stripping. A motel room backdrop: bed, chipped stucco walls, sombrero lamps and a bullfight poster on the closet door. Tijuana, pure and simple.

Danny felt Claire's hand hovering. The blonde rolled her eyes to heaven; she'd just seen her co-star's cock – huge, veiny, hooked at the middle like a dowsing rod. She salaamed before him, hit her knees and started sucking. The camera caught her acne scars and his needle tracks. She sucked while the hophead gyrated his hips; he pulled out of her mouth and sprayed.

Danny looked away; Claire touched his thigh. Danny flinched, tried to relax but kept flinching; Claire fingered a ridge of coiled muscle inches from his stuff. Hophead screwed Pimples from behind, the insertion close in. Danny's stomach growled – worse than when he was on a no-food jag. Claire's hand kept probing; Danny felt himself shriveling – cold shower time where you shrunk down to nothing.

The blonde and the Mexican fucked with abandon; Claire kneaded muscles that would not yield. Danny started to cramp, grabbed Claire's hand and squeezed it to his knee, like they were back at the jazz club and he was calling the shots. Claire pulled away; the movie ended with a close-up of the blonde and the Mex tongue-kissing.

Film snapped off the cylinder; Claire got up, hit the lights and exchanged reels. Danny uncramped into his best version of Ted Krugman at ease – legs loosely crossed, hands laced behind his head. Claire turned and said, 'I was saving this for aprés bed, but I think we might need it now.'

Danny winked – his whole head twitching – lady-killer Ted. Claire turned the projector on and the lights off; she came back to the couch and snuggled down again. The second half of their double feature hit the screen.

No music, no opening credits, no subtitles like in the old silents – just blackness – gray flecks, the only indication that film was running. The darkness broke down at the corners of the screen, a shape took form and a dog's head came into focus: a pit bull wearing a mask. The dog snapped at the camera, the screen went black again, then slowly dissolved into white.

Danny remembered the dog breeder and his tale of Hollywood types buying pits to film; he jumped to the masked men at Felix Gordean's house; he saw that he'd shut his eyes and was holding his breath, the better to think who knew what, said what, lied what. He opened his eyes, saw two dogs ripping at each other, animated red splashed in surreal patterns across black-and-white celluloid, disappearing and coloring the real blood its real color, a spritz fogging the camera lens, gray first, cartoon red next. He thought of Walt Disney gone insane; as if in answer, an evil-looking Donald Duck flashed on the screen, feathered phallus hanging to its webbed feet. The duck hopped around, impotent angry like the real Donald; Claire laughed; Danny watched the snapping dogs circle each other and charge, the darker dog getting a purchase on the speckled dog's midsection, plunging in with his teeth. And he knew his killer, whoever he was, had gone crazy watching this movie.

A black screen; Danny going light-headed from holding his breath, sensing Claire's eyes on him. Then all color footage, naked men circling each other just like the dogs, going for each other with sucking mouths, 69 close-ups, a pullback shot and Felix Gordean in a red devil costume, capering, prancing. Danny got hard; Claire's hand went there – like she *knew*. Danny

339

squirmed, tried to shut his eyes, *couldn't* and kept looking.

A quick cut; then Pretty Boy Christopher, naked and hard, pointing his thing at the camera, the head nearly eclipsing the screen like a giant battering ram, white background borders looking just like parted lips and teeth holding the image intact through rigor mortis –

Danny bolted, double-timed to the front of the house, found a bathroom and locked the door. He got his shakes chilled with a litany: BE A POLICEMAN BE A POLICEMAN BE A POLICEMAN; he made himself think *facts*, flung the medicine cabinet open and got one immediately: a prescription bottle of sodium secobarbital, Wiltsie's and Lindenaur's death ticket in a little vial, Reynolds Loftis' sleep pills administered by D. Waltrow, MD, 11/14/49. Fumbling through shelves of ointments, salves and more pills got him nothing else; he noticed a second door, ajar, next to the shower stall.

He pushed it open and saw a little den all done up cozy, more bookshelves, chairs arranged around a leather ottoman, another desk with another cluttered blotter. He checked the clutter – mimeographed movie scripts with hand scrawl in the margins – opened drawers and found stacks of Claire De Haven stationery, envelopes, rolls of stamps and an old leather wallet. Flipping through the sleeves, he saw expired Reynolds Loftis ID: library card, membership cards to Pinko organizations, a '36 California driver's license with a tag stuck to the back side, Emergency Medical Data – allergic to penicillin, minor recurring arthritis, *O+ blood*.

HIM?

Danny closed the drawers, unlocked the bathroom door, wiped a towel across his face and slow-walked back to the screening room. The lights were on, the screen was blank and Claire was sitting on the couch. She said, 'I didn't think a tough boy like you would be so squeamish.'

Danny sat beside her, their legs brushing. Claire pulled away, then leaning forward. Danny thought: *she*

340

knows, she can't know. He said, 'I'm not much of an aesthete.'

Claire put a warm hand to his face; her face was cold. 'Really? All my friends in the New York Party were mad for New Drama and Kabuki and the like. Didn't the movie remind you of Cocteau, only with more sense of humor?'

He didn't know who Cocteau was. 'Cocteau never jazzed me. Neither did Salvador Dali or any of those guys. I'm just a square from Long Island.'

Claire's hand kept stroking. It was warm, but the to-die-for softness of last night was all gone. 'I used to summer in Easthampton when I was a girl. It was lovely.'

Danny laughed, glad he'd read Considine's tourist brochure. 'Huntington wasn't exactly Easthampton, sweetie.'

Claire cringed at the endearment, started to let her hand go, then made with more caresses. Danny said, 'Who filmed that movie?'

'A brilliant man named Paul Doinelle.'

'Just for friends to see?'

'Why do you say that?'

'Because it's smut. You can't release films like that. It's against the law.

'You say that so vehemently, like you care about a bourgeois law that abridges artistic freedom.'

'It was ugly. I was just wondering what kind of man would enjoy something like that.'

'Why do you say 'man'? I'm a woman, and I appreciate art of that nature. You're strictured in your views, Ted. It's a bad trait for people in our cause to have. And I *know* that film aroused you.'

'That's not true.'

Claire laughed. 'Don't be so evasive. Tell me what you want. Tell me what you want to do with me.'

She was going to fuck him just to get what he knew, which meant she knew, which meant –

Danny made Claire a blank frame and kissed her neck and cheeks; she sighed – phony – sounding just like a

Club Largo girl pretending stripping was ecstasy. She touched his back and chest and shoulders – hands kneading – it felt like she was trying to restrain herself from gouging him. He tried to kiss her lips, but her mouth stayed crimped; she reached between his legs. He was frozen and shriveled there, and her hand made it worse.

Danny felt his whole body choking him. Claire took her hands away, reached behind her back and removed her sweater and bra in one movement. Her breasts were freckled – spots that looked cancerous – the left one was bigger and hung strange and the nipples were dark and flat and surrounded by crinkled skin. Danny thought of traitors and Mexicans sucking them; Claire whispered, 'Here, babe,' a lullaby to mother him into telling what he knew, who he knew, what he lied. She fondled her breasts towards his face; he shut his eyes and couldn't; thought of boys and Tim and HIM and couldn't –

Claire said, 'Ladies' man? Oh Teddy, how were you ever able to pull that charade off?' Danny shoved her away, left the house slamming doors and drove home thinking: *SHE CANNOT KNOW WHO I AM*. Inside, he went straight for his copy of the grand jury package, prowled pages to prove it for sure, saw 'Juan Duarte – UAES brain trust, extra actor/stagehand at Variety Intl Picts' on a personnel sheet, snapped to Augie Duarte choking on his cock on a morgue slab, snapped to the three Mexes on the *Tomahawk Massacre* set the day he questioned Duane Lindenaur's KAs, snapped on Norm Kostenz taking his picture after the picket line brawl. Snap, snap, snap, snap to two final snaps: the Mex at the morgue who eyed him funny was a Mex actor on the movie set he had to be an Augie Duarte relative, Juan Duarte the spic Commie actor/stagehand. The crossout on the meeting ledger had to be his name, which meant that he saw Kostenz' picture and told Loftis and Claire that Ted Krugman was a police detective working on Augie's snuff.

Which meant that the ledger was a setup alibi.

Which meant that the movie was a device to test his reactions and find out what he knew.

Which meant that the Red Bitch was trying to do to him what Mal Considine set him up to do to her.

WHICH MEANT THAT THEY KNEW WHO HE WAS.

Danny went for the shelf over the refrigerator, the place where he stashed his Deputy D. Upshaw persona. He picked up his badge and handcuffs and held them to himself; he unholstered his .45 revolver and aimed it at the world.

CHAPTER THIRTY

Chief of Detectives Thad Green nodded first to Mal, then to Dudley Smith. 'Gentlemen, I wouldn't have called you in this early in the morning if it wasn't urgent. What I'm going to tell you has not been leaked yet, and it will remain that way.'

Mal looked at his LAPD mentor. The man, rarely grave, was coming on almost funereal. 'What is it, sir?'

Green lit a cigarette. 'The rain caused some mudslides up in the hills. About an hour ago, a body was found on the access road going up to the Hollywood Sign. Sergeant Eugene Niles, Hollywood Squad. Buried, shot in the face. I called Nort Layman in for a quick one, and he took two .38's out of the cranial vault. They were fired from an Iver-Johnson Police Special, which you know is standard LAPD/LASD issue. Niles was last seen day before yesterday at Hollywood Station, where he got into a fistfight with your grand jury chum Deputy Daniel Upshaw. You men have been working with Upshaw, and I called you in for your conclusions. Mal, you first.'

Mal made himself swallow his shock, think, then speak. 'Sir, I don't think Upshaw is capable of killing a man. I reprimanded him on Niles night before last, and he took it like a good cop. He seemed relieved that Niles was off his Homicide detail, and we all know that Niles was in up to here on Brenda Allen. I've heard he ran bag for Jack Dragna, and I'd look to Jack and Mickey before I accused a brother officer.'

Green nodded. 'Lieutenant Smith.'

Dudley said, 'Sir, I disagree with Captain Considine. Sergeant Mike Breuning, who's also working that Homicide detail with Upshaw, told me that Niles was afraid of the lad and that he was convinced that Upshaw had committed a break-in in LAPD territory in order to get evidence. Niles told Sergeant Breuning that Upshaw lied about how he came to get word of the second and third victims, and that he was going to try to accrue criminal charges against him. Moreover, Niles was convinced that Upshaw had a very strange fixation on these deviant killings he's so concerned with, and Niles calling Upshaw a 'queer' was what precipitated their fight. An informant of mine told me that Upshaw was seen threatening a known queer pimp named Felix Gordean, a man who is known to heavily pay off Sheriff's Central Vice. Gordean told my man that Upshaw is crazy, obsessed with some sort of homo conspiracy, and that he made extortion demands on him – threatening to go to the newspapers unless he gave him special information – information that Gordean asserts does not even exist.'

Mal took the indictment in. 'Who's your informant, Dudley? And Why do you and Breuning care so much about Upshaw?'

Dudley smiled – a bland shark. 'I would not want that lad's unstable violent behavior to upset his work for our grand jury, and I would no more divulge the names of my snitches than you would, Captain.'

'No, but you'd smear a brother officer. A man who I think is a dedicated and brilliant young policeman.'

'I've always heard you had a soft spot for your operatives, Malcolm. You should be more circumspect in displaying it, though. Especially now that you're a captain.

I personally consider Upshaw capable of murder. Violence is often the province of weak men.'

Mal thought that with the right conditions and one drink too many, the kid could shoot in cold blood. He said, 'Chief, Dudley's persuasive, but I don't make Upshaw for this at all.'

Thad Green stubbed out his cigarette. 'You men are too personally involved. I'll put some unbiased officers on it.'

CHAPTER THIRTY-ONE

The phone rang. Danny reached for the bedside extension, saw that he'd passed out on the floor and tripped over dead bottles and file folders getting to it. 'Yeah? Jack?'

Jack Shortell said, 'It's me. You listening?'

Danny blinked away wicked sunlight, grabbed paper and a pencil. 'Go.'

'First, Breuning's tails were all fake. I called in an old favor at LAPD Homicide, checked the work sheets for the men Dudley uses regularly and found out they were all working regular assignments full-time. I looked around for Gene Niles to see if I could sweet-talk him and get some more dope on it, but that bastard is nowhere. LAPD canvassed the area where Duarte's body was found – they caught the squeal and some rookie squadroom dick out of Central hopped on it. Nothing so far. Doc Layman's grid-searching for trace elements there – he wants complete forensics on Duarte so he can put him in his next textbook. He thinks the rain will kibosh it, but he's trying anyway, and on the autopsy it's the same story as the first three: sedated, strangled, mutilated after death. I called the other men on your tailing list, and they're going on little vacations until this blows over. Danny, did you know that guy Hartshorn you told me about killed himself?'

Danny said, 'Yeah, and I don't know if it plays with our case or not.'

'Well, I went by Wilshire Station and checked the report, and it looks clean – no forced entry, no struggle. Hartshorn's daughter said Pops was despondent over your grand jury.'

Danny was getting nervous; the scene with De Haven was coming back: she knew, they knew, no more Red Ted. 'Jack, have you got anything hot?'

Shortell said, 'Maybe a scorcher. I was up all night on the wolverine thing, and I got a great lead on an old man named Thomas Cormier, that's C-O-R-M-I-E-R. He's an amateur naturalist, famous, I guess you'd call him. He lives on Bunker Hill, and he rents weasel genus things to the movies and animal shows. He has a batch of individually penned-up wolverines, the only known batch in LA. Now listen, because this is where it gets good.

'Last night I went by the West Hollywood Substation to talk to a pal of mine who just transferred over. I heard the girl at the switchboard ragging you to the watch sergeant, and I played nice and sweet-talked her. She told me she was dragging her heels on her set of dental queries because she thought you were just using her. She gave me a list that had notes on it – negative on the killer's description, but positive on the animal teeth – Joredco Dental Lab on Beverly and Beaudry. They do animal dentures for taxidermists, and they're the only lab in LA that works with actual animal teeth – that lead you had that said all taxidermists use plastic teeth was wrong. And Beverly and Beaudry is seven blocks from Thomas Cormier's house – 343 South Corondelet.'

Red hot and biting.

Danny said, 'I'm rolling,' and hung up. He put muscling Felix Gordean aside, cleaned up and stashed his files, cleaned up his person and dressed as Daniel T.

Upshaw, policeman, replete with badge, gun and official ID. Ted Krugman dead and buried, he drove to Bunker Hill.

343 South Corondelet was an eaved and gabled Victorian house sandwiched between vacant lots on the west edge of the Hill. Danny parked in front and heard animal yapping; he followed the sounds down the driveway and around to a terraced back yard with a picture postcard view of Angel's Flight. Lean-tos with corrugated metal roofs were arranged in L-shapes, one to each level of grass; the structures were fronted by heavy wire mesh, and the longest L had what looked like a generator device built onto its rear side. The whole yard reeked of animals, animal piss and animal shit.

'The smell getting to you, Officer?'

Danny turned around. The mind reader was a grizzled old man wearing dungarees and hipboots, walking toward him waving a fat cigar that blended in perfectly with the shit stink and made it worse. He smiled, adding bad breath to the effluvia. 'Are you from Animal Regulation or Department of Health?'

Danny felt the sun and the smell go to work on his skinful of booze, sandpapering him. 'I'm a Sheriff's Homicide detective. Are you Thomas Cormier?'

'I am indeed, and I've never killed anyone and I don't associate with killers. I've got some killer mustelids, but they only kill the rodents I feed them. If that's a crime, I'll take the blame. I keep my mustelidae in captivity, so if they called a bum tune, I'll pay the piper.'

The man looked too intelligent to be an outright loony. Danny said, 'Mr. Cormier, I heard you're an expert on wolverines.'

'That is the God's truth. I have eleven in captivity right this instant, my baby refrigeration unit keeping them nice and cool, the way they like it.'

Danny queased on cigar smoke and halitosis; he willed himself pro. 'This is why I'm here, Mr. Cormier. Four men have been killed between New Year's and now.

They were mutilated by a man wearing denture plates with wolverine teeth attached. There's a dental lab several blocks from here – the only one in LA that manufactures actual animal dentures. I think that's a strange coincidence, and I thought maybe you could help me out with it.'

Thomas Cormier snuffed his cigar and pocketed the butt. 'That is just about the strangest thing I have heard in my entire time on this planet, which dates back to 1887. What else have you got on your killer?'

Danny said, 'He's tall, middle-aged, gray-haired. He knows the jazz world, he can purchase heroin, he knows his way around male prostitutes.' He stopped, thinking of Reynolds Loftis, wondering if he'd get anything that wasn't circumstantial on him. 'And he's a homosexual.'

Cormier laughed. 'Sounds like a nice fellow, and sorry I can't help you. I don't know anybody like that, and if I did, I think I'd keep my back to the wall and my trusty rifle out when he came to call. And this fellow's enamored of *Gulo luscus*?'

'If you mean wolverines, yes.'

'Lord. Well, I admire his taste in mustelids, if not the way he displays his appreciation.'

Danny sighed. 'Mr. Cormier, do you know anything about the Joredco Dental Lab?'

'Sure, just down the street. I think they make animal choppers.'

A clean take. Danny saw takes from Claire De Haven's movie, pictured HIM seeing it, getting aroused, wanting more. 'I'd like to see your wolverines.'

Cormier said, 'Thought you'd never ask,' and walked ahead of Danny to the refrigeration shed. The air went from warm to freezing; the yapping became snarling; dark shapes lashed out and banged the mesh fronts of their pens. Cormier said, '*Gulo luscus*. Carcajou – evil spirit – to the Indians. The most insatiable carnivore alive and pound for pound the meanest mammal. Like I said, I admire your killer's taste.'

Danny found a good sun angle – light square on a

middle pen; he squatted down and looked, his nose to the wire. Inside, a long creature paced, turning in circles, snapping at the walls. It's teeth glinted; its claws scraped the floor; it looked like a coiled muscle that would not stop coiling until it killed and slept in satiation – or died. Danny watched, feeling the beast's power, feeling HIM feeling it; Cormier talked. '*Gulo luscus* is two things; smart and intractable. I've known them to develop a taste for deer, hide in trees and toss nice edible bark down to lure them over, then jump down and rip the deer's jugular out clean to the windpipe. Once they get a whiff of blood, they will not stop persisting. I've heard of wolverines stalking cougars wounded in mating battles. They'll jab them from behind, take nips out and run away, a little meat here and there until the cougar nearly bleeds to death. When the poor fellow's almost dead, *Gulo* attacks frontally, claws the cougar's eyes out of his head and eats them like gumballs.'

Danny winced, transposing the image: Marty Goines, HIM, the creature he was watching. 'I need to look at your records. All the wolverines you've lent out to movies and animal shows.'

Cormier said, 'Officer, you can't lend *Gulos* out, much as I'd like to make the money. They're my private passion, I love them and I keep them around because they shore up my reputation as a mustelidologist. You lend *Gulos* out, they'll attack anything human or animal within biting range. I had one stolen out of its pen five or six years ago, and my only consolation was that the stealer sure as hell got himself mangled.'

Danny looked up. 'Tell me about that. What happened?'

Cormier took out his cigar butt and fingered it. 'In the summer of '42 I worked nights at the Griffith Park Zoo, resident zoologist doing research on nocturnal mustelid habits. I had an earlier bunch of wolverines that were getting real fat. I knew somebody must have been feeding them, and I started finding extra mouse and hamster carcasses in the pens. Somebody was lifting

349

the food latches and feeding my *Gulos*, and I figured it for a neighborhood kid who'd heard about my reputation and thought he'd see for himself. Truth be told, it didn't bother me, and it kind of gave me a cozy feeling, here's this fellow *Gulo* lover and all. Then, late in July, it stopped. I knew it stopped because there were no more extra carcasses in the cages and my *Gulos* went back to their normal weights. About a year and a half or so went by, and one night my *Gulo* Otto was stolen. I laughed like hell. I figured the feeder had to have a *Gulo* for himself and stole Otto. Otto was a pistol. If the stealer got away with keeping him, I'm sure Otto bit him real good. I called hospitals around here to see if they stitched a bite victim, but it was no go, no Otto.'

Bit him real good.

Danny thought of sedation – a wolverine Mickey Finned and stolen – HIM with his own evil mascot – *the story might just play*. He looked back in the pen; the wolverine noticed something and lashed the wire, making screechy blood W noises. Cormier laughed and said, 'Juno, *you're* a pistol.' Danny put his face up to the mesh, tasting the animal's breath. He said, 'Thanks, Mr. Cormier,' pulled himself away and drove to the Joredco Dental Lab.

He was almost expecting a neon sign facade, an animal mouth open wide, the address numbers done up as teeth. He was wrong: the lab was just a tan stucco building, a subtly lettered sign above the door its only advertisement.

Danny parked in front and walked into a tiny receiving area: a secretary behind a desk, a switchboard and calendar art on the walls – 1950 repeated a dozen times over, handsome wild animals representing January for local taxidermist's shops. The girl smiled at him and said, 'Yes?'

Danny showed his badge. 'Sheriff's. I'd like to speak to the man in charge.'

'Regarding?'

'Regarding animal teeth.'

The girl tapped an intercom switch and said, 'Policeman to see you, Mr. Carmichael.' Danny looked at pictures of moose, bears, wolves and buffalos; he noticed a sleek mountain cat and thought of a wolverine stalking it, killing it off with sheer ugly persistence.

A connecting door swung open; a man in a bloody white smock came in. Danny said, 'Mr. Carmichael?'

'Yes, mister?'

'It's Deputy Upshaw.'

'And this regards, Deputy?'

'It regards wolverine teeth.'

No reaction except impatience – the man obviously anxious to get back to work. 'Then I can't help you. Joredco is the only lab in Los Angeles that fashions animal dentures, and we've never done them for a wolverine.'

'Why?'

'Why? Because taxidermists do not stuff wolverines – they are not an item that people want mounted in their home or lodge. I've worked here for thirteen years and I've never filled an order for wolverine teeth.'

Danny thought it over. 'Could someone who learned the rudiments of animal-denture making here do it himself?'

'Yes, but it would be bloody and very slapdash without the proper tools.'

'Good. Because I'm looking for a man who likes blood.'

Carmichael wiped his hands on his smock. 'Deputy, what is this in regard to?'

'Quadruple homicide. How far back do your employment records go?'

The 'quadruple homicide' got to Carmichael – he looked shaken under his brusqueness. 'My God. Our records go back to '40, but Joredco employs mostly women. You don't think – '

Danny was thinking Reynolds Loftis wouldn't sully

351

his hands in a place like this. 'I think maybe. Tell me about the men you've had working here.'

'There haven't been many. Frankly, women work for a lower wage. Our current staff has been here for years, and when we get rush orders, we hire bums out of day labor and kids from Lincoln and Belmont High School to do the scut work. During the war, we hired lots of temporaries that way.'

The Joredco connection felt – strangely – like it was clicking in, with Loftis clicking out. 'Mr. Carmichael, do you have a medical plan for your regular employees?'

'Yes.'

'May I see your records?'

Carmichael turned to the receptionist. 'Sally, let Deputy whatever here see the files.'

Danny let the remark slide; Carmichael went back through the connecting door. Sally pointed to a filing cabinet. 'Nasty prick, if you'll pardon my French. Medicals are in the bottom drawer, men in with the women. You don't think a real killer worked here, do you?'

Danny laughed. 'No, but maybe a real live monster did.'

It took him an hour to go through the medical charts.

Since November '39, sixteen men had been hired on as dental techs. Three were Japanese, hired immediately after the Jap internment ended in '44; four were Caucasian and now in their thirties; three were white and now middle-aged; six were Mexican. All sixteen men had, at one time or another, given blood to the annual Red Cross Drive. Five of the sixteen possessed O+ blood, the most common human blood type. Three of the men were Mexican, two were Japanese – but Joredco still felt right.

Danny went back to the shop and spent another hour chatting up the techs, talking to them while they pried teeth out of gum sections removed from the heads of elk, deer and Catalina Island boar. He asked questions about tall, gray-haired men who acted strange; jazz;

heroin; guys with wolverine fixations. He breathed blood and animal tooth infection and stressed strange behavior among the temporary workers who came and went; he threw out teasers on a handsome Hollywood actor who just might have made the scene. The techs deadpanned him, no'd him and worked around him; his only lead was elimination stuff: most of the temps were Mex, wetbacks going to Belmont and Lincoln High sans green cards, veterans of the Vernon slaughterhouses, where the work was twice as gory and the money was even worse than the coolie wages Mr. Carmichael paid. Danny left thinking Reynolds Loftis would faint the second he hit the Joredco line; thinking the actor might be circumstantial linkage only. But Joredco/Cormier still felt right; the blood and decay smelled like something HE would love.

The day was warming up; heat that felt all the worse for coming after heavy rain. Danny sat in the car and sweated out last night's drunk; he thought elimination, thought that the day labor joints kept no records in order to dodge taxes, that the high school employment offices were long shots he had to try anyway. He drove to Belmont High, talked to the employment counselor, learned that her records only went back to '45 and checked the Joredco referrals – twenty-seven of them – all Mexes and Japs. Even though he knew the age range was wrong, he repeated the process at Lincoln: Mexes, Japs and a mentally deficient white boy hired because he was strong enough to haul two deer carcasses at a time. Gooser. But the rightness kept nagging him.

Danny drove to a bar in Chinatown. After two shots of house bonded, he knew this was his last day as Homicide brass: when he told Considine Ted Krugman was shot, he'd be shot back to the West Hollywood Squad, packing some large blame if Ellis Loew thought he'd jeopardized the chance for a successful grand jury. He could keep looking for HIM on his off-hours – but there was a good chance Felix Gordean would talk to his golf buddies Sheriff Biscailuz and Al Dietrich and he'd get

353

dumped back into uniform or jail duty. He'd made an enemy of Gene Niles and pissed off Dudley Smith and Mike Breuning; Karen Hiltscher wouldn't play pratgirl for him anymore; if Niles could prove he B&E'd 2307, he'd be in real trouble.

Two more shots; warm wisps edging out the gloom. He had a friend with rank and juice – if he could make up for blowing his decoy job, he could still ride Considine's coattails. A last shot; HIM again, HIM pure and abstract, like there was never a time when he didn't exist, even though they'd been together only a few weeks. He thought of HIM free of Reynolds Loftis and last night with Claire, taking it back chronologically, stopping at Augie Duarte dead on a stainless steel slab.

The facial cuts. Jump forward to last night's file work. His instinct: the killer knew Marty Goines' pal – the youth with the bandaged face – and drew sexual inspiration from him. Jump to Thomas Cormier, whose wolverines were overfed – worshiped? – during the summer of '42, Sleepy Lagoon summer, when zoot sticks were most in use. Cormier's interpretation: a neighborhood kid. Jump to Joredco. They hired youths, maybe youths out of skid row day labor, where they didn't keep records. The burn boy was white; all the high school referrals were Mex and Jap, except for the non-play retard. Maybe the workers he talked to never met the kid because he only worked there briefly, maybe they forgot about him, maybe they just didn't notice him. Jump forward to now. The burned-face boy was a burglar – Listerine Chester Brown tagged him as burglarizing with Goines circa '43 to '44, his face bandaged. If he was the one who stole Thomas Cormier's wolverine some eighteen months after his summer of '42 worship, and he was a local kid, he might have committed other burglaries in the Bunker Hill area during that time period.

Danny drove to Rampart Station, the LAPD division that handled Bunker Hill felonies. Mal Considine's name got him the squad lieutenant's attention; a few minutes later he was in a musty storeroom checking boxes of discarded occurrence reports.

The boxes were marked according to year; Danny found two grocery cartons stencilled '1942'. The reports inside were loose, the multi-page jobs stapled together with no carbons in between. There was no rhyme or reason to the order they were filed in – purse snatchings, muggings, petty thefts, burglaries, indecent exposures and loiterings were all lumped together. Danny sat down on a box of '48 reports and dug in.

He scanned upper right corners for penal code numbers – Burglary, 459.1. The two boxes for '42 yielded thirty-one; location was his next breakdown step. He carried the reports into the squadroom, sat at an empty desk facing a wall map of Rampart Division and looked for Bunker Hill street names to match. Four reports in, he got one; six reports in, three more. He memorized the ten north-south and eight east-west blocks of the Hill, tore through the rest of the pages and ended with eleven burglaries, unsolved occurrences, on Bunker Hill in the year 1942. And the eleven addresses were all within walking distance of Thomas Cormier's house and the Joredco Dental Lab.

Next was dates.

Danny flipped through the reports again quickly; the time and date of occurrence were typed at the bottom of each first page. May 16, 1942; July 1, 1942; May 27, 1942; May 9, 1942; June 16, 1942, and six more to make eleven: an unsolved burglary spree, May 9 to August 1, 1942. His head buzzing, he read 'Items Stolen' – and saw why Rampart didn't put out beaucoup men to catch the burglar:

Trinkets, family portraits, costume jewelry, cash out of purses and wallets. A deco wall clock. A cedar cigar humidor. A collection of glass figurines. A stuffed ring-neck pheasant, a stuffed bobcat mounted on rosewood.

More HIM, more not Loftis HIM. It had to be.

Danny tingled. like he was being dangled on electric strings. He went back to the storeroom, found the '43 and '44 boxes, looked through them and got zero Bunker Hill trinket jobs – the only burglary occurrence reports for those years denoted *real* 459.1's, real valuables taken; burglary reports resulting in arrest had already been checked City- and Countywide. Danny finished and kicked at the boxes; two facts kicked him.

The killer was ID'd as middle-aged; he had to be connected to the wolverine-worshiping burglar – a youth – who was emerging from today's work. Chester Brown told him that Marty Goines and his burned-face accomplice B&E'd in the San Fernando Valley '43 to '44; station houses out there might have occurrence reports – he could roll there after he muscled a certain Commie stagehand. And summer '42 was the height of the wartime blackout, curfew was rigidly enforced and field interrogation cards were written up on people caught out after 10:00 P.M. – when the wolverine lover was most likely prowling. If the cards were saved –

Danny tore the storeroom apart, throwing empty boxes; he sweated out his booze lunch, got sprayed with cobwebs, mildew and mouse turds. he found a box marked 'FI's '41-'43,' thumbed back the first few cards and saw that they were – amazingly – in chronological order. He kept flipping; the late spring and summer of '42 yielded eight names: eight white men aged nineteen to forty-seven stopped for being out after curfew, questioned and released.

The cards were filled out slapdash: all had the name, race and date of birth of the interrogee; only half had home addresses listed – in most cases downtown hotels. Five of the men would now be middle-aged and possibles for HIM; the other three were youths who could be the burned-face boy pre-burns – or – if *he* was tangential to the case – Thomas Cormier's neighborhood kid wolverine lover.

Danny pocketed the cards, drove to a pay phone and called Jack Shortell at the Hollywood squadroom. The squad lieutenant put the call through; Shortell came on the line sounding harried. 'Yeah? Danny?'

'It's me. What's wrong?'

'Nothing, except I'm getting the fisheye from every City bull in the place, like all of a sudden I'm *worse* than worse than poison. What have you got?'

'Names, maybe a hot one right in the middle. I talked to that Cormier guy and hit Joredco, and I couldn't put them straight together, but I'm damn sure our guy got kissing close to Cormier's wolverines. You remember that old burglary accomplice of Marty Goines I told you about?'

'Yeah.'

'I think I've got a line on him, and I just about think he plays. There was a bunch of unsolved burglaries on Bunker Hill, May to August of '42. Mickey Mouse stuff clouted, right near Cormier and Joredco. LAPD was enforcing curfew then, and I picked out eight possible FI cards from the area – May through August. I've got a hunch the killings stem from then – the Sleepy Lagoon killing and the SLDC time – and I need you to do eliminations – current address, blood type, dental tech background, criminal record and the rest.'

'Go, I'm writing it down.'

Danny got out his cards. 'Some have addresses, some don't. One, James George Whitacre, DOB 10/5/03, Havana Hotel, Ninth and Olive. Two, Ronald NMI Dennison, 6/30/20, no address. Three, Coleman Masskie, 5/9/23, 236 South Beaudry. Four, Lawrence Thomas Waznicki with a K–I, 11/29/08, 641 1/4 Bunker Hill Avenue. Five, Leland NMI Hardell, 6/4/24, American Eagle Hotel, 4th and Hill Streets. Six, Loren Harold Nadick, 3/2/02, no address. Seven, David NMI Villers, 1/15/04, no address. And Bruno Andrew Gaffney, 7/29/06, no address.'

Shortell said, 'All down. Son, are you getting close?'

Another electric jolt: the Bunker Hill burglaries ended on August 1, 1942; the Sleepy Lagoon murder – *the victim's clothes zoot stick slashed* – occurred on August 2. 'Almost, Jack. Some right answers and luck and that fucker is mine.'

Danny got to Variety International Pictures just as dusk was falling and the picket lines were breaking up for the day. He parked in plain view, put an 'Official Police Vehicle' sign on his windshield and pinned his badge to his coat front; he walked to the guard hut, no familiar faces, pissed that he was ignored. The gate man buzzed him in; he walked straight back to Set 23.

The sign on the wall had *Tomahawk Massacre* still in production; the door was open. Danny heard gunfire, looked in and saw a cowboy and an Indian exchange shots across papier-mâché foothills. Lights were shining down on them; cameras were rolling; the Mexican guy he'd seen outside the morgue was sweeping up fake snow in front of another backdrop: grazing buffalos painted on cardboard.

Danny hugged the wall going over; the Mex looked up, dropped his broom and took off running, right in front of the cameras. Danny ran after him, sliding on soap flakes; the moviemaking stopped; someone yelled, 'Juan, goddamn you! Cut! Cut!'

Juan ran out a side exit, slamming the door; Danny ran across the set, slowed and eased the door open. It was slammed against him, reinforced steel knocking him back; he slid on phony snow, hauled outside and saw Duarte racing down an alley toward a chain-link fence.

Danny ran full out; Juan Duarte hit the fence and started climbing. He snagged his trouser legs; he kicked, pulled and twisted to get free. Danny caught up, yanked him down by his waistband and caught a hard right hand in the face. Stunned, he let go; Duarte collapsed on top of him.

Danny kneed upward, a jerky shot; Duarte hit down, missing, smashing his fist on the pavement. Danny rolled away, came up behind him and pinned him with his weight; the Mex gasped, 'Puto fascist shitfuck fascist cop fascist shitfuck.' Danny fumbled out his cuffs, ratcheted Duarte's left hand and attached the spare bracelet to a fence link. The Mex flopped on his stomach and tried to tear the fence down, spitting epithets in Spanish;

Danny got his breath, let Duarte shake and shout himself out, then knelt beside him. 'I know you saw my picture, and you saw me at the morgue and you snitched me to Claire. I don't care and I give a fuck about UAES and the fucking Red Menace. I want to get Augie's killer and I've got a hunch it goes back to Sleepy Lagoon. Now you can talk to me, or I'll nail you for Assault on a Police Officer right here. Call it now.'

Duarte shook his cuff chain; Danny said, 'Two to five minimum, and I don't give a shit about the UAES.' A crowd was forming in the alley; Danny waved them back; they retreated with sidelong looks and slow head shakes. Duarte said, 'Take these things off me and *maybe* I'll talk to you.'

Danny unlocked the cuffs. Duarte rubbed his wrist, stood up, got rubber-legged and slid down to a sitting position, his back against the fence. He said, 'Why's a hired gun for the studios give a damn about my dead fag cousin?'

Danny said, 'Get up, Duarte.'

'I talk better on my ass. Answer me. How come you care about a maricón who wanted to be a puto movie star like every other puto in this puto town?'

'I don't know. But I want the guy who killed Augie nailed.'

'And what's that got to do with you trying to get next to Claire De Haven?'

'I told you I don't care about that.'

'Norm Kostenz said you sure care. When I told him you were the fucking law, he said you should get a fucking Oscar for your bonaroo portrayal of Ted Krug – '

Danny squatted by Duarte, holding the fence. 'Arc you going to spill or not?'

Duarte said, 'I'll spill, pendejo. You said you thought Augie's snuff went back to Sleepy Lagoon, and that got my interest. Charlie Hartshorn thought that too, so – '

Danny's hand shook the fence; he braced his whole body into it to stay steady. 'What did you say?'

'I said Charlie Hartshorn thought the same thing maybe, so maybe talking to a puto cop ain't all poison.'

Danny slid down the fence so he could eyeball Duarte close. 'Tell me all of it, slow and easy. You know Hartshorn killed himself, don't you?'

Duarte said, 'Maybe he did. You tell me.'

'No. You tell me, because I don't know and I've got to know.'

Duarte stared at Danny, squinty-eyed, like he couldn't figure him out. 'Charlie was a lawyer. He was a maricón, but he wasn't a swish or nothing. He worked Sleepy Lagoon, filing briefs and shit for free.'

'I know that.'

'Okay, here's what you don't know, and here's the kind of guy he was. When you saw me at the morgue it was my second time there. I got a call from a buddy who works there, maybe one in the morning, and he told me about Augie – the zoot cuts, all of it. I went to Charlie's house. He had legal juice, and I wanted to see if he'd goose the cops so they'd give Augie's snuff a good investigation. He told me he'd been goosed by some cop about the death of a guy named Duane Lindenaur, even though the cop pretended he didn't care about that. Charlie read this scandal rag that said Lindenaur and some clown named Wiltsie got cut up by a zoot stick, and my morgue buddy said Augie got chopped like that, too. I told Charlie, and he got the idea all three snuffs went back to Sleepy Lagoon. He called the cops and spoke to some guy named Sergeant Bruner or something – '

Danny cut in. 'Breuning? Sergeant Mike Breuning?'

'Yeah, that's him. Charlie told Breuning what I just told you and Breuning said he'd come to see him at his crib right away to talk to him about it. I took off then. So if Charlie thought there was something to this Sleepy Lagoon theory, maybe you ain't such a cabrón.'

Danny's brain stoked on overdrive:

Breuning's curiosity on the zoot stick queries, his making light of them. His strange reaction to the four surveillance names – Augie Duarte singled out – because he was Mex, a KA of a Sleepy Lagoon Committee member? Mal telling him that Dudley Smith asked to join the grand jury team, even though, as an LAPD Homicide lieutenant, there was no logical reason for him to work the job. Mal's story: *Dudley brutally interrogating Duarte/Sammy Benavides/Mondo Lopez, stressing the Sleepy Lagoon case and the guilt of the seventeen youths originally charged with the crime – even though the questioning tack was not germane to UAES.*

Hartshorn mentioning 'zoot stick' on the phone to Breuning.

Jack Shortell's oral report: Dudley Smith and Breuning were seen hobnobbing at Wilshire Station the night before last – the night Hartshorn killed himself. Did they make a quick run to Hartshorn's house – a scant mile from the station – kill him and return to the Wilshire squadroom, hoping that no one saw them leave and return – a perfect cop alibi?

And why?

Juan Duarte was looking at him like he was from outer space; Danny got his brain simmered down to where he could talk. 'Think fast on this. Jazz musicians, burglary, wolverines, heroin, queer escort services.'

Duarte slid a few feet away. 'I think they all stink. Why?'

'A kid who worships wolverines.'

Duarte put a finger to his head and twirled it. 'Loco mierda. A wolverine's a fucking rat, right?'

Danny saw Juno's claws lashing out. 'Try this, Duarte. Sleepy Lagoon, the Defense Committee, '42 to '44 and Reynolds Loftis. Think slow, go slow.'

Duarte said, 'Easy. Reynolds and his kid brother.'

Danny started to say, 'What?', stopped and thought. He'd read the entire grand jury package twice on arrival and twice last night; he'd read the psychiatric files twice before Considine took them back. In all the paperwork there was no mention of Loftis having a brother. But there was a gap – '42 to '44 – in Loftis' shrink file. 'Tell me about the kid brother, Duarte. Nice and slow.'

Duarte spoke rapidamente. 'He was a punk, a lame-o. Reynolds started bringing him around around the time the SLDC was hot. I forget the kid's name, but he was a kid, eighteen, nineteen, in there. He had his face bandaged up. He was in a fire and he got burned bad. When he got his burns healed up and the bandages and gauze and shit came off, all the girls in the Committee thought he was real cute. He looked just like Reynolds, but even handsomer.'

The new facts coming together went tap, tap, tap, knocks on a door that was still a long way from opening. A Loftis burn-faced brother put the actor back in contention for HIM, but contradicted his instinct that the killer drew sex inspiration from the youth's disfigurement; it played into Wolverine Prowler and Burn Face as one man and tapped the possibility that he was a killing accomplice – one way to explain the new welter of age contradictions. Danny said, 'Tell me about the kid. Why did you call him a punk?'

Duarte said, 'He was always sucking up to the Mexican guys. He told this fish story about how a big white man killed José Diaz, like we were supposed to like him because he said the killer wasn't Mexican. Everybody knew the killer was Mexican – the cops just railroaded the wrong Mexicans. He told this crazy story about seeing the killing, but he didn't have no real details, and when guys pressed him, he clammed up. The SLDC got some anonymous letters saying a white guy did it, and you could tell the kid brother sent them – it was crazy-man stuff. The kid said he was running from the killer, and once I said, "Pendejo, if the killer's looking for you, what the fuck you doing coming to these rallies where he could grab your crazy ass?" The kid said he had special protection, but wouldn't tell me no more. Like I said, he was a lame-o. If he wasn't Reynolds' brother, nobody woulda tolerated him at all.'

Tap, tap, tap, tap, tap. Danny said, 'What happened to him?'

Duarte shrugged. 'I don't know. I haven't see him since the SLDC, and I don't think nobody else has either. Reynolds don't talk about him. It's strange. I don't think I've heard Chaz or Claire or Reynolds talk about him in years.'

'What about Benavides and Lopez? Where are they now?'

'On location with some other puto cowboy turkey. You think this stuff about Reynolds' brother has got something to do with Augie?'

Danny brainstormed off the question. Reynolds Loftis' brother was the burn-faced burglar boy, Marty Goines' burglar accomplice, very possibly the Bunker Hill prowler/wolverine lover. The Bunker Hill B&Es stopped August 1, 1942; the next night, José Diaz was killed at the Sleepy Lagoon, three miles or so southeast of the Hill. The kid brother alleged that he witnessed a 'big white man' killing José Diaz.

Tap, tap, tap. Jump, jump, jump.

Dudley Smith was a big white man with a bone-deep cruel streak. He joined the grand jury team out of a desire to keep incriminating Sleepy Lagoon testimony kiboshed, thinking that with access to witnesses and case paperwork, he could get the jump on damaging evidence about to come out. Hartshorn's zoot stick call to Mike Breuning scared him; he and Breuning or one of them alone drove over from Wilshire Station to talk to the man: Hartshorn got suspicious. Either premeditatedly or on the spur of the moment, Smith and/or Breuning killed him, faking a suicide. Tap, tap, tap – thunder loud – with the door still closed on the most important question: *How did Smith killing José Diaz, his attempts to keep possible evidence quashed and his killing Charles Hartshorn connect to the Goines/Wiltsie/Lindenaur/Duarte murders? And why did Smith kill Diaz?*

Danny looked around at set doors spilling glimpses: the wild west, jungle swampland, trees in a forest. He said, 'Vaya con Dios,' left Duarte sitting there and drove home to hit the grand jury file, thinking he'd finally made detective in the eyes of Maslick and Vollmer. He walked in his building, light as air; he pushed the elevator button and heard footsteps behind him. Turning, he saw two big men with guns drawn. He reached for his own gun, but a big fist holding a set of big brass knucks hit him first.

He came awake handcuffed to a chair. His head was woozy, his wrists were numb and his tongue felt huge. His eyes homed in on an interrogation cubicle, three fuzzy men seated around a table, a big black revolver lying square in the middle. A voice said, '.38's are standard issue for your Department, Upshaw. Why do you carry a .45?'

Danny blinked and coughed up a bloody lunger; he blinked again and recognized the voice man: Thad Green, LAPD Chief of Detectives. The two men flanking Green fell into focus; they were the biggest plainclothes cops he'd ever seen.

'I asked you a question, Deputy.'

Danny tried to remember the last time he had a drink, came up with Chinatown and knew he couldn't have gone crazy while fried on bonded. He coughed dry and said, 'I sold it when I made detective.'

Green lit a cigarette. 'That's an interdepartmental offense. Do you consider yourself above the law?'

'No!'

'Your friend Karen Hiltscher says otherwise. She says you've manipulated her for special favors ever since you made detective. She told Sergeant Eugene Niles you broke into 2307 Tamarind and knew that two murder victims had recently been killed there. She told Sergeant Niles that your story about a girlfriend near the doughnut stand on Franklin and Western is a lie, that she phoned you the information off the City air. Niles was going to inform on you, Deputy. Did you know that?'

Danny's head woozed. He swallowed blood; he recognized the man to Green's left as the knuck wielder. 'Yeah. Yes, I knew.'

Green said, 'Who'd you sell your .38 to?'

'A guy in a bar.'

'That's a misdemeanor, Deputy. A criminal charge. You really don't care much for the law, do you?'

'Yes, yes, I care! I'm a policeman! Goddamn it, what is this!'

The knuck man said, 'You were seen arguing with a known homo procurer named Felix Gordean. Are you on his payroll?'

'No!'

'Mickey Cohen's payroll?'

'No!'

Green took over. 'You were given command of a Homicide team, a carrot for your grand jury work. Sergeant Niles and Sergeant Mike Breuning found it very strange that a smart young officer would be so concerned about a string of queer slashes. Would you like to tell us why?'

'No! What the fuck is this! I B&E'd Tamarind! What do you fucking want from me!'

The third cop, a huge bodybuilder type, said, 'Why did you and Niles trade blows?'

'He was ditzing me with Tamarind Street, threatening to rat me.'

'So that made you mad?'

'Yes.'

'Fighting mad?'

'Yes!'

Green said, 'We heard a different version, Deputy. We heard Niles called you a queer.'

Danny froze, reached for a comeback and kept freezing. He thought of ratting Dudley and kiboshed it – they'd never believe him – *yet*. 'If Niles said that, I didn't hear it.'

The knuck cop laughed. 'Strike a nerve, Sonny?'

'Fuck you!'

The weightlifter cop backhanded him; Danny spat in his face. Green yelled, 'No!'

The knuck man put his arms around weightlifter and held him back; Green chained another cigarette, butt to tip. Danny gasped, *'Tell me what this is all about.'*

Green waved the strongarms to the back of the cubicle, dragged on his smoke and stubbed it out. 'Where were you night before last between 2:00 and 7:00 A.M.?'

'I was at home in bed. Asleep.'

'Alone, Deputy?'

'Yes.'

'Deputy, during that time Sergeant Gene Niles was shot and killed, then buried in the Hollywood Hills. Did you do it?'

'No!'

'Tell us who did.'

'Jack! Mickey! Niles was fucking rogue!'

The knuck cop stepped forward; the weightlifter cop grabbed him, mumbling, 'Spit on my Hathaway shirt you queer-loving hump. Gene Niles was my pal, my good buddy from the army, you queer lover.'

Danny dug his feet in and pushed his chair against the wall. 'Gene Niles was an incompetent bagman son of a bitch.'

Weightlifter charged, straight for Danny's throat. The cubicle door opened and Mal Considine rushed in; Thad Green shouted commands impossible to hear. Danny brought his knees up, toppling the chair; the monster cop's hands closed on air. Mal crashed into him, winging rabbit punches; the knuck cop pulled him off and wrestled him out to the corridor. Shouts of 'Danny!' echoed; Green stationed himself between the chair and the monster, going, 'No, Harry, no,' like he was reprimanding an unruly monster dog. Danny ate linoleum and cigarette butts, heard, 'Get Considine to a holding tank', was lifted, chair and all, to an upright position. The knuck man went behind him and unlocked his cuffs; Thad Green reached for his .45 on the table.

Danny stood up, swaying; Green handed him his gun. 'I don't know if you did it or not, but there's one way to find out. Report back here to City Hall, room 1003, tomorrow at noon. You'll be given a polygraph test and sodium pentothal, and you'll be asked extensive questions about these homicides you're working and your relationships with Felix Gordean and Gene Niles. Good night, Deputy.'

Danny weaved to the elevator, rode to the ground floor and walked outside, his legs slowly coming back. He cut across the lawn toward the Temple Street cabstand, stopping for a soft voice.

'Lad.'

Danny froze; Dudley Smith stepped out of a shadow. He said, 'It's a grand night, is it not?'

Small talk with a murderer. Danny said, 'You killed José Diaz. You and Breuning killed Charles Hartshorn. And I'm going to prove it.'

Dudley Smith smiled. 'I never doubted your intelligence, lad. Your courage, yes. Your intelligence, never. And I'll admit I underestimated your persistence. I'm only human, you know.'

'Oh, no you're not.'

'I'm skin and bone, lad. Eros and dust like all us frail mortals. Like you, lad. Crawling in sewers for answers you'd be better off without.'

'You're finished.'

'No, lad. You are. I've been talking to my old friend Felix Gordean, and he painted me a vivid picture of your emergence. Lad, next to myself Felix has the finest eye for weakness I've ever encountered. He knows, and when you take that lie detector test tomorrow, the whole world will know.'

Danny said, 'No.'

Dudley Smith said, 'Yes,' kissed him full on the lips and walked away whistling a love song.

Machines that know.

Drugs that don't let you lie.

Danny took a cab home. He unlocked the door and went straight for his files: facts you could put together for the truth, Dudley and Breuning and HIM nailed by 11:59, a last-minute reprieve like in the movies. He hit the hall light, opened the closet door. No file boxes, the rugs that covered them neatly folded on the floor.

Danny tore up the hall carpet and looked under it, dumped the bedroom cabinet and emptied the drawers, stripped the bed and yanked the medicine chest off the bathroom wall. He upended the living room furniture, looked under the cushions and tossed the kitchen drawers until the floor was all cutlery and broken dishes. He saw a half-full bottle by the radio, opened it, found his throat muscles too constricted and hurled it, knocking down the venetian blinds. He walked to the window, looked out and saw Dudley Smith haloed by a streetlight.

And he knew he knew. And tomorrow they would all know.

Blackmail bait.

His name in sex files.

His name bandied in queer chitchat at the Chateau Marmont.

Machines that know.

Drugs that don't let you lie.

Polygraph needles fluttering off the paper every time they asked him why he cared so much about a string of queer fag homo fruit snuffs.

No reprieve.

Danny unholstered his gun and stuck the barrel in his mouth. The taste of oil made him gag and he saw how it would look, the cops who found him making jokes about why he did it that way. He put the .45 down and walked to the kitchen.

Weapons galore.

Danny picked up a serrated-edged carving knife. He tested the heft, found it substantial and said goodbye to Mal and Jack and Doc. He apologized for the cars he stole and the guys he beat up who didn't deserve it, who

368

were just there when he wanted to hit something. He thought of his killer, thought that he murdered because someone made him what he himself was. He held the knife up and forgave him; he put the blade to his throat and slashed himself ear to ear, down to the windpipe in one clean stroke.

3

Wolverine

CHAPTER THIRTY-TWO

A week later Buzz went by the grave, his fourth visit since LASD hustled the kid into the ground. The plot was a low-rent number in an East LA cemetery; the stone read:

Daniel Thomas Upshaw
1922–1950

No beloved whatever of.

No son of whoever.

No crucifix cut into the tablet and no RIP. Nothing juicy to catch a passerby's interest, like 'Cop Killer' or 'Almost DA's Bureau Brass.' Nothing to spell it out true to whoever read the half-column hush job on the kid's accidental death – a slip off a chair, a nose dive onto a kitchen cutlery rack.

Fall Guy.

Buzz bent down and pulled out a clump of crabgrass; the butt of the gun he'd killed Gene Niles with dug into his side. He stood up and kicked the marker; he thought that 'Free Ride' and 'Gravy Train' and 'Dumb Okie Luck' might look good too, followed by a soliloquy on Deputy Danny Upshaw's last days, lots of details on a tombstone skyscraper high, like the ones voodoo nigger pimps bought for themselves. Because Deputy Danny Upshaw was voodooing him, little pins stuck in a fat little Buzz Meeks voodoo doll.

Mal had called him with the word. The rain dug up Niles' body, LAPD grabbed Danny as a suspect, rough-housed him and cut him loose with orders to report for a lie detector test and sodium pentothal questioning the next day. When the kid didn't show, City bulls hit his pad in force and found him dead on the living room floor, throat slashed, the pad trashed. Nort Layman, distraught, did the autopsy, dying to call it a 187; the evidence wouldn't let him: fingerprints on the knife and the angle of the cut and fall said 'self-inflicted,' case closed. Doc called the death wound 'amazing' – no hesitation marks, Danny Upshaw wanted out bad and now.

LASD double-timed the kid graveside; four people attended the funeral: Layman, Mal, a County cop named Jack Shortell and himself. The homo investigation was immediately disbanded and Shortell took off for a vacation in the Montana boonies; LAPD closed the book on Gene Niles, Upshaw's suicide their confession and trip to the gas chamber. City-County police relations were all-time bad – and he skated, thin-icing it, trying to fix an angle to save both their asses, no luck, too late to do the kid any good.

Free Ride.

What kept nagging at him was that he fixed Audrey's skim spree first. Petey Skouras paid Mickey back the dough the lioness bilked; Mickey was generous and let him off with a beating: Johnny Stomp and a little blackjack work on the kidneys. Petey took off for Frisco then – even though the Mick, impressed with his repentance, would have kept him on the payroll. Petey had played into his fix by skedaddling; Mickey, Mr. Effusiveness, had upped his payoff on the dope summit guard gig to a grand, telling him the charming Lieutenant Dudley Smith would also be standing trigger. More cash in his pocket – while Danny Upshaw climbed the gallows.

Dumb Okie Luck.

Mal took it hard, going on a two-day drunk, sobering up with a direct frontal attack on the Red Menace. A strongarmed lefty told Dudley Smith that Claire De Haven made 'Ted Krugman' as a cop; Mal was enraged, but the consensus of the team was that they now had enough snitch testimony to take UAES down without Upshaw's covert dirt. Docket time was being set up; if all went well, the grand jury would convene in two weeks. Mal had gone off the deep end, crucifying Reds to perk his juice for *his* court battle. He'd turned Nathan Eisler's diary upside down for names, turning out snitches from four of the men Claire De Haven serviced to start her union. His flop at the Shangri-Lodge Motel now looked like Ellis Loew's living room: graphs, charts and cross-referenced hearsay, Mal's ode to Danny Upshaw, all of it proving one thing: that Commies were long on talk. And when the grand jury heard that talk, they probably wouldn't have the brains to think it out one step further: that the sad, deluded fuckers talked because they didn't have the balls to do anything else.

Buzz kicked the gravestone again; he thought that Captain Mal Considine almost had himself convinced that UAES was a hot damn threat to America's internal security – that he had to believe it so he could keep his son and still call himself a good guy. Odds on the Hollywood Commies subverting the country with their cornball propaganda turkeys, rallies and picket line highjinks: thirty trillion to one against, a longshot from Mars. The entire deal was a duck shoot, a play to save the studios money and make Ellis Loew District Attorney and Governor of California.

Bagman.

Fixer.

He'd been skating since the moment Mal called him with the news. Ellis told him to run background checks on the names in Eisler's diary; he called R&I, got their dope and let it go at that. Mal told him to conduct phone interviews with HUAC snitches back east; he gave a third of the numbers cursory calls, asked half the questions he was supposed to and edited the answers down to two pages per man, easy stuff for his secretary to type up. His big job was to locate Dr. Saul Lesnick, the grand jury's boss fink; he'd skated entirely on that gig – and kept skating in general. And always in the same direction – toward Danny Upshaw.

When he knew the hush was in, he drove up to San Bernardino for a look-see at the kid's past. He talked to his widowed mother, a faded ginch living on Social

Security; she told him she didn't attend the funeral because Danny had been curt with her on his last several visits and she disapproved of his drinking. He got her talking; she painted a picture of Danny the child as smart and cold, a youngster who read, studied and kept to himself. When his father died, he expressed no grief; he liked cars and fix-it things and science books; he never chased girls and always kept his room spotless. Since he became a policeman, he visited her only on Christmas and her birthday, never more, never less. He got straight B's in high school and straight A's in junior college. He ignored the floozies who chased after him; he tinkered with hot rods. He had one close friend: a boy named Tim Bergstrom, now a phys ed teacher at San Berdoo High.

Buzz drove to the school and badged Bergstrom. The man had seen the newspaper plant on Upshaw's Death, said Danny was born to die young and elaborated over beers in a nearby bar. He said that Danny liked to figure things like motors and engines and arithmetic out, that he stole cars because he loved the danger, that he was always trying to prove himself, but kept quiet about it. You could tell he was crazy inside, but you couldn't figure out how or why; you could tell he was really smart, but you didn't know what he'd end up doing with his brains. Girls liked him because he was mysterious and played hard to get; he was a terrific street fighter. Years ago, drunk, Danny told him a story about witnessing a murder; that was when he got hipped on being a cop, hipped on scientific forensic stuff. He was a cold drunk: booze just made him more inside, more mysterious and persistent, and sooner or later you knew he'd persist with the wrong guy and get himself shot – what surprised him was that Danny died accidentally. Buzz let that one go and said, 'Was Danny a queer?' Bergstrom flushed, twitched, sputtered into his beer and said, 'Hell, no' – and two seconds later was whipping out pictures of his wife and kids.

Buzz drove back to LA, called a County pal, learned

that Danny Upshaw's Personnel file had been yanked and that for all intents and purposes the kid was never a member of the Los Angeles County Sheriff's Department. He took a trip by the West Hollywood Substation, talked to the guys on the squad, learned that Danny never accepted bribes or trade pussy; he never moved on his snitch Janice Modine or on switchboard Karen Hiltscher – both of whom were dying to give it to him. Upshaw's fellow deputies either respected his brains or wrote him off as an idealistic fool with a mean streak; Captain Al Dietrich was rumored to like him because he was methodical, hard-working and ambitious. Buzz thought of him as a kid graduating from machines to people at the wrong time, fishing for WHY? in a river of shit, getting the worst answer two bad cases had to give and ending up dead because he couldn't lie to himself.

Daniel Thomas Upshaw, 1922–1950. Queer.

Turner Prescott Meeks, 1906–? Free ride because the kid couldn't take it.

'It' couldn't be anything else. Danny Upshaw didn't kill Gene Niles. Mal said Thad Green and two hardnoses roughed him up; they probably recounted Niles calling him a queer and went over what Dudley Smith told Mal and Green: that Danny was seen shaking down Felix Gordean. With a poly test and silly syrup pending, Green let the kid go home with his gun, hoping he'd spare LAPD the grief of a trial and Niles as a Dragna bagman coming out. Danny had obliged – but for the wrong reason and not with his gun.

Scapegoat.

Who got some kind of last laugh.

He couldn't sleep for shit; when he did put three or four hours together he dreamed of all the crappy stunts he'd pulled: farm girls coerced into Howard's bed; heroin bootjacked and sold to Mickey, cash in his pocket, the junk sidetracked on its way to some hophead's arm. Sleeping with Audrey was the only cure – she'd played her string since Niles like a trouper – and

377

touching her and keeping her safe kept the kid away. But their four nights in a row at Howard's place was dangerous too, and every time he left her he got scared and knew he had to do something about it.

Keeping his take on Danny away from Mal was one way. The cop couldn't believe the kid killed Niles, and he was pretty shrewd in tagging Cohen gunmen for the job – he'd watched Danny question a Dragna hump named Vinnie Scoppettone, who spilled on the shooting at Sherry's: LAPD shooters. But that was as far as his reconstruction went, and he still idealized Upshaw as a smart young cop headed for rank and glory. Keeping the kid's secret was the beginning.

Buzz cocked a finger at the gravestone and made up his mind around two facts. One, when LAPD crashed Upshaw's pad, they found it thoroughly trashed; Nort Layman did a forensic, came up with Danny's prints on a shitload of tossed furniture and pegged him going crazy in the last moments of his life. LAPD's property report – the contents of the apartment inventoried – carried no mention of the grand jury paperwork *or* the personal file Danny kept on his homicides. He broke into the place and tossed it extra good; no files were secreted anywhere inside the four rooms. Mal was there when the body was discovered; he said LAPD sealed the crib tight, with only Danny and the knife leaving the premises. Two, the night before he died, Danny called him: he was amazed that his two cases had crossed at the juncture of Charles Hartshorn and Reynolds Loftis.

'Deputy, are you tellin' me Loftis is a suspect for your killin's?'

'I'm telling you maybe. Maybe real strong. He fits the killer's description . . . and he fits.'

No way was Danny Upshaw a murder victim. No way did the file thief wreck his apartment. Dudley Smith had a strange fix on the kid, but there was no reason for him to steal the files, and if he did he would have faked a burglary.

378

Person or persons unknown – a good starting point for some payback.

Buzz found Mal in Ellis Loew's back yard, sitting on a sunbleached sofa, going over papers. He looked skinny beyond skinny, like he was starving himself to make the bantamweight limit. 'Hey, boss.'

Mal nodded and kept working. Buzz said, 'I want to talk to you.'

'About what?'

'Not some Commie plot, that's for damn sure.'

Mal connected a series of names with pencil lines. 'I know you don't take this seriously, but it is serious.'

'It's a serious piece of gravy, I'll give you that. And I sure want my share. It's just that I've got some other boogeymen on my mind right now.'

'Like who?'

'Like Upshaw.'

Mal put his paper and pencil down. 'He's LAPD's boogeyman, not yours.'

'I'm pretty sure he didn't kill Niles, boss.'

'We've been over that, Buzz. It was Mickey or Jack, and we'd never be able to prove it in a million years.'

Buzz sat down on the couch – it stank of mildew and some Red chaser had burned the arms with cigarette butts. 'Mal, you remember Upshaw tellin' us about his file on the queer snuffs?'

'Sure.'

'It was stolen from his apartment, and so was his copy of the grand jury package.'

'What?'

'I'm certain about it. You said LAPD sealed the pad and didn't take nothin', and I checked Upshaw's desk at West Hollywood Station. Lots of old paperwork, but zilch on the 187's and the grand jury. You been so absorbed chasin' pinkers you probably didn't even think about it.'

Mal tapped Buzz with his pencil. 'You're right, I didn't, and where are you fishing? The kid's dead and buried, he was in trouble over that B&E he pulled, he was probably finished as a cop. He could have been the best, and I miss him. But he dug his own grave.'

Buzz clamped down on Mal's hand. 'Boss, *we* dug his grave. You pushed him too hard on De Haven, and I . . . oh fuck it.'

Mal pulled his hand free. 'You what?'

'The kid had a fix on Reynolds Loftis. We talked on the phone the night before he died. He'd read about Charles Hartshorn's suicide, the paper made him as a Sleepy Lagoon lawyer and Upshaw had him as a lead on his homicides – Hartshorn was blackmailed by one of the victims. I told him Loftis was rousted with Hartshorn at a queer bar back in '44, and the kid went nuts. He didn't know Hartshorn was involved with Sleepy Lagoon, and that sure did seem to set him off. I asked him if Loftis was a suspect, and he said, "Maybe real strong".'

Mal said, 'Have you talked to that County man Shortell about this?'

'No, he's in Montana on vacation.'

'Mike Breuning?'

'I don't trust that boy to answer straight. Remember how Danny told us Breuning fluffed the job and was jerkin' his chain?'

'Meeks, you sure took your time telling me this.'

'I've been thinkin' it over, and it took me a while to figure out what I was gonna do.'

'Which is?'

Buzz smiled, 'Maybe Loftis is a hot suspect, maybe he ain't. Whatever, I'm gonna get me that queer slasher, whoever he is.'

Mal smiled. 'And then what?'

'Then arrest him or kill him.'

Mal said, 'You're out of your mind.'

Buzz said, 'I was sorta thinkin' about askin' you to join me. A captain out of his mind has got more juice than a loaner cop with a few loose.'

'I've got the grand jury, Meeks. And day after tomorrow's the divorce trial.'

Buzz cracked his knuckles. 'You in?'

'No. It's crazy. And I don't feature you as the dramatic gesture type, either.'

'I owe him. *We* owe him.'

'No, it's wrong.'

'Think of the angles, skipper. Loftis as a psycho killer. You pop him for that before the grand jury convenes and UAES'll go in the toilet so large they'll hear it flush in Cleveland.'

Mal laughed; Buzz laughed and said, 'We'll give it a week or so. We'll put together what we can get out of the grand jury file and we'll talk to Shortell and see what he's got. We'll brace Loftis, and if it goes bust, it goes bust.'

'There's the grand jury, Meeks.'

'A Commie like Loftis popped for four 187's makes you so large that no judge in this state would fuck you over on your custody case. Think of that.'

Mal broke his pencil in two. 'I need a continuance, *now*, and I won't frame Loftis.'

'That mean you're in?'

'I don't know.'

Buzz went for the kill. 'Well, shit there, *Captain*. I thought appealin' to your career would get you, but I guess I was wrong. Just think about Danny Upshaw and how bad he wanted it, and how you got your rocks off sendin' him after Claire De Haven. Think how maybe her and Loftis played with that cherry kid right before he cut his fuckin' throat. Then you – '

Mal slapped Buzz hard in the face.

Buzz sat on his hands so he wouldn't hit back.

Mal threw his list of names on the grass and said, 'I'm in. But if this fucks up my grand jury shot, it's you and me for real. For keeps.'

Buzz smiled. 'Yessir, Captain.'

CHAPTER THIRTY-THREE

Claire De Haven said, 'I take it this means all pretenses are off.'

A weak intro – he knew she had Upshaw made and the grand jury on track. Mal said, 'This is about four murders.'

'Oh?'

'Where's Reynolds Loftis? I want to talk to him.'

'Reynolds is out, and I told you before that he and I will not name names.'

Mal walked into the house. He saw the front page of last Wednesday's *Herald* on a chair; he knew Claire had seen the piece on Danny's death, Sheriff's Academy picture included. She closed the door – *her* no pretense – she wanted to know what *he* had. Mal said, 'Four killings. No political stuff unless you tell me otherwise.'

Claire said, 'I'll tell you I don't know what you're talking about.'

Mal pointed to the paper. 'What's so interesting about last week's news?'

'A sad little obituary on a young man I knew.'

Mal played in. 'What kind of young man?'

'I think frightened, impotent and treacherous describes him best.'

The epitaph stung; Mal wondered for the ten millionth time what Danny Upshaw and Claire De Haven did to each other. 'Four men raped and cut up. No political stuff for you to get noble about. Do you want to get down off your high Commie horse and tell me what you know about it? What Reynolds Loftis knows?'

Claire walked up to him, perfume right in his face. 'You sent that boy to fuck information out of me and now *you* want to preach decency?'

Mal grabbed her shoulders and squeezed them; he got

his night's worth of report study straight in his head. 'January 1, Marty Goines snatched from South Central, shot with heroin, mutilated and killed. January 4, George Wiltsie and Duane Lindenaur, secobarbital sedated, mutilated and killed. January 14, Augie Luis Duarte, the same thing. Wiltsie and Duarte were male whores, we know that certain men in your union frequent male whores and the killer's description is a dead ringer for Loftis. Still want to play cute?'

Claire squirmed; Mal saw her as something wrong to touch and let go. She wheeled to a desk by the stairwell, grabbed a ledger and shoved it at him. 'On January first, fourth and fourteenth, Reynolds was here in full view of myself and others. You're insane to think he could kill anybody, and this proves it.'

Mal took the ledger, skimmed it and shoved it back to her. 'It's a fake. I don't know what the crossouts mean, but only your signature and Loftis' are real. The others are traced over, and the minutes are like Dick and Jane join the Party. It's a fake, and you had it out and ready. Now you explain that, or I go get a material witness warrant for Loftis.'

Claire held the ledger to herself. 'I don't believe that threat. I think this is some kind of personal vendetta with you.'

'Just answer me.'

'My answer is that your young Deputy Ted kept pressing me about what Reynolds was doing on those nights, and when I discovered that he was a policeman I thought he must have convinced himself that Reynolds did something terrible. Reynolds was here then for meetings, so I left this out for the boy to see, so he wouldn't launch some awful circumstantial pogrom.'

A perfect right answer. 'You didn't know a graphologist would eat that ledger up in court?'

'No.'

'And what did you think Danny Upshaw was trying to prove against Loftis?'

'I don't know! Some kind of treason, but not sex murders!'

Mal couldn't tell if she'd raised her voice to cover a lie. 'Why didn't you show Upshaw your real ledger? You were taking a risk that he'd spot a fake one.'

'I couldn't. A policeman would probably consider our real minutes treason.'

'Treason' was a howler; profundity from a roundheels who'd spread for anything pretty in pants. Mal laughed, caught himself and stopped; Claire said, 'Care to tell me what's so amusing?'

'Nothing.'

'You sound patronizing.'

'Let's change the subject. Danny Upshaw had a file on the murders, and it was stolen from his apartment. Do you know anything about that?'

'No. I'm not a thief. Or a comedienne.'

Getting mad shaved ten years off the woman's age. 'Then don't give yourself more credit than you're worth.'

Claire raised a hand, then held it back. 'If you don't consider my friends and me serious, then why are you trying to smear us and ruin our lives?'

Mal fizzled at a wisecrack; he said, 'I want to talk to Loftis.'

'You didn't answer my question.'

'I'm doing the asking. When's Loftis coming back?'

Claire laughed. 'Oh, mein policeman, what your face just said. You know it's a travesty, don't you? You think we're too ineffectual to be dangerous, which is just about as wrong as thinking we're traitors.'

Mal thought of Dudley Smith; he thought of the Red Queen eating Danny Upshaw alive. 'What happened with you and Ted Krugman?'

'Get your names straight. You mean Deputy Upshaw, don't you?'

'*Just tell me.*'

'I'll tell you he was naive and eager to please and all bluff where women were concerned, and I'll tell you you shouldn't have sent such a frail American patriot after us. Frail and clumsy. Did he *really* fall on a cutlery rack?'

Mal swung an open hand; Claire flinched at the blow and slapped back, no tears, just smeared lipstick and a welt forming on her cheek. Mal turned and braced himself against the banister, afraid of the way he looked; Claire said, 'You could just quit. You could denounce the wrongness of it, say we're ineffectual and not worth the money and effort and still sound like a big tough cop.'

Mal tasted blood on his lips. 'I want it.'

'For what? Glory? You're too smart for patriotism.'

Mal saw Stefan waving goodbye; Claire said, 'For your son?'

Mal, trembling, said, 'What did you say?'

'We're not the fools you think we are, recently promoted Captain. We know how to hire private detectives and they know how to check records and verify old rumors. You know, I'm impressed with the Nazi you killed and rather surprised that you can't see the parallels between that regime and your own.'

Mal kept looking away; Claire stepped closer to him. 'I understand what you must feel for your son. And I think we both know the fix is in.'

Mal pushed himself off the railing and looked at her. 'Yeah. The fix is in, and this conversation didn't happen. And I still want to talk to Reynolds Loftis. And if he killed those men, I'm taking him down.'

'Reynolds has not killed anyone.'

'Where is he?'

Claire said, 'He'll be back tonight, and you can talk to him then. He'll convince you, and I'll make you a deal. I know you need a continuance on your custody trial, and I have friends on the bench who can get it for you. But I don't want Reynolds smeared to the grand jury.'

'You can't mean that.'

'Don't make a career out of underestimating me. Reynolds was hurt badly in '47, and I don't think he'd be able to go through it again. I'll do everything I can to help you with your son, but I don't want Reynolds hurt.'

'What about you?'

'I'll take my knocks.'

'It's impossible.'

'Reynolds has not killed anyone.'

'Maybe that's true, but he's been named as a subversive too many times.'

'Then destroy those depositions and don't call those witnesses.'

'You don't understand. His name is all over our paperwork a thousand goddamn times.'

Claire held Mal's arms. 'Just tell me you'll try to keep him from being hurt too badly. Tell me yes and I'll make my calls, and you won't have to go to trial tomorrow.'

Mal saw himself doctoring transcripts, shuffling names and realigning graphs to point to other Commies, going mano a mano: his editorial skill versus Dudley Smith's memory. 'Do it. Have Loftis here at 8:00 and tell him it's going to be ugly.'

Claire took her hands away. 'It won't be any worse than your precious grand jury.'

'Don't go noble on me, because I know who you are.'

'Don't cheat me, because I'll use my friends to ruin you.'

A deal with a real red devil: the continuance buying him time to un-nail a subversive, nail a killer and nail himself as a hero. And just maybe cross Claire De Haven. 'I won't cheat you.'

'I'll have to trust you. And can I ask you something? Off the record?'

'What?'

'Your opinion of this grand jury.'

Mal said, 'It's a goddamn waste and a goddamn shame.'

CHAPTER THIRTY-FOUR

Mickey Cohen was pitching a tantrum; Johnny Stompanato was fueling it; Buzz was watching – scared shitless.

They were at the Mick's hideaway, surrounded by muscle. After the bomb under the house went off, Mickey sent Lavonne back east and moved into the Samo Canyon bungalow, wondering who the fuck wanted him dead. Jack D. called to say it wasn't him – Mickey believed it. Brenda Allen was still in jail, the City cops had settled into a slow burn and cop bombers played like science fiction. Mickey decided it was the Commies. Some Pinko ordnance expert got word he was fronting the Teamsters, popped his cork and planted the bomb that destroyed thirty-four of his custom suits. It was a Commie plot – it couldn't be anything else.

Buzz kept watching, waiting by the phone for a call from Mal Considine. Davey Goldman and Mo Jahelka were prowling the grounds; a bunch of goons were oiling the shotguns stashed in the fake panel between the living room and bedroom. Mickey had started squawking half an hour ago, topics ranging from Audrey not giving him any to passive resistance on the picket line and how he was going to fix the UAES's red wagon. Comedy time until Johnny Stomp showed up and started talking *his* conspiracy.

The guinea Adonis brought bad news: when Petey Skouras blew to Frisco he took a week's worth of receipts with him – Audrey told him when he picked up the Southside front's cash take. Buzz horned in on the conversation, thinking the lioness couldn't be stupid enough to try to play Petey's splitsville for a profit – Petey himself had to have done it – his bonus atop the thousand-dollar beating. Johnny's news got worse: he took a baseball bat to a guy on the welcher's list, who told him Petey was no skimmer, Petey would never protect a girlfriend's brother because Petey liked boys – young darky stuff – a habit he picked up in a U.S. army stockade in Alabama. Mickey went around the twist then, spraying spit like a rabid dog, spitting obscenities in Yiddish, making his Jew strongarms squirm. Johnny had to know that his story contradicted Buzz's story; the fact that he wouldn't give him an even eyeball clinched it. When Mickey stopped ranting and started thinking, he'd snap to that, too – then he'd start asking questions and it would be another convoluted epic to his *boy-friend's* brother, how he didn't want poor Greek Petey smeared as taking it Greek. Mickey would believe him – probably.

Buzz got out his notepad and wrote a memo to Mal and Ellis Loew – abbreviated skinny from three trigger-men moonlighting as picket goons. Their consensus: UAES still biding its time, the Teamster rank and file on fire to whomp some ass, the only new wrinkle a suspicious-looking van parked on Gower, a man with a movie camera in the back. The man, a studious bird with Trotsky glasses, was seen talking to Norm Kostenz, the UAES picket boss. Conclusion: UAES wanted the Teamsters to rumble, so they could capture the ass-whomping on film.

His skate work done, Buzz listened to Mickey rant and checked his real notes – the grand jury and shrink files read over and put together with a few records prowls and a brief talk with Jack Shortell's partner at the San Dimas Substation. Shortell would be returning from Montana tomorrow; he could hit him for a real rundown on Upshaw's case then. The partner said that Jack said Danny seemed to think the killings derived from the time of the Sleepy Lagoon murder and the SLDC – it was the last thing the kid talked up before LAPD grabbed him. That in mind, Buzz matched the theory to his file facts.

He got:

Danny told him Reynolds Loftis fit his killing suspect's

description – and in general – 'he fits.' Charles Hartshorn, a recent suicide, was rousted with Loftis at a local fruit bar in '44.

Two identical names and an R&I and DMV check got him Augie Duarte, snuff victim number four, and his cousin, SLDC/UAES hotshot Juan Duarte, currently working at Variety International Pictures – on a set next to the room where victim number three, Duane Lindenaur, worked as a rewrite man. SLDC Lawyer Hartshorn was blackmailed by Lindenaur years ago – a check on the crime report led him to an LASD Sergeant named Skakel, who had also talked to Danny Upshaw. Skakel told him that Lindenaur met Hartshorn at a party thrown by fag impresario Felix Gordean, the man Danny said the killer had a fix on.

The first victim, Marty Goines, died of a heroin over-jolt. Loftis' fiancée Claire De Haven was a skin-popper; she took Dr. Terry Lux's cure three times. Terry said Loftis copped H for her.

From Mal's report on the Sammy Benavides/Mondo Lopez/Juan Duarte questioning:

Benavides shouted something about Chaz Minear, Loftis' fag squeeze, buying boys at a 'puto escort service' – Gordean's?

Also on Minear: in his psych file, Chaz justified snitching Loftis to HUAC by pointing to a third man in a love triangle – 'If you knew who he was, you'd understand why I did it.'

Two strange-o deals:

The '42 to '44 pages were missing from Loftis' psych file and Doc Lesnick couldn't be found. At the three Mexes' questioning, one of the guys muttered an aside – the SLDC got letters tapping a 'big white man' for the Sleepy Lagoon murder.

Strange-o stuff aside, all circumstantial – but too solid to be coincidence.

The phone rang, cutting through Mickey's tirade on Commies. Buzz picked it up; Johnny Stomp watched him talk.

'Yeah. Cap, that you?'

'It's me, Turner, my lad.'

'You sound happy, boss.'

'I just got a ninety-day continuance, so I am happy. Did you do your homework?'

Stompanato was still staring. Buzz said, 'Sure did. Circumstantial but tight. You talk to Loftis?'

'Meet me at 463 Canon Drive in an hour. We've got him as a friendly witness.'

'No shit?'

'No shit.'

Buzz hung up. Johnny Stomp winked at him and turned back to Mickey.

CHAPTER THIRTY-FIVE

Headlights bounced over the street, caught his windshield and went off. Mal heard a car door slamming and tapped his highbeams; Buzz walked over and said, 'You do *your* homework?'

'Yeah. Like you said, circumstantial. But it's there.'

'How'd you fix this up, Cap?'

Mal held back on the De Haven deal. 'Danny wasn't too subtle hitting up Claire for Loftis' whereabouts on the killing dates, so she faked a meeting diary – Loftis alibied for the three nights. She says there were meetings, and he was there, but they were planning seditious stuff – that's why she sugar-coated the damn thing. She says Loftis is clean.'

'You believe it?'

'Maybe, but my gut tells me they're connected to the whole deal. This afternoon I checked Loftis' bank records going back to '40. Three times in the spring and summer of '44 he made cash withdrawals of ten grand. Last week he made another one. Interesting?'

Buzz whistled. 'From old Reynolds' missing-file time.

It's gotta be blackmail, there's blackmail all over this mess. You wanna play him white hat-black hat?'

Mal got out of the car. 'You be the bad guy. I'll get De Haven out of the way, and we'll work him.'

They walked up to the door and rang the bell. Claire De Haven answered; Mal said, 'You go somewhere for a couple of hours.'

Claire looked at Buzz, lingering on his ratty sharkskin and heater. 'You mustn't touch him.'

Mal hooked a thumb over his back. 'Go somewhere.'

'No thank yous for what I did?'

Mal caught Buzz catching it. 'Go somewhere, Claire.'

The Red Queen brushed past them out the door; she gave Buzz a wide berth. Mal whispered, 'Hand signals. Three fingers on my tie means hit him.'

'You got the stomach for this?'

'Yes. You?'

'One for the kid, boss.'

Mal said, 'I still don't make you for the sentimental gesture type.'

'I guess old dogs can learn. What just happened with you and the princess?'

'Nothing.'

'Sure, boss.'

Mal heard coughing in the living room; Buzz said, 'I'll kick-start him.' A voice called, 'Gentlemen, can we get this over with?'

Buzz walked in first, whistling at the furnishings; Mal followed, taking a long look at Loftis. The man was tall and gray per Upshaw's suspect description; he was dashingly handsome at fifty or so and his whole manner was would-be slick – a costume of tweed slacks and cardigan sweater, a sprawl on the divan, one leg hooked over the other at the knee.

Mal sat next to him; Buzz thunked a chair down a hard breath away. 'You and that honey Claire are gettin' married, huh?'

Loftis said, 'Yes, we are.'

Buzz smiled, soft and homespun. 'That's sweet. She gonna let you pork boys on the side?'

Loftis sighed. 'I don't have to answer that question.'

'The fuck you don't. You answer it, you answer it now.'

Mal came in. 'Mr. Loftis is right, Sergeant. That question is not germane. Mr. Loftis, where were you on the nights of January first, fourth and the fourteenth of this year?'

'I was here, at meetings of the UAES Executive Committee.'

'And what was discussed at those meetings?'

'Claire said I didn't have to discuss that with you.'

Buzz snickered. 'You take orders from a woman?'

'Claire is no ordinary woman.'

'She sure ain't. A rich bitch Commie that shacks with a fruitfly sure ain't everyday stuff to me.'

Loftis sighed again. 'Claire told me this would be ugly, and she was correct. She also told me your sole purpose was to convince yourselves that I didn't kill anyone, and that I did not have to discuss the UAES business that was transacted on those three nights.'

Mal knew Meeks would figure out the Claire deal before too long; he joined his partner on the black hat side. 'Loftis, I don't think you did kill anybody. But I think you're in deep on some other things, and I'm not talking politics. We want the killer, and you're going to help us get him.'

Loftis licked his lips and knotted his fingers together; Mal touched his tie bar: *go in full*. Buzz said, 'What's your blood type?'

Loftis said, 'O positive.'

'That's the killer's blood type, boss. You know that?'

'It's the most common blood type among white people, and your friend just said I'm no longer a suspect.'

'My friend's a soft touch. You know a trombone man named Marty Goines?'

'No.'

392

'Duane Lindenaur?'

'No.'

'George Wiltsie?'

Tilt: Loftis crossing and recrossing his legs, licking his lips. 'No.'

Buzz said, 'Horse fucking pucky, you don't. *Give*.'

'I said I never knew him!'

'Then why'd you describe him in the past tense?'

'Oh God – '

Mal flashed two fingers, then his left hand over his right fist: *He's mine, no hitting*. 'Augie Duarte, Loftis. What about him?'

'I don't know him' – a dry tongue over dry lips.

Buzz cracked his knuckles – loud. Loftis flinched; Mal said, 'George Wiltsie was a male prostitute. Did you ever traffic with him? Tell the truth or my partner will get angry.'

Loftis looked down at his lap. 'Yes.'

Mal said, 'Who set it up?'

'Nobody set it up! It was just . . . a date.'

Buzz said, 'A date you paid for, boss?'

'No.'

Mal said, 'Felix Gordean set you up with him, right?'

'No!'

'I don't believe you.'

'No!'

Mal knew a straight admission was out; he jabbed Loftis hard on the shoulder. 'Augie Duarte. Was he just a date?'

'No!'

'Tell the truth, or I'll leave you alone with the sergeant.'

Loftis pinched his knees together and hunched his shoulders down. 'Yes.'

'Yes what?'

'Yes. We dated once.'

Buzz said, 'You sound like a one-night stand man. A date with Wiltsie, a date with Duarte. Where'd you meet those guys?'

'Nowhere . . . at a bar.'

'What bar?'

'The Oak Room at the Biltmore, the Macombo, I don't know.'

'You're rattlin' my cage, boy. Duarte was Mex and those joints don't serve spics. So try again. Two goddamn queer slash murder victims you got between the sheets with. Where'd you meet them?'

Reynolds Loftis stayed crimped up and silent; Buzz said, 'You paid for them, right? It ain't no sin. I've paid for pussy, so why shouldn't somebody of your persuasion pay for boys?'

'No. No. No, that's not true.'

Mal, very soft. 'Felix Gordean.'

Loftis, trembling. 'No no no no no.'

Buzz twirled a finger and smoothed his necktie – the switcheroo sign. 'Charles Hartshorn. Why'd he kill himself?'

'He was tortured by people like you!'

Mal's switcheroo. 'You copped horse for Claire. Who'd you get it from?'

'Who told you that?' – Loftis actually sounding indignant.

Buzz leaned over and whispered, 'Felix Gordean'; Loftis jerked back and banged his head on the wall. Mal said, 'Duane Lindenaur worked at Variety International, where your friends Lopez, Duarte and Benavides are working. Juan Duarte is Augie Duarte's cousin. You used to appear in Variety International movies. Duane Lindenaur was blackmailing Charles Hartshorn. Why don't you put all that together for me.'

Loftis was sweating; Mal caught a twitch at *blackmail*. 'Three times in '44 and once last week you withdrew ten grand from your bank account. Who's blackmailing you?'

The man was oozing sweat. Buzz flashed a fist on the QT; Mal shook his head and gave him the switch sign. Buzz said, 'Tell us about the Sleepy Lagoon Defense Committee. Some strange stuff happened, right?'

Loftis wiped sweat off his brow; he said, 'What strange stuff?', his voice cracking.

'Like the letters the Committee got that said a big white man snuffed José Diaz. A deputy pal of ours seemed to think these here killings went back to Sleepy Lagoon – zoot stick time. All the victims were cut with zoot sticks.'

Loftis wrung his hands, popping more sweat; his eyes were glazed. Mal could tell Meeks went for a soft shot – innocuous stuff from his interrogation notes – but came up with a bludgeon. Buzz looked bewildered; Mal tamped down his black hat. 'Loftis, who's blackmailing you?'

Loftis squeaked, 'No'; Mal saw that he'd sweated his clothes through. 'What happened with the SLDC?'

'No!'

'Is Gordean blackmailing you?'

'I refuse to answer on the grounds that my answ – '

'You're a slimy piece of Commie shit. What kind of treason are you planning at your meetings? Cop on that!'

'Claire said I didn't have to!'

'Who's that piece of tail you and Chaz Minear were fighting over during the war? Who's that piece of fluff?'

Loftis sobbed and keened and managed a squeaky singsong. 'I refuse to answer on the grounds that my answers might tend to incriminate me, but I never hurt anybody and neither did my friends so please don't hurt us.'

Mal made a fist, Stanford ring stone out to do maximum damage. Buzz put a hand on his own fist and squeezed it, a new semaphore: *don't hit him or I'll hit you*. Mal got scared and went for big verbal ammo: Loftis didn't know Chaz Minear ratted him to HUAC. 'Are you protecting Minear? You shouldn't, because he was the one who snitched you to the Feds. He was the one who got you blacklisted.'

Loftis curled into a ball; he murmured his Fifth Amendment spiel, like their interrogation was legal and defense counsel would swoop to the rescue. Buzz said,

'You dumb shit, we coulda had him.' Mal turned and saw Claire De Haven standing there. She was saying, 'Chaz,' over and over.

CHAPTER THIRTY-SIX

The picket line action was simmering.

Buzz watched from the Variety International walkway, three stories up. Jack Shortell and Mal were supposed to call; Ellis Loew had called him at home, yanking him out of another Danny nightmare. The DA's command: convince Herman Gerstein to kick an additional five thou into the grand jury war chest. Herman was out – probably muff-diving Betty Grable – and there was nothing for him to do but stew on Considine's foul-up and scope the prelim to slaughter down on the street.

You could see it plain:

A Teamster goon with a baseball bat was lounging near the UAES camera van; when the shit hit the fan and the film rolled, he'd be Johnny on the spot to neutralize the cinematographer and bust up his equipment. Teamster pickets were carrying double and triple banner sticks, taped grips, good shillelaghs. Four muscle boys were skulking by the Pinkos' lunch truck – just the right number to tip it over and coffee-scald the guy inside. A minute ago he saw a Cohen triggerman make an on-the-sly delivery: riot guns with rubber-bullet attachments, wrapped in swaddling cloth like Baby Jesus. Over on De Longpre, the Teamsters had *their* moviemaking crew at the ready: actor/picketers who'd wade in, provoke just the right way and make sure a few UAES pickets whomped them; three camera guys in the back of a tarp-covered pickup. When the dust cleared, Mickey's boys would survive on celluloid as the good guys.

Buzz kept posing Mal against the action. The Cap had

almost shot Doc Lesnick's confidentiality on the psych files – blowing the whistle on Minear squealing Loftis – just when they were getting close on the blackmail angle and Felix Gordean. He'd hustled him out of the house quicksville, so he wouldn't keep trashing the team's cover – if they were lucky, De Haven and Loftis figured a HUAC source gave them the dope on Minear. For a smart cop, Captain Malcolm Considine kept making stupid moves: it was twenty to one he'd cut a deal with Red Claire for the custody case continuance; ten to one his attack on Loftis came close to deep sixing it. The old nance was no killer, but the '42 to '44 gap in his psych file – a time he was terrified remembering – talked volumes, and he and De Haven were looking like prime suspects on the snatch of the kid's paperwork. And Doc Lesnick being noplace was starting to look as wrong as Mal fucking up his own wet dream.

The Teamster men were passing around bottles; UAES was marching and shouting its sad old refrain: 'Fair Wages Now,' 'End the Studio Tyranny.' Buzz thought of a cat about to pounce on a mouse nibbling cheese on the edge of a cliff; he gave the matinee a pass and walked into Herman Gerstein's office.

Still no mogul; the switchboard girl at the plant knew to forward his calls to Herman's private line. Buzz sat behind Gerstein's desk, sniffed his humidor, admired his starlet pics on the wall. He was speculating on his grand jury bonus when the phone rang.

'Hello.'

'Meeks?'

Not Mal, not Shortell – but a familiar voice. 'It's me. Who's this?'

'Johnny.'

'Stompanato?'

'How soon they forget.'

'Johnny, what're you callin' me for?'

'How soon they forget their good deeds. I owe you one, remember?'

Buzz remembered the Lucy Whitehall gig – it seemed like a million years ago. 'Go, Johnny.'

'I'm paying you back, you cracker shitbird. Mickey knows Audrey's the skimmer. I didn't tell him, and I even kept hush on what you pulled with Petey S. It was the bank. Audrey put her skim in the Hollywood bank where Mick puts his race wire dough. The manager got suspicious and called him. Mickey's sending Fritzie over to get her. You're closer, so we're even.'

Buzz saw Icepick Fritzie carving. 'You knew about us?'

'I thought Audrey looked nervous lately, so I tailed her up to Hollywood, and she met you. Mickey doesn't know about you and her, so stay icy.'

Buzz blew a wet kiss into the phone, hung up and called Audrey's number; he got a busy signal, hauled down to the back lot and his car. He ran red lights and yellow lights and took every shortcut he knew speeding over; he saw Audrey's Packard in the driveway, jumped the curb and skidded up on the lawn. He left the motor running, pulled his .38, ran to the door and shouldered it open.

Audrey was sitting on her bargain basement lounge chair, hair in curlers, cold cream on her face. She saw Buzz and tried to cover herself; Buzz beelined for her and started kissing, getting all gooey. He said, 'Mickey knows you skimmed him,' between kisses; Audrey squealed. 'This isn't fair!' and 'You're not supposed to see me this way!' Buzz thought of Fritzie K. gaining ground, grabbed the lioness and slung her out to her car. He gasped, 'Ventura by Pacific Coast Highway, and I'm right behind you. It ain't the Beverly Wilshire, but it's safe.'

Audrey said, 'Five minutes to pack?'

Buzz said, 'No.'

Audrey said, 'Oh shit. I really liked LA.'

Buzz said, 'Say goodbye to it.'

Audrey popped off a handful of curlers and wiped her face. 'Bye-bye, LA.'

The two-car caravan made it to Ventura in an hour ten. Buzz ensconced Audrey in the shack at the edge of his farmland, hid her Packard in a pine grove, left her all his money except a tensky and a single and told her to call a friend of his on the Ventura Sheriff's for a place to stay – the man owed him almost as much as he owed Johnny Stompanato. Audrey started crying when she realized it really was bye-bye LA, bye-bye house, bank account, clothes and everything else except her bagman lover; Buzz kissed off the rest of her cold cream, told her he'd call his buddy to grease the skids and ring her at the guy's place tonight. The lioness left him with a dry-eyed sigh. 'Mickey was good with a buck, but he was lousy in bed. I'll try not to miss him.'

Buzz drove straight into Oxnard, the next town south. He found a pay phone, called Dave Kleckner at the Ventura Courthouse, made arrangements for him to pick up Audrey and dialed his own line at Hughes Aircraft. His secretary said Jack Shortell had called; she'd forwarded him to Herman Gerstein's office and Mal Considine's extension at the Bureau. Buzz changed his dollar into dimes and had the operator ring Madison–4609; Mal answered, 'Yes?'

'It's me.'

'Where are you? I've been trying to get you all morning.'

'Ventura. A little errand.'

'Well, you missed the goodies. Mickey went nuts. He gave his boys on Gower Gulch carte blanche, and they're busting heads as we speak. I just got a call from a Riot Squad lieutenant, and he said it's the worst he's ever seen. Want to place bets?'

Odds on him getting the lioness out of the country: even money. 'Boss, Mickey's nuts on Audrey, that's what probably ripped his cork. He found out she was skimmin' at his shark mill.'

'Jesus. Does he know about – '

'Ixnay, and I wanta keep it that way. She's stashed up here for now, but it can't last forever.'

Mal said, 'We'll fix something. Are you still hot on payback?'

'More than ever. You talk to Shortell?'

'Ten minutes ago. Do you have something to write on?'

'No, but I got a memory. Shoot me.'

Mal said, 'The last thing Danny worked was a connection between the Joredco Dental Lab on Bunker Hill – they make animal dentures – and a naturalist who raises wolverines a few blocks away. Nort Layman identified bite marks on the victims as coming from wolverine teeth – that's what this is all about.'

Buzz whistled. 'Christ on a crutch.'

'Yeah, and it gets stranger. One, Dudley Smith never put tails on those men Danny wanted under surveillance. Shortell found out, and he doesn't know if it means anything or not. Two, Danny's fix on the Sleepy Lagoon killing and the SLDC ties in to some burglary accomplice of Marty Goines – a youth back in the early '40s – a kid with a burned face. Bunker Hill had a lot of unsolved B & Es the summer of '42, and Danny gave Shortell eight names from FI cards – curfew was being enforced then, so there were plenty of them. Shortell ran eliminations on the names and came up with one man with O+ blood – Coleman Masskie, DOB 5/9/23, 236 South Beaudry, Bunker Hill. Shortell thinks this guy may be a good bet as Goines' burglar buddy.'

Buzz got the numbers down. 'Boss, this Masskie guy ain't even twenty-seven years old, which sorta contradicts the middle-aged killer theory.'

Mal said, 'I know, that bothers me too. But Shortell thinks Danny was close to cracking the case – and *he* thought this burglary angle was a scorcher.'

'Boss, we gotta take down Felix Gordean. We were gettin' close last night, when you . . .'

Silence, then Mal sounding disgusted. 'Yeah, I know. Look, you take the Masskie lead, I'll shake Juan Duarte.

I put four Bureau men out to find Doc Lesnick, and if
he's alive and findable, he's ours. Let's meet tonight
in front of the Chateau Marmont, 5:30. We'll stretch
Gordean.'

Buzz said, 'Let's do it.'

Mal said, 'Did you figure out De Haven and me?'

'Took about two seconds. You don't think she'll cross
you?'

'No, I've got the ace high hand. You and Mickey
Cohen's woman. Jesus.'

'You're invited to the wedding, boss.'

'Stay alive for it, lad.'

Buzz took Pacific Coast Highway down to LA, Wilshire
east to Bunker Hill. Dark clouds were brewing, threatening a deluge to soak the Southland, maybe unearth a
few more stiffs, send a few more hardnoses out for
payback. Two thirty-six South Beaudry was a low-rent
Victorian, every single shingle weatherstripped and
splintered; Buzz pulled up and saw an old woman raking
leaves on a front lawn as jaundiced as the pad.

He got out and approached her. Closer up, she
showed a real faded beauty: pale, almost transparent
skin over haute couture cheekbones, full lips and the
comeliest head of gray-brown hair he'd ever seen. Only
her eyes were off – they were too bright, too protruding.

Buzz said, 'Ma'am?'

The old girl leaned on her rake; there was all of one
leaf caught on the tines – and it was the only leaf on the
whole lawn. 'Yes, young man? Are you here to make a
contribution to Sister Aimee's crusade?'

'Sister Aimee's been out of business awhile, ma'am.'

The woman held out her hand – withered and arthritic
looking – a beggar's paw. Buzz dropped some odd dimes
in it. 'I'm lookin' for a man named Coleman Masskie.
Do you know him? He used to live here seven, eight
years ago.'

Now the old girl smiled. 'I remember Coleman well.
I'm Delores Masskie Tucker Kafesjian Luderman Jensen

401

Tyson Jones. I'm Coleman's mother. Coleman was one of the staunchest slaves I bore to proselytize for Sister Aimee.'

Buss swallowed. 'Slaves, ma'am? And you certainly do have a lot of names.'

The woman laughed. 'I tried to remember my maiden name the other day, and I couldn't. You see, young man, I have had many lovers in my role as child breeder to Sister Aimee. God made me beautiful and fertile so that I might provide Sister Aimee Semple McPherson with acolytes, and the County of Los Angeles has given me many a Relief dollar so that I might feed my young. Certain cynics consider me a fanatic and a welfare chiseler, but they are the devil speaking. Don't you think that spawning good white progeny for Sister Aimee is a noble vocation?'

Buzz said, 'I certainly do, and I was sorta thinkin' about doin' it myself. Ma'am, where's Coleman now? I got some money for him, and I figure he'll kick some of it back to you.'

Delores scratched the grass with her rake. 'Coleman was always generous. I had a total of nine children – six boys, three girls. Two of the girls became Sister Aimee followers, one, I'm ashamed to say, became a prostitute. The boys ran away when they turned fourteen or fifteen – eight hours a day of prayer and Bible reading was too strenuous for them. Coleman remained the longest – until he was nineteen. I gave him a dispensation: no prayer and Bible reading because he did chores around the neighborhood and gave me half the money. How much money do you owe Coleman, young man?'

Buzz said, 'Lots of it. Where is Coleman, ma'am?'

'In hell, I'm afraid. Those who rebuke Sister Aimee are doomed to boil forever in a scalding cauldron of pus and Negro semen.'

'Ma'am, when did you last see Coleman?'

'I believe I last saw him in the late fall of 1942.'

A half-sane answer – one that played into Upshaw's timetable. 'What was old Coleman doin' then, ma'am?'

Delores pulled the leaf from her rake and crumbled it to dust. 'Coleman was developing worldly ways. He listened to jazz records on a Victrola, prowled around in the evenings and quit high school prematurely, which angered me, because Sister Aimee prefers her slaves to have a high school diploma. He got a dreadful job at a dental laboratory, and quite frankly he became a thief. I used to find strange trinkets in his room, but I let him be when he confessed his transgressions against private property and pledged ten percent of his proceeds to Sister Aimce.'

The dental lab, Coleman as a burglar – Upshaw's theory coming through. 'Ma'am, was this '42 when Coleman was doin' his thievery?'

'Yes. The summer before he left home.'

'And did Coleman have a burned face? Was he disfigured somehow?'

The old loon was aghast. 'Coleman was male slave beauty personified! He was as handsome as a matinee idol!'

Buzz said, 'Sorry for impugnin' the boy's looks. Ma'am, who was Masskie? He the boy's daddy?'

'I don't really recall. I was spreading myself quite thin with men back in the early nineteen twenties, and I only took the surnames of men with large endowments – the better for when I chanted my breeding incantations. Exactly how much money do you owe Coleman? He's in hell, you know. Giving me the money might win a reprieve for his soul.'

Buzz forked over his last ten-spot. 'Ma'am, you said Coleman hightailed in the fall of '42?'

'Yes, that's true, and Sister Aimee thanks you.'

'Why did he take off? Where did he go?'

Delores looked scared – her skin sank over her cheekbones and her eyes bugged out another couple of inches. 'Coleman went looking for his father, whoever he was. A nasty man with a nasty brogue came around asking for him, and Coleman became terrified and ran away. The brogue man kept returning with questions on Coleman's whereabouts, but I kept invoking the power of Sister Aimee and he desisted.'

Sleepy Lagoon killing time; Dudley Smith asking to join the grand jury team; Dudley's off-the-track hard-on for the José Diaz murder and the SLDC. 'Ma'am, are you talkin' about an Irish brogue? A big man, late thirties then, red-faced, brown hair and eyes?'

Delores made signs, hands to her chest and up to her face, like she was warding off vampires in an old horror movie. 'Get behind me, Satan! Feel the power of Foursquare Church, Angelus Temple and Sister Aimee Semple McPherson, and I will not answer another single question until you provide adequate cash tribute. Get behind me or risk hell!'

Buzz turned out his pockets for bubkis; he knew a brick wall when he saw one. 'Ma'am, you tell Sister Aimee to hold her horses – I'll be back.'

Buzz drove home, ripped a photo of then-Patrolman Dudley Smith out of his LAPD Academy yearbook and rolled to the Chateau Marmont. Dusk and light rain were falling as he parked on Sunset by the front entrance; he was settling into a fret on the lioness when Mal tapped the windshield and got in the car.

Buzz said, 'Gravy. You?'

'Double gravy.'

'Boss, it plays like a ricochet, and it contradicts "middle-aged" again.'

Mal stretched his legs. 'So does my stuff. Nort Layman called Jack Shortell, he called me. Doc's been grid-searching the LA River near where Augie Duarte's body was found – he wants a complete forensic for some book he's writing. Get this: he found silver-gray wig strands with O+ blood – obviously from a head scratch – at the exact spot where the killer would have had to scale a fence to get away. That's why your ricochet plays.'

Buzz said, 'And why Loftis doesn't. Boss, you think somebody's tryin' to frame that old pansy?'

'It occurred to me, yes.'

'What'd you get off Juan Duarte?'

'Scary stuff, worse than goddamn wolverine teeth. Danny talked to Duarte, did you know that?'

'No.'

'It was right before LAPD grabbed him. Duarte told Danny that around the SLDC time Reynolds Loftis had a much younger kid brother hanging around – who looked just like him. At first, the kid had his face bandaged, because he'd been burned in a fire. Nobody knew how much he resembled Loftis until the bandages came off. The kid blabbed at the SLDC rallies – about how a big white man killed José Diaz – but nobody believed him. He was supposed to be running from the killer, but when Duarte said, "How come you're showing up here where the killer might see you," the brother said, "I've got special protection." Buzz, there are no notations on a Loftis kid brother in any of the grand jury files. And it gets better.'

Buzz thought: I know it does; he wondered who'd say 'Dudley Smith' first. 'Keep going. My stuff fits right in.'

Mal said, 'Duarte went to see Charles Hartshorn right before his alleged suicide, to see if he could get the cops to put some juice into investigating Augie's murder. Hartshorn said he'd been ditzed on Duane Lindenaur's killing – you, partner – and he read about the zoot stick mutilations on the other victims in a scandal sheet and thought the snuffs might be SLDC connected. Hartshorn called the LAPD then, and talked to a Sergeant Breuning, who said he'd be right over. Duarte left, and the next morning Hartshorn's body was found. Bingo.'

Buzz said it first. 'Dudley Smith. He was the big white man and he joined the team so he could keep the SLDC testimony watchdogged. That's why he was interested in Upshaw. Danny was hipped on the zoot stick mutilations, and Augie Duarte – Juan's cousin – was on his surveillance list. That's why Dudley blew off the tails. He went with Breuning to see Hartshorn, and somebody said the wrong thing. Necktie party, bye-bye, Charlie.'

Mal hit the dashboard. 'I can't fucking believe it.'

'I can. Now here's a good question. You been around Dudley lots more than I have lately. Is he tied to the queer snuffs?'

Mal shook his head. 'No. I've been racking my brain on it, and I can't put the two together. Dudley wanted Upshaw to join the team, and he couldn't have cared less about dead homos. It was when Danny pushed on "zoot stick" and "Augie Duarte" that Dudley got scared. Wasn't José Diaz a zooter?'

Buzz said, 'His threads were slashed with a zoot stick, I think I remember that. You got a motive for Dudley killin' Diaz?'

'Maybe. I went with Dudley to visit his niece. Apparently she's got a bent for Mexes and Dudley can't stand it.'

'Pretty slim, boss.'

'Dudley's insane! What the fuck more do you want?'

Buzz squeezed his partner's arm. 'Whoa, boy, and just listen to my stuff. Coleman Masskie's crazy mama and I had a little chat. She had lots of different kids by different daddies, she don't know who's whose. Coleman left home in the late fall of '42. He was a burglar, he loved jazz, he worked at the dental lab. All that fits Upshaw's scenario. Now, dig this: fall of '42, a big man with a brogue comes around askin' for Coleman. I describe Dudley, the ginch gets terrified and clams. I say Coleman's the one runnin' from the big white man, who's Dudley, who bumped José Diaz – and Coleman saw it. I say we stretch Gordean now – then go back and ply that old girl and try to tie her to Reynolds Loftis.'

Mal said, 'I'm taking Dudley down.'

Buzz shook his head. 'You take another think on that. No proof, no evidence on Hartshorn, an eight-year-old spic homicide. A cop with Dudley's juice. You're as nuts as he is if you think that plays.'

Mal put on a lilting tenor brogue. 'Then I'll kill him, *lad*.'

'The fuck you will.'

'I've killed a man before, Meeks. I can do it again.'

Buzz saw that he was out to do it – enjoying the view off the cliff. 'Partner, a Nazi in the war ain't the same thing.'

'You knew about that?'

'Why'd you think I was always afraid it was you 'stead of Dragna set me up? A mild-mannered guy like you kills once, he *can* do it again.'

Mal laughed. 'You ever kill anyone?'

'I stand on the Fifth Amendment, boss. Now you wanta go roust that queer pimp?'

Mal nodded. '7941's the address – I think it's back in the bungalow part.'

'You be the bad guy tonight. You're good at it.'

'After you, lad.'

Buzz took the lead. They walked through the lobby and out a side door to the courtyard; it was dark, and high hedges hid the individual bungalows. Buzz tracked the numbers marked on wrought-iron poles, saw 7939 and said, 'It's gotta be the next one.'

Gunshots.

One, two, three, four – close, the odd-numbered side of the walkway. Buzz pulled his .38; Mal pulled and cocked his. They ran to 7941, pinned themselves to the wall on opposite sides of the door and listened. Buzz heard footsteps inside, moving away from them; he looked at Mal, counted one, two, three on his fingers, wheeled and kicked the door in.

Two shots splintered the wood above his head; a muzzle flickered from a dark back room. Buzz hit the floor; Mal piled on top of him and fired twice blindly; Buzz saw a man spread-eagled on the carpet, his yellow silk robe soaked red from sash to collar. Cash wrapped in bank tabs surrounded the body.

Mal stumbled and charged. Buzz let him go, heard thumping, crashing, glass breaking and no more shots. He got up and checked the stiff – a fancy man with a neat beard, a neat manicure and not much of a torso left. The bank tabs were marked Beverly Hills Federal, and there was at least three thousand in half-grand packets within grabbing distance. Buzz resisted; Mal came back, panting. He wheezed, 'Car waiting. Late model white sedan.'

Buzz kicked a pack of greenbacks; they hit an embroidered 'F.G.' on the dead man's sleeve. 'Beverly Hills Fed. That where Loftis withdrew his money?'

'That's the place.'

Sirens in the distance.

Buzz waved goodbye to the cash. 'Loftis, Claire, the killer, what do you think?'

'Let's hit their place now. Before the Sheriffs ask us what we're – '

Buzz said, 'Separate cars,' and took off running as fast as he could.

Mal got there first.

Buzz saw him standing across the street from the De Haven house, U-turned and killed his engine. Mal leaned in the window. 'What took you?'

'I run slow.'

'Anybody see you?'

'No. You?'

'I don't think so. Buzz, we weren't there.'

'You're learnin' this game better every day, boss. What'd you get here?'

'Two cold cars. I looked in a window and saw De Haven and Loftis playing cards. They're clean. You make the killer for it?'

Buzz said, 'Nix. It's wrong. He's a psycho fuckin' rat worshiper, and it's my considered opinion that psycho rat worshipers don't carry guns. I'm thinkin' Minear. He fits with Loftis, and there was a line on him from the files, said he liked to buy boys.'

'You could be right. The Masskie woman next?'

'236 South Beaudry, boss.'

'Let's do it.'

Buzz got there first; he rang the bell and went eyeball

to eyeball with Delores in a long white robe. She said, 'Did you bring monetary tribute for Sister?'

Buzz said, 'My bagman's comin' in a minute.' He took out the picture of Dudley Smith. 'Ma'am, is this the fella who was inquirin' after Coleman?'

Delores blinked at the photograph and crossed herself. 'Get behind me, Satan. Yes, that's him.'

Seven come eleven, one more for Danny Upshaw. 'Ma'am, do you know the name Reynolds Loftis?'

'No, I don't think so.'

'Anybody named Loftis?'

'No.'

'Any chance you messed with a man named Loftis around the time Coleman was born?'

The old girl harumphed. 'If by "messed" you mean engaged in breeding activities for Sister Aimee, the answer is no.'

Buzz said, 'Ma'am, you told me Coleman went lookin' for his daddy when he took off in '42. If you didn't know who his daddy was, how'd the boy know where to look?'

Delores said, 'Twenty dollars for Sister Aimee and I'll show you.'

Buzz slid off his high school ring. 'Yours to keep, sweetie. Just show me.'

Delores examined the ring, pocketed it and walked away; Buzz stood on the porch wondering where Mal was. Minutes dragged; the woman returned with an old leather scrapbook. She said, 'The genealogy of my slave breeding. I took pictures of all the men who gave me their seed, with appropriate comments on the back. When Coleman decided he had to find his father, he looked at this book for pictures of the men he most resembled. I hid the book when the brogue man came by, and I still want twenty dollars for this information.'

Buzz opened the scrapbook, saw that the pages contained stapled-on photographs of dozens of men, held it up to the porch light and started looking. Four pages down, a picture caught his eye: a spellbinder youthful, spellbinder handsome Reynolds Loftis in a tweed

409

knicker suit. He pulled the photo out and read the writing on the back.

'Randolph Lawrence (a nom de guerre?), summer stock actor, the Ramona Pageant, August 30, 1922. A real Southern gentleman. Good white stock. I hope his seed springs fertile.'

1942: burglar, tooth technician, rat lover Coleman witnesses Dudley Smith killing José Diaz, sees this picture or others and locates Daddy Reynolds Loftis. 1943: Coleman, his face burned in a fire???, hangs out at SLDC rallies with his father/phony brother, talks up the big white man, nobody believes him. 1942 to 1944: Loftis' psych file missing. 1950: killer Coleman. Was the psycho trying to frame Daddy/Reynolds for the queer murders, dressed up like Loftis himself – Doc Layman's wig fragments the final kicker?

Buzz held out the picture. 'That Coleman, ma'am?'

Delores smiled. 'Rather close. What a nice-looking man. A shame I can't remember spawning with him.'

A car door slammed; Mal got out and trotted up the steps. Buzz took him aside and showed him the photo. 'Loftis, 1922. AKA Randolph Lawrence, summer stock actor. He's Coleman's father, not his brother.'

Mal tapped the picture. 'Now I'm wondering how the boy got burned and why the brother charade. And you were right on Minear.'

'What do you mean?'

'I called the DMV. Minear owns a white '49 Chrysler New Yorker sedan. I went by his place in Chapman Park on my way here. It was in his building's garage, warm, and it looked just like the car at the Marmont.'

Buzz put an arm around Mal's shoulders. 'Gifts in a manger, and here's another one. That crazy woman in the doorway ID'd Dudley from a picture I got. He's the brogue man.'

Mal looked over at Delores. 'Do you think Dudley copped Danny's files?'

'No, I think he'd have faked a burglary. Coleman's our killer, boss. All we gotta do now is find him.'

410

'Shit. Loftis and Claire won't talk. I know it.'

Buzz took his arm away. 'No, but I bet we could squeeze Chaz beauty. He was tight with Loftis back in '43, '44, and I know a good squeeze artist to help us. You give that lady a double-saw and I'll go give him a call.'

Mal went for his billfold; Buzz walked into the house and found a phone by the kitchen door. He called Information, got the number he wanted and dialed it; Johnny Stompanato's slick guinea baritone oiled on the line. 'Talk to me.'

'It's Meeks. You wanta make some money? Number-one muscle on a strongarm job, make sure my buddy don't go crazy and hurt someone?'

Johnny Stomp said, 'You're a dead man. Mickey found out about you and Audrey. The neighbors saw you hustling her away, and I'm lucky he didn't figure out I tipped you. Nice to know you, Meeks. I always thought you had style.'

Move over Danny Upshaw, fat man coming through. Buzz looked at Mal paying off the rat killer's mother; he got an idea – or the idea got him. 'Contract out?'

'Ten grand. Fifteen if they get you alive so Mickey can get his jollies.'

'Chump change. Johnny, you wanna make twenty grand for two hours' work?'

'You slay me. Next you'll be offering me a date with Lana Turner.'

'I mean it.'

'Where you gonna get that dough?'

'I'll have it inside two weeks. Deal?'

'What makes you think you'll live that long?'

'Ain't you a gambler?'

'Oh shit. Deal.'

Buzz said, 'I'll call you back,' and hung up. Mal was standing beside him, shaking his head. 'Mickey knows?'

'Yeah, Mickey knows. You got a couch?'

Mal gave Buzz a soft punch on the arm. 'Lad, I think people are starting to get your number.'

411

'Say what?'
'I figured out something today.'
'What?'
'You killed Gene Niles.'

CHAPTER THIRTY-SEVEN

Mal's take on Johnny Stompanato: two parts olive-oil charm, two parts hepcat, six parts plug-ugly. His take on the whole situation: Buzz was doomed, and his voice talking to Audrey on the phone said he knew it. Coleman arrested for four sex murders plus grand jury indictments added up to Stefan dropped on his doorstep like a Christmas bundle. The *Herald* and *Mirror* were playing up the Gordean killing, no suspects, puff pieces on the victim as a straight-arrow talent agent, no mention of the bank money – the catching officers probably got fat. The papers made UAES the instigators of the riot the Teamsters started; Buzz was impressed with his shot in the dark on Gene Niles and believed his promise not to spill on it. The fat man was going to brace Dudley's niece while he and Stompanato braced Chaz Minear, and when they had Coleman placed, he'd call his newspaper contacts so they could be in on the capture: first interviews with Captain Malcolm E. Considine, captor of the Wolverine Monster. And then Dudley Smith.

They were sitting in Stompanato's car, 8:00 A.M., a cop-crook stakeout. Mal knew his scenario; Buzz had filled Johnny in on his and had greased the doorman of Minear's building. The man told him Chaz left for breakfast every morning at 8:10 or so, walked over Mariposa to the Wilshire Derby and returned with the newspaper around 9:30. Buzz gave him a C-note to be gone from 9:30 to 10:00; during that half hour they'd have a wide-open shot.

Mal watched the door; Stompanato gave himself a pocketknife manicure and hummed opera. At 8:09 a small man in tennis sweater and slacks walked out the entrance of the Conquistador Apartments; the doorman gave them the high sign. Stompanato sliced a cuticle and smiled; Mal jacked his plug-ugly quotient way up.

They waited.

At 9:30, the doorman tipped his cap, got into a car and drove off; at 9:33 Chaz Minear walked into the building holding a newspaper. Stompanato put his knife away; Mal said, 'Now.'

They quick-marched into the lobby. Minear was checking his mail slot; Johnny Stomp strode ahead to the elevator and opened the door. Mal dawdled by a wall mirror, straightening his necktie, getting a reverse view of Minear grabbing letters, Stompanato keeping the elevator door open with his foot, smiling like a good neighbor. Little Chaz walked over and into the trap; Mal came up behind him, nudged Johnny's foot away and let the door close.

Minear pushed the button for three. Mal saw his door key already in his hand, grabbed it and rabbit-punched him. Minear dropped his newspaper and mail and doubled over; Johnny pinned him to the wall, a hand on his neck. Minear went purply blue; it looked like his eyes were about to pop out. Mal talked to him, a mimic of Dudley Smith. 'We know you killed Felix Gordean. We were his partners on the Loftis job, and you're going to tell us allll about Reynolds and his son. Allll about it. *Lad.*'

The door slid open; Mal saw '311' on the key and an empty hallway. He walked out, located the apartment four doorways over, unlocked the door and stood back. Stompanato forced Minear inside and released his neck; Chaz fell down rasping for breath. Mal said, 'You know what to ask him. Do it while I toss for the files.'

Minear coughed words; Johnny stepped on his neck. Mal took off his jacket, rolled up his sleeves and tossed.

The apartment had five rooms: living room, bedroom,

kitchen, bathroom, study. Mal hit the study first – it was the furthest from Stompanato and the nance. A radio went on, the dial skimming across jazz, commercial jingles and the news, stopping at an opera, a baritone and a soprano going at each other over a thunderous orchestra. Mal thought he heard Minear scream; the music was turned up.

Mal worked.

The study – desk, filing cabinets and a chest of drawers – yielded stacks of movie scripts, carbons of Minear's political letters, correspondence to him, miscellaneous memoranda and a .32 revolver, the cylinder empty, a cordited barrel. The bedroom was pastel-appointed and filled with piles of books; there was a wardrobe closet crammed with expensive clothes and rows of shoes arrayed in trees. An antique cabinet featured drawers spilling propaganda tracts; there was nothing but more shoes under the bed.

The opera kept wailing; Mal checked his watch, saw 10:25, an hour down and two rooms clean. He gave the bathroom a cursory toss; the music stopped; Stompanato popped his head in the doorway. He said, 'The pansy spilled. Tell Meeks he better stay alive to get me my money.'

The hard boy looked green at the gills. Mal said, 'I'll do the kitchen and talk to him.'

'Forget it. Loftis and Claire what's her face got the files. Come on, you've gotta hear this.'

Mal followed Johnny into the living room. Chaz Minear was sitting prim and proper in a rattan chair; there were welts on his cheeks and blood had congealed below his nostrils. His tennis whites were still spotless, his eyes were unfocused, he was wearing an exhausted, almost slaphappy grin. Mal looked at Stompanato; Johnny said, 'I poured half a pint of Beefeater's into him.' He tapped the sap hooked into his belt. 'In vino veritas, capiche?'

Danny Upshaw had said the same thing to him – the

one time they drank together. Mal took a chair facing Minear. 'Why did you kill Gordean? Tell me.'

Minear, an easy mid-Atlantic accent. 'Pride.'

He sounded proud. Mal said, 'What do you mean?'

'Pride. Gordean was tormenting Reynolds.'

'He started tormenting him back in '44. It took you a while to get around to revenge.'

Minear focused on Mal. 'The police told Reynolds and Claire that I informed on Reynolds to the House Committee. I don't know how they knew, but they did. They confronted me about it, and I could tell Reynolds' poor heart was broken. I knew Gordean was blackmailing him again, so I did penance. Claire and Reynolds and I had gotten so close again, and I imagine you could present a case for me acting in my own self-interest. It was good having friends, and it was awful when they started hating me.'

The rap was falling on him – he was the one who snitched the snitch. 'Why didn't you take the money?'

'Oh Lord, I couldn't. It would have destroyed the gesture. And Claire has all the money in the world. She shares so generously with Reynolds . . . and with all her friends. You're not really a criminal, are you? You look more like an attorney or an accountant.'

Mal laughed – a kamikaze queer romantic had his number. 'I'm a policeman.'

'Are you going to arrest me?'

'No. Do you want to be arrested?'

'I want everyone to know what I did for Reynolds, but . . .'

'But you don't want them to know why? Why Gordean was blackmailing Loftis?'

'Yes. That's true.'

Mal threw a switcheroo. 'Why did Reynolds and Claire steal Upshaw's files? To protect all of you from the grand jury?'

'No.'

'Because of Reynolds' kid brother? *His son*? Was it Upshaw's *homicide* file they were most interested in?'

Minear sat mute; Mal waved Stompanato toward the back of the apartment. 'Chaz, you've said it once. Now you have to say it to me.'

No answer.

'Chaz, I'll make you a deal. I'll make sure everyone knows you killed Gordean, but I won't let Reynolds get hurt anymore. All you'll get is what you want. Reynolds will know you had courage and you paid him back. He'll love you again. He'll forgive you.'

'Love you' and 'forgive you' made Minear cry, sputters of tears that he dried with his sweater sleeves. He said, 'Reynolds left me for him. That's why I informed to HUAC.'

Mal leaned closer. 'Left you for who?'

'For *him*.'

'Who's "him"?'

Minear smiled, 'Reynolds' little brother was really his son. His mother was a crazy religious woman Reynolds had an affair with. She got money from him and kept the boy. When Coleman was nineteen, he ran away from the woman and found Reynolds. Reynolds took him in and became his lover. He left me to be with his own son.'

Mal pushed his chair back, the confession a horror movie he wanted to run screaming from. He said, 'All of it,' before he bolted for real.

Minear raised his voice, like he was afraid of his confessor running; he speeded up, like he was anxious to be absolved or punished. 'Felix Gordean was blackmailing Reynolds back in '44 or so. Somehow he figured out about him and Coleman, and he threatened to tell Herman Gerstein about it. Gerstein hates men like us, and he would have ruined Reynolds. When that policeman came around questioning Felix about the first three killings, Felix put things together. George Wiltsie had been with Reynolds, Marty Goines and Coleman were both jazz men. Then Augie Duarte was killed, and more details had been in the newspapers. The policeman had let some things slip and Felix knew Coleman had to be the killer. He renewed his blackmail demands, and Reynolds gave him another ten thousand.

'Claire and Reynolds confided in me, and I knew I could make up for informing. They knew after the first three killings that it had to be Coleman – they read a tabloid that had details on the mutilations, and they knew from the names of the victims. They knew about it before the policeman tried to infiltrate UAES, and they were looking for Coleman to try to stop him. Juan Duarte saw Upshaw at the morgue when Augie was there, and recognized him from a picture Norm Kostenz took. He told Claire and Reynolds who Upshaw really was, and they got scared. They had read that the police were looking for a man who resembled Reynolds, and they thought Coleman must be trying to frame his father. They left out clues to exonerate Reynolds, and I followed Upshaw home from Claire's house. The next day, Claire got Mondo Lopez to pick the lock of his apartment and look for things on the killings – things that would help them find Coleman. Mondo found his files and brought them to Claire. She and Reynolds were desperate to stop Coleman and keep the . . .'

Keep the whole horror epic from ruining Reynolds Loftis worse than the grand jury ever could.

Mal thought of Claire – terrified of a harmless Sleepy Lagoon remark the first time they talked; he thought of Coleman's burn face, put it aside and went straight for the woman. 'Claire and Coleman. What's between them?'

The queer redeemer glowed. 'Claire nurtured Coleman back in the SLDC days. He was in love with her, and he told her he always thought about her when he was with Reynolds. She heard out all his ugly, violent fantasies. She forgave them for being together. She was always so strong and accepting. The killings started a few weeks after the papers ran the wedding announcements. When Coleman learned that Reynolds was getting Claire forever, it must have made him crazy. Are you going to arrest me now?'

Mal couldn't make himself say no and break the rest of Chaz Minear. He couldn't say anything, because Johnny Stompanato had just walked into the room with his olive-oil charm back in place, and all he could think of was that he could never keep Stefan safe from the horror.

CHAPTER THIRTY-EIGHT

Mary Margaret Conroy was coming across as a major league Mexophile.

Buzz had tailed her from her sorority house to a hand-holding kaffeeklatch at the UCLA Student Union; she was a simpering frail in the presence of a handsome taco bender named Ricardo. Their conversation was all in Spanish, and all he recognized were words like 'corazon' and 'felicidad,' love stuff he knew from the juke box music at Mexican restaurants. From there, Dudley Smith's dough-faced niece went to a meeting of the Pan American Students' League, a class in Argentine history, lunch and more fondling with Ricardo. She'd been sequestered in a classroom with 'Art of the Mayans' for over an hour now, and when she walked out he'd pop the question – shit or get off the pot time.

He kept checking his flank, seeing bad guys everywhere, like Mickey with the Commies. Only his were real: Mickey himself, Cohen goons armed with icepicks and saps and garottes and silencered heaters that could leave you dead in a crowd, a heart attack victim, square-johns summoning an ambulance while the triggerman walked away. He kept checking faces and kept trying not to cut odds, because he was too good an oddsmaker to give himself and Audrey much of a chance.

And he had a monster hangover.

And his back ached from boozy catnaps on Mal Considine's floor.

They'd been up most of the night, planning. He called

Dave Kleckner in Ventura – Audrey was safely tucked in at his pad. He'd called Johnny Stomp with details on the Minear squeeze and gave Mal the lowdown on Gene Niles. Mal said he'd tagged him as the killer on a hunch – that payback for Danny was so antithetical to his style that he knew the debt had to be huge. Mal got weepy on the kid, then went loony on Dudley Smith – Dudley made for José Diaz, Charles Hartshorn, suppression of evidence and a fuckload of conspiracy raps, Dudley sucking gas up at Q. He never made the next jump: the powers that be would never let Dudley Smith stand trial for anything – his rank, juice and reputation were diplomatic immunity.

They talked escape routes next. Buzz held back on his idea – it would have sounded as crazy as Mal taking down Dudley. They talked East Coast hideouts, slow boats to China, soldier of fortune gigs in Central America, where the local strongmen paid gringos good pesos to keep the Red Menace in check. They talked the pros and cons of taking Audrey, leaving Audrey, the lioness stashed someplace safe for a couple of years. They came to one conclusion: he'd give payback another forty-eight hours tops, then go in a hole somewhere.

A classroom bell sounded; Buzz got pissed: Mary Margaret Conroy would never blab, only confirm by her actions – all he was doing was humoring Mal's hump on Dudley. 'Art of the Mayans' adjourned in a swirl of students, Mary Margaret the oldest by a good ten years. Buzz followed her outside, tapped her shoulder and said, 'Miss Conroy, could I talk to you for a second?'

Mary Margaret turned around, hugging her armload of books. She eyed Buzz with distaste and said, 'You're not with the faculty, are you?'

Buzz forced himself not to laugh. 'No, I'm not. Sweetie, wouldn't you say Uncle Dudley went a bit too far warnin' José Diaz away from you?'

Mary Margaret went sheet white and passed out on the grass.

Dudley for Diaz.

Buzz left Mary Margaret on the grass with a firm pulse and fellow students hovering. He got off the campus quick and drove to Ellis Loew's house to play a hunch: Doc Lesnick's absence while UAESer lunacy raged on all fronts was too pat. The four Bureau dicks trying to find the man were filing reports at the house, and there might be something in them to give him a spark atop the hunch and the flicker that caused it: all the psych files ended in the summer of '49, even though the brain trusters were still seeing Lesnick. The fact reeked of wrong.

Buzz parked on Loew's front lawn, already crowded with cars. He heard voices coming from the back yard, walked around and saw Ellis holding court on the patio. Champagne was cooling on an ice cart; Loew, Herman Gerstein, Ed Satterlee and Mickey Cohen were hoisting glasses. Two Cohen boys were standing sentry with their backs to him; nobody had seen him yet. He ducked behind a trellis and listened.

Gerstein was exulting: yesterday's picket brawl was blamed on the UAES; the Teamster film crew leaked their version of the riot to Movietone News, who'd be captioning it 'Red Rampage Rocks Hollywood' and shoving it into theaters nationwide. Ellis came on with his good news: the grand jury members being appointed by the City Council looked mucho simpatico, his house was packed with great evidence, mucho indictments seemed imminent. Satterlee kept talking about the climate being perfect, the grand jury a sweetheart deal that was preordained by God for this time and place only, a deal that would never come again. The geek looked about two seconds away from asking them to kneel in prayer; Mickey shut him up and not too subtly started asking questions about the whereabouts of Special Investigator Turner 'Buzz' Meeks.

Buzz walked to the front of the house and let himself in. Typists were typing; clerks were filing; there was enough documentation in the living room to make confetti for a thousand ticker tape parades. He moved to the report board and saw that it had been replaced by a whole wall of photographs.

Federal evidence stamps were attached to the borders; Buzz saw 'SLDC' a dozen times over and looked closer. The pics were obviously the surveillance shots Ed Satterlee was trying to buy off a rival clearance group; another scope and he noticed *every* photo was marked SLDC, with '43 and '44 dates tagged at the bottom, the pictures arranged chronologically, probably waiting for some artwork: circling the faces of known Commies. Buzz thought: Coleman, and started looking for a face swathed in bandages.

Most of the photos were overhead group shots; some were enlarged sections where faces were reproduced more clearly. The quality on all of them was excellent – the Feds knew their stuff. Buzz saw some blurry, too white faces in the earlier pics, crowd shots from the spring of '43; he followed the pictures across the wall, hoping for Coleman sans gauze and dressings, an aid to ID the rat killer in person. He got bandage glimpses through the summer of '43; little looks at Claire De Haven and Reynolds Loftis along the way. Then – blam! – a Reynolds Loftis view that was way off; the handsome queer too, too short in the tooth, with too much hair.

Buzz checked the date – 8/17/43 – rechecked the Loftis glimpses, rechecked the clothes on the bandaged man. Reynolds had noticeably thinning hair throughout; the too young Reynolds sported a full head of thick stuff. In three of the overhead shots, bandage man was wearing a striped skivvy shirt; in the close-up, too young Reynolds was wearing the same thing. Juan Duarte had told Mal that Reynolds' 'kid brother' looked just like him – but *this man* was Reynolds in every respect except the hair, every facial plane and angle exactly like his father – a mirror image of Daddy twenty years younger.

Buzz thought semantics, thought 'just like' might be an uneducated greaseball's synonym for 'identical twin'; Delores Masskie called the resemblance 'rather close'.

421

He grabbed a magnifying glass off a typist's desk; he followed the pictures, looking for more Coleman. Three over he got a close shot of the boy with a man and a woman; he put the lens up to it and squinted for all he was worth.

No burn scars of any kind; no pocked and shiny skin; no uneven patches where flesh was grafted.

Two photos over, one row down. November 10, 1943. The boy standing sideways facing Claire De Haven, shirtless. Deep, perfectly straight scars on his right arm, a row of them, scars identical to scars he saw on the arm of an RKO actor who'd had his face reconstructed after an auto wreck, scars that actor had pointed to with pride, telling him that only Doctor Terry Lux did arm grafts, the skin there was the best, so good that it was worth upper body tissue removal. The actor said that Terry made him look *exactly* like he did before the accident – when he looked at himself even he couldn't tell the difference.

Terry Lux dried Claire De Haven out at his clinic three times.

Terry Lux had workers who slaughtered chickens with zoot sticks.

Terry Lux told him Loftis used to cop H for Claire; Marty Goines was snuffed by a heroin overjolt. Terry Lux diluted the morphine for his dope cures on the premises at his clinic.

Buzz kept the magnifying glass to the wall, kept scanning. He got a back view of Coleman shirtless, saw a patchwork of perfectly straight scars that made him think of zoot stick wounds; he found another set of group shots that looked like Coleman fawning all over Claire De Haven. Hard evidence: Coleman Masskie Loftis was plastic surgery altered to look more like his father. He resembled his father enough to ID him from Delores' pictures before; now he *was* him. His 'special protection' from Dudley Smith was being disguised as Loftis.

Buzz ripped the best Coleman pic off the wall, pocketed it and found a table stacked with reports from the

Bureau men. He quick-skimmed the latest update; all the officers had accomplished was a shakedown of Lesnick's parolee daughter – she said the old man was just about gone from his lung cancer and was thinking about checking into a rest home to check out. He was about to pocket a list of local sanitoriums when he heard 'Traitor,' and saw Mickey and Herman Gerstein standing a few feet away.

Cohen with a clean shot, but a half dozen witnesses spoiling his chance. Buzz said, 'I suppose this means my guard gig's kaput. Huh, Mick?'

The man looked hurt as much as he looked mad. 'Goyishe shitheel traitor. Cocksucker. Communist. How much money did I give you? How much money did I set up for you that you should do me like you did?'

Buzz said, 'Too much, Mick.'

'That is no smart answer, you fuck. You should beg. You should beg that I don't do you slow.'

'Would it help?'

'No.'

'There you go, boss.'

Mickey said, 'Herman, leave this room'; Gerstein exited. The typers kept typing and the clerks kept clerking. Buzz gave the little hump's cage a rattle. 'No hard feelin's, huh?'

Mickey said, 'I will make you a deal, because when I say "deal", it is always to trust. Right?'

'Trust' and 'deal' were the man's bond – it was why he went with him instead of Siegel or Dragna. 'Sure, Mick.'

'Send Audrey back to me and I will not hurt a hair on her head and I will not do you slow. Do you trust my word?'

'Yes.'

'Do you trust I'll get you?'

'You're the odds-on favorite, boss.'

'Then be smart and do it.'

'No deal. Take care, Jewboy. I'll miss you. I really will.'

Pacific Sanitarium – fast.

Buzz turned off PCH and beeped his horn at the gate; the squawk box barked, 'Yes?'

'Turner Meeks to see Dr. Lux.'

Static sounds for a good ten seconds, then: 'Park off to your left by the door marked "Visiting," go through the lounge and take the elevator up to the second floor. Doctor will meet you in his office.'

Buzz did it, parking, walking through the lounge. The elevator was in use; he took stairs up to the second floor, saw the connecting door open, heard, 'Okie baboon' and stopped just short of the last step.

Terry Lux's voice: '. . . but I have to talk to him, he's a pipeline to Howard Hughes. Listen, there should be something in the papers today I'm interested in – a guy I used to do business with was murdered. I just heard about it on the radio, so go get me all the LA dailies while I talk to this clown.'

Odds on Lux-Gordean business: six to one in favor of. Buzz retraced his steps to the car, grabbed his billy club, stuck it down the back of his pants and took his time walking inside. The elevator was empty; he pushed the button for 2 and glided up thinking how much Terry loved money, how little he cared where it came from. The door opened; the dope doc himself was there to greet him. 'Buzzy, long time no see.'

The administrative corridor looked nice and deserted – no nurses or orderlies around. Buzz said, 'Terry, how are you?'

'Is this business, Buzz?'

'Sure is, boss. And on the extra QT. You got a place where we can talk?'

Lux led Buzz down the hall, to a little room with filing cabinets and facial reconstruction charts. He closed the door; Buzz locked it and leaned on it. Lux said, 'What the hell are you doing?'

Buzz felt the billy club tickling his spine. 'Spring of '43 you did a plastic job on Reynolds Loftis' son. Tell me about it.'

'I don't know what you're talking about. Check my '43 files if you like.'

'This ain't negotiable, Terry. This is you spill all, Gordean included.'

'There's nothing to negotiate, because I don't know what you're talking about.'

Buzz pulled out his baton and hit Lux behind the knees. The blow sent Lux pitching into the wall; Buzz grabbed a fistful of his hair and banged his face against the door jamb. Lux slid to the floor, trailing blood on polished mahogany, sputtering, 'Don't hit me. Don't hit me.'

Buzz backed up a step. 'Stay there, the floor looks good on you. Why'd you cut the boy to look like his old man? Who told you to do that?'

Lux tilted his head back, gurgled and shook himself like a dog shedding water. 'You scarred me. You . . . you scarred me.'

'Give yourself a plastic. And answer me.'

'Loftis had me do it. He paid me a lot, and he paid me never to tell anybody about it. Loftis and the psycho had essentially the same bone structure, and I did it.'

'Why'd Loftis want it done?'

Lux moved into a sitting position and massaged his knees. His eyes darted to an intercom phone atop a filing cabinet just out of reach; Buzz smashed the contraption with his stick. 'Why? And don't tell me Loftis wanted the boy to look like him so he could be a movie star.'

'He did tell me that!'

Buzz tapped the baton against his leg. 'Why'd you call Coleman a psycho?'

'He did his post-op here, and I caught him raiding the hatchery! He was cutting up the chickens with one of those zoot sticks my men use! He was drinking their goddamn blood!'

Buzz said, 'That's a psycho, all right'; he thought Terry *had* to be clean on snuff knowledge: the fool

425

thought chickens were as bad as it got. 'Boss, what kind of business did you do with Felix Gordean?'

'I didn't kill him!'

'I know you didn't, and I'm pretty damn sure you don't know who did. But I'll bet you hipped him to something about Reynolds Loftis back around '43, '44 or so, and Gordean started collectin' hush money on it. That sound about right?'

Lux said nothing; Buzz said, 'Answer me, or I'll go to work on your kidneys.'

'When I tell Howard about this, you'll be in trouble.'

'I'm finished with Howard.'

Lux made an overdue move. 'Money, Buzz. That's what this is about, right? You've got an angle you want to buy in on and you need help. Am I right?'

Buzz tossed his stick out, holding the end of the thong. The tip hit Lux in the chest; Buzz jerked it back like a yo-yo on a string. Lux yipped at the little wonder; Buzz said, 'Coleman, Loftis and Gordean. Put them together.'

Lux stood up and straightened the folds of his smock. He said, 'About a year after the reconstruction on Coleman I went to a party in Bel Air. Loftis and his so-called kid brother were there. I pretended not to know them, because Reynolds didn't want anyone to know about the surgery. Later on that night, I was out by the cabanas. I saw Coleman and Loftis kissing. It made me mad. I'd plasticed the kid for an incestuous pervert. I knew Felix liked to put the squeeze on queers, so I sold him the information. I figured he blackmailed Loftis. Don't look so shocked, Meeks. You would have done the same thing.'

Minear's file quote: 'If you knew who *he* was, you'd know why I snitched' – the one reference Doc Lesnick let slip into the grand jury team's hands – *the half-dead old stoolie had to know the whole story*. Buzz looked at Lux culling back his dignity, pushed him into the wall and held him there with his stick. 'When's the last time you saw Coleman?'

Lux's voice was high and thin. 'Around '45. Daddy

426

and Sonny must have had a spat. Coleman came to me with two grand and told me he didn't want to look so much like Daddy anymore. He asked me to break his face up scientifically. I told him that since I enjoy inflicting pain, I'd only take a grand and a half. I strapped him into a dental chair, put on heavy bag gloves and broke every bone in his face. I kept him on morph while he recovered down by the chicken shed. He left with a teeny weeny little habit and some not so teeny little bruises. He started wearing a beard, and all that was left of Reynolds was the set of his eyes. Now, do you want to take that goddamn club off of me?'

Bingo – the Goines heroin angle. Buzz held off on the baton. 'I know you dilute your own morph here on the grounds.'

Lux took a scalpel from his pocket and started cleaning his nails. 'Police sanctioned.'

'You told me Loftis copped horse for Claire De Haven. Did you and him use the same suppliers?'

'A few of them. Coloreds with cop connections down in southtown. I only deal with officially sanctioned lackeys – like you.'

'Did Coleman have info on them?'

'Sure. After the first surgery, I gave him a list. He had a crush on Claire, and he said he wanted to help her get the stuff, make the runs himself so she wouldn't have to truck with niggers. When he left after my second surgery, he probably used them for his own habit.'

A round of applause for Coleman Loftis: he kicked morph and took up rat worship slaughter. 'I want that list. Now.'

Lux unlocked the filing cabinet by the demolished phone. He pulled out a slip of lined paper and reached for some blank sheets; Buzz said, 'I'll keep the original,' and grabbed it.

The doctor shrugged and went back to cleaning his nails. Buzz started to tuck his baton away; Lux said, 'Didn't your mother tell you it's not polite to stare?'

Buzz kept quiet.

'The strong, silent type. I'm impressed.'

'I'm impressed with you, Terry.'

'How so?'

'Your recuperative powers. I'll bet you got yourself convinced this little humiliation didn't really happen.'

Lux sighed. 'I'm Hollywood, Buzz. Easy come, easy go, and it's already a dim memory. Got a sec for a question?'

'Sure.'

'What's this about? There has to be money in it somewhere. You don't work for free.'

Adios, Terry.

Buzz kidney-punched Lux, his hardest stick shot. The scalpel fell from the doctor's hand. Buzz caught it, kneed Lux in the balls, smothered him into the wall and placed his right palm against it Jesus style. Lux screamed; Buzz rammed the scalpel into the hand and pounded it down to the hilt with his baton. Lux screamed some more, his eyes rolling back. Buzz shoved a handful of pocket cash into his mouth. 'It's about payback. This is for Coleman.'

CHAPTER THIRTY-NINE

Mal made another circuit of the De Haven house, wondering if they'd ever leave and give him a crack at the files, wondering if they'd got the word on Gordean yet. If Chaz Minear had called, they would have run to him; the killing was front page and all over the radio, and friends of theirs had to know that Loftis at least knew the man. But both cars stayed put and there was nothing he could do but keep waiting, moving, waiting to swoop.

Canon Drive to Elevado, Comstock to Hillcrest to Santa Monica and around again – sitting surveillance was an invitation for the ubiquitous Beverly Hills cops to roust him, out of his jurisdiction and getting ready to pull a Class B felony. Every time around the house he imagined more horrors inside – Loftis and his own son, a knife to the part of him that lived to protect Stefan. Two hours of circling had him dizzy; he'd called Meeks' switchboard and left a message: meet me on Canon Drive – but Buzz's Caddy hadn't showed and it was getting to the point where he was close to going in the door gun first.

Santa Monica around to Canon. Mal saw a paperboy tossing newspapers on front porches and lawns, hooked an idea, pulled over three houses up from Claire's and fixed her porch in his rearview. The boy hurled his bundle and hit the door; the door opened and an androgynous arm scooped the newspaper up. If they didn't already know, they soon would – and if their brains held over their fear they'd think *Chaz*.

A slow minute passed. Mal fidgeted and found an old sweater in the back seat – a good window punch. Another slow bunch of seconds, then Claire and Loftis hurrying out to the Lincoln in the driveway. She got behind the wheel; he sat beside her; the car backed out and headed south – the direction of Minear's place.

Mal walked over to the house – a tall, dignified man in a three-piece suit carrying a loosely folded sweater. He saw a side window by the door, punched it in, reached around and picked the lock. The door snapped open; Mal let himself in, closed the door and threw the top bolt.

There were at least fifteen rooms to toss. Mal thought: closets, dens, places with desks – and hit the writing table by the stairwell. He pulled out a half dozen drawers, rummaged in a coat closet adjacent, feeling for folders and loose paper as much as looking.

No loot.

Back to the rear of the house; two more closets. Vacuum cleaners and carpet sweepers, mink coats, a prayer to his old Presbyterian God: please don't let them keep it in a safe. A den off a rear bathroom, bookshelves, a desk there – eight drawers of potpourri

– movie scripts, stationery, old Loftis personal papers and no false bottoms or secret compartments.

Mal left the den by a side door and smelled coffee. He followed the scent to a large room with a movie screen and projector set up at the rear. A drop leaf table holding a coffeepot and a scattering of papers was stationed square in the middle, two chairs tucked under it – a study scene. He walked over, started reading and saw how good Danny Upshaw could have been.

The kid block-printed cleanly, thought intelligently, wrote with clarity and would have cracked the four killings easy if LAPD had given him an extra day or so. It was right here on his first summary report, page three, his second eyewitness on the Goines snatch. Claire and Reynolds had circled the information, confirming what Minear said: they were trying to find Loftis' son.

Page three.

Eyewitness Coleman Healy, questioned by Danny Upshaw on his first full day working the case.

He was late twenties – the right age. *He* was described as tall, slender and wearing a beard, which was undoubtedly a fake, one that he took off when he impersonated his father/lover. He *front-view*-confirmed a bartender's side view description of himself, filling in the middle-aged part. *He* was the first – and only, according to Jack Shortell – witness to identify Marty Goines as a homosexual, Upshaw's first homo lead outside of the mutilations. Put makeup on Coleman, and he could look middle-aged; put it all together with Doc Layman's silver wig strands found by the LA River and you had Coleman Masskie/Loftis/Healy committing murders out of his own blood lust and some kind of desire for revenge on incest raper Reynolds.

But one thing didn't play: Danny had questioned Coleman and met Reynolds. Why didn't he snap to their obvious resemblance?

Mal went through the rest of the pages, feeling the kid giving him juice. Everything was perfectly logical and boldly intelligent: Danny was beginning to get the killer's psyche down cold. There was a six-page report on his Tamarind Street break-in – he *did* do it – devil take the hindmost, fuck City/County strictures; he was afraid LAPD would ruin him for it, so he didn't take the polygraph that would have cleared him on Niles and night-trained it instead. Photographs showing blood patterns were mixed in with the reports; Danny had to have taken them himself, he'd risked a forensic in enemy territory. Mal felt tears in his eyes, saw himself building Ellis Loew's prosecution with Danny's evidence, making his own name soar on it. The Wolverine Killer in the gas chamber – sent there by the two of them and the unlikeliest best friend a ranking cop ever had: Buzz Meeks.

Mal dried his eyes; he made a neat stack of the pages and photographs. He saw feminine script in the margins of a jigtown canvassing list: Southside hotels, with jazz clubs check-marked against Danny's printing. He stuffed that page in his pocket, bundled the rest of the file up and walked to the front door with it. Tripping the bolt, he heard a key go in the lock; he opened the door bold, like Danny Upshaw at Tamarind Street.

Claire and Loftis were there on the porch; they looked at the broken glass, then at Mal and his armful of paper. Claire said, 'You broke our deal.'

'Fuck our deal.'

'I was going to kill him. I finally figured out there was no other way.'

Mal saw a bag of groceries in Loftis' arms; he realized they didn't have time to see Minear. 'For justice? People's justice?'

'We just talked to our lawyer. He said there's no way you can prove any kind of homicide charges against us.'

Mal looked at Loftis. 'It's all coming out. You and Coleman, all of it. The grand jury and Coleman's trial.'

Loftis stepped behind Claire, his head bowed. Mal glanced streetside and saw Buzz getting out of his car. Claire embraced her fiancé; Mal said, 'Go look after Chaz. He killed a man for you.

CHAPTER FORTY

Down to darktown in Mal's car, Lux's list of heroin pushers and the Danny/Claire list taped to the dashboard. Mal drove; Buzz wondered if he'd killed the Plastic Surgeon to the Stars; they both talked.

Buzz filled in first: Mary Margaret's swooning confirmation and Lux minus the crucifixion. He talked up the plastic surgery on Coleman, a ploy to keep him safe from Dudley and fulfill his father's perv; Lux shooting Gordean the incest dope for blackmail purposes, the story of the burned face a device to hide the perv from Loftis' fellow lefties, the bandages simply the surgery scars healing. Buzz saved Lux rebreaking Coleman's face for last; Mal whooped and used the point to segue to sax man Healy, questioned by Danny Upshaw on New Year's Day – that was why the kid never snapped to a perfect Loftis/Coleman resemblance – it didn't exist anymore.

From there, Mal talked Coleman. Coleman's intro lead on Marty Goines as a fruit, Coleman stressing the tall, gray man, Coleman wearing a gray wig and probably makeup when he glommed his victims, shucking the beard Upshaw saw on him. Loftis and Claire had Mondo Lopez steal Danny's files when they found out he was working the homo killings – Juan Duarte had snitched him as a cop. Mal recounted the Minear interrogation, Coleman the third point of the '42-'44 love triangle, Chaz shooting blackmailer Gordean to redeem himself in Claire and Loftis' eyes, Claire and Loftis searching for Coleman. And they both agreed: Marty Goines, a longtime Coleman pal, was probably a victim of opportunity – he was there when the rat man *had* to kill. Victims two, three and four were to tie in to Daddy Reynolds – a hellish smear tactic.

432

They hit the Central Avenue Strip, daytime quiet, a block of spangly facades: the Taj Mahal, palm trees hung with Christmas lights, sequined music clefs, zebra stripes and a big plaster jigaboo with shiny red eyes. None of the clubs appeared to be open: bouncer-door-men and parking lot attendants sweeping up butts and broken glass were the only citizens out on the street. Mal parked and took the west side; Buzz took the east.

He talked to bouncers; he talked to auto park flunkies; he handed out all the cash he didn't stuff down Terry Lux's throat. Three of the darkies gave him 'Huh?'; two hadn't seen Coleman the alto guy in a couple of weeks; a clown in a purple admiral's tunic said he'd heard Healy was gigging at a private sepia club in Watts that let whiteys perform if they were hep and kept their lily-white meathooks off the colored trim. Buzz crossed the street and started canvassing toward his partner; three more 'Huh?'s' and Mal came trotting over to him.

He said, 'I talked to a guy who saw Coleman last week at Bido Lito's. He said he was talking to a sickly old Jewish man about half dead. The guy said he looked like one of the old jazz fiends from the rest home on 78th and Normandie.'

Buzz said, 'You think Lesnick?'

'We're on the same track, lad.'

'Quit callin' me lad, it gives me the willies. Boss, I read a Bureau memo at Ellis' house. Lesnick's daughter said Pops was thinkin' about checkin' in to a rest bin to kick. There was a list of them, but I couldn't grab it.'

'Let's hit that Normandie place first. You get anything?'

'Coleman might be playin' his horn at some private jig club in Watts.'

Mal said, 'Shit. I worked 77th Street Division years ago, and there were tons of places like that. No more details?'

'Nix.'

'Come on, let's move.'

They made it to the Star of David Rest Home fast,

Mal running yellow lights, busting the speed limit by twenty miles an hour. The structure was a low tan stucco; it looked like a minimum security prison for people waiting to die. Mal parked and walked straight to the reception desk; Buzz found a pay phone outside and looked up 'Sanitariums' in the Yellow Pages.

There were thirty-four of them on the Southside. Buzz tore the page of listings out; he saw Mal standing by the car and walked over shaking his head. 'Thirty-four bins around here. A long fuckin' day.'

Mal said, 'Nothing inside. No Lesnick registered, nobody dying of lung cancer on the ward. No Coleman.'

Buzz said, 'Let's try the hotels and pushers. If that's no go, we'll get some nickels and start callin' the sanitariums. You know, I think Lesnick's a lamster. If that was him with Coleman, he's in this somehow, and he wouldn't be registered under his own name.'

Mal tapped the hood of the car. 'Buzz, Claire wrote that hotel list out. Minear said she and Loftis have been trying to find Coleman. If they've already tried – '

'That don't mean spit. Coleman's been seen around here inside a week. He could be movin' around, but always stayin' close to the music. Somethin's goin' on with him and music, 'cause nobody made him for playin' an instrument, now these boogies down here say he's a hot alto sax. I say we hit hotels and H men while it's still light out, then come dark we hit those jig joints.'

'Let's go.'

The Tevere Hotel on 84th and Beach – no Caucasians in residence. The Galleon Hotel on 91st and Bekin – the one white man staying there a three-hundred-pound rummy squeezed into a single room with his negress wife and their four kids. Walking back to the car, Buzz checked the two lists and grabbed Mal's arm. 'Whoa.'

Mal said, 'What?'

'A matcher. Purple Eagle Hotel, 96th and Central on Claire's list. Roland Navarette, Room 402 at the Purple Eagle on Lux's.'

'It took you a while.'

'Ink's all smudged.'

Mal handed him the keys. 'You drive, I'll see what else you missed.'

They drove southeast. Buzz ground gears and kept popping the clutch; Mal studied the two lists and said, 'The only matchup. You know what I was thinking?'

'What?'

'Lux knows Loftis and De Haven, and Loftis used to cop Claire's stuff. They could have access to Lux's suppliers, too.'

Buzz saw the Purple Eagle – a six-story cinderblock dump with a collection of chrome hood ornaments affixed above a tattered purple awning. He said, 'Could be,' and double-parked; Mal got out first and practically ran inside.

Buzz caught up at the desk. Mal was badging the clerk, a scrawny Negro with his shirt cuffs buttoned full in a sweltering lobby. He was muttering, 'Yessir, yessir, yessir,' one eye on Mal, one hand reaching under the desk.

Mal said, 'Roland Navarette. Is he still in 402?'

The hophead said, 'Nossir, nossir,' his hand still reaching; Buzz swooped around and pinned his wrist just as he was closing in on a junk bindle. He bent the fingers back; the hophead went, 'Yessir, yessir, yessir'; Buzz said, 'A white man, late twenties, maybe a beard. A jazz guy. He glom horse from Navarette?'

'Nossir, nossir, nossir.'

'Boy, you tell true or I break the hand you geez up with and throw you in the cracker tank at the Seven-Seven.'

'Yessir, yessir, yessir.'

Buzz let go and laid the bindle out on the desk. The clerk rubbed his fingers. 'White man, white woman here askin' same thing twenty minutes 'go. I tol' them, I tell you, Roland straighten up, fly right, don't sell no sweet horsey nohow.'

The punk's eyes strayed to a house phone; Buzz

ripped it out and chucked it on the floor. Mal ran for the stairs.

Buzz huffed and puffed after him, catching up on the fourth-floor landing. Mal was in the middle of a putrid-smelling hallway, gun out, pointing to a doorway. Buzz got his breath, pulled his piece and walked over.

Mal ticked numbers; at three they kicked in the door. A Negro in soiled underwear was sitting on the floor sticking a needle in his arm, pushing the plunger down, oblivious to the noise and two white men pointing guns at him. Mal kicked his legs and pulled the spike out of his arm; Buzz saw a C-note resting under a fresh syringe on the dresser and knew Claire and Loftis had bought themselves a hot lead.

Mal was slapping the H man, trying to bring him back from cloud nine; Buzz knew that was futile. He hauled him away from Mal, dragged him to the bathroom, stuck his head in the toilet and flushed. Roland Navarette came back to earth with shakes, shivers and sputters; the first thing he saw out of the bowl was a .38 in his face. Buzz said, 'Where'd you send them white people after Coleman?'

Roland Navarette said, 'Man, this a humbug.'

Buzz cocked the gun. 'Don't make me.'

Roland Navarette said, 'Coleman gigging at this after-hours on One-O-Six an' Avalon.'

Watts, code three without a siren. Buzz fingered his billy club; Mal leadfooted through twilight traffic. One hundred an sixth and Avalon was the heart of the heart of Watts: every tarpaper shack on the block had goats and chickens behind barbed-wire fences. Buzz thought of crazed darkies sacrificing them for voodoo rituals, maybe inviting Coleman over for some wolverine stew and a night of jazz hot. He saw a string of blue lights flickering around the doorway of a corner stucco; he said, 'Pull over, I see it.'

Mal swung hard right and killed his engine at the curb. Buzz pointed across the street. 'That white car was in

436

De Haven's driveway.' Mal nodded, opened the glove compartment and took out a pair of handcuffs. 'I was going to let the papers in on this, but I guess there's no time.'

Buzz said, 'He might not be here. Loftis and Claire might be waitin' him out, or there'd of been grief already. *You* ready?'

Mal nodded. Buzz saw a group of Negroes line up by the blue-lit door and start filing in. He motioned Mal out of the car; they hurried across the sidewalk and rode the last jazzbo's coattails.

The doorman was a gigantic shine in a blue bongo shirt. He started to block the way in, then stepped back and bowed – an obvious police courtesy.

Buzz went in first. Except for blue Christmas bulbs taped to the walls and a baby spot illuminating the bar, the joint was dark. People sat at card tables facing the stage and a combo back-lit by more blue lights: blinkers covered with cellophane. The music was ear-splitting shit, one step down from noise. The trumpet, bass, drums, piano and trombone were Negro guys in blue bongo shirts. The alto sax was Coleman, no beard, a cracked blue bulb blinking across the set of Daddy Reynolds' eyes.

Mal nudged Buzz and spoke loud in his ear. 'Claire and Loftis at the bar. Over in the corner, tucked away.'

Buzz pivoted, saw the two, half shouted to make himself heard: 'Coleman can't see 'em. We'll take him when this goddamn noise shuts off.'

Mal moved to the left side wall, ducking his head, moving up toward the bandstand; Buzz followed a few feet behind, doing a little shuffle: I'm not conspicuous, I'm not a cop. When they were almost to the edge of the stage, he looked back at the bar. Claire was still there; Loftis wasn't; a door on the right side of the room was just closing, showing a slice of light.

Buzz tapped Mal; Mal pointed over like he already knew. Buzz switched his gun from his holster to his right pants pocket; Mal had his piece pressed to his leg. The jigs quit playing and Coleman flew solo: squeals, rasps, honks, barks, growls, squeaks – Buzz thought of giant rats ripping flesh to the beat. There was a keening noise that seemed to go on forever, Coleman pitching his sax to the stars. The blue lights died; the keen went low note shuba-shuba-shuba in darkness and died. Real lights went on and the audience stampeded the bandstand, applauding.

Buzz pushed into the crush of bodies, Mal beside him, extra tall on his tiptoes. Everyone surrounding them was black; Buzz blinked for white and saw Coleman, sax held above his head, going through the right side door.

Mal looked at him; Buzz looked back. They pushed, punched, shoved, elbowed and kneed their way over, getting elbows, shoves and tossed drinks in their faces. Buzz came up on the door wiping bourbon sting out of his eyes; he heard a scream and a shot on the other side – and Mal went through the door gun first.

Another shot; Buzz ran after Mal's shadow. A smelly linoleum corridor. Two shapes struggling on the floor twenty feet down; Mal aiming, gun hand braced. A black guy turned a side corner and tried to block his aim; Mal shot him twice. The man careened off the walls and went down face first; Buzz got a look at the two on the floor. It was Loftis being strangled by Coleman Healy, big ugly pink dentures with fangs attached in his mouth. Coleman's chest was bloodied; Loftis was soaked dark red at the legs and groin. A revolver lay beside them.

Mal yelled, 'Coleman, get back!' Buzz slid down the wall, .38 out, looking for a clean shot at the rat man. Coleman made a denture-muffled bleat and bit off his father's nose; Mal fired three times, hitting Loftis in the side and chest, pitching him away from the thing attacking him. Coleman wrapped his arms around Daddy like an animal starved for food and went for his throat. Buzz aimed at his gorging head; Mal blocked his arm and fired again, a ricochet that tore the walls with zigzags. Buzz got free and squeezed a shot; Coleman grabbed his shoulder; Mal fumbled out his handcuffs and ran over.

Buzz threw himself prone and tried to find a shot; Mal's legs and flapping suitcoat made it impossible. He stumbled up and ran himself; he saw Coleman grab the gun on the floor and aim. One, two, three shots – Mal lifted clean off his feet and spun around with his face blown away. The body collapsed in front of him; Buzz walked to Coleman; Coleman leered behind bloody fangs and raised his gun. Buzz shot first, emptying his piece at the wolverine toothwork, screaming when he finally got an empty chamber. He kept screaming, and he was still screaming when a shitload of cops stormed in and tried to take Mal Considine away from him.

4

The Red Chaser Blues

CHAPTER FORTY-ONE

Ten days went by; Buzz hid out at a motel in San Pedro. Johnny Stompanato brought him information and bothered him for his fee on the Minear squeeze; the chink restaurant down the street delivered three greasy squares a day; the newspapers and radio supplied more info. He called Audrey in Ventura every night, spinning her tall tales about Rio and Buenos Aires, where the U.S. government couldn't extradite and Mickey was too cheap to send men. He fretted on the last and craziest money-making scheme of his LA career, wondering if he'd survive to spend the proceeds. He listened to hill-billy music; and Hank Williams and Spade Cooley did terrible things to him. He missed Mal Considine wicked bad.

After the shootout, an LAPD army got the citizens quelled and the bodies removed. Four dead: Coleman, Loftis, Mal and the back door bouncer he shot. Claire De Haven disappeared – she probably sent Reynolds on his lunatic mission, heard the shots, decided one redemption for the night was sufficient and calmly caught a cab home to plan more People's Revolts, Beverly Hills style. He followed Mal to the morgue and gave a statement at the Seven-Seven squadroom, tying in the Healy/Loftis deaths to the homo snuffs and insisting the late Deputy Danny Upshaw get credit for cracking the case. His statement glossed the illegalities he and Mal pulled; he didn't mention Felix Gordean, Chaz Minear, Dudley Smith or Mike Breuning at all. Let fruitfly Chaz live to enjoy his redemption; crazy Dud was too large to tap for the José Diaz kill or Charles Hartshorn's 'suicide.'

Reading between newspaper lines, you could follow the upshot: the Gordean killing unsolved, no suspects;

the shootout explained as Mal and himself 'following up a lead on an old case'; the dead boogie attributed to Coleman. No Commie or queer homicide angle on it at all – Ellis Loew had beaucoup press connections and hated complications. Reynolds and his son-lover were dismissed as 'old enemies settling a grudge' – the howler to top all howlers.

Mal Considine got a hero's funeral. Mayor Bowron attended, as did the entire LA City Council, Board of Supervisors and selected LAPD brass. Dudley Smith gave a moving eulogy, citing Mal's 'grand crusade' against Communism. The *Herald* ran a picture of Dudley chucking Mal's kid Stefan under the chin, exhorting him to 'be a trouper.'

Johnny Stomp was his conduit for dope on the grand jury, Ellis Loew to Mickey to him – and it looked like 24-karat stuff on all fronts:

Loew would begin his presentation of evidence next week – perfect timing – the UAES was still bearing the brunt of radio and newspaper editorials blaming them for the Gower Gulch bloodshed. Herman Gerstein, Howard Hughes and two other studio heads had told Loew they woud oust UAES the day the grand jury convened – violating the union's contract on the basis of fine-print clauses pertaining to expulsion for subversive activities.

Johnny's other glad tidings: Terry Lux had suffered a stroke – the result of 'prolonged oxygen deprivation' caused by a mouthful of money and a popped artery in his right hand. He was recuperating well, but ruined tendons in that hand would prevent him from performing plastic surgery again. Mickey Cohen had upped the ante on the Meeks contract to $20,000; Buzz jacked his payoff on the Minear job to $25,000 so Stompanato wouldn't put a bullet in his head. The Mick was pulling his hair out over Audrey; he'd erected a shrine out of Audrey memorabilia: her stripper publicity pics, the costumes she wore when she headlined the Burbank in '38. Mickey locked the stuff up in his bedroom at the hideaway and spent hours mooning over it. Sometimes you could hear him crying like a baby.

And Turner Meeks himself, holder of the Va Va Voom Girl's real true love, was getting fat, fat, fatter on moo shu duck, sweet and sour pork, shrimp chop suey and beef kowloon – a shitload of condemned man's last meals. And with his money shot a day away, he knew there were two things he wanted to know before he stuck his head in the noose: the whole story on Coleman and why the UAES hadn't played its extortion scheme against the studios – whatever it was – yet. And he had a hunch he knew where to get the answers.

Buzz went to the motel office, changed a five into nickels and walked to the phone booth in the parking lot. He got out the list of rest homes he'd torn from the Yellow Pages the day of the shootout and started calling, impersonating a police officer. He figured Lesnick would be hiding under an alias, but he hit the flunkies he talked to with his real name anyway, along with 'old,' 'Jewish,' 'dying of lung cancer.' He was $3.10 poorer when a girl said, 'That sounds like Mr. Leon Trotsky.' She went on to say that the oldster had checked out against medical advice and left a forwarding address: the Seaspray Motel, 10671 Hibiscus Lane, Redondo Beach.

A cheap Commie joke making it easy for him.

Buzz walked to a U-Drive and rented an old Ford sedan, thinking it looked pretty long in the tooth for a getaway car. He paid a week's fee in advance, gave the clerk a look at his driver's license and asked him for a pen and paper. The clerk complied; Buzz wrote:

Dr. Lesnick –
I was in with the grand jury for a while. I was there when Coleman and Reynolds Loftis were killed and I know what happened with them '42-'44. I didn't let any of that information out. Check the newspapers if you don't believe me. I have to leave Los Angeles because of some trouble I've gotten into and I would like to talk to you about Coleman. I won't tell what

445

you tell me to the grand jury – I would get hurt if I
did.

                                                    T. Meeks.

Buzz drove to the Seaspray Motel, hoping Mal's death
kiboshed the Bureau men looking for Lesnick. It was
an auto court at the tail of a dead-end street facing the
beach; the office was shaped like a rocket ship pointed
at the stars. Buzz walked in and punched the bell.

A youth with godawful pimples came in from the
back. 'You want a room?'

Buzz said, 'Mr. Trotsky still alive?'

'Barely. Why?'

Buzz handed him the note and a five-spot. 'Is he in?'

'He's always in. Here or the beach. Where's he gonna
go? Jitterbugging?'

'Give him the paper, sonny. Keep the five. If he says
he'll talk to me, Abe Lincoln's got a brother.'

The pimple boy motioned Buzz outside; Buzz stood
by his car and watched him walk to the middle of the
court and knock on a door. The door opened, the boy
went in; a minute later he came out lugging two beach
chairs, a stooped old man holding his arm. The hunch
played – Lesnick wanted some friendly ears on his way
out.

Buzz let them come to him. The old man had a hand
extended from ten yards away; his eyes were bright with
sickness, his face was muddy beige and everything about
him looked caved-in. His voice was strong – and the
smile that went with it said he was proud of the fact.
'Mr Meeks?'

Buzz gave the hand a little tug, afraid of breaking
bones. 'Yessir, Doctor.'

'And what is your rank?'

'I'm not a policeman.'

'Oh? And what were you doing with the grand jury?'

Buzz handed the clerk a fiver and grabbed the beach
chairs. The boy walked off smiling; Lesnick held Buzz's

arm. 'Why, then? I had thought Ellis Loew's minions were all policemen.'

Lesnick's weight on his was almost nothing – a stiff breeze would blow the fucker to Catalina. Buzz said, 'I did it for money. You wanta talk on the beach?'

Lesnick pointed to a spot near some rocks – it was free of glass and candy bar wrappers. Buzz shepherded him over, the chairs more of a strain than the man. He set the seats down facing each other, close, so he could hear if the Doc's voice went bum; he settled him in and watched him hunch into folds of terrycloth. Lesnick said, 'Do you know how I was convinced to become an informant?'

True snitch behavior – he had to justify himself. Buzz sat down and said, 'I'm not sure.'

Lesnick smiled, like he was glad he could tell it. 'In 1939 representatives of the Federal government offered me a chance to secure my daughter's release from Tehachapi Prison, where she was incarcerated for vehicular manslaughter. I was the official CP analyst in Los Angeles then, as I have remained. They told me that if I gave them access to my psychiatric files for evaluation by the 1940 State Attorney General's probe and other probes that might come up, they would release Andrea immediately. Since Andrea had a minimum of four more years to serve and had told me terrible stories of the abuse the matrons and her fellow inmates inflicted, I did not hesitate one second in agreeing.'

Buzz let Lesnick catch some breath – and cut to Coleman. 'And the reason you didn't kick loose with Loftis' file from '42 to '44 was because Coleman was smeared all over it. That right?'

Lesnick said, 'Yes. It would have meant much unnecessary suffering for Reynolds and Coleman. Before I turned the files over in toto I checked for other Coleman references. Chaz Minear alluded to Coleman, but only elliptically, so his file I relinquished. I did that same sort of editing when I gave my files to the HUAC investigators, but I lied and told them the Loftis file had

been lost. I didn't think Ellis Loew woud believe that
lie, so I just secreted Reynolds' file portion and hoped
I would die before they asked me for it.'

'Why didn't you just chuck the damn thing?'

Lesnick coughed and hunched deeper into his robe.
'I had to keep studying it. It compelled me greatly. Why
did you leave the grand jury? Was it moral qualms over
Ellis Loew's methods?'

'I just didn't think UAES was worth the trouble.'

'Your statement on the newspapers gives you credibility, and I find myself wondering exactly how much
you know.'

Buzz shouted over a sudden crash of waves. 'I worked
the killings *and* the grand jury! What I don't know is
the history!'

The ocean noise subsided; Lesnick coughed and said,
'You know all . . .'

'Doc, I know the incest stuff, and the plastic surgery
and all about Coleman tryin' to frame his daddy. The
only other guy who knew was that DA's captain who
was killed at the jazz club. And I think you wanta tell
what you got, or you wouldn't of pulled that juvenile
"Trotsky" number. Make sense, headshrinker?'

Lesnick laughed, coughed, laughed. 'You understand
the concept of subliminal motivation, Mr. Meeks.'

'I got a half-assed brain, boss. Wanta hear my theory
why you held the files back from summer '49 on?'

'Please expound.'

'The UAESers who knew were talkin' about Reynolds
and Claire gettin' married and how Coleman would take
it. That right?'

'Yes. I was afraid the investigators would seize the
Coleman references and try to locate him as one of
their friendly witnesses. Claire tried to keep news of the
wedding out of the papers so Coleman wouldn't see it,
but she did not succeed. At a terrible price, as I'm sure
you know.'

Buzz stared at the water, stone quiet: his favorite trick
to open suspects up. After a minute or so, Lesnick

said, 'When the second two victims were reported in the scandal tabloids, I knew the killer had to be Coleman. He was my analysand during the SLDC time. I knew he would have to be living somewhere near the Central Avenue jazz clubs, and I located him. We were close once, and I thought I could reason with him, get him to a locked institution and stop his senseless slaughter. Augie Duarte proved me wrong, but I tried. *I tried.* Think of that before you judge me too harshly.'

Buzz looked at the walking dead man. 'Doc, I'm not judgin' anybody in this fuckin' thing. I'm just leavin' town in a day or so, and I sure would like you to fill in what I don't know.'

'And nobody else will be told?'

Buzz threw Lesnick some crumbs. 'You tried to spare your friends grief while you played the game, and I've pulled tricks like that too. I've got these two friends who'd like to know why, but they ain't ever gonna. So could you maybe just tell me?'

Saul Lesnick told. It took him two hours, with many long pauses to suck in air and keep himself fueled. Sometimes he looked at Buzz, sometimes he looked out at the ocean. He faltered at some of the worst of it, but he always kept telling.

1942.

Wartime blackouts in LA, 10:00 P.M. curfew. Coleman was nineteen, living on Bunker Hill with his crazy mother Delores and two of his quasi-sisters. He used the surname 'Masskie' because slave breeder mommy needed a paternal monicker to get Relief payments for her son and the seven letters jibed with Sister Aimee's dictates on numerology. Coleman dropped out of Belmont High when they wouldn't let him play in the school band; he was heartbroken when the band teacher told him the stupid saxophone flubbing he did was just noise that indicated no talent, only strong lungs.

Coleman tried to join the army two months after Pearl Harbor; he flunked the physical on trick knees and a

449

spastic colon. He passed out handbills for Angelus Temple, earned enough money to buy himself a new alto sax and spent hours running chords and improvisational charts that sounded good only to him. Delores wouldn't let him practice at home, so he took his horn to the Griffith Park hills and honked at the squirrels and coyotes and stray dogs that trucked there. Sometimes he walked to the downtown library and listened to Victrola records with earphones. His favorite was 'Wolverine Blues,' sung by an old coon named Hudson Healy. The jig mushed words, and you could hardly hear him; Coleman invented his own words, dirty stuff about wolverines fucking, and sometimes he sang alone under his breath. He listened to the record so much that he wore down the grooves to where you could hardly hear anything, and he started singing a little bit louder to make up for it. Finally, the old biddy who ran the Victrola Room got wind of his lyrics and gave him the boot. For weeks he jerked off to fantasies of Coleman the Wolverine butt raping her.

Delores kept bothering Coleman for Sister Aimee money; he took a job at the Joredco Dental Lab and gave her a percentage tithe. The work was pulling animal teeth out of decapitated trophy heads, and he loved it. He watched the more skilled workers make dentures with the teeth, fashioning plastic and mortar paste into choppers that could bite for eternity. He stole a set of bobcat plates and played with them when he honked his sax up in the hills. He pretended he was a bobcat and that Delores and his phony brothers and sisters were afraid of him.

Joredco laid Coleman off when the boss found a wetback family who'd work for an extra-low group rate. Coleman was hurt and tried to get a job at a couple of other dental labs, but found out Joredco was the only one that made dentures with *real* animal teeth. He took to prowling around after dark – *real* dark – everybody shut in behind blackout curtains so the Japs wouldn't see all the lights and do LA like they did Pearl Harbor.

Coleman composed music in his head while he prowled; curiosity about life behind the curtains almost drove him crazy. There was a list on the wall at a local barber shop: Bunker Hill citizens who were *good* citizens working defense jobs. The list said who was working days, swing and graveyard. Coleman took the names to the phone book and matched them to addresses; from there he made phone calls – a phony census poll – and figured out who was married and who wasn't. Unmarried and graveyard meant a Coleman foray.

He forayed a bunch of times: in through an unlocked window, busting open a woodbox door, sometimes chiseling a door jamb. He took little things and money to keep Delores off his back. His best catch was a stuffed bobcat. But Coleman liked just *being* in the empty houses best. It was fun to pretend to be an animal that could appreciate music. It was fun to be in dark places and pretend you could see in the dark.

Early in June, Coleman was on the Hill Street trolley and heard two guys talking about a strange-o named Thomas Cormier and the smelly animals he kept behind his house on Carondelet. One man recited the names: weasels, ferrets, badgers, otters and wolverines. Coleman got excited, census-called Thomas Cormier and learned he worked nights at the Griffith Park Zoo. The next night, armed with a flashlight, he visited the wolverines and fell in love with them.

They were nasty. They were vicious. They took shit from no one. They tried to chew through the front of their cages to get at him. They had a snarl that sounded like the high notes on his sax.

Coleman left; he didn't burglarize the house, because he wanted to keep coming back for more visits. He read up on the lore of the wolverine and reveled in tales of its savagery. He set rat traps in Griffith Park and brought his catch back for the wolverines to eat dead. He brought hamsters and fed them to the wolverines live. He shone his flashlight on the wolverines and watched them gorge

451

on his goodies. He came without touching himself while he watched.

Coleman's summer was marred by Delores pestering him for more money. Late in July, he read in the paper about a local bachelor who working swing shift at Lockheed and owned a valuable coin collection. He decided to steal it, sell it and parcel the money out to Delores so she'd leave him alone.

On the night of August 2, Coleman tried – and was captured inside the house by the owner and two friends of his. He went for the owner's eyes like a good wolverine – unsuccessfully – but managed to get away. He ran the six blocks home, found Delores and a strange man going 69 on the couch with the lights on, was repulsed and ran back outside in a panic. He tried to run for the wolverine house, but the coin collection man and his pals – trawling in a car – found him. They drove him out to Sleepy Lagoon Park and beat him; the coin collection man wanted to castrate him, but his friends held him back. They left him there beaten bloody, composing music in his head.

Coleman stumbled over to a grassy knoll and saw – *or thought he saw* – a big white man beating a Mexican youth with his fists, slashing at his clothes with a razor-bladed two-by-four. The white man railed in a thick brogue: 'Spic filth! I'll teach you to traffic with clean young white girls!' He ran the boy down with a car and drove away.

Coleman examined the Mexican youth and found him dead. He made it home, lied to Delores about his injuries and spent time recuperating. Seventeen Mexican boys were indicted for the Sleepy Lagoon killing; a social ruckus over their innocence ensued; the boys were quickly put on trial and languished in jail. Coleman sent the LA Police Department anonymous letters during the trial – he described the monster he had come to call the Scotch Voice Man and told what really happened. Months passed; Coleman played his sax, afraid to burglarize, afraid to visit his wolverine friends. He worked skid row day labor and kicked back most of the scratch to keep Delores off his case. Then one day the Scotch Voice Man himself came walking up the steps of 236 South Beaudry.

Delores and his half sisters were gone for the day; Coleman hid out, realizing what must have happened: he left fingerprints on the letters and Scotch Voice retrieved the notes and compared the prints against the prints in his Selective Service file. Coleman hid out all that day and the next; Delores told him an 'evil man' was looking for him. He knew he had to run, but had no money; he got an idea: check crazy momma's scrapbook of old flames for men that he resembled.

Coleman found four photographs of a summer-stock actor named Randolph Lawrence – the dates on the back of the pictures and a strongish facial resemblance said this was his daddy. He copped two of the snapshots, hitchhiked to Hollywood and told a fish story to a clerk at the Screen Actors Guild. She believed his abridged tale of parental abandonment, checked the Guild files and informed him that Randolph Lawrence was really Reynolds Loftis, a character actor of some note: 816 Belvedere, Santa Monica Canyon.

The child showed up at his father's door. Reynolds Loftis was touched, pooh-poohed the story of the Scotch Voice Man, admitted his parentage and gave Coleman shelter.

Loftis was living with a screenwriter named Chaz Minear; the two men were lovers. They were members of the Hollywood leftist community, they were party-hopping devotees of avant-garde cinema. Coleman spied on them in bed – he both loved and hated it. He went with them to parties thrown by a Belgian filmmaker; the man screened movies featuring naked men and snapping dogs that reminded him of his wolverines – and the films obsessed him. Reynolds was generous with money and didn't mind that he spent his days in the back yard honking his alto. Coleman started hanging out at jazz clubs in the Valley and met a trombone player named Mad Marty Goines.

Mad Marty was a heroin fiend, a reefer seller, a burglar and a second-rate horn. He was a lowlife's lowlife, with a legitimate gift: teaching thievery and music. Marty taught Coleman how to hot-wire cars and really blow alto, showing him how to shape notes, read music, take his repertoire of noises and powerful lungs and use them to make sounds that meant something.

It was now the winter of '43. Coleman was shedding his baby fat, getting handsome. Reynolds became demonstrative to him, physically affectionate – lots of hugs and kisses on the cheek. He suddenly credited the story of the Scotch Voice Man. He joined the Sleep Lagoon Defense Committee – a hot lefty item now that the seventeen boys had been convicted – to prove his faith in Coleman.

Reynolds told Coleman to be quiet about the Scotch Voice Man – nobody would believe him, and the important thing was to get the poor prosecuted boys out of jail. He told him Scotch Voice would never be caught, but the evil man was probably still looking for Coleman – who needed protective coloration to remain safe from him. Reynolds took Coleman to Dr. Terence Lux and had his face physically altered to his own specifications. While recuperating at the clinic, Coleman went crazy, killing chickens in the hatchery, pretending he was a wolverine while he drank their blood. He got leaves from the clinic and pulled burglaries with Mad Marty, his face bandaged like a movie monster; he went to SLDC rallies with his attentive father – and against his wishes told the story of José Diaz and the Scotch Voice Man. Nobody believed him, everyone patronized him as Reynold Loftis' nutty kid brother burned in a fire – lies his father told him to go along with. Then the bandages came off and Coleman *was* his father twenty years younger. And Reynolds seduced his own youthful mirror image.

Coleman went with it. He knew he was safe from

Scotch Voice; while recovering from the surgery he did not know how his new face would look, but he knew now that he was beautiful. The perversion was awful but continually exciting, like being a wolverine prowling in a strange dark house twenty-four hours a day. Acting the part of a platonic kid brother was an intriguing subterfuge; Coleman knew Daddy was terrified of their secret coming out and kept mum – he knew also that Reynolds was going to rallies and donating money to causes because he felt guilty for seducing him. Maybe the surgery was not for his safety – just for the seduction. Chaz moved out – bitter over the horrific cuckolding – spurning Reynolds' offer to make it a menage à trois. Minear went on a sex bender then, a different Felix Gordean male prostitute every night – Reynolds lived in terror of his ex-lover telling them of the incest and tricked with a bunch of prosties himself, for the sex and to keep his ear down. Coleman was jealous, but kept still about it, and his father's sudden frugality and displays of nervousness convinced him that Reynolds was being blackmailed. Then Coleman met Claire De Haven and fell in love with her.

She was Reynolds' friend and confrere in various left-ist organizations, and she became Coleman's confidante. Coleman had begun to find sex with his father intoler-able; he pretended the man was Claire to get through their nights together. Claire heard Coleman's horror story out and convinced him to see Dr. Lesnick, the CP's approved psychiatrist – Saul would never violate confidentiality with an analysand.

Lesnick heard Coleman out – in a series of arduously detailed two-hour sessions. He believed the Sleepy Lagoon story to be fabricated on two levels: Coleman needing to justify his search for his father and his own latent homosexuality; Coleman wanting to curry favor with SLDC Latins by saying the killer was white – not the unfound Mexican gang members the leftist com-munity asserted the slayers to be. That aside, he believed

Coleman's narratives, comforted him and urged him to break off the affair with his father.

Lesnick was also seeing Loftis as a patient; he knew Reynolds was guilt-crazed over the affair, giving more and more money to more and more causes – especially the SLDC – an adjunct of the lever of manipulation he had applied to get Coleman to consent to the plastic job. Coleman felt reality closing in and began visiting Thomas Cormier's wolverines again, feeding and loving them. One night he felt an incredible urge to pet and hold one. He opened a pen, tried to embrace the beast and was bitten all over his arms. He and the wolverine fought; Coleman won with a stranglehold. He took the carcass home, skinned it, ate its flesh raw and made dentures out of its teeth, wearing them in his private hours, pretending to be the wolverine – stalking, fucking, killing.

Time passed.

Reynolds, convinced by Claire and Lesnick, broke off the liaison with Coleman. Coleman resented his sex power being usurped and started hating Daddy outright. The boys convicted of the Sleepy Lagoon killing were exonerated and released from prison – the SLDC largely responsible for securing the piece of justice. Claire and Coleman continued to talk, but now sporadically. Coleman copped Southside heroin for her to dally with; Claire was more disturbed than pleased by the gesture, but she did give Coleman a two-thousand-dollar loan he asked for. He used the money to buy himself a second Terry Lux surgery, the doctor going at his face with weighted boxing gloves, then holing him up at the hatchery with morphine and syringes to keep himself painless. Coleman read anatomy and physiology texts there; he left the clinic, kicked the drug cold turkey and showed up at Claire's door black and blue, but not looking like his father. When he asked Claire to sleep with him, she ran away in horror.

1945.

Coleman moved out of Los Angeles, Claire's revulsion a hot wind at his back. He bummed around the country and played alto with pickup bands, taking Hudson Healy's surname. In '47, Reynolds Loftis went before HUAC, refused to inform and was blacklisted; Coleman read about it and was delighted. Coleman was living in a world of impacted rage: fantasies of hurting his father, possessing Claire, raping men who looked at him the wrong way and eating their flesh with the wolverine teeth he still carried everywhere. Composing music and playing it was the only thing holding him glued. Then, back in LA at the end of '49, he read that Daddy and Claire were getting married. His threadbare, jerry-built world crashed in.

Coleman's fantasies escalated to where he couldn't even think of music. He knew he had to act on the fantasies and build a purpose around them, clear and precise like what his music meant to him. He found out about Reynolds' UAES membership and learned when the union held its Executive Committee meetings. He decided to kill sex partners of his father's – ones he remembered from the time of Daddy's breakup with Chaz. Coleman recalled George Wiltsie and Latin lover Augie by face and name, but they would never be able to identify him: at the time he was protectively colored as a lowly kid brother. He remembered other Reynolds conquests strictly by face, but knew the bars they frequented. Finding victims would be easy, the rest of it more difficult.

The plan:

Kill the Reynolds lovers on UAES meeting nights, disguised as Reynolds, spreading Reynolds' identical O+ seed, dropping clues to point to Reynolds as the killer, forcing him to – at worst – be implicated in the murders, or – milder punishment – cough up his treasonous UAES meetings as alibis. Daddy could be convicted of the crimes; he could be a suspect and have to admit his homosexuality to the police; he might get smeared in the press, and if he used his precious union soirees

457

as alibis, he might ruin his newly resurrected movie career on grounds of Pinko associations.

Coleman knew he needed money to finance his killing spree, and he was only making chump change gigging on Central Avenue. On Christmas Eve he ran into his old pal Marty Goines at Bido Lito's. Marty was surprised – and happy – it was the first time he'd seen Coleman post-bandages, years had gone by, the boy had become a man with a new face – and was not a bad alto. Coleman suggested they pull another B & E string; Mad Marty agreed. They made plans to talk after New Year's; then, early New Year's Eve, Goines saw Coleman outside Malloy's Nest and told him he'd called a Quentin buddy in Frisco, Leo Bordoni, and invited him to join their gang. Coleman, enraged at not being consulted – but not showing it – determined that Goines hadn't mentioned him or described him to Bordoni and decided that his old jazz mentor was prime wolverine bait. He told Marty to meet him at 67th and Central at 12:15, and to be quiet about it – there was a reason.

Coleman went to his room and got the Reynolds gray wig and makeup kit he'd brought. He fashioned a zoot stick from a plank he found in the garbage and a Gillette five-pack. He snapped that UAES was holding a party/meeting that night, copped four H bindles and a hypo from his old source Roland Navarette, pegged an unlocked Buick on 67th as his wheels, played his last gig at the Zombie, walked into the men's can at the Texaco Station on 68th as Coleman, walked out as Daddy.

Marty was right on time, but drunk – he didn't even blink at Coleman's disguise. Coleman coldcocked him on the sidewalk, slung him against his shoulder like a boozed-out buddy, got him into the Buick and hot-wired it. He geezed Marty up with a heavy junk load, drove him to his crib in Hollywood, shot him with the other three bindles and stuffed the hood of a terrycloth robe in his mouth so he wouldn't vomit blood on him when his cardiac arteries burst. Marty's heart popped big;

Coleman strangled the rest of his life out, zoot slashed his back, pulled out his eyes like he tried to with the coin collection man back at Sleepy Lagoon. He raped those bare sockets; he put on his wolverine teeth and feasted, spraying blood on the walls to wild alto riffs in his head. When he was finished he left the eyeballs in the Frigidaire, dressed Goines in the white terry robe, carried him downstairs and propped him up in the back seat of the Buick. He adjusted the rear-view mirror so he could watch Marty with his eyeless head lolling; he drove to Sunset Strip in the rain, thinking of Daddy and Claire reamed to their teeth in every orifice. He deposited Marty nude in a vacant lot on Allegro, prime fruit territory, a corpse on display like the Black Dahlia. If he was lucky, victim number one would get just as much ink.

Coleman went back to his music, his other life. The Goines kill did not reap the publicity he hoped it would – the Dahlia was a beautiful woman, Marty an anonymous transient. Coleman rented U-Drive cars and patrolled 2307 Tamarind at odd times; no cops showed up – he could use the place again. He got George Wiltsie's address from the phone book and decided that Wiltsie would be victim number two. He spent nights cruising queer bars near the pad, saw Wiltsie at the dives, but always in the company of his squeeze, a guy he called 'Duane.' He almost decided to let the bastard live – but thinking of the possibilities a duo kill presented made him tingly and reminded him of Delores and the man going 69. Then Duane mentioned to a barman that he worked at Variety International – old Daddy turf.

Providence.

Coleman approached George and Duane, carying a little kill kit he'd concocted: secobarbital caps bought from Roland Navarette, and strychnine from the drug-store. Two to one, barbiturate to poison – pinpricks on the capsules for a quick effect. Coleman suggested a party at 'his place' in Hollywood; George and Duane accepted. On the ride over in his U-Drive, he gave them a pint of rye to slug from. When they were half gassed, he asked them if they'd like to try some real Spanish Fly. Both men eagerly swallowed death pills; by the time they got to Marty's dump they were so woozy Coleman had to help them upstairs. Lindenaur was DOA, Wiltsie in a deep slumber. Coleman undressed them and went to work zooting the dead guy.

Wiltsie woke up and fought to live. Coleman slashed one of the fruiter's fingers off defending himself and killed him with a knife thrust to the throat. With both men dead, he zooted, wolverined, raped the standard way and drew music pictures and a trademark W on the walls. He put Wiltsie's digit in the icebox; he showered Duane and George free of blood, wrapped them in spare blankets, carried them down and drove to Griffith Park, his old sax-honking territory. He stripped them and carried them up to the hiking trail; he 69'd them for the world to see. If *he* was seen, he was seen as his father.

Two events coincided.

Dr. Saul Lesnick, near death and wanting to somehow recoup his moral losses, read a scandal tabloid account of the Wiltsie/Lindenaur murders. He recalled Wiltsie as a name bandied in a Reynolds Loftis psychiatric session years before; the zoot slashing reminded him of Coleman's fantasies regarding the Scotch Voice Man and the weapons at Terry Lux's hatchery. What finally convinced him that Coleman was the killer was the hunger behind the obliquely described bite marks. Coleman was hunger personified. Coleman wanted to be the most vicious, insatiable animal on earth, and now he was proving that he was.

Lesnick knew the police would kill Coleman if they caught him. Lesnick knew he had to try to get him to a locked-ward institution before he killed anyone else or took it in mind to go after Reynolds and Claire. He knew Coleman had to be close to the music, and found him playing at a club on Central Avenue. He regained Coleman's confidence as the one person who had never hurt him, secured him a cheap apartment in Compton and talked, talked, talked to him, hiding with him when a friend in the leftist community told him Reynolds and Claire were also seeking Coleman out. Coleman was experiencing moments of clarity – a classic behavior pattern in sexual psychopaths who had succumbed to murder to satisfy their lusts. He poured out the story of his first three killings; Lesnick knew that chauffeuring a dead man in the back seat and the second victims brought to Tamarind Street were a pure subconscious attempt to be caught. Psychological craters existed for a skilled psychologist to drive wedges into – Saul Lesnick's redemption for ten years of informing on people he loved.

Coleman was fighting his urges inchoately, with music. He was working on a long solo piece filled with eerie silences to signify lies and duplicities. The riffs would spotlight the unique high sounds he got with his sax, loud at first, then getting softer, with longer intervals of silence. The piece would end on a scale of diminishing notes, then unbroken quiet – which Coleman saw as being louder than any noise he could produce. He wanted to call his composition The Big Nowhere. Lesnick told him that if he got to a hospital, he would survive to perform it. The doctor saw Coleman faltering, clarity gaining. Then Coleman told him about Danny Upshaw.

He'd met Upshaw the night after he killed Marty Goines. The detective was on a routine canvassing assignment, and Coleman brazened him out with his 'I was in plain view all night' alibi, knowing Upshaw believed it. That belief meant Goines had kept mum about meeting him, and Coleman took the opportunity to lie about Marty being fruit and drop clues on tall, gray Daddy. He put Upshaw out of his mind and went on with his plan, killing Wiltsie and Lindenaur, wavering between Augie Duarte or another Daddy squeeze he knew as victim number four. But he'd started having dreams about the young detective, steamy stuff that said he really was what Daddy tried to make him. Coleman made a decision to murder Reynolds and Claire if he couldn't smear Daddy to the rafters – he thought that potential added blood to his stew would spice him up and make him dream about the women he once loved.

The plan didn't work. Coleman had more Upshaw dreams, more Upshaw fantasies. He was Daddy-garbed and in the process of staking out Felix Gordean's office for leads on old Reynolds lovers when he spotted Upshaw holding down his own surveillance; he was nearby when Upshaw phoned the DMV Police Information Line. He caught the gist of his talk, and tailed Upshaw in the Pontiac he'd stolen – just to get close to him. Upshaw spotted the tail; a chase followed; Coleman got away, stole another car, called the DMV and pretended to be the deputy's partner. One of the names the clerk read back to him was Augie Duarte; Coleman decided it was providence again and settled on him as victim four then and there. He drove to Gordean's beach house, spotted Upshaw's car, hid and listened to Gordean and one of his musclemen talking. The pimp/queer expert said, 'That policeman is coming out of the closet. I know it.'

The next day, Coleman let himself into Upshaw's apartment and savored it. He saw no mementoes of women, nothing but a too-tidy, impersonal pad. Coleman *knew* then, and began to feel a complete identification with Upshaw, a symbiosis. That night, Lesnick left the apartment to get medicine at County General, thinking Coleman's Upshaw fixation would break him down on his homosexuality, stymie and stalemate him. He was wrong. Coleman picked up Augie Duarte at a downtown bar, sedated him and took him to an abandoned garage in Lincoln Heights. He strangled him and hacked him and ate him and emasculated him like Daddy and all the others had tried to do to him. He left the body in the LA River wash, drove back to Compton and told Lesnick he had finally put Upshaw in perspective. He was going to compete with the man, killer against detective. Saul Lesnick left the apartment and

462

took a cab back to his rest home, knowing Coleman Healy would wreak slaughter until he was slaughtered himself. And the frail old headshrinker had been trying to get up the guts for a mercy killing ever since.

Lesnick ended his narrative with a deft storyteller's flourish, pulling a revolver from the folds of his robe. He said, 'I saw Coleman one more time. He had read that Upshaw died accidentally and was very disturbed by it. He had just purchased opiates from Navarette and was going to kill another man, a man who had been an extra on one of Reynolds' films, an opium dabbler. The man had had a brief fling with Reynolds and Coleman was going to kill him. He told me, like he thought I would do nothing to stop it. I bought this gun at a pawn shop in Watts. I was going to kill Coleman that night, but you and Captain Considine got to him first.'

Buzz looked at the piece. It was old and rusted and would probably misfire, like the shrinker's nutso take on Sleepy Lagoon as a fantasy. Coleman would have slapped it out of his bony hand before Pops could pull the trigger. 'You pleased the way it turned out, Doc?'

'No. I am sorry for Reynolds.'

Buzz thought of Mal shooting straight at Daddy – wanting Coleman alive for his career and maybe something to do with his own kid. 'I've got a cop question, Doc.'

Lesnick said, 'Please. Ask me.'

'Well, I thought Terry Lux hipped Gordean to all the stuff Gordean blackmailed Loftis with. Your story makes me think Chaz Minear told Felix some details, details that he put together when he blackmailed Loftis a second time just lately. Stuff that made him think Coleman was killin' people.'

Lesnick smiled. 'Yes, Chaz told Felix Gordean many things about Coleman's clinic stay that could be construed as clues when put together with newspaper facts. I read that Gordean was murdered. Was it Chaz?'

'Yeah. Does that please you?'

'It's a small happy ending, yes.'

'Any thoughts on Claire?'

'Yes. She'll survive your grand jury pogrom like a Tigress. She'll find another weak man to protect and other causes to champion. She'll do good for people who deserve good done for them, and I will not comment on her character.'

Buzz said, 'Before things got out of control, it looked like the UAES had some kind of extortion scheme brewin' against the studios. Were you playin' both ends? Holdin' back stuff you heard as a psychiatrist to help the union?'

Lesnick coughed and said, 'Who wants to know?'

'Two dead men and me.'

'And who else will hear?'

'Just me.'

'I believe you. Why, I don't know.'

'Dead men got no reason to lie. Come on, Doc. Spill.'

Lesnick fondled his pawnshop piece. 'I have verified information on Mr. Howard Hughes and his penchant for underaged girls, and much information on various RKO and Variety International actors and the narcotics cures they periodically undergo. I have information on the underworld associations of many studio executives, including one RKO gentleman who ran down a family of four in his car and killed them. The arrest was fixed, and it never went to trial, but that allegation by itself would be most embarrassing. So the UAES is not without weapons, you see.'

Buzz said, 'Boss, I pimped them girls to Howard and fixed up most of them dope cures. I got that RKO guy off the hook and ran the payoff to the judge that woulda arraigned them. Doc, the papers would never print what you got and the radio would never put it on the air. Howard Hughes and Herman Gerstein would laugh your extortion right back in your face. I'm the best fixer this town ever saw, and believe me the UAES is crucified.'

Saul Lesnick got to his feet, wobbled, but stayed standing. He said, 'And how will you fix that?'

Buzz walked on the question.

When he got back to his motel, there was a note from the manager on the door: 'Call Johnny S.' Buzz went to the pay phone and dialed Stompanato's number.

'Talk to me.'

'It's Meeks. What's up?'

'Your number, but hopefully not my money. I just got a lead, through a friend of Mickey's. LAPD did a routine ballistics run-through on that jazz club shootout you were in. That hotshot coroner Layman examined the report on the pills they took out of that rat guy you told me about. It looked familiar, so he checked back. Bullets from your gun matched the pills they took out of Gene Niles. LAPD makes you for the Niles snuff, and they're out to get you in force. Shoot to kill. And I hate to mention it, but you owe me a lot of money.'

Buzz sighed. 'Johnny, you're a rich man.'

'What?'

Buzz said, 'Meet me here tomorrow at noon,' and hung up. He dialed an East LA number and got, 'Quien? Quien es?'

'Speak English, Chico, it's Meeks.'

'Buzz! My Padrone!'

'I'm changin' my order, Chico, No thirty-thirty, make it a sawed-off.'

'.12 gauge, Padrone?'

'Bigger, Chico. The biggest you got.'

CHAPTER FORTY-TWO

The shotgun was a .10 gauge pump with a foot-long barrel. The slugs held triple-aught buckshot. The five rounds in the breech were enough to turn Mickey Cohen's haberdashery and the dope summit personnel into dog food. Buzz was carrying the weapon in a venetian blind container covered with Christmas wrapping paper.

His U-Drive clunker was at the curb a half block south of Sunset. The haberdashery lot was packed with Jew canoes and guinea gunboats; one sentry was stationed by the front door shooing away customers; the man by the back door looked half asleep, sitting in a chair catching a full blast of late-morning sun. Two neutral triggers accounted for – Dudley and the fourth man had to be inside with the action.

Buzz waved at the guy up on the corner – his prepaid accomplice recruited from a wine bar. The guy walked into the lot looking furtive, trying Caddy and Lincoln door handles, skirting the last row of cars by the fence. Buzz eased up slowly, waiting for the sentry to take note and pounce.

It took the sunbird almost half a minute to stir, get wise and tread over, a hand inside his jacket pocket. Buzz ran full speed, fat lightning on sneakered feet.

The sentry turned around at the last second; Buzz swung the Christmas box in his face and knocked him against the hood of a '49 Continental. The man pulled his gun; Buzz kneed him in the nards, popped his nose with a flat palm and watched the .45 auto hit the black-top. Another knee spear put him down and keening; Buzz kicked the gun away, whipped off the box and used the butt of his sawed-off to beat him quiet.

The accomplice was gone; the sentry was bleeding at the mouth and nose, deep off in dreamland – maybe for keeps. Buzz pocketed the loose cannon, walked over to the back door and let himself in.

Laughter and hail-fellow dialogue booming; a short corridor lined with dressing rooms. Buzz inched up to a curtain, pulled a corner back and looked.

The summit was in full swing. Mickey Cohen and Jack Dragna were glad-handing each other, standing by a table laid out with cold cuts, bottles of beer and liquor. Davey Goldman, Mo Jahelka and Dudley Smith were knocking back highballs; a line of Dragna humps was standing by the front window curtains. Johnny Stompan-ato was nowhere to be seen because Johnny Stompanato was probably halfway to Pedro by now, hoping a certain fat man survived the morning. Over by the left wall, the real business was happening: two Mex National types counting a suitcase full of money while one Mickey guy and one Jack guy taste-tested the white-brown powder stuffed into reinforced paper bags in another suitcase. Their smiles said the stuff tasted good.

Buzz pulled the curtain aside and joined the party, sliding a round into the chamber to get some attention. The noise caused heads to turn, drinks and plates of food to drop; Dudley Smith smiled; Jack Dragna eyed the barrel. Buzz saw a cop type by the Mexes. Twenty to one he and Dudley were the only ones heeled; Dud was much too smart to try something. Mickey Cohen looked hurt. He said, 'As God is my witness I will do you worse than I did the guy who did Hooky Rothman.'

Buzz felt his whole body floating away from him. The Mexes were starting to look scared; a rap on the window would bring the outside man. He stepped over to where he could see every face in the room and trained his muzzle for a blast spread: Jack and Mickey vaporized the second he pulled the trigger. 'The money and the dope in one of your garment bags, Mick. Now and slow.'

Mickey said, 'Davey, he'll shoot. *Do it!*'

Buzz saw Davey Goldman cross his vision and start talking low Spanish to the Mexes. He caught a slant view of paper sacks and greenbacks being ladled into a zippered hanger bag, tan canvas with red piping and Mickey Cohen's face embossed on the front. Mickey said, 'If you send Audrey back to me I will not harm a hair on her head and I will not do you slow. If I find her with you, mercy I cannot promise. Send her back to me.'

A million-dollar deal blown – and all Mickey Cohen could think of was a woman. 'No.'

The bag was zipped up; Goldman walked it over extra slow. Buzz held his left arm out straight; Mickey was

467

shaking like a hophead dying for a fix. Buzz wondered what he'd say next; the little big man said, '*Please*.'

The garment bag settled; Buzz felt his arm buckling. Dudley Smith winked. Buzz said, 'I'll be back for you, lad. Diaz and Hartshorn.'

Dudley laughed. 'You won't live the day.'

Buzz backed into the curtains. 'Don't go out the rear door, it's booby-trapped.'

Mickey Cohen said, '*Please*. You can't run with her. Not a hair on her head will I hurt.'

Buzz getawayed.

Johnny Stompanato was waiting for him at the motel, lying on the bed listening to an opera on the radio. Buzz dropped the garment bag, unzipped it and pulled out ten ten-thousand-dollar bank stacks. Johnny's jaw dropped; his cigarette hit his chest and burned a hole in his shirt. He snuffed the butt with a pillow and said, 'You did it.'

Buzz threw the money on the bed. 'Fifty for you, fifty for Mrs. Celeste Considine, 641 South Gramercy, LA. You make the delivery, and tell her it's for the kid's education.'

Stompanato hoarded the money into a tight little pile and gloated over it. 'How do you know I won't keep it all?'

'You like my style too much to fuck me.'

Buzz drove up to Ventura, parked in front of Deputy Dave Kleckner's house and rang the bell. Audrey answered. She was wearing an old Mickey shirt and dungarees, just like she was the first time he kissed her. She looked at the garment bag and said, 'Planning to stay awhile?'

'Maybe. You look tired.'

'I was up all night thinking.'

Buzz put his hands to her face, smoothing a wisp of stray hair. 'Dave home?'

'Dave's on duty until late, and I think he's in love with me.'

'Everybody's in love with you.'

'Why?'

'Because you make them afraid to be alone.'

'Does that include you?'

'Me especially.'

Audrey jumped into his arms. Buzz let go of the garment bag and kicked it for luck. He carried his lioness into the front bedroom and made a swipe at the light switch; Audrey grabbed his hand. 'Leave it on. I want to see you.'

Buzz got out of his clothes and sat on the edge of the bed; Audrey slow-grinded herself naked and leaped on him. They kissed ten times as long as they usually did and strung out everything else they'd ever done together. Buzz went into her fast, but moved extra slow; she pushed up with her hips harder than she did their first time. He couldn't hold it and didn't want to; she went crazy when he did. Like the first time, they thrashed the sheets off the bed and held each other, sweating. Buzz remembered how he'd hooked a finger around Audrey's wrist so they'd still be touching while he caught his breath. He did it again, but this time she squeezed his whole hand like she didn't know what the gesture meant.

They curled up, Audrey nuzzling. Buzz looked around the strange bedroom. Passport applications and stacks of South American tourist brochures were resting on the nightstand and boxes of women's clothing were arrayed by the door next to a brand-new suitcase. Audrey yawned, kissed his chest like it was sleep time and yawned again. Buzz said, 'Sweetie, did Mickey ever hit you?'

A drowsy head shake in answer. 'Talk later. *Lots* of talk later.'

'Did he ever?'

'No, only men.' Another yawn. 'No Mickey talk, remember our deal?'

'Yeah, I remember.'

Audrey gave him a squeeze and settled into sleep. Buzz picked up the brochure closest to him, a huckster job for Rio de Janeiro. He flipped pages, saw that Audrey had circled listings for guest cottages offering newlywed rates and tried to picture an on-the-lam cop-killer and a thirty-seven-year-old ex-stripper basking in the South American sun. He couldn't. He tried to picture Audrey waiting for him while he attempted to lay off twenty-five pounds of heroin to some renegade mob guy who hadn't already heard of the heist and the contract that went with it. He couldn't. He tried to picture Audrey with him when the LAPD closed in, hard-on glory cops holding their fire because the killer was with a woman. He couldn't. He thought of Icepick Fritzie finding them together, going icepick crazy on Audrey's face – and that picture was easy. Mickey saying 'Please' and going mushy with forgiveness was even easier.

Buzz listened to Audrey's breath; he felt her sweaty skin cooling. He tried to picture her getting some kind of bookkeeper's job, going home to Mobile, Alabama, and meeting a nice insurance man looking for a Southern belle. He couldn't. He made a big last try at the two of them buying their way out of the country with a nationwide cop-killer APB on his head. He tried extra, extra hard on that one – and couldn't find a way to make it stick.

Audrey stirred and rolled away from him. Buzz saw Mickey tired of her in a few years, cutting her loose for some younger stuff, a nice cash money separation gift. He saw Sheriff's, City cops, Feds and Cohen goons chasing his okie ass to the moon. He saw Ellis Loew and Ed Satterlee on easy street and old Doc Lesnick hounding him with, 'And how will you fix that?'

Lesnick was the kicker. Buzz got up, walked into the living room, grabbed the phone and had the operator get him Los Angeles CR–4619. A voice answered, 'Yeah?'

It was Mickey. Buzz said, 'She's at 1006 Montebello

Drive in Ventura. You hurt her and I'll do you slower than you ever thought of doin' me.'

Mickey said, 'Mazel tov. My friend, you are still dead, but you are dead very fast.'

Buzz let the receiver down gently, went back to the bedroom and dressed. Audrey was in the same position, her head buried in the pillow, no way to see her face. Buzz said, 'You were the one,' and turned off the light. He grabbed his garment bag on the way out and left the door unlocked.

Dawdling on back roads got him to the San Fernando Valley just after 7:30 – full evening, black and starry. Ellis Loew's house was dark and there were no cars parked out front.

Buzz walked around to the garage, broke a clasp on the door and pushed it open. Moonlight picked out a roof bulb at the end of a string. He pulled the cord and saw what he wanted on a low shelf: two double-gallon cans of gasoline. He picked them up, found them near full, carried them to the front door and let himself in with his special-investigator's key.

A flick of the overhead light; the living room jarring white – walls, tables, cartons, shelves and odd mounds of paper – Loew and company's once-in-a-lifetime shot at the political moon. Graphs and charts and thousands of pages of coerced testimony. Boxes of photographs with linked faces to prove treason. A big fuckload of lies glued together to prove a single theory that was easy to believe because believing was easier than wading through the glut of horseshit to say, 'Wrong.'

Buzz doused the walls and shelves and tables and stacks of paper with gasoline. He soaked the Sleepy Lagoon Committee photos. He ripped down Ed Satterlee's graphs, emptied the cans on the floor and made a gas trail out to the porch. He lit a match, dropped it and watched the white whoosh into red and explode.

The fire spread back and upward; the house became a giant sheet of flame. Buzz got in his car and drove away, red glow lighting up the windshield. He took back streets northbound until the glow disappeared and he heard sirens whirring in the opposite direction. When the noise died, he was climbing into the foothills, Los Angeles just a neon smear in his rear-view mirror. He touched his future there on the seat: sawed-off, heroin, a hundred and fifty grand. It didn't feel right, so he turned on the radio and found a hillbilly station. The music was too soft and too sad, like a lament for a time when it all came cheap. He listened anyway. The songs made him think of himself and Mal and poor Danny Upshaw. Hardcases, rogue cops and Red chasers. Three dangerous men gone for parts unknown.